Lagging Indicators

a novel

Jennifer Anglade Dahlberg

Lagging Indicators
Jennifer Anglade Dahlberg
ISBN 978-1-77342-050-9

Produced by IndieBookLauncher.com
www.IndieBookLauncher.com
Cover Design: Saul Bottcher
Interior Design and Typesetting: Saul Bottcher

The body text of this book is set in Adobe Caslon.

Also Available
EPUB edition, ISBN 978-1-77342-048-6
Kindle edition, ISBN 978-1-77342-049-3

For my sister, Dominique

lagging indicator
(lægɪŋ ɪndɪkeɪtər)

Word forms:
(regular plural) lagging indicators

noun

(Finance : Economics)
A lagging indicator is an economic indicator that changes
following a change in the economy, such as unemployment.

Source: Collins English Dictionary

1.

October 2009

"So"—I glanced quickly at the name on top of the resume—
"Ashley. What makes you think you can sell?"

Ashley, smiling widely, met my gaze. "I'd say that selling
is in my blood. My father owns a clothing store and I worked
on the floor, pushing product, ever since junior high. Selling or
trading financial instruments would be the ultimate sales job
in the most dynamic industry in the world. And having the
opportunity to work on Wall Street would be a dream come
true."

Of course.

"What about your personality will make you a good trader?"

"I'm quick, self-motivated, analytical, not afraid to take
risks ..."

Blah, blah, blah. Ashley was a senior at a prestigious university and my colleagues and I had been bombarded with
eager, fresh-faced undergraduates all week. It was interview
season on Wall Street and the recent financial crisis had only
increased the number of candidates applying for jobs at the
company I worked for, Atlas Capital. We were a boutique trading and investment advisory firm, but the financial crisis and
implosion of many larger competitors had resulted in fewer
opportunities, so positions at small, stable firms like Atlas had
become highly-coveted.

The room fell silent and Ashley looked at me expectantly.

Snapping back to the present, I nodded and said, "Now, tell me about a situation in which it was difficult to obtain information you needed and how you dealt with that?"

I'd been asking that question three times a day now for the past five days. Well, multiply that by ten, which is the numbers of years I'd worked at Atlas and had the dubious honor of conducting these interviews. *One hundred and fifty.* These questions hadn't change and I could recite them from memory. They hadn't evolved with the colossal challenges facing Wall Street and were embarrassingly out-of-step with today's savvy recruits. When I interviewed at a Top Firm in the Nineties, I had spent weeks studying the company, its strategy and key executives. There had been no guide beyond the unwritten rules on how we were expected to look, behave and dress. But today's candidates were raised on the Internet and regurgitated canned, nearly identical answers to our questions. I could almost predict Ashley's response, but decided to give her the benefit of the doubt. *Come on, surprise me.*

"Well, it involved a case study my classmates and I were doing last semester . . . " she began.

I reined in my laughter. Which case would it be this time? The devaluation of the Thai baht? Or maybe the dotcom bust? I hadn't heard that one in, oh, at least two days. I stole a glance at my BlackBerry on the conference table. There was only an hour left until the markets closed and I decided to bring this tedious procedure to an end. No more generic questions.

"Ashley," I said, interrupting her monologue. "Do you think executing actual trades will be anything like what you've studied about it in school?"

"No, but I think my education and summer internships

will prepare me for the job," she answered, without missing a beat. "I think I've got the tool kit to succeed in this business."

I leaned back and appraised Ashley, something I hadn't done thoroughly when I entered the conference room earlier, impatient and five minutes late. She was a petite brunette with tasteful makeup, professionally turned out in a charcoal gray skirt suit and cream silk blouse.

"Self-confidence will certainly go a long way," I said, "but nothing really prepares you for the stress, the constant action, the highs and lows." I paused for effect. "I go to bed every night worried about my positions. I wake up every morning worried about my positions. Vacations will become a privilege, not a right. Your Bloomberg terminal will become your best friend . . ."

Ashley's eyes assumed a determined glint. "That's what I want."

"Being a trader these days is very different from what it used to be." I was thirty-five and with ten years in the industry, couldn't help imparting some words of wisdom. "You might not be the most popular person at a cocktail party. Why do you want do this at all?"

Her face relaxed. "Because I think there should be more women in this business. If there were more of us out there"— she pointed to herself and then to me—"maybe we wouldn't have gotten into this financial mess. I think women in general are better at managing risk. We don't let our egos get in the way of decisions."

Touché. A response Ashley probably wouldn't have given to one of my male colleagues.

"But you still need a healthy ego. It's the nature of the

beast." I evened out the edges of her resume and letters of recommendation on the tabletop. "You do know what the upside is, right?"

She nodded. "If you're good, you have the potential to make a lot of money—your own money."

Sliding back my chair back and rising, I added, "And that, for a woman, is not a bad thing."

I neglected to say *single woman* because that's inevitably what it would come down to, but Ashley would have to figure that one out on her own.

Back at my desk, I frowned at the Bloomberg information on two of my four computer screens. These screens were my lifeblood, providing me with real-time news and prices for every tradable instrument in the market from stocks and bonds to commodities and currencies. Jagged lines on the upper left hand corner showed a downward trend in the stocks I was monitoring. I had been buying stocks in large, "blue chip" companies, established household names that even ordinary folks would recognize. In uncertain times, businesses that were familiar and could offer a proven product for good value were almost always a sure bet. As Head of Equities, I had instructed my team of nine traders to "long" or increase our stake in a half dozen blue chips, predicting their stock prices would rise in the near future.

Atlas Capital had survived the worst crisis since the Great Depression on account of one simple fact: My boss, Peter Branco, didn't believe in overleveraging the firm. As a result, we hadn't been as heavily exposed to the subprime mortgages and credit default swaps that had crippled the larger banks. We were also able to exploit inefficiencies in the market, purchasing undervalued stocks for a low price and then selling high when the market started to rally again. While others struggled, Atlas cemented its reputation as a firm for sophisticated investors who valued stability.

Then why were my mature, historically reliable companies falling? Sighing loudly, I took a sip of VitaminWater. It was flavored with dragon fruit and I drank several bottles of it a day, on top of my morning cappuccino, lunchtime latte and afternoon espresso. I stayed alert, over-caffeinated and super-hydrogenated, but the side-effects also had me running to the bathroom more than I had time for.

"What's up, Mia?" asked Nick Vamvakis, the bond trader who sat across from me.

Atlas employed ten equity and eight fixed-income traders and we sat side-by-side in two rows facing each other in the middle of a large, rectangle room. There was absolutely no privacy; no place to retreat if you were having a bad day. High ceilings sharpened the acoustics and we became accidental bystanders to each other's conduct and conversation, professional or otherwise. Coupled with the noise from the televisions mounted on the wall and the frenzy of buying and selling, I often felt like I was in the middle of rush-hour traffic.

"Just trying to understand why my blue chips are trending downward."

Nick shrugged. "Market's not that excited about toothpaste or cereal."

"These companies will be standing long after we're gone."

"I bet they said the same thing about Lehman Brothers."

"Ouch."

"So, whaddya think of her?"

Clicking up a six-month earnings chart for a leading food and beverage company, I asked, "Who?"

"The girl you guys interviewed today."

"Oh. Ashley. I thought she seemed very smart and motivated."

"You know what Tripp asked her?"

"What?" I asked. Tripp Armsden was the newest member of my equities team. Peter had hired him without my knowledge several months ago, soon after the venerable bank Tripp worked for filed for bankruptcy. Peter claimed that "time was of the essence" and he was handing me "one of the sharpest trading minds out there on a silver platter," but I was still irritated that he had left me out of the selection process.

"He asked her to guess how much money he had in his wallet."

"That question is borderline harassment!"

"You know what she answered?"

"Something rude, I hope."

"She told him he probably had no cash since he seemed like a Platinum card kind of guy!" Nick tried to laugh, but it came out more like a snort.

"Ha ha! Do you think Tripp got the subtle insult?" I always felt silly saying his name. Why had his parents gone through the trouble of giving him the illustrious title of William Arthur Armsden, III, if he would only be known by the more pedestrian "Tripp?"

"I don't think so. If he did then he wouldn't have bragged

about it."

I chuckled. "True."

"Do you think Peter will make her an offer?" Nick asked.

I thought back to Ashley's last words. "I hope so. I think she'd be a good trader's assistant to start with."

"She's probably better off working for you. She'd just be a distraction to the other guys."

I crinkled my brows, an unconscious habit I'd noticed only after lines had taken up permanent residence on my fore-head. "Because she's pretty?"

Nick's expression became sheepish, as though he knew he was treading very close to the edge of political incorrectness. "Sorry."

In the trading world, there was an archaic myth that the mere presence of estrogen took a male trader's eyes off his business. Against his better judgment, he'd end up dating this woman, or worse, marry her. She would then have to quit her job and have been of little use to the firm in the first place. Perhaps my being an African-American woman kept such thoughts at bay among my white male colleagues or, rather, as Head of Equities, I was strictly off-limits. About a third of Atlas's staff was female, distributed in analysis, operations and human resources. I was the only female trader in a field of eighteen males, but I preferred to see my profession as gender-neutral. I wanted to be judged by my results, the volume of my trades and how much money I made for the firm. Trading was still the ultimate boys club, but it was also objective. Money was the ultimate signifier.

"What's your P&L?" Nick asked, getting back to basics.

His question was innocent enough. Measuring the profit

and loss of a day's trading was standard operating procedure. Since Nick traded bonds, he reported to my counterpart in fixed income but we had been "neighbors" on the desk for the past two years. A burly, easy-going guy who had played football for Duke, we shared a nice rapport, but a nagging sense of caution prevented me from stating the truth, so I kept my poker face on.

"I'm down a bit, but I think I can make it up," I replied.

"I'm sure you'll be back in positive territory again."

I nodded. I was actually down ten percent, a $1.5 million loss for the day, on my book alone.

I cursed Peter for making me interview Ashley. Shares in a beverage company had plunged in my absence and I missed an opportunity to sell when I was down by two dollars a share. Now, I was down two-fifty. My losses had grown over the last three days in steady hundred thousand dollar increments. When was the last time I had been down so much in such a short period of time?

During those first, precarious months of the financial meltdown, my group's trades had fallen and then risen and then fallen again, mirroring the madness in the marketplace. Most of our counterparties were flooded with sub-prime mortgages and I didn't sleep for more than four hours a night for several weeks. We kept vigil at the office, scouring our systems to determine how widespread our exposure to the mushrooming catastrophe was. The shared panic galvanized Atlas and by the end of that defining year, we were out of intensive care and breathing on our own again. Storied banks had fallen, but Atlas, the small shop founded by Peter Branco—a contrarian who always believed the Wall Street establishment was too cocky and bloated for its own good—was still standing. Having survived the market meltdown, my current predicament was baffling. But the markets aren't rational. There are black swans flying around and, sooner or later, they will turn against you.

Shortly after five o'clock, I heard Nick turn off his screens. He got up and stretched his hands above his head, displaying two hundred and fifty pounds of bulk. He'd been a star football player at Duke, but fallen short of the NFL. He had, however, caught the attention of well-connected Duke alumni who facilitated the proper introductions on Wall Street. Nick's career progression typified Wall Street's "old boy network," a fact that irked me to no end. I had worked two—if not three—times as hard for my current position, but guys like Nick seemed to coast by without as much effort. Former jock? Check. Golf nut? Check. Smart, but not intimidating? Check. Perky wife and house in Connecticut? Check.

"A couple of us are gonna grab a beer down the street. Care to join?" he asked.

I also forgot to mention he was affable and a team player. I really had to shake off the negativity, but the day's losses were making me cranky.

"I better stay here and regroup, but thanks anyway."

Nick stopped by Tripp's desk and the two of them sauntered towards the front door, picking up three more traders along the way. The five of them were dressed in khaki pants, button-downs, and navy blue fleece vests, the uniform of choice for male traders and hedge fund managers. The vests were emblazoned with the Atlas logo, a variation of the Greek god kneeling on one knee, supporting a huge globe on his shoulders. Everyone assumed Peter had named the firm in homage to Ayn Rand's capitalist tome, *Atlas Shrugged*, but he was fascinated by Greek mythology and wanted to convey strength and globalism. I always thought Atlas Capital was an enlightened choice, particularly since Peter had resisted the impulse to name the firm after himself. I had gotten one of those fleece vests at a company off-site, but refused to wear it. The very idea of *sleeveless fleece* seemed like an oxymoron.

I reviewed the results for the trades my team had made that day. We had analysts who were responsible for plugging in all the numbers, but I still liked to see where we stood at the close. My million and a half dollar loss was a professional embarrassment, particularly since a losing streak had a dangerous way of replicating itself.

The rest of the team had made some profitable trades, having correctly bet on some positive news in the oil industry. Retail stocks were bringing us down, but that was no surprise since the buying frenzy that typified the last couple of years had leveled off. Tripp's supposed expertise was evaluating tech stocks and his book showed some gains with the usual suspects who dominated the industry, but an unfamiliar company caught my attention: Touchnology Systems.

"What the hell—" I muttered. The equities team always discussed the status of our positions at daily morning meetings and I had never heard of Touchnology Systems. Nevertheless, Tripp had bought 300,000 shares at sixty-five dollars per share. He had committed $19.5 million without my knowledge or approval.

Dumbfounded, I pored over Touchnology's company profile on my Bloomberg. They were a seven-year old outfit based in La Jolla, California, that developed, manufactured and marketed a line of touch screen products "with diverse applications in smartphones, video games, electronic readers and satellite navigation systems." The company went public two years ago, just as the capital markets fizzled, raising only $150 million. With tech companies vying to invent devices that could handle e-mail, e-commerce, entertainment and social media in the palm of your hand, Touchnology should have been sitting pretty, but last year's earnings were a mediocre $15 million. What on earth did Tripp see in this company?

My BlackBerry vibrated. It was Drago, my personal trainer. He was a former Serbian kickboxing champion and tortured me three times a week, showing no sympathy for my aches and pains or whether I had lost a million dollars. Drago was like a benevolent dictator and under his regime, I had built lean leg muscles, tightened my abdomen and sculpted my arms.

"Mia!" he shrieked, his voice stewing with the authority of a boot camp general. "Where are you? You are ten minutes late!"

"I'll be there in twenty minutes. Can you stay a little later today?"

"You will have to do extra lunges and sit-ups!" he barked, punishing me with my most-hated exercises, and hung up.

I checked on the closing price for Touchnology; it had dipped from sixty-five dollars per share to fifty-eight. It made no sense. Tripp Armsden had casually closed shop and gone out for a beer—after losing $2.1 million on a stock I never authorized.

2.

My doubts about Tripp intensified after we were formally introduced, but I never divulged them to Peter. Throughout my career, I had mastered the art of the placid expression, the opaque smile when facing potential adversaries. And make no mistake: my instincts warned me that Tripp was an adversary. Wall Street was all about defending one's turf and the sudden, secretive circumstances by which Tripp joined Atlas gave him a special status as Peter's new "wunderkind" around the firm. Fielding questions from the other guys, I pretended to know more about his background than I actually did, but had gleaned some useful information on LinkedIn. Peter was right; on paper, Tripp was perfect.

He had grown-up in the affluent suburb of Bernardsville, New Jersey; attended Deerfield Academy; and graduated from Trinity College with a degree in economics. He then made his way to Wall Street, moving up the ranks as a trader for a couple of big firms, before taking a break from the finance world and investing in a small technology company. Two years later, he was back at the trading desk, becoming the top tech trader for a British bank until the subprime mortgage crisis ushered its collapse. I noted with some strange satisfaction that, unlike me, Tripp didn't have an MBA.

Peter had treated us to lunch at Bobby Van's on Broad Street, a steakhouse near the office and a favorite among Wall Street types. The steaks were huge and accompanied by sides of creamy potatoes and vegetables that would abolish a week's worth of my training with Drago. In a decadent mood, Peter ordered a little of everything, including a bottle of Opus One.

We were seated at a table for four, but one chair had been taken away and I made sure to claim the one next to Peter so that we both sat opposite Tripp. I first worked with Peter straight out of college as an analyst at Morgan Stanley and could have never predicted the outsized role he would play in my life. He became my mentor, giving me opportunities where others might not have seen my potential, and entrusted me with more and more responsibility at his beloved firm. Peter had just turned sixty, but he brandished a poufy mane of dark hair and favored the chalk-striped, three-piece suits that symbolized a more civilized era on Wall Street.

Watching Tripp strum his square-shaped fingers on the table, I ran my eyes from his hands to his face. I wished he hadn't looked so predictable, that he hadn't conformed to my notions of an overgrown preppy. During my undergraduate years at Wellesley, Boston had been littered with them and my girlfriends had tripped over themselves to catch the attention of guys like, well, Tripp. Gangly, with high cheekbones, his dirty blond hair was shaped into a side part. I made note of his faintly reddish skin and the two thin knot bracelets on his right wrist. Was it wrong to assume he sailed and probably spent summer weekends at an exclusive yacht club? When we shook hands for the first time, the bright smile on his face didn't quite reach his brown eyes. His confidence was intertwined with an air of entitlement since *I* wasn't the one he needed to impress. The job was already his. I was a mere formality.

"Peter, tell me. How did you hear about Tripp?" I asked.

"Tripp's been on my radar screen for a while now," Peter replied. "The timing—"

"And circumstances—"Tripp added.

"Have just never been right," Peter finished.

"But your old bank went under and changed all of that," I noted.

"You might say it sped the process along,"Tripp answered, "but I'd been contemplating a change for a while."

"I noticed you've been with many different banks throughout your career . . ." I let my words trail so Peter could interpret their full meaning. He seemed so smitten with Tripp. How could he be so sure his new hire wouldn't leave Atlas at the next best opportunity?

"Back then, I focused solely on how much money I could make. If I got a better offer, I jumped ship," Tripp explained, with no shred of regret. "Then I started to really get into the tech industry and wanted to do more than just sit at the periphery and trade. I wanted the chance to build something."

"But you only stayed two years at that start-up," I said.

"Mia, business is ever-changing," Peter interrupted, waving his right hand in the air. "It's very rare to find people today with the kind of company loyalty you have."

"Is that such a bad thing?" I asked, miffed.

"Of course not!" he said quickly. "Tripp, when I started Atlas, Morgan Stanley insisted I sign a non-poaching agreement and not approach anyone from the firm for a year. When that year was up, the first person I called was Mia."

"Impressive," Tripp remarked, which might have been more for Peter's benefit than mine.

"But there's still a lot left to do at Atlas and I'm counting on the two of you to bring us to the next level," Peter gushed, raising his glass. "Cheers!"

We clinked, but I only took a baby sip of wine. My internal alarm, finely honed after a career spent jabbing elbows on Wall Street, pinged repeatedly. I needed to keep my wits about me.

"Peter?" I came into his office later that day, after most of the staff had already gone home. "Can I ask you a question?"

"Go ahead—shoot," he said, looking up from the *Financial Times* he had been reading. His eyelids hung like a wilting flower, leftovers from the three glasses of wine at lunch.

"Who does Tripp report to? Me, right?"

"Erm, yes. But he's also, erm, kind of independent, sort of running his own desk too."

"A desk of one?"

Peter's head jerked forward and then backwards, flustered back to life. "No, that's not what I meant! He definitely reports to you for strategy, etc., but it's also a dual reporting relationship, so he reports to me too."

"How's that going to work? He's going to be working with stocks, right?"

"Yes."

"Then I think it's pretty simple: I manage him and the eight other guys on the equity team."

"Mia, it's complicated. I had to promise Tripp some autonomy in order to get him over here."

"What are we paying him?"

"The standard base plus performance bonus."

"Did you also give him a signing bonus?"

"That wouldn't be unusual for someone with his experience."

"How much?"

Peter stared at his newspaper. "Half a buck."

"*Five hundred thousand dollars!*" No wonder Tripp had looked so smug at lunch. "He hasn't made a dime for the firm yet and there are plenty of smart people out there looking for jobs who would've joined us for nothing."

"Trust me, Mia, Tripp will be good for the firm." He folded his *FT* in quadrants and smiled. "And I know I can count on you, right?"

Reluctantly, I nodded. There was really nothing else to say that would have made a difference.

The equities group had assembled for our final morning meeting of the week. These daily forums gave us the opportunity to assess the market and our positions and to anticipate how financial reports or events would impact our business. After almost fifteen years, they still gave me a rush and reminded me of why I got into trading in the first place. I majored in International Relations at Wellesley, expecting to work at the UN or pursue a career in the foreign service, but coursework in Economics—and my student loans—drove me to apply for an analyst job at an investment bank. At Morgan Stanley, I worked in the energy sector, reading research reports and inputting data onto spreadsheets, but I also got to drop in on the department's morning meetings. It soon became clear that I had underestimated the level of thought required to make a trade. I presumed traders were loud, impatient and anti-intellectual, operating primarily from their gut instinct. But good traders always do their homework. Good traders use their gut *and* their head. I listened to their quick, sharp banter—shorthand for a string of financial terms I was just beginning to understand—and their discussions ranged on everything from how an election in the Ukraine could affect natural gas prices to whether the Yankees' playoff run signaled a bull market. I eventually came to this conclusion: Everything circled back to the markets and I wanted to be in on the action in a concrete way, not on the sidelines as an embassy bureaucrat or a talking head at a think tank. Some of my Wellesley friends considered my about-face an affront, calling it the pursuit of dirty money, but their objections seemed naïve and idealistic. Sooner or later we would have to leave our ivory towers and join the real world.

A few minutes past eight, I signaled for the meeting to begin. "Okay, guys. Is everyone here? I'd like to get started." I did a quick headcount. Only eight traders were present; Tripp was late.

"It looks like the market's going to open lower today. Asia's down a half percent, the euro's down three-quarters. Gold is up . . ." I ran down my list of indicators and then asked, "Would anyone like to add something?"

Tom Schultz, a veteran trader who specialized in durable goods, raised his pen. He was a dying breed; a scrappy guy who had talked his way into a job as a floor clerk for the New York Stock Exchange in the Seventies, straight out of Brooklyn's Thomas Jefferson High School and long before MBAs, PhDs and complex computer algorithms invaded Wall Street. He joined Atlas soon after I did, preferring the entrepreneurial atmosphere to the inertia at the big banks, and had never been interested in securing a fancy title. Tom had seen it all and liked to invoke Black Monday in '87—the biggest fall of the Dow in a single day—whenever we bemoaned the current state of the market.

"Labor and housing are still soft, and all signs indicate this trend will continue, so I'm cautious—if not outright negative—on home improvement stocks."

"Good point, Tom. Seems like a never-ending story."

"I'm still bullish on China," added Jack Wong, another top performer who had lived in Shanghai and spoke fluent Mandarin. "Their telecom stocks are a good buy right now."

I nodded. "In spite of the global slowdown, we can't count them out." Surveying the room, I added, "Anything else?"

The guys turned to each other and a few shook their heads before Tom said, "No, I think we're good."

Sighing, I put down my notes and looked at the group. "I want to talk about yesterday's P&L," I began. "We're down much more than I'd like to be. There's still a lot of volatility out there so we need to think about our long positions. A lot of companies have missed their earnings targets, unemployment is high . . . I know you all think I'm the biggest bear out there"—I heard a few chuckles—"but I feel like the market's still overvalued, so remember to be steady. You know what your price stops are, so have an exit strategy in place."

I was telling them things they already knew, but my losses and Tripp's enormous position had left me rattled. Until this week, our team had been enjoying a relatively good run. I wanted to remind everyone to avoid reckless behavior, but the person to whom that really applied wasn't even in the room.

"Did you guys have a late night?" I asked Nick once I was back at my desk.

"Not all," he answered. "I managed to get on the 7:16

train. Why?"

"Just wondering. Tripp wasn't at our morning meeting."

"He's here now. I saw him sitting at his desk."

I glanced at the time on my screen. 9:00AM. How gracious of Tripp to show up half an hour before the opening bell. Skipping the morning meeting without informing me demonstrated a nonchalance verging on disrespect and I refused to let him get away with it. Grabbing my BlackBerry, I walked the perimeter of the room until I reached the back of Tripp's chair. I watched him strike the keyboard with his index fingers for a few seconds and said, "Tripp."

He swiveled his chair halfway. "Oh. Hi, Mia. How are you?"

"Good, thanks. Can I chat with you for a few minutes?"

He quickly turned back to his screen and clicked down a window.

"Would you mind waiting until lunch? The market's about to open."

"I've been here since 7:30, so I have a little time to spare."

My subtle dig did not go unnoticed.

He shrugged and smiled. "Sure."

"I think the main conference room is free."

I stepped aside so he could disengage his long limbs from the chair.

"Lead the way," he said.

I softened my steps and the vise-like hold I kept on my BlackBerry. Had it been anyone else in the office, I would have made small-talk, but I couldn't come up with anything of polite insignificance to say to Tripp. He made no effort either and we plodded ahead in leaden silence.

I entered the dark conference room and turned on the

recessed lighting, grimacing at the bright wattage.

Tripp, hands in pockets, asked, "So, what's up?"

"You weren't at the morning meeting. Any particular reason?"

"Didn't I tell you? I had a dentist's appointment. Had to get a crown removed."

I looked at Tripp's top row of straight teeth, doubting they had needed much work since prep school. "No, you didn't tell me and, in the future, I'd appreciate an email if you can't make it. Those meetings are really the only time the team can meet as one."

"I apologize for my oversight," he conceded.

"Was it also an oversight that you neglected to run Touchnology Systems by me?"

"No," he deadpanned, "that was a calculated trade."

"Then why didn't you discuss with me first? Or did you think I'd object to your buying $19.5 million worth of stock on a company that made $15 million last year?"

"You know revenues aren't always an accurate sign of growth or potential."

"Maybe so, but I also think they can serve as a warning. Your position is too big and risky. It's almost a third of what we have outstanding right now and you can't just place trades like that without talking to me first."

"I've placed larger trades than that in my career."

"Atlas is not like the other firms. We have to think about risk control."

"But I thought Peter wanted to take more chances."

"My desk has never had that kind of mentality."

"Maybe it's time your desk took on more risk. I noticed

that your strategy is to play it safe. You run from a position the minute things get a little hairy."

"*Excuse me?* What are you implying?"

He shrugged. "Nothing. I'm just callin' it the way I see it. And for your information, I didn't arbitrarily buy Touchnology shares. Peter approved the trade."

Peter approved the trade.

I tried to contain my surprise and decided not to give him the satisfaction by delving further. "You should have given me the heads-up anyway. That's how it works on my team and I expect you to follow the same rules as everybody else."

"I think you and I have a very different view of my role here."

"Your role is not to lose any more money. Touchnology was down ten percent yesterday and we lost over two million. If the stock goes below fifty-six a share, I want you to get out. Understood?"

"Mia, I know this industry. Touchnology's seriously undervalued—"

"Below fifty-six and you're out. Are we aligned?"

"I don't think that'll happen, so I guess we're safe."

"Let's hope so."

Tripp looked at his watch. "I need to get back before the opening bell. Are we done?"

No, we've only just begun, I thought, but said, "Yes."

His lengthy strides had him out the door in seconds. Yanking a chair from under the table, I sat down and tried to collect my thoughts before the market opened. Instead of devising a strategy to recoup my losses, I had to meditate on Tripp's surprising revelation that Peter had signed off on his

Touchnology position. How could Peter have forgotten to tell me about it? He outlined broader market themes for us, areas where he saw the best opportunities, but seldom got involved in day-to-day trading activities. Approving a trade of Touchnology's size required a series of discussions; one-on-one sessions that had taken place without me. Tripp must have initiated them and that could only mean one thing: The prick was conspiring against me. He was out for my job.

It was something I'd suspected from the beginning. Peter was spending more time at his second home in Connecticut and had made a few comments in the last year about wanting to scale back. It was only natural he would want someone else to oversee the daily operations of the business, the internal headaches and challenges that grew tiresome with age. I'd always assumed that I was the front-runner to take on that role. Atlas didn't have a Chief Operating Office and my seniority, knowledge of the business and insight into Peter's psyche made me ideally suited. But now, instead of being appointed COO, I had to audition for the job. I didn't know what Peter had promised Tripp, but it was becoming increasingly evident we were competing against each other. Maybe Peter *had* forgotten to tell me about the Touchnology position, but Tripp's omission had been intentional. He knew I would criticize the trade. He wanted me to blow a fuse and look weak in front of Peter, but I had a flash of inspiration and laughed out loud.

Sorry, Tripp, but you're not as slick as you think.

I called Peter's cell. He usually left for the country on Thursday evenings and worked from there on Fridays.

"Mia!" he answered after two rings. "How's the city treatin' ya? The leaves are already changing color up here and I've just fed the goats ..."

Peter's twenty-acre property in Washington, Connecticut, could best be described as a gentleman's farm. A long, Belgian block driveway culminated in a ten-thousand square foot Adirondack-style "cabin" with stables and a fenced enclosure for cows, goats and chickens. Atlas's company retreats took place on the estate and Peter loved to turn milking cows or picking apples into team-building activities. I tried to be chipper, but found these off-sites messy and exhausting and couldn't get back to the city fast enough.

"Sounds wonderful," I enthused. "Listen, I just spoke to Tripp about his Touchnology Systems trade."

I expected an apology for not keeping me in the loop, but Peter simply replied, "Oh, that one! What do you think?"

"It's a huge position, but if Tripp's bet holds, we stand to make a bundle."

"My thoughts exactly! So you're on board with our Touchnology strategy?"

"Yes," I said, reveling in the genius of flipping the script on Tripp, never once imagining that this obscure little company would be my undoing.

3.

"Your usual, *cara*?" asked Guilio, the tattooed waiter with close-cropped brown hair at Sant Ambroeus, the West Village Italian eatery where I was a regular for Saturday brunch.

I perused the menu again, torn between my standard *omelette della casa* or something different. "I'll try the *crostino milanese* today," I said, unable to resist scrambled eggs with vine-ripened tomatoes and parmesan on a homemade roll.

"Excellent choice," he said. "With cappuccino and orange juice?"

"Yes, please."

He smiled, took my menu and slipped away. I sighed, at peace. All was right in my world: a bright, fall day, brunch at my favorite *pasticceria* and, best of all, ten hours of sleep the night before. For all my energy and discipline during the week, I needed a good weekend sleep-in to maintain my sanity. As a woman-of-color in a white, male-dominated profession, I had to work overtime to prove that I deserved to be Head of Equities. The highs and lows of the market were a given, but the energy required to stay cool under pressure—and to control my emotions—had me wound tighter than a ball of rubber bands. Yet the more senior my position, the more suspicious I became, jeopardizing the very self-confidence that had gotten me there in the first place. The weekends were my only exemption; prized hours when I answered to no one and could indulge my guilty pleasures like eating a pint of ice cream in bed.

Guilio set down my cappuccino and I admired the leaf-like design in the frothy milk. When I looked up again, he was in the same spot, a curious expression on his face.

"*Cara*, why are you always alone? Every Saturday? Pretty woman like you? Doesn't make sense!" he lamented, his torso rocking with each sentence.

I smiled. "Guilio, I like to come here by myself."

"What? No boyfriend?"

"Not one . . . several," I said. "Just kidding."

Guilio stared at me for several seconds, shook his head and then scurried away. Self-conscious, I sipped my cappuccino, daintily wiping the foam from my lips. I wondered if the rest of the wait staff thought I was pathetic, coming for brunch *da sola* Saturday after Saturday. Surely, I must have come across as successful and fulfilled? Besides, I was surrounded by men all the time. I actually had the privilege of working with some of the city's most eligible bachelors—presentable, economically stable men whom dozens of women would have considered the ideal partner. Ironically, that proximity had only resulted in turning me off of them completely. Access to dozens of uncensored conversations on the trading floor had only confirmed many of my assumptions about the men who worked on Wall Street. They considered themselves a universe apart, light years away from those who didn't earn million dollar paychecks. A girl entered at her own risk and could expect an outsized ego; short attention span; cancelled dates; a belief that his time was more precious than hers; plenty of excess but little romance; and, in the worst case, serial dating or compulsive cheating. By their very nature, these guys were transactional players and always on the lookout for the Bigger Better Deal.

When Guilio came back with my *crostino milanese*, he avoided eye contact, perhaps afraid he had said too much.

But his comments had roused old memories and my thoughts strayed to two years ago, a time when the markets were crumbling, but my personal life seemed almost perfect.

David Warren and I weren't introduced at a bar or restaurant. Our paths didn't cosmically cross scrambling for the same taxi during rush hour. We met at an event typical for overworked, time-strapped urban professionals: a 3.5 mile charity run around Central Park. A full year would pass before worldwide markets teetered on the brink of collapse, but there were already signs that summer—falling housing prices and a rise in foreclosures—that the economic winds were changing. But it was difficult to tell from the gamesmanship taking place at registration, as bankers and lawyers bragged about their training regimens and fastest times around the park. Having run track in high-school, I had faith in my ability, but was shriveling in the June heat. Muggy as only New York can be, I felt lethargic at the start and beads of perspiration dotted my chest. My plan was to run at a steady pace, cross the finish line and then cab it back to my apartment.

Naturally things didn't proceed as I'd hoped. An overeager runner rammed into me and my legs buckled on impact. I crashed to the ground as a gust of wind whisked across my face. The throng barreled ahead and I didn't know how to escape the impending stampede until a guy grabbed me by the armpits and dragged me to the sidelines. This Good Samaritan quickly swung into action, checking to see if anything was broken, but only my wrist throbbed from trying to stop the fall.

After securing an ice pack from a first aid volunteer, he introduced himself and I tactfully began to check him out, curious about this stranger who had interrupted his run to rescue me. David was tall and wiry, with the well-defined leg muscles of a dedicated runner, and I was tempted to touch the wavy ridges in his dark hair as he put the cold compress on my blistering skin, but what really struck me was his voice. It was an announcer's voice, fluent and clear, calming my moans of pain and mortification. I must have looked like a hot mess, too; my hair was coiled into a tight knot and I'd gone make-up free to avoid sweaty streaks of foundation. But David asked for my telephone number before re-entering the race and, although he repeated it a few times, I doubted I would hear from him ever again. When he did call later that evening to check up on me—and explained that he didn't work on Wall Street, but was a Manhattan Assistant District Attorney—I couldn't help grinning on the other end, delighted by my luck.

David was Chief in the Investigation Division, the department investigating financial fraud, corruption and racketeering. He spent a large part of his time going after people in my industry, but crimes committed by those with the money and position to know better intrigued me. I also felt an obligation to show him that not everyone on Wall Street was a greedy monster, so our early conversations were quite heated. Nonetheless something had clicked over the phone lines and we made a date for dinner at The River Café in Brooklyn. Since David had only seen me in a disheveled state, there was no way I would meet him again without careful preparation. After a Bliss Spa oxygen facial, fresh blowout and a new Alaïa dress, I entered the restaurant gleaming but unsure if we could sustain our telephone chemistry in person. David was already seated at the bar, drink in hand. When we exchanged that first, tentative glance and then started laughing about how this latest encounter was so different from our first, my misgivings evaporated. Dinner was delicious, the city views stunning and we talked non-stop.

Almost everyone I met in New York came from someplace else, but David was a true New Yorker, a native of Cobble Hill, the Brooklyn neighborhood inhabited by immigrants from Ireland, Italy and the Middle East before an influx of displaced Manhattanites looking for "up-and-coming" areas moved in. The blocks had long been inhabited by police officers and firefighters and David wasn't the least bit impressed by Manhattan's moneyed ruling class. He came from a large, close-knit family and had attended Fordham University on a full basketball scholarship. He was also active in his local chapter of the Boys & Girls Club, the place where he had first learnt to shoot hoops. David was an interesting dichotomy, a hard-nosed prosecutor with a big heart and a strong moral code.

We both had busy work schedules, so our date nights were limited to weekends. They usually consisted of casual dinners and movies on the Upper West Side where David lived, or more fashionable affairs at downtown spots near my Battery Park apartment. After about a month, our Friday dinners blossomed into Saturday mornings, wonderful, lazy mornings where we would wake up groggily in each other's arms. David loved to make a big breakfast—omelets, smoothies, pancakes and bacon—so we never left the apartment for brunch. During those first weeks of passion and discovery, we never went out much, but once we settled into a cozy routine, I wanted to let the outside world in again. There was so much going on that I wanted to share with David: new restaurants, movies, concerts, art exhibits. But he had little interest in the city's flashier side and said he loved nothing more than going for a run in the morning and then relaxing at home with me. I teased him about being a homebody until he finally agreed to a spattering of charity events and parties.

After we had been dating for about eight months, I booked a weekend for us at The Raleigh in South Beach. It was a gloomy time of year and we had been inundated with work. Our most recent date had been Chinese take-out and a DVD, but we fell asleep before the movie ended. I was afraid we were entering a premature rut and wanted to recapture the spark, but David lashed out at me for assuming he could just drop everything and take off. He also let it slip that I was spoiled and had no concept of the word "budget," especially since people were losing their jobs left and right. His criticism reverberated like a hammer to my heart. Nothing in my life had been handed to me on a silver platter and I'd worked hard for every last cent in my bank account. I made no apologies for my salary, one that was almost ten times larger than David's. And that's when it hit me. I asked if my lifestyle made him uncomfortable because I earned more money than he did. He denied it at first, arguing he was just as successful as I was, but that society placed little value on the kind of work that actually made a difference—teachers, nurses, police officers. All I did, he pronounced, was move money around. I produced nothing and helped no one.

I remembered sinking onto my couch—a plush, Italian symbol of my extravagance—and wondered if I should feel ashamed, if I should apologize for some crime I wasn't quite sure I'd committed. David had negated my identity, excoriating everything I'd struggled for and accomplished into a sham. He had always told me that he respected my career, loved the fact that I was independent and ambitious. His previous girlfriends had complained about his long hours, but I understood. Had all of that been a lie? Did he really clump me with those white-collar con-artists he wrangled with every day? I sought a cutting one-liner to lob back at him, but none came. I merely buried my head in my hands, shielding my hurt and disappointment.

David, realizing he had gone too far, finally crouched down and took my hands in his. "I'm sorry. That was totally uncalled for." He laughed nervously. "But I can't keep up with you."

"Why didn't you say anything before?"

His head drooped. "Male pride, I suppose. Mia, you know what ADAs make. I'm still paying off my student loans!"

"I don't mind treating for the dinners or trips. It doesn't matter who pays. I just wanted us to do those things together."

"But *I* mind. I don't want you to think I'm taking advantage of you."

"You've never made me feel that way," I said and began to consider the possibility that I had been trying to change David into something he wasn't. His normalness and lack of affectation were the very qualities that had appealed to me in the first place. With me, I never felt like he was looking for the Bigger Better Deal. Maybe I needed to take his concerns to heart and not be as demanding.

He tucked a piece of hair behind my ear. "I love you. I'm

sorry for being so grumpy."

David had told me he loved me five months into our relationship. When I responded in kind, I saw no imbalance between us, no signs that my salary could nurture his insecurity.

"It's Okay. We've both been under a lot of stress." Although this new layer in our relationship was troubling, I was willing to put it behind us.

"There *is* something I wanted to talk to you about."

"What now?" I asked, pulse quickening.

"I'm thinking of running for office next year."

"What?" I exclaimed. "Where did this come from?"

The presidential election was still a year away, but the nation was at a crucial crossroads with two wars and the floundering economy. David and I had spent many Saturday and Sunday mornings sifting through the *New York Times*, discussing the fate of our country, but I had never considered him anything more than a political junkie, certainly not someone with an appetite for political office.

"The congressman in the district where I grew up is retiring and my name has been mentioned as a candidate to replace him. I think it's time for me to take everything I believe in to the next level."

I thought of David's twelve years at the DA's office, his community service, photogenic looks and captivating voice. He wasn't a carpetbagger either, but a local boy who had never forgotten his roots. He could have easily accepted a job at a cushy, corporate law firm, but chose to serve the city.

I sighed. "You'd probably be perfect."

"But I don't want to do it alone. I want you by my side." He paused. "We'd make the perfect team."

"I wouldn't be good at politics—the fundraising, all the empty promises and pandering . . . "

"My campaign will be different. I'll have the highest ethical standards. I won't just pay lip service to—"

"But where will I find the time to help you?" I cut in. "I have my job and the market seems unstable. Things could get crazy."

"That's also what I wanted to talk to you about. I'm about to make a big change and want to know if you're willing to make one too."

"What kind of change?"

"Would you consider leaving Atlas and changing careers?"

"Changing careers?"

"Seriously, Mia, how much do you really enjoy what you do? You're tired and stressed out—you've said so yourself. You're a brilliant woman with so much more to offer than what you're doing now . . . "

"Stop it!" I shouted. "First my spending and now my career! You don't respect anything about me!"

"That couldn't be further from the truth! I'm saying this for your own good: Wall Street has shot itself in the foot. Your business isn't sustainable. It's all a house of cards, believe me. I plan to make financial reform a big part of my platform. Get out while you can."

I had heard this all before. Wall Street was a familiar punching bag and I had never taken it personally—until now.

"Is this for my benefit or yours?" I asked.

"What are you talking about?"

"For my benefit of yours?" I repeated. "Won't it look better for you if you have a girlfriend who doesn't work on Wall

Street?"

David looked down, realizing he had been caught. "Yes. It would make my message consistent."

"Have you poll-tested that? Because this is all about you, not me. You want a partner, all right, one who puts aside her goals to work on your dreams. Well, guess what David? I have my own dreams too and I'm not willing to give them up."

"Are you saying, then, that those dreams don't include me?" he asked.

I thought of David's parents whom I had met a few times, a cute couple married for almost forty years. His father was a retired municipal worker and had supported a family of five on his government salary. David's mother took a job as an administrative assistant only when her youngest began junior high. The eldest of three kids, David basked in his family's adulation; he represented all their hopes and aspirations. How could I have missed the signs? We had grown up so differently. I was an only child, brought up by a working mom after my father perished in a factory fire when I was three. My mother had never remarried and I saw first-hand the importance of having your own career and becoming financially independent. David wanted someone who wasn't emotionally invested in her own job and would willingly drop it all to follow his lead. He had been wired to shine; any woman by his side would have to live with the afterglow.

"Oh, David," I said. "I thought they did. I wanted them to, but if you want to be with me, you have to accept me for who I am: my job, my quirks, my lifestyle . . ."

"Please," he pleaded. "Go on this journey with me."

My throat tightened. Was I throwing away my chance

at happiness? Of marriage and having a family of my own? I looked into eyes; beautiful, brown eyes that had shown such compassion in the middle of that chaotic race in Central Park, but saw only a future I would no longer control, a life dictated by appearances and a lack of spontaneity.

"I'm sorry," I whispered, "but I can't."

We spent that final night together, tender hours where we both laughed and cried in the darkness, but when morning came, our differences were still insurmountable.

Four months later, I read in the Weddings & Celebrations section of the *Times* that David had married a Special Education teacher from Westchester. She was twenty-eight and conventionally pretty, with a dimpled smile that made her seem very malleable. Her father was also a prominent businessman and political fundraiser. I don't know what tore me up more, the fact that David had moved on so quickly or the withering suspicion this woman might have been waiting in the wings all along. He won the Congressional seat that pivotal election year, riding the winds of change and railing against Wall Street. I had spent almost a year with David, but never understood the full extent of his ambition. He epitomized the modern-day politician to a T—brilliant, calculating and so convinced of his own righteousness, he was blind to the casualties he left behind.

It was just as well we ended things. The markets went berserk shortly thereafter and I wouldn't have had the time to stroke David's ego. It was a relief to focus solely on my job again, with no digressions or self-reproach. When we were together, he had infiltrated my thoughts at the most inconvenient times and I could daydream about our weekends in bed or click on an affectionate text message again and again. The global economic meltdown left no space to ruminate over what could have been. Atlas required my full attention and, with David gone, I felt like myself again—in control, in front of my computer screens. Maybe I functioned better in a world of facts and figures; emotions were too erratic. Immersing myself in the labyrinth of a financial crisis, where billions of dollars and peoples' livelihoods were at stake, seemed like a worthy cause. Contrary to David's ominous prediction, Atlas survived. My leadership kept my team together and, most importantly, no one had been laid off.

Like David, I had been groomed to succeed and standing silently beside him at a political event with a plastic smile on my face would have contradicted everything I worked for.

I would not be fooled again.

4.

By eight o'clock Sunday night, I sat in my home office, officially out of weekend mode. It was Monday morning in Asia and the Japanese and South Korean markets had already been open for an hour. By 9:00PM New York time, Singapore and Hong Kong would follow suit. My strongest currency was information and trading trends from the major exchanges in that region were usually good indicators for what direction the US market would take. CNBC Asia droned on from the flat-screen television in the center of a custom-built bookcase. A reporter with an Australian accent provided updates from a panoramic glass-windowed studio in Hong Kong, where a morning fog hovered over the ultra-modern skyline of Victoria Harbor. I tightened my eyes to better capture the data from the ticker that ran across the lower part of the TV. This feature was jam-packed with symbols and figures, transmitting the latest news on securities and indices.

My office was the second-largest of the three bedrooms in my apartment. It was my favorite room in the whole place, the one that I had designed without the help of the tony decorator, who had completed the job late and over-budget. I knew this room would be the place where I would spend most of my time, so it was filled with the books and objects that made me the most happy. Unlike the tranquil grays and beiges that dominated my abode, these walls were clad in David Hicks's purple and white hexagon wallpaper. Two computer monitors stood on the brass Gabriella Crespi desk I found on *1stdibs* and photographs of my mother, godchildren and friends were dispersed on the bookshelves and window ledges. My extensive collection of coffee table books, with their striking, multicolored covers, brightened the sober navy and maroon spines of my business manuals. I often fell asleep on the tufted leather daybed pushed beneath the window and a small refrigerator stocked with nuts, dark chocolate and water was concealed inside one of the bookshelf cabinets. This office was a more luxurious version of my college dorm and I was still up late, studying.

Trading so far was brisk and the anchorwoman disclosed that two chemical giants had begun merger talks. Looking at her lustrous black hair and bright red lipstick, I wondered if she had ever made a split-second decision with millions of dollars on the line. Had she ever felt that knot in her stomach after losing money? The wobbly hands when you weren't sure whether to buy or sell?

Exhaling, I took off my glasses and rubbed my eyes. My vision had worsened after spending countless hours in front of the computer and fatigue was setting in, despite my peaceful weekend. The last two, turbulent years were finally taking their toll. I had pivoted from a painful break-up with David to the financial crisis with absolutely no time to catch my breath. My main priority had been to stay afloat—emotionally, professionally, financially—and it finally seemed like there was light at the end of the tunnel. December was two months away, commencing the start of bonus season.

Despite last year's debacle, Peter hadn't eliminated our bonuses. It was a middling sum compared to the previous three years when Wall Street seemed to ooze money, but not one person complained. In the wake of massive layoffs and dying firms, we were all grateful to have jobs. Mortgages and school fees could be paid and Peter's goodwill solidified our loyalty to him. I had some savings that carried me through the year, but I was counting on this year's bonus as much as everyone else. Yes, this was in the shadow of government bailouts and rising unemployment, but Atlas hadn't received any taxpayer money and I firmly believed our team's appreciable performance deserved to be recognized. Although my P&L had been down the last couple of weeks, I was sure I could make up those losses in the next two months. I had also made some shrewd bets earlier in the year and, if I continued making prudent trades— and had a bit of luck on my side—I was poised to receive a hefty bonus check.

My base salary of $250,000 was still a huge sum, an amount that would have taken my mother three years to earn at the height of her career. In college, I considered $100,000 the benchmark, the number which would announce that I'd arrived. Two hundred and fifty thousand was considered upper middle class—maybe even rich—for most of the country, but in Manhattan it barely covered my yearly expenses. The city had changed since the Nineties when I moved in. It was no longer the haven for idiosyncratic retailers; struggling artists in seedy downtown lofts; or recent college grads trying to get a break in fashion or publishing. It had become a homogenized, sanitized playground for the wealthy. Without a trust fund, you needed money to live in the city. Real money. Wall Street money.

Gone were the days when, fresh out of Wellesley, I shared an apartment with three other girls on East 96th Street and we each paid $500 a month in rent. It was technically a two-bedroom, but we put up drywall dividers and made it a four-bed-room. I ate cheap Dominican food from a restaurant in Spanish Harlem a few blocks up from my apartment. Organic food, gourmet coffee, a *cell phone*—they were all luxuries I couldn't afford. Fun, when my grueling schedule permitted, consisted of a movie or museum visits to MoMA and the Met when admission was free. Occasionally I would hit a bar with twenty dollars in my purse and buy a drink or two. Yet I never felt poor or inferior; slogging through New York became a badge of honor.

Ten years later, my responsibilities had morphed beyond recognition. I needed that bonus to pay my mortgage and maintenance; cover my bills and expenses; set up a nest egg for the future; and maintain a lifestyle that only seemed to balloon with each passing year. I was also on the Leadership Council of the Sherwood Forest Foundation, a non-profit started by a billionaire trader to fight poverty in New York City, and was expected to make a generous donation every year. Its annual gala was Wall Street's biggest event; a glitzy affair that brought the worlds of finance, fashion, art, sports and entertainment together, raising tens of millions of dollars in a single night. Sherwood Forest doubled its donations at the apex of the Wall Street bubble and its fundraiser the spring before the market meltdown was the snazziest on record. Jimmy Fallon's light-hearted jokes warmed up the exacting crowd, while Mary J. Blige's soulful voice and sublime beats had everyone gyrating on the dancefloor. We later learned that the whole extrava-ganza had been underwritten by one of the board members.

That evening, on my way to the ladies room at Cipriani Wall Street, I ran into a former classmate from Wharton, a cocky guy who had stood out among the more studious types with his penchant for openly challenging the professors. Unsurprisingly, he managed a very successful hedge fund and was regularly featured in *Alpha* magazine. I was amazed he recognized me at all, but he looked me up and down and declared, unapologetically, that I looked better now than I did in grad school. Ignoring the barb, I responded with all the insouciance I could muster, that I didn't look better, only more expensive. He laughed knowingly and mumbled before walking away, "Don't we all."

I think he had reacted to the outward signs of my success: the designer clothes and statement jewelry, my name on the Sherwood Forest Foundation's program. I had acquired all the trappings of the single-income woman with no kids: the three-bedroom co-op, reservations at the smartest restaurants, personal shoppers, vacations at exclusive resorts and spas, entry to prestigious organizations. Perhaps he could also intuit all the effort and contortions it had taken me to finally get a seat at the table. Now that I had joined the inner circle, it became paramount for me to stay there.

For the next half hour, I read back issues of the *FT* and *Wall Street Journal*, waiting for Hong Kong to open. When I turned up the volume again, the female anchor had been replaced by a spiky-haired Asian reporter in a tie and shirt-sleeves, commenting directly from the exchange. Unlike the controlled chaos of New York, where loud, jostling brokers and paper-strewn floors ruled, traders on the HKEX sat in neat rows at their computer terminals.

"Hong Kong shares opened 0.82 percent lower, with the benchmark Hang Seng index dropping 200.50 points to

24,219.12 in the first minutes of trading, driven mostly by a dip in technology stocks," he said, listing the stocks that led the downturn.

Scowling, I clicked on my Bloomberg screen. The Nasdaq futures index was down one and a quarter percent. Since most high-tech companies traded on Nasdaq, this was a worrying sign indeed. The tech sector was always evolving and prone to volatility, but the potential for growth also made those companies more attractive to investors. Our book of trades was heavily reliant on tech, with Tripp's Touchnology Systems the most exposed stock of all.

I pictured several different scenarios for tomorrow's open and quickly typed out an email to Tripp: Tech looks very weak. Keep in mind your stop-limit for Touchnology at 56.

Tripp's response came back immediately: Message received, Boss.

I paused and read the words again. I was advising him on how to avoid a major loss and he was being cute? Did Tripp think I would answer back in a huff? After several seconds of kicking around testy comebacks, I decided not to humor him and let the comment slide. I finally shut off the television and retired to my bedroom. I needed to save my energy for the trading day ahead.

I normally wake up on Monday mornings filled with optimism and an eagerness for the coming week. Previous mistakes were duly noted, but I didn't dwell on them and chose to focus on the present with a positive outlook. Maybe Tripp and I could call a truce and form a productive working relationship. Personality clashes were keeping us from our shared goal: making money for Atlas. I bounded out of bed as soon as the six o'clock alarm went off and took my BlackBerry into the bathroom with me. I checked Reuters, but within seconds, my good mood deteriorated. The markets were down. The tech dip in Asia had infected Europe, the Middle East, and Africa and now the blue chips were taking a beating. New York was waking up to another day of market turmoil.

I hustled down the hall to my office and turned on all my screens, condensing as much information as I could. The loss leader was Jihyun in South Korea, one of the world's largest electronics companies. Jihyun manufactured phones, televisions as well as the memory components for devices that didn't have their brand name on it. A market bellwether, they had warned of "lighter than expected" demand for their products and that technology spending was not as "robust" as previously thought. The CEO also cautioned that the "uncertainty" could persist for the next quarter. As Jihyun's stock tumbled, it displaced a host of other technology shares with it, renewing concerns about the health of the broader market. While I slept like a baby, a moderate decline had turned into a sharp nosedive, changing the day's trajectory. I compiled my positions and went through them one by one. I had taken a hit, but my trades were diversified and I could limit the damage. Unfortunately, my P&L would suffer another blow.

I couldn't afford to ratchet up more losses; my bonus depended on it. I emailed all of my traders and asked them to print out a status report by the morning meeting. Eight out of the nine traders—everyone except Tripp—got back to me within ten minutes. Tripp traded the tech sector exclusively, so his non-response must have been on purpose. His trades would bring down the whole equity group if we didn't map out a plan of action and, whether he liked it or not, he would have to listen to me. I checked the time and realized I only had half an hour to shower, dress and make the ten-minute walk to work.

Not exactly the calm, uplifting start to the week I had hoped for.

5.

I let Jack Wong, our Asian market specialist, conduct the morning meeting. He had lost a chunk of change on his Chinese telecom stocks, but made up for it by betting against a Japanese chip maker. Watching him hold court, I wondered why Peter hadn't hired another trader like Jack. He was so level-headed and exhibited a rare talent for breaking facts and figures down to their most understandable components.

"It looks like Europe might close with smaller than expected losses, so maybe our day won't be as bad we think," he said.

"Jack, what's your take on the stocks we should watch out for?" I asked.

"Right now, I'd short semiconductors. I also think software companies are overvalued and consumer electronics aren't going up any time soon," he said, ticking off each point with his fingers.

"What about small tech stocks?" I asked.

Jack shrugged. "There are opportunities out there, but they've got to be cheap. There's no need to overpay for anything. That's just stupid."

I nodded. "Well, thank you, Jack, for bringing us up to speed."

He broke into a slight smile. "Sure. No problem."

I scribbled down some notes while the other traders left the conference room. Once the clamor of feet and voices petered out, I was jolted by the grinding sound of the chair next to mine. Tripp lowered his loose-jointed arms and legs into it, his cheeks broiling with red-hot anger.

"Was that for me?" he growled.

"I don't know what you're talking about."

"That little show. Your questions to Jack."

Satisfied, I made a production of slowly closing my note-book and twisting my Mont Blanc pen shut, the same pen my mother had given me as a parting gift when she dropped me off at Wellesley for the first time. I carried that pen with me throughout college and grad school and would never surrender it, no matter how digitalized our world became. "At least I finally got your attention."

"You've had my attention. We just have a difference of opinion."

"Tripp, you've seen the numbers, you heard Jack. Tech's taking a hell of a beating and you can't lose any more money on Touchnology. Things are bad enough as it is and we can't handle anything below fifty-six."

The angry muscles in his face slackened and his chestnut eyes held mine for several seconds. "Mia, just trust me," he said, his mouth breaking into a simpering smile. "This one's a winner."

After ignoring my emails and snubbing my more senior role on the desk, Tripp now thought he could charm me with a cheesy statement.

"No. I've run the numbers. You know what the game plan is." I packed up my things and walked out.

I spent the rest of the morning attached to my headset, trading and comparing notes with our counterparties. Wall Street sometimes operates with a herd mentality, so the falling indices, coupled by a sudden rise in the price of oil, made people nervous. This motivated them to dump more shares, which decreased prices and brought the market down even further. It was a vicious cycle, making it difficult to know when you've hit bottom.

"Mia, here's that latte and sandwich you ordered," Nick said around lunchtime, handing over a paper bag and large coffee cup from a cardboard box. He had volunteered to phone in and pick up everyone's order from the café across the street.

"Thanks, Nick. You're a lifesaver."

"You look like you need a break," he said, ignoring his Greek salad and going straight for a bag of salt and vinegar chips.

"It's been a crazy day," I admitted, biting into my avocado and chicken wrap. "At least you're in positive territory."

He grinned. "Slow growth, tame inflation, record low interest rates . . . They've been perfect for my bonds."

"Feel free to rub it in."

"Returned over ten percent so far this year."

"When interest rates go up again, you won't be smiling."

"That won't be happening any time soon."

We chatted like this throughout lunch and, batteries recharged, I checked the European markets again. They ended a bit higher as Jack predicted, but not enough to rally the US market. Sipping my cold latte, I looked at our equity positions and nearly spit out my coffee. The whole desk was down fifteen percent. Panic-stricken, I quickly called up the current price for Touchnology Systems and saw that the stock had gone down to fifty-two dollars a share, four dollars below Tripp's stop-limit price. The size of the loss meant that Tripp had held on to the shares. He was sitting on a sinking stock and was willing to take the entire group down with him. Why had I believed he would follow my guidance? Why was he so hell-bent on defying me at every turn?

"That idiot!" The words flew out of my mouth before I could stop them.

"Mia, is something wrong?" Nick asked, looking up from his screens.

"You better believe something's wrong!" Taking my BlackBerry, I sprinted over to Tripp's desk.

"What the hell are you doing?" I demanded.

He craned his neck to look at me and replied, "Do you have a problem, Mia?"

"*You're* the one with the problem. You're down twenty percent and still sitting on the Touchnology position!"

He jumped from his seat, towering above me. "Yes, that's right. I made a decision not to dump the stock."

"We've discussed this time and time again! What is it that's not sinking in?" I asked, batting the side of my head with an index finger.

"I can't follow instructions I don't agree with."

His arrogance had made it clear that he considered me his inferior, holder of a job title he questioned. Our relationship had been infected from the very beginning, as soon as Peter brought him in without consulting me. My opinion had not mattered then, so why would it now?

"No, that's not it. You can't follow instructions from a woman!" I spat out, the last word shooting through the air like a bullet. The other traders, who had made pretense of doing their work, were now openly watching us.

Crossing his arms, he asked, "Do you throw that around whenever it's convenient?"

"I've never had a reason to say that before!" Taking a deep breath, I tried to regain the professional high ground. "Listen, Tripp, you're not just trading for yourself. You're jeopardizing our whole equity portfolio by being so reckless."

He unclamped his mouth to speak, but stopped abruptly. I waited, hoping we could get past this ugly spectacle and have a rational discussion. Instead, Tripp shrugged and turned, dismissing me and any authority I had as Head of Equities. Once I saw the backside of his blue fleece vest, I exploded.

"Don't turn your back on me!"

The whole room fell silent. My colleagues' bewilderment permeated the room, but I was impervious to their shock, never taking my eyes off of Tripp.

He spun to face me again with such haste, he bumped against his chair. "You need to calm down! Who do you think you're talking to? You run this desk like an uptight schoolmarm, it's a miracle you make any money at all!"

Uptight schoolmarm. I had been called many things, but this one surpassed them all. Before I could respond, I heard what sounded like snickering in the background. It was soon followed by another, and then another. They were laughing at me. Tripp had turned me into an object of ridicule.

"YOU. ARE. FIRED!" I roared. "Is that calm enough for you?" Glaring at those within earshot, I dared them to laugh at me again, but jaws dropped in stunned silence. I had never aired my dirty laundry in public before, but this rage I felt, my antipathy towards Tripp, was completely alien.

"Mia! Tripp! In my office *now!*" Peter screamed, cutting through the stalemate.

Our heads rotated in unison. I hadn't seen Peter all morning and wondered how much of my confrontation with Tripp he had witnessed. Tripp had pushed my buttons since the moment I met him. Once I explained it all, Peter would see that I'd had no choice. I tried to calm down as the three of us marched to Peter's office, but my boss startled me by slamming the door.

"Peter, I can't work like this, with *him*," I sputtered, heart ticking. "He's insubordinate and doesn't care about the team, only himself!"

"She's a verbally abusive prima donna!" Tripp shouted. "I can't work with someone who doesn't respect me."

"I don't respect you? You don't respect me!"

"The two of you better find a way to work together! And you, Mia—" Peter thrust his finger in my direction. "I won't tolerate that kind of outburst ever again on *my* trading floor!"

"Tripp instigated this, not me!"

Peter sat down, but didn't offer us a seat. Tripp and I stood like two unruly students called to the principal's office.

"What's the problem?" he asked wearily.

Tripp and I began speaking at the same time, but Peter cut us off.

"Mia, you first."

"The problem centers on Tripp's Touchnology position. He's already lost $3.9 million, ignored the stop-limit I gave him and shows absolutely no regard for my seniority. Enough is enough already!" I said.

"Mia and I fundamentally disagree about where this stock

is headed. You and I"—Tripp nodded in Peter's direction— "both agreed it was a good buy."

"Tripp's hanging on to that stock out of desperation. Just admit you don't want to dump it because that would prove I was right."

"Now I've heard it all."

"Peter, let's settle this, once and for all," I implored. "You're the only one Tripp will listen to. If he doesn't cut his losses today, Atlas stands to lose millions."

Peter steepled his fingers together, assessing us both.

"Mia, I know the last couple of years have been trying for you," he said at last.

It was an odd statement, delivered very matter-of-factly. What was Peter alluding to? The market meltdown? David?

Puzzled, I replied, "No more so than for anyone else."

"And the last few weeks have not been your best. Some of your positions haven't had the outcomes we'd hoped for," he added.

"The market's been in a free-fall, but I'm getting back on track. I always do," I said. "But that has nothing to do with Touchnology. My instincts tell me we need to pull out."

"You're acknowledging, then, that you've been having a tough time?" Peter pressed.

"Okay, fine—yes! But if everyone on my team was on the same page, things would be a hell of a lot easier."

"Mia, I think Tripp should be in charge of the equity desk going forward," Peter announced.

"Excuse me, Peter, but what did you say?" I asked, certain my ears were deceiving me.

"I said that I would like Tripp to lead the equity team

now," he repeated.

This couldn't be happening. Was the person I had just fired going to take over my job?

"Peter, I have to respectfully disagree."

"Mia, you know how much I care about you," he said, softening his tone. "This has nothing to do with us. I'm only thinking about the firm."

"Peter, you and I have worked together for almost fifteen years! You know what I can do. You know that I can turn things around!" I wanted to remind Peter of our bond—of how I had helped him build this firm—but he set his mouth into a thin line. I pointed scornfully at Trip and asked, "Who is this guy? *Who is he?* He doesn't care about the firm, only himself. *You know me.*"

"Mia, I think we'll be better positioned to take advantage of the opportunities in the market if Tripp takes over," Peter said.

"Peter, please just give me more time. I don't think we should be taking on more risk right now." I paused and envisaged the future: Meetings run by Tripp, trading strategy devised by Tripp, my bonus determined by Tripp . . . It was all too much and my rage bubbled over. "There's no way I'm going to report to—to *him!*"

"You don't have a choice," Tripp scoffed.

I looked at him and Peter. Two men—one was my mentor, the other my nemesis—but at that moment, they were interchangeable.

"Have you guys been planning to push me out all along?" I asked.

"Absolutely not," Peter said. "This is purely a business decision, based on your track record of late."

I had spent the bulk of my career—my most productive years—working for this man. I helped him bring in clients, set up his trading system, hired his staff. I saw his eyes well up when he showed me pictures of his first grandchild. I watched him enrich himself on the backs of traders like me, and calmed his fears when he thought Atlas would go under during the financial crisis. I had stood by him, through good times and bad, and that made me uniquely qualified to sniff out when he wasn't being completely forthright.

"Prove it to me then," I said. "It's either me or him."

"Mia, please don't go there," he said.

"Why not? It's either me or him."

"You're not being rational. Now you're the one being insubordinate," Peter said.

"I don't think so. You have to decide who's more important to this firm. Me"—I touched my chest—"or him." I pointed to Tripp.

"Well, if that's what it comes down to. If you're giving *me* an ultimatum," Peter retorted, "then I have to ask *you* to leave."

I didn't think he would call my bluff. I had expected him to take me aside and reassure me, reiterate how essential I was to the firm. Or, at a minimum, reprimand Tripp for provoking me. Dumb things were said in the heat of the moment and then forgotten once everyone cooled down, but Peter's voice was hard, devoid of any allegiance to our history together.

"Peter—" I began, but Tripp interrupted me.

"Didn't you hear what he just said?" he asked.

"Let's talk this through, Peter," I begged, all self-respect gone. "I helped you build this firm for God's sake!"

Out of the blue, I felt a slight pressure on my elbow and the acid heat of Tripp's breath on my check.

"I think everything's already been said. It's time for you to go," he hissed, nudging me towards the door.

I wrenched my arm away. "Let go of me! I am not fucking going anywhere with you!"

"Mia!" Peter cried. "Get a hold of yourself!"

"All that drama got you off the desk," Tripp sneered. "Show some dignity."

Every inch of my body rumbled, like a volcano about to erupt. I looked down and saw a plastic cup of water on Peter's desk. In that moment, I made a snap decision that was completely out of character. I reached for the cup, aimed and let the liquid fly in the air and onto Tripp's face, rejoicing as water splashed against his nose and dripped down his chin. Blinking wildly, Tripp tried to dry himself, but he flailed about like the stilt man in a circus. I crushed the cup in my hand, hurled it across the room and took off.

Avoiding the uncomfortable stares of my now-former colleagues, I proceeded to my desk, but CJ, the security guard whom I always said hello to, was already there. Although this shouldn't have made a difference, the ugly turn of events felt particularly humiliating because CJ was also black. He had told me numerous times how proud he was that a black woman had succeeded in the white, male-dominated world of trading. I had taken his daughter, now a senior in high school, out to lunch last summer to discuss colleges and careers. I, successful trader and pillar of the financial community, had even offered to write her a letter of recommendation. How I wished I could explain what happened! *I haven't let you down, CJ,* I thought.

Maybe the deck was always stacked against me. It was a miracle I lasted this long.

"CJ, I don't need a babysitter."

He shifted from one foot to another, as if weighing where his loyalty should lie. Finally, he said, "I have strict orders from Mr. Branco to escort you out the door."

In an instant, I had become a threat. Whenever a trader leaves a firm for good—whether it's forced or voluntary—he or she is asked to exit the premises at once, sometimes under the supervision of other traders or a security guard. In the worst case, a disgruntled trader could do untold damage with access to the firm's trading system.

Across the table, Nick had been watching me and asked, "Mia, what the fuck is going on?"

I thought back to our lunchtime chat an hour ago. I could always count on Nick for a good laugh or to commiserate with me over a bad day. I wanted to believe he respected me—maybe we were even friends—but wasn't he cast from the same privileged clay as Peter and Tripp? When push came to shove, wouldn't he take their side?

"Ask Tripp," I snapped.

Inside my right pant pocket, I thumbed the buttons of my BlackBerry. Strangely enough, it hadn't tooted or whirred throughout this whole ugly episode and I hoped CJ wouldn't remember to ask for it back. That phone was the only tangible thing left of my job.

Straightening my shoulders, I summoned what was left of my disintegrating pride and said, "I'm ready to go now."

Following CJ to the large mahogany doors, I departed Atlas Capital for the last time.

6.

The sound of CNBC's "Squawk on the Street" woke me up the next morning. The reporters' booming voices could only signify one thing: It was past 9:00AM, the market was about to open—if it hadn't already—and I was late, horribly late, for work. I flung off the duvet cover, stood straight up and realized I had slept in only my bra and underwear. I sunk back down on the edge of the bed and tried to stunt the tempest brewing in my system, a bizarre mixture of nausea, heat and a splitting headache. With so much to do at the office, I had no time to be sick. And what mysterious illness would make me feel like I had a hangover? I turned to the digital clock on my bedside table and screamed. Not only was it ten-thirty, but an empty wine glass and a carton of Häagen-Dazs Dulce de Leche ice cream (on a weekday!) were squished between the tissue box and a Diptyque candle. I studied the items in confusion until a messy pile of clothes also came into view: rumpled black trousers and a blue silk blouse. My BlackBerry was strewn atop like the cherry on a sundae and I was catapulted back to reality.

I'd been fired. I didn't set the alarm because I had nowhere to go. "Squawk on the Street" had started the trading day without me. Yesterday's humiliating events rushed back mercilessly, pestering me to relive every painful moment of my dismissal. How had events gotten so out-of-control? Why hadn't I kept my composure? Did I really curse Tripp out in full view of the trading floor? He had sabotaged me with every purchase of Touchnology stock and I walked right into his trap. My stomach lurched when I thought of Peter's betrayal. I only wanted what was best for the firm. How could he have thrown me under the bus like that?

Picking up my tainted, jilted clothes, I tried to piece together what happened after I got kicked out of Atlas. I remembered riding the elevator in a daze and stepping out into the October chill. I had no coat, no purse, no money. Only my company-issued BlackBerry, but who could I call? I hugged myself to stave off the cold and walked down Rector Street shell-shocked. Passersby shot strange glances in my direction, as though my dismissal were printed on my forehead. Why on earth would a professional-looking woman wander down the street—without a coat in brisk, forty-degree weather—unless she was drunk or disturbed?

By the time I reached my apartment building in Battery Park, I was shivering and the chief doorman, Vladimir, who had been signing for a package, rushed to my side, his normally cheerful face contracting in worry as he fired off questions:

"Ms. Lewis, is everything OK?"

I think I gave an unconvincing nod.

"Did anything happen? Were you mugged?" He led me to the lobby's seating area and urged me to sit down.

I obeyed.

"Should I call the police?"

"No, thank you."

"What is it?"

Vladimir presided over a building where the cheapest apartment sold for two million dollars. In that price-bracket, residents expected him to go above and beyond the call of duty. Discretion was foremost, so he turned a blind eye to a drunken stupor or a loud, bickering couple. But getting fired? People who lived in this building didn't get fired. They made decisions, moved markets, served on distinguished boards. If Vladimir knew I'd been fired, his concerned eyes would turn to pity and it was more than I could take.

I tried to eke out a few coherent words. "I felt really sick and had to come home right away."

"Would you like some water?"

The unfortunate incident with the cup on Peter's desk sprang to mind and I shook my head vigorously. "I just need to go upstairs and rest."

"Of course. Let me help you get up."

He offered his hand for support and we took small steps towards the elevator.

"There's one more thing," I added. "Can I have my spare set of keys? I forgot my bag at the office."

Once inside my apartment, I finally released the torrent of tears that had been pressing so feverishly against my eyes. I think I wolfed down my first glass of Cabernet soon after and then rifled through the refrigerator for something sweet, finding the ice cream behind a bag of vegetables in the freezer. I must have been disoriented when I finally threw off my clothes and crawled into bed, reflexively putting on the TV for company. Hours later, here I stood, almost naked, shaking out the wrinkles from yesterday's clothes and laying them neatly on the bench at the foot of my bed, as though they needed to be preserved for another day at the office.

I cradled the BlackBerry uncertainly in my hand. It was my lifeline, my extra appendage, the only number I had handed out to friends and business associates for the past ten years. I pushed a few keys and the phone lit up. Hopeful, I reached for my dormant landline and called my BlackBerry. A sharp signal was followed by an automated message: "The person you are trying to reach is not accepting any calls at this time. Please try your call again later." I couldn't even leave a voicemail. Since I was in a punishing mood, I also called my direct line at the office, but it went straight to the receptionist.

I showered, changed into an old pair of sweats, and set up a command post in my home office. First, I tried logging on to my Atlas email. My user name was invalid. I was also denied access to the firm's Intranet. When I brought up Atlas's homepage and clicked on "Management Team," I was no longer listed on the employee roster. Tripp's name had replaced mine as Head of Equities. I stiffened, staring at the computer screen. My phone and email accounts had been cancelled. All proof of my ten years at Atlas Capital had been wiped out. I was shocked by how quickly they had formalized my termination. Tech support was notoriously slow when it came to fixing a computer glitch, but they had scampered like ants to expunge me from the system. Their orders must have come directly from Peter. What would he tell my clients? My team?

I had bought into the notion that Peter was a man of integrity, but his self-confidence bordered on hubris. His mood could swing with every fluctuation of the Dow, but as long as I followed orders, my career flourished. This enabled me to stand silently while he ingratiated himself with potential clients or disparaged underperformers whom he considered dead weight. I never cared when spiteful employees claimed that I had really started out as his secretary or implied that I had slept with him to become Head of Equities. When I was top, when I thought Peter had my back, I laughed off these false assumptions. I must have been doing really well if I could inspire such malicious gossip.

After dedicating nearly all my waking hours to Atlas Capital and making millions of dollars for the firm, how *dare* Peter fire me? Tripp's losses were much worse than mine, why was I being made the scapegoat? My head spun as I searched for a plausible explanation and I kept returning to the same sorry conclusion: Peter had cut me loose because I was a woman. Tripp's unexpected hire had been the first step in his calculated plan to phase me out. The chain of events followed a familiar, highly effective pattern, one that scores of women on Wall Street have experienced. It begins harmlessly enough when male colleagues "forget" to give you important information. You try not to be paranoid and believe them when they tell you it was just an "oversight." Next they stop including you in meetings and nights out with clients, using the old "it was a last-minute thing" excuse when you object. They'll inevitably remark that your numbers are down too, but when you complain about the lack of support and resources, they'll accuse you of being "too sensitive." Finally, when the firm posts a loss or needs to downsize, you'll be the first to go and you're out the door before you can rationally process what really happened.

The financial crisis had been brutal for a handful of high-ranking women who had risen to the executive suite at several banks. The most depressing firing of all had been that of Theresa Breeze, a charismatic M&A banker and the highest-paid woman on Wall Street. Not only had Theresa shepherded the most lucrative deals of the decade, she was raising three kids to boot. But when Theresa clashed with her bank's new president, he fired her as she boarded a flight to San Francisco for a client meeting. If Theresa Breeze hadn't been spared, some women argued, none of us was safe. But I had seen no reason to worry. Peter supported me; my position at Atlas was secure.

Unfortunately for Peter, I wasn't going quietly into the night. I would contact a lawyer and sue Atlas for wrongful termination or sexual discrimination or racial bias—anything to make them pay for sacking me and disgracing me in front of the whole firm. But first, I had some business to do. I set up a Gmail account and rejoined the digital universe. Luckily, I had backed up all of my professional contacts on my home desktop and transferred all that information to my new Gmail address book. I wrote an email to my clients, Wall Street counterparties, professional associations and the Sherwood Forest Foundation informing them that Atlas Capital and I had parted ways. I was surprised by how quickly the words flowed, but I was confident about what I could offer a new firm. I had a solid reputation as a straight-shooter among the other traders in the marketplace and many of them had tried to poach me from Atlas in the past, but I always touted my loyalty to Peter. I emphasized my "proven track record" in the industry as well as my strong personal relationships. I finished off with a statement about "wanting to leverage my fifteen years of experience with new opportunities" and sent it off. The only thing left to do was wait.

Five hours later, sprawled out on my bed again, laptop by my side, I still hadn't received any responses to my email. I had banned CNBC—it was a painful reminder of what I had just lost—and tolerated daytime talk shows and reality television. To make matters worse, Vladimir called to say I had a delivery and when I went downstairs to pick it up, it was nothing more than a box with my handbag and other personal belongings from Atlas. Before emptying the box, I glanced at my email again. I had a new message! Leila Benghazi, Head of Equity Strategy at Komura Securities, had written me back. A fellow Wharton grad, Leila had been in the business for over twenty years. We often met at industry functions and alumnae events and she had always been a good source of advice. The subject line of her email was empty. The only text in the body of the message was "Call me" and a link to *marketmaker.com*, the Wall Street gossip site.

Market Maker professed to cover breaking news in the financial industry, but it actually spent a disproportionate amount of time tracking the movements, fumbles and follies of Wall Street personalities. The site was run by JoJo Katz, a thirty year-old English Lit grad who had dabbled on Wall Street for a few years before giving it all up to write. Instead of penning the next Great American Novel, she created a blog at the height of the Wall Street bubble when bankers were still respected and envied. In the aftermath of the financial crisis, Market Maker had taken a crude, satirical turn; fair criticism had warped into ridicule. But everyone on the Street read *marketmaker.com*— even if they were loath to admit it—and many of the reader comments were off-color. A well-known hedge fund manager once became so irritated by JoJo's negative articles, he wrote her a scathing letter. JoJo thought nothing of publishing it on Market Maker, certain his unintelligible sentences would only cause further damage.

Therefore, I clicked on the link with a boding sense of doom.

Mia's Meltdown

Hot-shot trader Mia Lewis is out at Atlas Capital. After a nasty tirade against fellow trader and tech expert Tripp Armsden—witnessed by everyone on the trading floor—Lewis was asked to leave the highly profitable niche firm she helped build with mentor and former Morgan Stanley powerhouse, Peter Branco. Ironically, the target of her wrath now has her job. One of the few women on the Street to head a trading desk, Lewis' book was said to be down by twenty percent and sources say her meltdown was painful to watch. If you don't believe me, click on the link below for the full audio-visual experience.

I clicked and saw a grainy version of myself mouthing off at Tripp. He stood still with his arms across his chest, so it seemed like I was the one on the attack. There was a pause in the recording after I fired him, but the next scene showed me again, defeated, being escorted out of Atlas with CJ.

I felt sick. One of my co-workers had secretly recorded the incident and was now using it to smear me. Tripp's insults and attitude had escalated the situation, but you couldn't tell from the video. I looked incoherent and unhinged, while he was the guiltless victim of my verbal abuse. It didn't get much worse than this. I'd been taken down on Market Maker. Everyone I emailed this morning must have seen JoJo's post or heard about it. I scrolled down to the Comments. Most of them were anonymous—or under a fake-sounding name—and there were forty-seven of them. Forty-seven!

"Too much sass, not enough class."

"I'm glad she's out of here!"

"Can somebody please just f**k her and put her out of her misery?!"

"This is what happens when you give women too much power. They can't handle it and go off the deep end."

Blurry-eyed, I couldn't see straight anymore. The viciousness of the comments was beyond anything I could ever conceive of. I didn't recognize the person they were writing about. Who were these people? Some of them must have been Atlas colleagues. Is this what they really thought of me? I had never hurt anyone; I was only doing my job. Sure, I was tough when necessary, but I was no different than the male traders out there. A woman on a trading desk had to fight for her professional survival every day. My career had ended because I wasn't afraid of standing up to Tripp.

Clicking out of Market Maker, I called Leila.

"Leila Benghazi."

"Leila, it's Mia," I said, trying to sound as upbeat as possible.

"Oh my gosh, Mia! How are you?" Leila asked. "Let me just close my door. How are you holding up?"

"I was okay until I read that post on Market Maker."

"I'm so sorry, but I thought you should know it's out there."

"Why would someone have recorded that?"

"No one's safe anymore with all the cell-phone cameras. You really have to watch everything you say and do."

"I looked like a banshee in that clip!"

"It was funny how you went off on Tripp!"

"Really? Did you read the Comments and all the mean things people wrote about me?"

"They're just losers with too much time on their hands."

"All this is happening because I let Tripp get the better of me!"

"You know, he interviewed here last year and took absolutely no responsibility for the losses at his old bank. My boss thought he was talented, but with a serious cowboy mentality."

"Well, my *old* boss seems to think that mentality is good for the firm."

"How old is Peter now?"

"He turned sixty this year. I was at his party. A big shindig his wife threw at The Pierre."

"Hmph. He's probably looking to retire soon, right? That always makes men do dumb things. He needs an heir-apparent. He's probably cheating on his wife too."

"The problem is," I began. "The problem is I thought I was his heir apparent."

"Oh, Mia, I'm so sorry—"

I couldn't disguise my despair anymore. It was too exhausting. "Leila, what am I going to do now? No one has gotten back to me except you."

"That's because all the firms have a hiring freeze right now. There won't be any jobs until the economy picks up."

I took a deep breath and asked, "How about Komura Securities? Are there any openings at your firm?"

"No, Mia, unfortunately we don't have any positions for someone at your level."

"I could work as a consultant or a staff trader. I don't need to head a group."

"Mia, I don't know how to tell you this because you're my friend and I hope that'll never change." She paused. "But I was specifically told not to hire you if you contacted me."

"*What?*" I croaked. "But I haven't done anything wrong!"

"I'm so sorry, Mia, but you've become persona non grata on Wall Street."

7.

It had taken less than an hour for my Wall Street career to go up in smoke. All the haters on Market Maker, along with flashbacks of my lethal faceoff with Tripp, destroyed any wishful thinking. A few people had emailed me back, but their responses were banal: Too bad...; Hang in there!; You're in my thoughts ☺. The smiley face didn't translate to a job offer.

I didn't leave my apartment, powerless to stop the miserable new existence closing in on me. Hours of nothingness, anxiety about the future, tormented me. Emotions veered from anger to disbelief to resentment as I replayed that cataclysmic scene in Peter's office again and again, wondering how I might have done things differently. And finally, when it all became too much, I swallowed two Nyquils and went to bed.

After over a week of self-pity, binge-eating and moving around without a purpose, I had already put on five pounds. I hadn't watched CNBC or read a newspaper either and I *always* stayed connected, even on vacation. I didn't know whether the markets were up or down and feared I had already relinquished brain cells. But hadn't I counseled dozens of the newly unemployed to pick themselves up and look ahead, no matter how bleak the future seemed? To take stock of their situation and start looking for a new job right away? Looking for a job required time and effort, I once advised, the equivalent of a full day at the office. If I was going to embark on an extensive job search, I needed to update my resume and get a new cell phone, so I finally dusted myself off and went outside.

Battery Park City was such a curious neighborhood, I observed, passing through Rector Park onto the Esplanade, the picturesque pedestrian walkway that extended along the Hudson River. It was a planned community at the southwestern tip of Lower Manhattan, fabricated by using tons of soil and rocks excavated during the construction of the World Trade Center, combined with sand dredged off of Staten Island. It was a recycled urban utopia, filled with high-achieving New Yorkers, shops and restaurants. The Esplanade was like an unexpected gift, a bountiful public space lined with parks, gardens and marinas. Whenever I jogged the length of it, I'd stop at the end and sit on one of the benches, taking in the muddy smell of the water, the dramatic views of the Statue of Liberty and Ellis Island—all of it an energy jolt, like New York itself. Midmorning on this autumn weekday, mainly parents, nannies and children packed the playgrounds or pushed baby carriages. The so-called professionals occupied the office buildings soaring above the Financial District. I had once been a member of that elite club. How could I have been so stupid and thrown it all away?

It had been so important for me to live in this odd stretch of Manhattan real estate. After 9/11—and the senseless loss of three Wharton classmates—it seemed essential to be a part of revitalizing the neighborhood, to support its efforts at normalcy again. Hundreds of Battery Park City residents hadn't been able to return to their homes for days following the attack. Airplane debris damaged one apartment building and toxic smoke from the World Trade Center fire filled the air for months. The developers of my building broke ground two years after 9/11 and the units were put on the market three years later. I purchased my apartment in 2006, the last year of the real estate boom, which meant I had definitely overpaid for it. Replete with bonus money to pay for half of my co-op in cash, I almost *thanked* the broker for accepting my offer.

I left the Esplanade and cut through the park again near West Thames Street, hastening my speed when I reached Rector, hoping I wouldn't run into anyone I knew. Or maybe they wouldn't recognize the woman in velour track pants and a Yankees cap who had taken over my body. I was entering the belly of the beast, the heart of the Financial District. The New York Stock Exchange stood straight ahead, with the Federal Reserve Bank a few blocks away. Tours of Wall Street had surged since the financial crisis; curiosity-seekers were eager to visit the mythical place that had almost bankrupted the country. Over the years, I became immune to the mystique, concentrating more on the time-critical, profit-making aspects of my job. I would sometimes visit Trinity Street Cemetery, the centuries-old graveyard on the corner of Wall and Broadway, and study the crumbling, engraved tombstones, unable to decipher the eerie cryptograms, but imagining what life was like in the seventeenth and eighteenth centuries. Several prominent early New Yorkers, like businessman John Jacob Astor, Sr., were buried at Trinity, a testament to how deeply finance and trade were embedded in the southern tip of the island. My favorite headstone belonged to Alexander Hamilton, the first Secretary of the Treasury. It seemed only fitting that his final resting place was at the center of the financial world.

When I finally made it to the Verizon store, about a dozen people were waiting to be served by two sales assistants who scuttled from one retail display of phones to another. I stood behind a guy dressed in a New York City Transit Authority uniform.

"Excuse me," I said to him tentatively.

He turned, looking at me through hooded eyelids. "Yeah?"

"How long have you been waiting?"

"About half an hour."

I looked at my watch and groaned—even though I had nothing but time to spare.

Two hours later—and a couple of hundred dollars poorer—I returned to my apartment. A good cellular package sure is expensive when you have to pay for it yourself. Atlas had upgraded my cell phone automatically every year with the full, deluxe plan: roaming, international long-distance, unlimited Internet, online subscriptions to Bloomberg and the *Wall Street Journal*. I couldn't bring myself to revert to a basic cell phone—technological regression would be the final insult—so I purchased the cheapest Blackberry I could find. Technically, I was still a trader and needed to look the part, but only signed up for the standard domestic plan. Long distance calls to Europe and Asia were out of the question.

I hadn't updated my resume in three years, not since being named Head of Equities at Atlas. The crowning achievement of my career, I hadn't been looking for another job. An article in the *Wall Street Journal* soon followed, and then a board member of the Sherwood Forest Foundation took me out to lunch and nominated me for their Leadership Council. Professionally, things had never looked better.

Where to begin? I assembled all the corporate action words I could think of: *manage, execute, supervise, increase.* I highlighted only the positives, of course, laboring over the font style and text size, but when I printed out the final version of my resume and held it in my hands, it felt like I had been reduced to that flat sheet of paper. Everything I had written, all my accomplishments, sounded like bullshit. An employer would certainly be able to read between the lines and ascertain what I had omitted. They would only have to Google my name and the vicious gossip about my demotion would flare like warning lights. I also couldn't ignore the crucial fact that Peter had been my only boss for the last ten years and a glowing reference from him would not be forthcoming. That might have been possible had I left on civil terms, but a ten-year trading career paled in comparison to a violent splash of water in Tripp's face.

I crumpled the resume and threw it in the garbage. Who was I kidding? The country was in the middle of the Great Recession and no one would hire me after the water-flinging rage in Peter's office. I had already contacted the top firms in the business in that first, urgent email and they wouldn't touch me with a ten-foot pole. My best option might be a back-office job at a bottom-tier firm.

And there was no way I was going to let that happen.

"So, Ms. Lewis, from what you're telling me, you have reason to believe that you were wrongfully terminated?" asked Eric Mannheimer, the labor lawyer who eagerly met with me a day after I contacted his office.

"Yes," I replied. "My job as Head of Equities for Atlas Capital—*one that I performed successfully for three years*—was taken away from me and given to a *male* trader who was hired to the firm a few months ago."

Mannheimer, the senior partner at this small employ-ment law firm, nodded sympathetically as he took notes with a ball-point pen on a yellow legal pad. He was in his late sixties; bald on half his head, but with bushy dark eyebrows; and a short, stocky physique. The practice operated out of an unlikely spot in the Garment District, with a creaky elevator and one of those frosted glass and wooden doors reminiscent of old de-tective movies. After researching lots of big, genteel firms that sounded impressive but impersonal, I had contacted an aggres-sive, inconspicuous one with a history of going after strong, establishment companies in the name of the weak, poor and underrepresented. Working as a well-paid trader didn't exactly put me in one of those categories, but I presumed a feisty law-yer like Mannheimer wouldn't resist a case where a Wall Street firm had fired a black, female executive in favor of a guy from *The Official Preppy Handbook*.

"And you're saying nothing in your job performance led to your termination?" he probed.

I grunted dismissively, smoothing down the lapels of my Escada jacket. I had dressed up for the first time in weeks, with full make-up and a neat bun to complement my game face.

"I don't need to tell you how volatile the market has been," I began, "so of course I suffered some unfortunate losses, but who hasn't? My overall performance had been consistent and, given enough time, I would have turned things around."

Mannheimer stopped writing and wagged his head from side to side. "When is all this bleeding going to stop? Those guys on Wall Street are crooks, nothing but crooks! Raping the average American while lining their pockets!"

I smiled awkwardly. Since the financial crisis, everyone had fiery opinions about Wall Street, even if they didn't know the difference between a stock and a bond. I wondered if my current predicament exempted me from the "crooks" label, but Mannheimer's zeal could only be good for my case, right?

He set down his pen and clawed his hands behind his head. "What do you want?" he asked.

"Excuse me?"

"*What do you want?*" he repeated, raising his shaggy eyebrows.

"Well," I began, giving myself time to think.

"Your old job? An apology? Damages? Severance?" Mannheimer egged me on.

Going back to Atlas wasn't an alternative. What I really wanted back was my former, irrefutable identity, the position and respect I had rightfully earned as a trader. Peter and Tripp had wrested that away from me and I no longer knew who I was without it. My job had been the very tool that directed my life and influenced all of my decisions. I felt directionless, unstructured and humiliated. I needed to reclaim my pride and self-confidence. If I didn't, then all the sacrifices I had made since I was thirteen would have been for nothing. *I* would be left with nothing.

I spoke with what I hoped was renewed resolve. "I'd like them to acknowledge that I was let go without due cause. I'd like to get my back pay and the bonus that's owed me. I'd also like a statement and positive reference that would enable me to get a comparable job at another firm." I paused. "I want my reputation— *my good name*—back."

Mannheimer nodded. "I want to see that fighting spirit

going forward because this case can go long and it can get ugly. Are you ready for that?"

I had called Mannheimer & Associates because I was ready for a fight, but just how strong was my case? I had purposely left out the water-flinging incident, hoping that by the time Mannheimer uncovered it, other factors would outweigh that momentary lapse of judgment. I took leave of my senses only *after* Peter's dismissal and Tripp's provocations. A fresh wave of anger coursed through me at the memory and I practically shouted, "Yes!"

"And how are you fixed for money? Do you have enough for a retainer and some savings to tide you over while I work on your case?" he asked.

I smiled widely and prayed my voice wouldn't betray me. "Of course."

As soon as I came home, I tossed the Escada jacket on a leopard chair in the foyer. It was one of two flanking the narrow console where I usually put my keys and mail on an orange lacquer tray. Who had picked out that furniture? Me or the bitchy decorator? All I remembered was how I had casually signed check after check to create a glamorous Manhattan showplace that I never spent any quality time in. In my current situation, none of these domestic trappings gave me any comfort. They were all liabilities, torturous reminders of how much money I had blown in conspicuous consumption during my years at Atlas Capital.

I made myself a foamy cup of Nespresso (at least I was

saving money by not going to Starbucks anymore) and entered the sanctuary of my home office, girding myself for the terrifying task I had been pushing out of my mind for the past week. I had licked my wounds with fattening foods and TV marathons, all the while knowing that I would have to face the cold, hard facts of my personal finances. I organized my bills and credit card statements from the last six months and entered all the expenses I could think of on a spreadsheet.

Monthly Budget

Mortgage ($2.5 million apartment)	$13600
Car Lease (Range Rover Sport)	$599
Whole Foods	$1000
Clothes / Shoes / Handbags	$6000
Dining & Entertainment	$2000
Hair	$800
Manicure / Pedicure	$400
Triple Oxygen Facial Treatment (Bliss Spa) 2 @ $160	$320
Massage (Dorit Baxter) 2 @ $89	$178
Personal Trainer (Drago)	$1200
Telephone	$150
Electricity	$500
Dry Cleaning	$800
Housekeeper (Eva)	$1600
Waxing	$200
Miscellaneous (Car Service, Taxis, Lunch, Gifts, Flowers)	$1000

total per month $30347

per year $364164

Yearly Expenses

Jewelry / Luxury Items	$25000
Insurance (Car, Apartment)	$5000
Vacations	$40000
Charitable Giving:	
Sherwood Forest Foundation	$50000
American Cancer Society	$25000
Wellesley	$10000
Wharton	$10000
Convent of the Sacred Heart	$5000
Art	$50000
Christmas Gifts	$10000
Tips	$5000
Emergency Fund / Savings	$50000
per year	**$285000**

After two hours of crunching numbers, I couldn't believe
my eyes, so I did it all over again. There had to be some mistake about the amount of money I spent each month, but my
American Express Platinum Card, the card I used exclusively
to earn points for membership rewards that I never actually re-
deemed, had conveniently broken down all of my expenses by
category and I saw just how much I spent a month on discre-
tionary items like spas, gourmet food and clothes. After adding
my mortgage, insurance, electricity, telephone and the Range
Rover that I barely used, I gaped at the sum before realizing
that I had left out the downtown garage where I kept the car.
That would add another bloodsucking $600 to my monthly
budget. In order to maintain this level of annual spending, I

went through about $55,000 a month. $660,000 a year. Six hundred and sixty thousand after-tax dollars to live in a flashy New York apartment and support a stable of stores, restaurants and service providers. I was like a small business with payroll. I had single-handedly kept the engine of the Manhattan consumer economy going. Facing those numbers on paper triggered more distress than when I'd been expelled from Atlas. Back then I still had a trace of hope that I could rebound. Now, I had no idea when I would work again.

The enormity of the digits was staggering, but I tried to find a silver lining. Not all of my expenses were shallow, self-serving pursuits. I gave $100,000 a year to charity. There was a price to pay for the privilege of being on the Leadership Council of the Sherwood Forest Foundation and the Board expected no less than $50,000 a year in support. My mother had died of pancreatic cancer when I was twenty-one and funding cancer research was a priority. Right out of college, I donated whatever I could, participating in walk-a-thons and donor drives, and as soon as I started earning a six-figure salary, I increased my donations accordingly. I was grateful for the scholarships and excellent education from the various schools I had attended. Those degrees had been the stepping stones to my career and the annual gifts were my way of saying thank you. I loved shopping for presents and stocked up on Christmas and birthday goodies for my friends and three godchildren months in advance. Generous Christmas tips spread a little joy to the housekeeper, personal trainer, doorman, mailman, superintendent, Fedex courier, Starbucks barista, dry cleaner, masseuse, skin therapist, hair stylist and nail technician who made my life that much easier and infinitely more attractive.

So I liked to share my wealth, what was the big deal?

Except that my year-end bonus had always paid for that largesse.

Bonuses were awarded based on personal as well as firm-wide performance. It was up to the individual trader to budget wisely and make that money last for the year. My base salary of $250,000 a year corresponded to a little under $13,000 a month after taxes. For the five years prior to the market meltdown, my bonuses had ranged from $650,000 to $1,250,000, the seven-figure number a direct result of heading the equities desk. I was a marketer's dream, the self-paying female, a single income earner with no dependents. *I'm worth it* had become my mantra. Personal shoppers had become friends. No wonder I was so susceptible to luxury advertisers, special offers and invitations to store openings and trunk shows. Hadn't my expensive wardrobe and accessories only validated my position as a top producer at Atlas? Hadn't all that stuff served as armor while I battled the evil knights and thieves at the office?

I'd been living on savings from my bonus of two years ago, waiting until December when this year's bonus was handed out and I could get back on track. And bonuses were taxed fifty-percent. Based on my calculations, I was burning $654,164 out of $777,500 in after-tax income.

I still had one last step and that was to check my bank account. I needed to see how liquid I was, just how much cash I had on hand. I logged onto Citibank and breathed a sigh of relief when I saw $48,562 in checking. Luckily, I had gotten paid half of my monthly salary on the fifteenth of the month and hadn't touched it yet. I had another $74,000 in savings. A total of one hundred and twenty-two thousand, five hundred and sixty two dollars in cash, but my stock portfolio and 401k had lost half of their value. With monthly expenses at around $35,000, I'd go through my savings in three and a half months. No, make that three months. I had already written Mannheimer a retainer check for ten thousand dollars.

The perverse facts drilled a hole in my brain. That, and the coffee I'd been drinking, churned my stomach. I grabbed my trash basket, bending my head over the brass rim, waiting for the acrid taste of panic to rise through my throat and straight into the cool black interior. What had happened to the rest of my money? After five years of making on average a million dollars a year, shouldn't I have had at least $500,000 saved up? That could have subsidized me until I cut back, got my finances in order and found a new job. After a long minute, nothing came up and I felt foolish. Returning the basket it to its proper spot near the printer, I surveyed the expensive computers, flat-screen television and bold contemporary art around me. My decision to pay for half of this apartment in cash had seemed like a good idea at the time. I refused to be like everyone else and buy a place that I couldn't afford. Plus Manhattan real estate was always a sound investment. Three years later, I had milked my savings on lavish decorating and similar units in this building were selling for a million dollars less than what I had paid for mine.

How could I, someone who worked with money, have screwed up so badly with my own finances? How had I let myself get sucked into the buying orgy? I was living on borrowed money, just like everyone else. Instead of getting lured into taking on an adjustable rate mortgage, I had bankrolled my lifestyle on a slippery number, counting on my year-end bonus to replenish my savings account. Shaking my head in shame and disbelief, I gulped what was left of my cold Nespresso and wondered how on earth I would get out of the ditch I had driven myself into.

There was no question I'd have to cut back and quickly assessed where I could save money.

"Sorry, Drago, but you have to go," I mumbled. I would learn to work out on my own or do exercise videos. I would enthusiastically adopt the world of do-it-yourself. Facials, flowers, massages, dining out and entertainment were crossed off unsentimentally. Hair and nails were a little trickier. I'd have to look my best for job interviews and hadn't done my own hair or nails in fifteen years. I'd just have to find cheaper alternatives, nail bars on the Lower East Side that offered mani/pedis for twenty-five dollars and Dominican hair salons in Spanish Harlem where blow-outs cost eighteen dollars. I could save $6,000 a month by eliminating clothes, shoes and handbags from my budget. Dry-cleaning bills would also disappear for the near term since I had no reason to wear any expensive work clothes. My food budget, however, survived. Organic greens, fruits and vegetables were pricey, but my body had gotten used to an all-natural, high-protein, low-carb diet. I couldn't scale back . . . at least not yet.

I also didn't want to give up my housekeeper, Eva. I had given her last week off with pay, so as not to raise her suspicion or concern. Originally from Honduras, Eva worked four days a week and had been with me for ten years. She not only cleaned, cooked and shopped for groceries, but organized my life (posting Christmas cards, arranging flowers, color-coding clothes, packing my suitcase, alphabetizing books and DVDs), anticipating what needed to be done and executing it with the utmost care and discretion. She worked for other clients too, but a few of them had either reduced her hours or let her go completely because they were downsizing. This meant she had less money to support her two kids who were enrolled at a Catholic school in Queens.

Heat emanating from the computer made me dizzy and I remembered that I hadn't eaten anything since breakfast. Most of the day was gone and I had no idea what to make for dinner. Toast? Cereal? Stretching my legs might help, so I slid my feet into a pair of broken-in Birkenstocks from my Wellesley days and rode the elevator down to the lobby, coming face-to-face with the burnished rows of slate grey mailboxes. I unlocked my box; the new issue of *Elle Décor* and a stack of envelopes tumbled to the floor. Picking them up one by one, I logged each sender's name: Con Edison (electricity), AT&T (telephone), Cablevision (I had also forgotten to add that one to my monthly budget), Wharton School of Business Alumni Fund (donation) and American Express. I leaned my head against the mailbox and let out a rueful laugh. The last ten days must have been some kind of cruel joke, a form of cosmic retribution for something I had done. Over-consumption? Standing up for myself at work?

Upstairs in my apartment, the place where it was becoming clearer by the second I could no longer afford, I ignored all the other bills and went straight for the Amex. Sliding a sterling silver letter opener across the envelope with more grace than I actually felt, I played a little game, daring myself to guess how much damage I had done in one month.

"Eight thousand," I said aloud.

When I saw that the amount due in twenty-eight days was $13,628.07, I nearly fell to the floor.

8.

I got a hold of myself and fetched another bottle of Cabernet. I poured a full glass and carried it, along with a bag of tortilla chips, to my immaculate, designer living room. I plunked onto the lush cream sofa; tucked an Hermès blanket under my legs; and pigged out—crumbs be damned. I was completely isolated; no one outside of my Wall Street circle knew of my professional disaster. I was ashamed of my dwindling finances and the burden of hiding everything was beginning to affect my health. The insomnia, sweaty palms and frequent heart palpitations—inverted bodily functions—alerted to how unbalanced I was. My eyes welled up again and I opened them wider, willing myself not to blink. *Don't cry. Don't cry. Don't cry!*

I finally succumbed, letting the tears flow. I was beyond crying for my job. My job had simply cushioned the emptiness that had surrounded me ever since my mother's death and, more recently, my break-up with David. The trauma of losing my mother never went away, an impossible longing to hear her voice or to feel the softness of her cheek, but I had learned to live with it, pushing it to the far, far reaches of my mind. For a long time after her death, my bitterness had sustained me. It centered on the unfairness of it all; the insidiousness of her cancer, and how, at twenty-one, I had become what a grief counselor called a "motherless daughter," the most horrible pairing of words I had ever heard. I was suddenly alone in the world and damn it, I was going to make something of myself.

My unyielding desire to make my mother proud had propelled me forward, dulling any doubts about the path I had chosen or the compromises I made. With every professional accomplishment—my graduation from Wellesley a mere four weeks after her death, my MBA, my success at Atlas—I had a silent dialogue with my mom, asking if she approved, thanking her for all she had done. I often felt her presence at the weirdest times, usually when I did something that unmasked a side of me she never knew. An image of her could appear directly after I'd had a casual fling with a guy. Or if I was rude to a cabbie, certain my gracious mother would have been appalled by my behavior. What would she say now? I know she'd be disappointed, but I wasn't sure if it would be over my rash behavior and subsequent firing, or if it would be about my sinking finances and the sense that I had, somehow, lost my way.

I needed to hear a comforting voice, one that was grounded and non-judgmental, before I swallowed the entire bottle of Cabernet and disappeared into another haze. My best friend, Christine Foley, and I met as analysts in the Equity Research department at Morgan Stanley. We survived the requisite all-nighters by sharing greasy takeout and covered for each other when one of us snuck out to take a nap. We fooled everyone by draping a suit jacket over our empty chair, pretending to still be at the office in case anybody asked. Things changed one evening at a downtown bar when Christine locked eyes with a scruffy-looking hipster. Three years later, she and Robert Hughes tied the knot; she quit Morgan Stanley; and the architecture firm Rob worked for transferred him to their Chicago office. Christine told me she had become so disenchanted with the "mercenary mentality" on Wall Street that choosing love over her career had been a no-brainer.

Soon after Christine's marriage, Peter asked me to join

him at Atlas. With both Peter and Christine gone, Morgan had become less interesting, all drudgery and politics, less camaraderie. Christine was the sister I never had. She was still the only friend with whom I could share all my vulnerabilities. I put down the bag of chips and dialed her number.

"This is Christine," she chirped after two rings.

"Hi, it's me," I said, sitting up on the couch.

"Mia! I've been thinking of you! So sorry you haven't heard from me lately, but I've been so busy running around with the kids . . ."

"No need to apologize. I totally understand. How are they?" I was godmother to Christine's three children: Lennox, Santana and Branson. I still had a hard time believing my simple, classic Christine had agreed to those names. Rob thought he was honoring his hipster past by giving them ready-made tags to start a rock band. But their kids were beautiful and they adored me, the merry auntie who flitted into their lives a few times a year bearing gifts.

"Everyone's fine. Santana just got placed in the first-grade advanced learning program! You'd be so proud of her. Lennox is playing tennis twice a week now and has matches every Saturday. I mean, do eight-year olds really need matches? Rob's really into it, but he's hardly home these days and I have to do all the driving. Branson's obsessed with that Nintendo DS you gave him for his fifth birthday. I feel so guilty letting him play with it so much, but sometimes I just need a break." She took a deep breath. "You must be swamped too, with third quarter earnings and guidance reports . . ."

Christine had been away from Wall Street for a decade, but was more inclined to quote the markets these days than she ever had during her final year at Morgan Stanley. Rob was now a partner at the architecture firm and many of his clients hailed from Chicago's business elite, so it made sense for her to keep up with the financial news. I wondered if now, with all three kids in school full-time, she wished she was back in the game.

"Things have been unusually slow."

"That's strange." Christine paused. "Is everything OK?"

"No. Things couldn't be worse."

"What is it?" She hesitated and added, "Are you sick?"

Christine knew how fanatical I was about my health, how terrified I was of developing the same cancer that had cut short my mother's life. "No. No. I'm not sick, thankfully. But I'm definitely—definitely on the verge of a nervous breakdown."

"What's wrong?" Christine's voice was now tinged with fear. "Can you talk about it?"

"I got fired."

"What?!"

"Peter told me to leave the firm."

"Whoa, whoa. Back up. Are you sure? Did you guys argue over a trade? Peter probably didn't mean it. You're hot-tempered; he's stubborn . . . I'm sure if you call him, everything will be fixed."

"No, that won't happen. This was more than a simple disagreement. Peter demoted me and when I questioned his decision, he let me go."

"But I just don't understand why he would do that! You've always been so loyal, one of his top producers. How could he just cut you loose like that?"

"That's what I've been asking myself for the past week."

"*The past week?* And you're just calling me now?"

"I was ashamed. I feel like a total failure."

"You said Peter demoted you. Who has your job now?"

"A guy named Tripp Armsden who was new to my group, so I just assumed I was his boss. My mistake. Apparently he reported directly to Peter."

"Wait a minute. Let's go through this," she said, going into analytical mode. "Peter let you go, the female head of a trading desk, a minority no less, in favor of a man? Did it ever occur to you that you've been wrongfully terminated? The victim of discrimination?"

"Yes, I've thought of that but ..."

"But what?"

"I'm scared to go *there*."

"You have no choice but to go there! The issue's pretty straightforward to me."

"I've never used my gender or played the race card in my entire career and I'm worried that if I make that claim they'll try to paint me as an 'angry black woman.' Then I'll really be damaged goods and no one will want to work with me ever again."

"Mia, for your own sake: don't be so naïve. Wall Street is a white, male-dominated world. No matter how hard you work, it will always be that way," she decreed.

"I'd like to think things have changed in the last ten years," I protested, referring to the decade Christine had been out of the industry. "I was successful because I worked my butt off. I made millions of dollars for that firm. That's what counts, not whether you're a man or woman ..."

"But if all those things are true, why did Peter let you go?"

"I don't know."

"Are they laying people off?"

"Not that I'm aware of."

"Was there any hint of a restructuring?"

"No."

"Then you just need to face the facts: They fired you with no cause and you have your rights. You're entitled to a severance package and some other form of compensation. If you go public with this, you'll blow the roof off of gender discrimination on Wall Street. You know that's one of the reasons I left, right? I just didn't see any long-term future there as a woman."

"Christine," I interrupted. "Before you get carried away, check out *marketmaker.com* and call me back. *Marketmaker.com* plus Mia Lewis." I hung up before she had time to ask for more specifics.

She called back five minutes later. "I loved it."

"Are you kidding me?"

"You're a little feisty. That's what makes you a good trader. I bet you have more guts in your little finger than that guy has in his whole skinny body."

"Christine, reality check: That clip has ruined my life. I've become a laughingstock. There's one part you don't see either."

"Which is?"

"Peter called us back into his office and when he fired me, I threw a cup of water in Tripp's face."

Christine burst out laughing. "That's priceless!"

"Christine, it's not funny! I just want to work again and I can't with *that* hanging over my head."

"Don't let getting fired crush you. Anybody can sail along in a job for twenty or thirty years. It takes a special kind of person to get fired." Christine was on a roll now. "One who has passion and won't take crap. That's you! Where's that girl? She needs to get out there again!"

That was the most twisted logic I'd ever heard. I started heaving; loud, hysterical spasms. "Christine, you're crazy!" I choked out.

"Crazy like a fox. And you should be too. Are you going to call a lawyer?"

I coughed to loosen the thickness in my throat and replied, "I already have."

"Whew! Thank God. I thought I had lost you there for a minute. What'd the lawyer say?"

"He's looking into it, to see if I have a case."

"I think you're doing the right thing. No second thoughts, okay?"

"Okay."

"You promise?"

"Yes."

"By the time you're done with Peter and his little firm, he won't know what hit him," she predicted.

I smiled, wishing I felt as positive as she did. "Thank you for listening. I should have called you sooner."

"That's right. I'm here for you, no matter what."

"I should let you go. You're probably about to start dinner."

"Wait! Before you hang up, do you need anything?" She hesitated and added, "How are you for money?"

I thought about hiding the truth again, but since I had already reached rock-bottom, it was futile. "My cash will run out soon. I can barely afford my mortgage and I'm drowning in bills. I was counting on my year-end bonus."

"Mia!" Christine shrieked. "Look at the mess those pricks have put you in! You've got to fight back."

Actually, my overspending put me in this mess.

"Rob and I can help out," she offered.

"You've already helped out by getting me all fired up," I joked.

"I'm being serious. Please don't get upset, I know how proud you are, but we want to help."

"Um, have you checked that out with Rob?" I asked, thinking back to the conversation Christine, Rob and I had last summer after a barbecue dinner at their Evanston home. Rob's business flourished during the construction boom, but the recession had put many of his projects on hold. To compensate, he was bidding for work in China and Dubai where the capital hadn't dried up yet, requiring more overseas travel and less time with his family. Christine was a stay-at-home mom and with three kids to provide for, they were pragmatic: Rob had to follow the jobs. I was only responsible for myself and had still mismanaged my finances. No matter how badly I might need the help, I could never accept money from them.

"Mia, you've done so much for our family, spoiling the kids, all those Easter trips to Casa de Campo, agreeing to take care of all three of them if anything happened to me and Rob . . . This is the least we can do."

"No, really it's OK. I'll figure something out. I'm on a serious austerity plan now."

"Are you sure? The offer is available for whenever you need it."

"Thank you, Christine, but I'm sure."

"I'm not giving up on this. I'm going to figure something out."

My goodbye to her was barely audible. I burrowed deeper in the couch and eased the blanket up to my chin. I don't know what shattered me more—Christine's unflappable support or my own downward spiral.

9.

When my new BlackBerry jingled, I stopped laying out sheets of tissue paper into an empty cardboard box. It was my lawyer, Eric Mannheimer.

"Mia Lewis." My tone was deliberately aloof; I hadn't heard from him since our first meeting over a week ago.

Mannheimer didn't bother with a greeting and got straight to the point. "Tripp Armsden says you're lucky he's not suing you."

"Excuse me?" I asked, stonewalling.

"He claims that you not only verbally abused him in the middle of the trading floor, but that you also *physically* assaulted him with a cup of water."

Mannheimer had finally uncovered my sin of omission and those few moments in Peter's office had stripped me of any credibility.

"That's not the way things happened. It's much more complicated than it sounds."

"Tripp has a witness, the firm's big boss, Peter Branco, who vouches that you threw a cup of water in his face."

"Tripp provoked me!" I cried and explained the run-up to the showdown in Peter's office. I expected Mannheimer to say that he could no longer represent me, but instead he chuckled.

"I didn't think that kind of behavior was your style," he said.

"It's not. I just went over the edge and something came over me."

"A smug knucklehead, perhaps?"

Had Mannheimer stood in front of me, I might have hugged him. "Perhaps."

"Listen, I'm not gonna lie to you. This incident muddles your case. When were you planning on telling me about it?"

"Um, when it came up?"

"I could've been caught with my pants down! I had already Googled you, so I'd seen the Market Maker clip, but this tidbit caught me totally off-guard."

"I'm sorry. You're right. I should have given you the heads-up, but I was afraid you wouldn't have taken my case."

"You had a strong case."

I annotated his use of the past tense. "*Had* a strong case?"

"You're not denying Tripp's claim and that complicates matters."

"I understand, but in what way specifically?"

"Well, for one thing, he could file a formal complaint with HR and make things even more hairy for you on the job front. He also has a couple of other traders from the firm who'll speak on his behalf, saying you were out to get him from the get-go and made it impossible for him to do his job properly."

"They're lying. Whoever those traders are, they switched loyalties because Tripp is now the Head of Equities."

"Could be."

"I was only trying to do my job and I'm willing to go all the way to prove that."

"Except that if you insist on pursuing this wrongful termination suit, Tripp, Peter and a whole team of Atlas lawyers will not only drag your name through the mud, they'll sue *you* for damages."

"That's absurd! Damages over what?"

"Defamation of character. Verbal abuse. Physical assault. Emotional distress."

"Tripp's not emotionally distressed! That's bullshit! You should see this guy. Nothing touches him. He's just cruised through life. I'm probably the first person who saw through his charade and now he's out to get me!"

"And it looks like he has."

"Are you saying that I've sabotaged any claim I have because I threw water in his face?"

"It's a strong possibility."

"That's not fair!" I shouted, thrashing my free hand in the air. "What the hell am I supposed to do? I have no job and no case. Where do I go from here?"

"I didn't say you didn't have a case. It's just not as strong because of, hmm, pardon my pun, Water-gate."

"If Tripp sues me, I'm ruined. I'll lose everything."

"Mia, I've never let a client down."

"So what are you telling me?"

"I warned you that this could get ugly and I was right. They were ready for you. They expected you to sue and already had a counterstrategy in place. This won't be the slam-dunk I thought it would be, but I'm not giving up on you."

"You're not?"

"No."

His simple response sounded so confident, it gave me a ray of hope. "Oh, thank you, Mr. Mannheimer! Thank you!"

"It's a little too early to start jumping for joy," he scolded. "And Mia?"

"Yes?"

"You're not keeping anything else from me, are you?"

"No!"

"Is that the truth?"

"Yes," I said. "Pinky swear."

"Good. Just get your life organized and start planning for the next six to twelve months. It's gonna be a long road ahead."

"This could take up to a year?" I moaned. "What am I supposed to do until then?"

"You're a bright, resourceful woman. I'm sure you'll figure something out. But let me get back to work. I have some more digging to do and I need to come up with a Plan B."

Mannheimer must have really thought that my act was together. I could hear it in the plain tones of his voice. An educated money-manager like myself must have some significant savings stashed away to carry me through this ugly lawsuit, because that would have just been the prudent thing to do, right?

If I was so prudent, then why was I surrounded by boxes, packing tape and a pile of designer handbags and shoes that I had just sold on eBay for a fraction of what they cost me? Some lucky girls in Seattle, Miami and Boston would be divvying up my Jimmy Choo, Prada and Gucci. As I struggled for a plan to pay my bills, the sight of my overflowing closet gave me agita. Low on cash, I had to do a bit of creative income generation, but eBay was bursting with other like-minded, cash-poor souls. People were selling everything: bags, shoes, watches, silver, boats, cars, art. It was a buyer's market and eBay had become one huge fire sale. The purses, heels and dresses I had meticulously photographed and described for my listings barely went above their minimum bids. I had never even worn the black Prada stilettos Rebecca in Boston would soon call her own.

I slashed my Amex bill by returning a pile of work clothes I had bought at the beginning of the season but never worn, their price tags still hanging on the designer labels. My personal shopper at Saks, Pamela, had griped about how the clothes were past the sixty-day return window and slated to go on sale in a couple of weeks to make room for resort. She then added, in a tone spiked with derision, that many customers had experienced buyer's remorse since the recession and had come running in with returns, trying to raise cash and ease their guilt. I threatened to call her manager if she didn't take back the clothes and reminded her of how much money in commissions she had earned from me over the years. As I waited, I tried to reconcile the woman making a fuss at the cash register with the one who had always treated me to a bottle of water or a cappuccino whenever I visited the store. Always complimentary, we would chat easily about the latest trends or gossip. But it was all fake. I was nothing more than a dollar sign. Or, was Pamela just as desperate as I was to make ends meet, protecting her commissions at all cost?

Almost five thousand dollars was credited back to my Amex account, but the whole encounter had been extremely uncomfortable. Pamela had seen right through the assertion that I had "just changed my mind." She could tell that I was either newly broke or freshly fired. The financial food chain was untangling fast and people like me were ruining her livelihood. I cancelled Drago, my personal trainer, via text message because I couldn't stomach speaking to him directly. Frankly, he scared me a bit—how else could he get me to do fifty crunches when I was bone-tired?

I ran the brown packing tape across the box intended for

Nicole in Miami and affixed one of the neatly printed address labels I had designed on my computer. Sitting cross-legged on the floor, I surveyed all the clothes and high-end accessories arranged on my bed. My housekeeper Eva had wailed "Ay Dios mio!" when I told her that I'd been "laid off." She lived in the real world, not the Wall Street bubble, and treated my jobless-ness for the tragedy that it was. She didn't try to downplay it or wield reassurances that I would soon "land on my feet." When she asked, glassy-eyed, what I planned to do, I tried to stay positive and explained how I had sent out my resume to dozens of firms. However, when I asked for help sorting through things to sell on eBay, Eva understood her days were numbered. It had been silly to think I could continue employ-ing her. There just wasn't enough money to go around and it was better to make an honest break.

I still had six piles of stuff to ship and would make about nine thousand dollars from my eBay auction, fifteen hundred more than what I had spent for the taupe brown Hermès Bir-kin that stood like an *objet d'art* on the top shelf of my closet. These handmade bags were marketed as "investment pieces" to be passed down from one generation to the next. Well, I had invested in them all right—the brown Birkin and a black Kelly—and they were going. But I wanted to get at least half of my purchase price, so I was selling them to a resale agent who specialized in Hermès, Chanel and haute couture. A small ad had been in the back of *New York* magazine and Beryl Kapnick was coming over in an hour. I needed to get out of my pajamas and look presentable.

Beryl Kapnick was one of those women who just didn't have the cognitive ability to talk and make eye contact at the same time. After we made our introductions, she immediately looked past my shoulder to the contents of my apartment.

"You have a nice place here," she said after a cursory inspection of the living room.

"Thank you," I replied with phony cheerfulness, livid that I had put myself in this demeaning position. "Do you want to look at the bags now?"

"Sure. Are they in your closet?"

I'm sure Beryl couldn't wait to get her beady little eyes on my closet.

"Have a seat," I said. "I'll bring them out."

Beryl was standing by an end table when I came out again and quickly put down a silver Buccellati flower bowl.

"You've accumulated some beautiful things," she remarked.

"Too many," I answered, before realizing what my words could mean to someone in Beryl's line of work.

"For many of my clients, consumption fills some kind of void."

That statement deadened the room and Beryl made no effort to fill the silence that followed.

"At least it's not drugs or alcohol," I replied at last.

"Well, some of them have those problems too," she said and smiled, looking me in the eye for the first time.

"Here they are," I said, removing the Birkin and Kelly out of their dust bags and parading them on my marble table. "I also have my receipts."

Beryl settled next to me on the couch and judged them from a distance.

"I'll give you five thousand for both," she said.

"You haven't even touched them!"

She shrugged. "I can see you either barely used them or you took immaculate care of them. They're in mint condition."

"Which is why I thought they'd be worth more."

"Mia, that's on the high end these days. I've been seeing four, five clients a week since the crisis who all want to unload their Hermès or their Cartier or their Vuitton . . . There's a lot of merchandise out there right now."

"I know." I paused. "How about six grand for both?"

"Deal."

Beryl wrote out the check and handed it to me. I put it on the table, placing a coaster over it. Although this was just a regular business transaction, it still felt unseemly. I wasn't used to money visibly changing hands. I preferred credit cards and electronic payments. I liked it better when money seemed to magically appear in my bank account.

"Do you have anything else that might be of interest to my clients?" Beryl asked.

I raised an eyebrow. "*Who* are your clients?"

Beryl threw back her head and laughed. "Oh, these days it's mostly Russians. Some Middle Eastern, but they prefer things to be spanking new."

"I guess they're the only ones who still have cash."

"Believe or not, some people here are still awash with cash too. They're just too afraid to flaunt it. They're also good for my business. Buying vintage or second hand makes them feel less guilty."

"I guess," I said. No longer one of them, my interest in the spending habits of the rich was waning by the minute.

"Mia, I'm parched. Could I trouble you for a glass of water?"

"Sure. I could also make you a cup of coffee if you'd like."

"The water's fine, dear."

I brought Beryl a glass of Evian and, approvingly, she reached for a coaster after the first sip.

"You don't seem so sad to be getting rid of your stuff," she remarked. "I've had some clients in tears."

"It's only stuff. I have more important things to think about."

"How long has it been?"

"Since what?"

"Since you lost your job."

"Is it that obvious?" I asked, and then looked down. "A couple of weeks. How can you tell?"

"Well, you live close to Wall Street. You seem very organized. Your apartment looks like a designer show house, so you were probably hardly ever at home. I'm also not sensing a male presence. Most of my clients' husbands have lost their jobs or have filed for bankruptcy. You've got tons of stuff, gifts to yourself that you're now disposing of because you don't think you have a right to keep them."

"I don't have much of a choice. I can't *afford* to keep them."

"Do you know how I got into this business?"

I shook my head. "How?"

"My husband left me twenty years ago for his secretary. I had spent our whole marriage taking care of him, our kids and our house and, in a flash"—she snapped her fingers—"it was gone."

"Oh, I'm sorry to hear that," I said, surprised by her candor.

"I wasn't as well-equipped as you either," Beryl continued. "I had a degree from a small community college and basically went from my parents' house to his house."

"So what did you do?"

"What you're doing now. I started selling things. The jewelry he gave me, the furs. I wanted to get rid of anything that reminded me of him and I needed the money. Then I started doing the same thing for my friends who were going through divorces. Through word of mouth, I traveled to places like Palm Beach and Newport, organizing estate sales and downsizing closets. I turned my anger and desperation into a new career, a new life for myself."

"You make it sound so easy."

"Look, I know it's not. It takes time. But if you try to wipe all the evidence of your old life away, you're denying the good parts too. The parts that made you successful. What did you work with?"

"I was a trader."

She raised her glass in a mock toast. "I knew you must have done something impressive."

I chuckled. "Not many people find traders so impressive anymore."

"Well, I find a *female trader* very impressive."

I smiled. "Thanks."

"Why don't you start trading for yourself?"

"What?"

"If you could trade for a firm, you could do it for yourself. What's the difference?"

"The difference is I take on all the risk."

"You're a smart cookie. I think you could handle it."

I shrugged. "Maybe."

"And then you could stop selling off your things because it'll take you a lifetime to assemble a collection like this again."

"Oh, I think I'm over all this stuff."

Beryl grinned, a twinkle in her eye. "That's what they all say."

10.

Not only had Beryl Kapnick presented me with a six-thousand dollar check for my guilt-wrenching Hermès bags, she voiced an idea I'd been toying with for days. Nothing whatsoever was happening with my job search and the prospect of lasting un-employment was becoming a grim reality. My canny redistri-bution of funds and eBay garage sale bought me some time, but even if I stuck to the bare essentials, my mortgage and monthly overhead would sap my cash reserves in three months. I could very well be out on the street. The mere thought of this sent shivers down my spine, but I couldn't wallow in it anymore. I needed income and I needed it fast. I had to draw on my natu-ral talents and professional skills. I had to utilize the one thing that had brought my success—and my downfall. I needed to start trading again.

The enormous personal risk I'd have to assume, and the fear of digging a deeper hole for myself, had been holding me back, but it made perfect sense. Supplementary income from trading could cover my cost of living until I settled my suit with Atlas. I had signed away the last ten years of my life, made millions of dollars for that ungrateful firm, and all my sacrifices had amounted to nothing. With my financial knowledge and experience, it was finally time to make the market *work for me*. I took the fifteen thousand dollars I earned selling my luxury items, withdrew another ten thousand from my savings and started a day trading account with a reputable online broker-age firm.

When I traded at Atlas, I usually took a long-term view

of the stocks in which I bought and sold shares. I could afford to withstand the frustrating price fluctuations until the stock moved up or down in the direction I had banked on. But as a day-trader, I would buy and sell a given stock within the same day. I would never hold on to it overnight. I wasn't interested in long-term growth or sitting tight until a stock regained value. Day trading was all about timing and taking advantage of small price movements. By buying or selling a stock soon after it had gone up or down and then unloading it again, I could make a neat profit. I'll admit it sounded too easy to be true. Too many people with too little experience considered day trading a chance to make fast money with the click of a button. But they were usually brash and untested and had no investment plan. They could scarcely read a chart or any other kind of technical analysis. They foolishly bet their savings on tenuous trades and, when those bets tanked, they lost everything.

I was not one of those people.

On the day I planned to start trading from home for the first time, I woke up at five o'clock in the morning. I drank my first cup of Nespresso while listening to CNBC's pre-market report and the latest trading news from Europe and Asia. There were strong upward trends everywhere and a sense of cautious optimism was creeping in. Maybe a real recovery was underway and things were about to change. It was a good omen. After an oatmeal breakfast, I took a quick shower and dressed in jeans and a sweater, forgoing my usual sweat pants.

I hadn't read the *Wall Street Journal* or *FT* in weeks. An office subscription had been one of my perks at Atlas. Now that I was an outsider, articles about bonuses and bailouts struck me as depressing and offensive, but I needed to cover all my bases before trading again. Stepping outside my building for the short walk to the newsstand, I fell in step with the rush hour crowd, but could no longer relate. These people seemed programmed; hired hands sacrificing their lives in the name of corporate America. I had finally been liberated from the soul-crushing shackles of Wall Street. I should have ventured out on my own long before Peter fired me, but had lacked the courage. Today was a new day and I could finally be myself. Whatever I earned would be mine to keep and working from home would give me the flexibility to manage my own time. Maybe I would take up yoga or learn how to knit, two hobbies I had always considered incompatible for someone with my Type A personality. If day trading went well, I wouldn't revert to my old, spend-thrift ways either. I would grow my nest egg thoughtfully and carefully. I bought the newspapers and splurged on a bouquet of white tiger lilies from the Korean deli to celebrate my new beginning.

On my first day of day trading, I made $1500. I bought stocks in a steel company at the opening bell and within minutes it went up by a quarter and I sold. I did this throughout the day with a variety of stocks, watching for incremental movements and trading accordingly. Although my profits were small, I felt a reassuring sense of triumph. I hadn't lost my killer instinct and making money again felt *good*. The market was on an upswing and I abandoned my customary contrarian outlook. Deep down, I still believed the market was overvalued and that we weren't out of the woods yet—a mere year after the worst financial crisis in modern history—but it wasn't my job to overanalyze. In spite of rising unemployment and tight credit, all indicators pointed to a recovery. Gold had advanced to record highs; the S&P 500 stock index was up; and the Nasdaq composite index kept gaining. The Fed Chairman had also reaffirmed support for the government's stimulus measures. My disdain for the herd mentality that inexplicably drove certain stocks up had only gotten me into trouble at Atlas, so I just went with the flow and kept on buying. The market continued to rally and I ended my first week as a day trader up fifty-percent.

As my confidence grew, the market sucked me in again.

I was afraid to leave my computer terminals for food or a bathroom break since things changed in seconds and I could lose money with the blink of an eye. I stayed up late, checking on Asia and Europe obsessively. I moved my Nespresso machine to the office and lost track of how many cups I drank a day. Christine called me several times, but I ignored her. A break in my concentration could spell personal financial ruin and the pressure left me both wired and exhausted. My reflexes became slower and I began to lose money. The losses weren't major at first. My gains had increased my trading account to $40,000, so a dent of a few hundred dollars didn't cause immediate panic. However, stocks fall in price much faster than they go up and, instead of dumping them as soon as they began to slide, I held on for too long. The gains I had accrued in my three weeks of day trading were wiped out.

How had I let that happen? But those trading profits were for my survival and I was determined to get them back. A few days before Thanksgiving, I purchased a slew of stocks in emerging markets. The US might be falling off a cliff, but South America, Asia and the Middle East had yet to peak. I continued my safe pattern of short-term buying and selling and steadily built up a small profit.

Everything changed on Thanksgiving Eve.

Dubai, the oil-rich Persian Gulf city-state that had become a tourist and shopping mecca, announced that its government-controlled company, Dubai World, would have trouble paying its $26 billion in debt. I had scary flashbacks to 2008. Like Lehman and AIG, Dubai World had tentacles everywhere and a default could send the markets into a tailspin all over again. I had no plans for Thanksgiving other than to catch up on sleep and clean my apartment, but an economic parasite spread through me like a virus. I was, unequivocally, on my own with no team to motivate or colleagues to lean on for comfort.

Dean & DeLuca was open on Thanksgiving Day and I ate a premade turkey dinner with all the fixings, listening to reports about Dubai from cable news and the international channels. I imagined traders all over Manhattan and Greenwich, held captive at elaborately staged tables, secretly checking their BlackBerrys while enduring small talk with relatives. They would probably have trouble keeping down their food since Wall Street was closed for the holiday and there was nothing to do but sit still as stocks plummeted in Europe and Asia. Maybe Peter would choke on an heirloom turkey from his farm.

On Friday, when the markets opened again for a shortened trading session, my worst fears were confirmed. Concerns about contagion from Dubai were so widespread, investors shied away from risky bets. My emerging market stocks were among the first to disintegrate. I couldn't give my shares away and lost almost everything.

I finally accepted it was time to call it quits and closed my day trading account the Monday after Thanksgiving. I deposited a little over two thousand dollars back to my savings, ending the month of November far worse than when it started. Most frightening of all, I had no back-up plan. I had taken from my safety net and squandered $23,000 on dicey trades. I lost $15,000 in profits. Day-trading was supposed to be my savior and it had turned out to be a disaster. *I* was a disaster and had no business playing the market ever again. The market had played *me*.

Sinking further and further into an abyss, I had to stop trading to maintain my sanity. But with the seductive high of making money gone, I really had nothing to fall back on.

11.

The persistent, annoying ring of my BlackBerry wrenched me from my wine-soaked coma. Seeing double, I reached for it, but the phone fell with a thud. Pawing the floor, inadvertently pressing buttons, I heard Christine's screechy voice.

"Mia!" she bellowed. "Are you there? Answer the friggin' phone!"

Gosh, she was loud. I tried to speak, but my mouth was dry.

"Hello," I murmured.

"If you didn't pick up, I was going to send the doorman up to bust open your door!" she shouted.

"You're hurting my ear," I moaned.

"Why haven't you called me back? I've left you tons of messages. What'd you do for Thanksgiving?"

"I've been busy."

"With what?"

I cackled like a crazy witch. "Do you really want to hear another sob story from me?"

"Don't say that. Of course I do."

"Dubai."

"You just came back from Dubai?"

I sighed. "Christine, forget it."

"No. What? I don't understand . . ."

I took the carafe of water I kept on the bedside table, gargled and then swallowed. "How's Rob's project going in Dubai? Is it down the tubes with everything happening over there?"

"Actually it's going really well."

"Really?" I asked, skeptical.

"I freaked out when I heard the news about Dubai World, but Rob says we have nothing to worry about. The sheikh he's working for is completely insulated from that mess."

"I just lost a shitload of money day trading because of the Dubai panic, so I'd be careful if I were you."

"*Day trading?!* Mia, what were you thinking?"

"That I needed to make some quick money!"

"I wish you had just answered my phone calls . . ."

"If I had, my trades would have tanked even sooner!" I paused. "I have to sell this apartment. It's the only equity I have and I can't afford to keep it."

"That's why I've been calling. I have a proposition for you."

"Unless you can get me an interview at an investment bank, I doubt it'll be of any help."

"Just listen. Do you remember Rob's friend Kevin Stackdale?"

"No."

"He was, like, manorexic, goatee, always wore that knit cap on his head?"

I cringed at her description. This Kevin Stackdale sounded like all of Rob's poser friends from the '90s. I still had no memory of him, but replied, "Vaguely."

"Well, he's a movie producer out in LA. Stacked Films. Ever heard of it?"

"No."

"They produced that movie about aid workers in Afghanistan that won the Oscar for Best Picture last year. Did you see it?"

No, Christine, I thought, *I did not see it because I was working my ass off to avert financial Armageddon last year. I did not*

*have time to sit at the movies and watch some overpaid Hollywood
actors pretend to be humanitarians in Afghanistan.*

"Must have missed that one," I said.

"It was brilliant. Who would've thought skinny Kev
would be an Oscar winner?"

An image of "skinny Kev" began to take shape in my
mind. "Was he the one who tried to impress me one night by
saying he drank 'mad tea'?"

Christine chuckled. "Yes! That was probably the worst
line ever. But he's evolved since then."

I felt nausea coming on—and not from last night's wine.
From irritation. And envy. A skull-capped slacker had finagled
his way to Hollywood and snagged an Academy Award. Had
Kevin even mentioned he was interested in filmmaking? This
is what getting fired had reduced me to: begrudging others
their hard-earned success.

"Well, he wasn't my type anyway."

"Kevin is quite the girl-magnet these days, as you can
imagine. Anyway, he's about to work on a new movie about
two families whose lives intersect after 9/11."

"Sounds heavy."

"Kevin told Rob he's scouting for an apartment in your
neighborhood and I immediately thought of you."

"You think I should sell my apartment to him?"

"Just sublet it for a year or for however long they're filming. *We're talking Hollywood money here.* His production company can pay top dollar."

"This all sounds very tempting, but assuming he likes my
apartment, where will I live?"

"Do you remember Rob's family cottage in Overlook?"

"That ramshackle place upstate?"

"It was renovated a few years ago, so it's in much better shape, but the people who've been renting it out as a weekend home didn't renew because they're cutting back. We don't think it's good for the house to sit empty. Rob and I wondered if you'd do us a favor and move in. You know look after the house and garden, etc . . . "

"Christine, I can't take care of a house! I've never lived in a house, not even growing up. My mom and I lived in a condo."

"It's not that hard. There's a handyman, a landscaper. They know what to do and you just call them if there's a problem. But it'd be great if someone was there to tell us if a pipe burst or if the ceiling leaked . . . "

"That doesn't sound very encouraging."

"I said *if!*" she cried. "We haven't had any problems lately."

Scenes of uprooting weeds, separating garbage and shoveling snow on an acre of land in the middle of nowhere repelled my urban sensibility.

"Christine, I appreciate all of this. Really I do, but I can't leave the city."

"Why not? You need to take a break from everything. You need to get some distance from all the bad vibes: Peter, Wall Street, your job search, the lawsuit . . . "

"If I leave the city, I'll really be cutting myself off. I need to be where the jobs are."

"Overlook is only an hour and a half from the city. You can take the train in when something comes up."

"Might as well be a continent away," I murmured.

"It's along the Hudson. Really beautiful. You said so yourself once."

"It's a nice place to visit!"

"Mia, don't be so hard-headed. I'm talking about subletting your place out to Kevin and living in Overlook rent-free! This is the perfect temporary solution for you until you get back on your feet."

"I hate that expression."

"What?"

"'Get back on your feet . . .'"

"I know, honey. I'm sorry it's come to this, but do you have a better option at this point?"

"No. I don't."

"Well, at least give Kevin a chance to look at your apartment and then we can take it from there."

"Okay. Will you arrange it?"

"I'm on it!"

I hung up and slung the duvet over my head.

Kevin Stackdale was no longer manorexic and the goatee was gone too. A Hollywood trainer had probably buffed him into shape and a stylist must have also chosen the slim jeans and soft black leather jacket that were meant to look nondescript, but screamed luxury. Hollywood, Wall Street—they were all part of the same dream factory America cooked up and I wondered just how high on the asshole quotient Kevin would score.

"Mia!" he said when I answered the door. "So nice to see you again!"

Kevin closed in for a bear hug and my nose was soon crushed against smooth lambskin.

"You too!" I said when I could breathe again.

"I'm so excited to see your place!"

"Please come in. I can't wait to give you the tour."

I escorted Kevin into the hallway and proceeded to go through the apartment, describing the orange columns of light that saturated the living room at sunrise (which I had only noticed since my firing) and the space-saving features in the kitchen (that still had not seen too much action, despite my abundance of time and lack of money). We paused outside my bedroom. I had made my bed and arranged the pillows for the first time in weeks.

Kevin walked inside and sat on the ottoman at the foot of the bed.

"Seems like a big place for one person," he remarked.

"Pardon?"

"Nothing," he answered quickly and got to his feet. "It's a great apartment. I like what you've done with it."

"It's not too feminine?" I asked.

"No. You've got some cool Art Deco stuff going on. I think Natasha will like it."

"Natasha?" I repeated. "Who's Natasha?" *Please let her be his personal assistant or location scout,* I prayed.

"A friend."

"So, uh, would the two of you be living here?"

"Sometimes. Would that be a problem?"

Beggars like me had no right to be choosy, so I smiled and said, "No problem at all."

We were interrupted by my apartment buzzer. It was the doorman, Vladimir.

"I have a Miss Natasha here to see you," he announced.

"Is it okay if I send her up?"

"Oh, send Miss Natasha right up," I said, watching Kevin, who finally had the self-awareness to blush.

Of course Natasha was tall and thin with long blonde hair, full lips and a perfectly symmetrical face. Her sky-high Louboutins click-clacked across the hardwood floors as she followed me into the kitchen, where Kevin drank the cup of Nespresso I had made him moments before her arrival. She put a possessive arm around his waist and kissed his cheek.

"Hi, babe," Kevin said. "Did you find your scarf at the restaurant?"

Natasha undid a few buttons of her black coat and showed off a red printed scarf. "The maître d' had put it aside for me," she replied, enunciating each word thoroughly, as though auditioning for a screen test.

"We were at Del Posto last night," Kevin explained.

"Oh, I love their risotto!" I glanced at Natasha. "Coffee? Sparkling water?"

"Do you have Pellegrino?"

"Yes, I do. Kevin, why don't you walk through the apartment again with Natasha while I fix that Pellegrino for her?" I said, shooing them away with my hands.

I took a glass from the cabinet, inspected it for spots and grabbed a bottle of Vintage seltzer from the fridge. It was like water on steroids, definitely much bubblier—and cheaper—than Pellegrino, but hopefully Natasha wouldn't notice. I filled the glass and shuffled to the living room where I heard their voices. Kevin and Natasha stood in front of a floor-to-ceiling window, studying the view.

"Natasha, here's your water," I said and they both turned

around.

She chugged half the glass and, seconds later, hiccupped.

"Oh!" she squealed.

I pretended not to notice. Vintage seltzer will do that to you sometimes.

"So, Tash, what do you think?" Kevin asked.

She shrugged. "It's nice, but it's so far away from everything."

Kevin winked at me. "Tash needs stores and restaurants close by."

"Well, the subway's close by," I suggested.

Kevin guffawed. "Ha! Tash, when was the last time you took the subway?"

Natasha stuck out her lips. "When was the last time *you* took the subway?"

I felt sorry for her. She clearly had no say in the matter. Kevin treated her like a Chihuahua in a crate—cute, light, and best put on display. I searched his face, but had a hard time imagining the sensitive producer who made compelling films about the decade's most important issues.

"We'll be filming in the neighborhood, so this place would be perfect," Kevin told me. "My assistant will call you to iron out all the details."

"Great," I responded, not sure if it was at all that great, but this Kevin option had taken on a momentum of its own. I knew it would be downright foolish of me to turn it down. I had to think of the big picture. I *could* manage a ninety minute train ride to the city if necessary and would have a better chance of keeping my apartment in the long run.

"We'll need it by January fifteenth and you'll rent it out

furnished, right?" he asked.

That was only a little over a month away. "Um, yes, that shouldn't be a problem. I'll want to store my personal items of course."

"Of course!" he agreed, with a big smile on his face. "C'mon, Tash. We have to go. I have a meeting uptown"—he looked at his watch—"in twenty minutes and I'm probably already late with all the traffic."

Kevin strode to the entry hall with me and Natasha bringing up the rear. Taking charge, he opened the front door and gently pushed Natasha ahead of him. "Tash, why don't you get the elevator?"

She gave him a dirty look and offered me her hand. "It was nice meeting you. Thank you for letting us rent your apartment."

"Nice meeting you too," I said. "And don't worry; the neighborhood's not that bad. I promise."

She smiled weakly and then wobbled up the corridor to the elevator bank.

Kevin gave me a farewell hug and then rocked on his heels, examining me like a strange painting he couldn't quite understand.

"I forgot to ask: What'll you do while we rent out your place?"

"Find myself," I said and tried not to laugh at the absurdity of it all. "You know how it is."

12.

I drove along Pittsfield Way with only my headlights illuminating the dark, winding road. Pittsfield seemed to go on forever and my new, second-hand Ford Escape (purchased after trading in the Range Rover Sport) was packed to the gills with clothes, laptop, toiletries and a few mementos from my apartment, but it had no GPS. My only guide this January night, a few weeks into the new decade, was a print out from MapQuest which was useless on these black roads. My last trip to Overlook had been years ago, when Christine and Rob still lived in the city. They had invited me and a bunch of his friends for the weekend, but none of us had access to a car, so we boarded a Metro-North train and then piled into taxis for the drive to the cottage. I was crushed between two guys who sang at the top of their lungs, between taking swigs of whisky from a pocket flask. With every sharp turn, one would pretend to fall on top of me and I pretended not to be annoyed. Needless to say, I hadn't paid much attention to the route.

I signaled before gliding over to the right shoulder of the double-lane road. I also made sure all the doors were locked and put on my warning blinkers. Flashing my BlackBerry over the directions, I flipped over to the third page: Drive on Pittsfield Way for 2.3 miles and then turn left onto Meadow Lane, the street where Rob's family cottage was located. It felt like I'd been driving for much longer and hadn't noticed a side street to the left. Sighing, I got back on Pittsfield and turned up the music, Michael Jackson's "Don't Stop Till You Get Enough." My head bopped to the pumping horns and bass, searching for

Meadow Lane from the corner of my eye.

Kevin Stackdale's "people" had wasted no time getting in touch with me and offered $18,000 per month to rent my apartment, fully furnished. That number was sufficiently high enough to squash any objections I had about him and Natasha frolicking on my bed. After the mortgage was paid, I'd have about $4,000 per month to live on and pay bills. My intention was to bank half the money. No more superfluous expenses. I would watch every single penny. I said a silent thank you to Christine and Rob again. Had I refused to meet Kevin, I'd still be hemorrhaging money in that flashy apartment, with no solution in sight. The next twelve months in Overlook would give me the peace of mind to craft some kind of viable future.

A green street sign came into view: MEADOW LANE. I signaled, turned left and proceeded to bounce down a road full of potholes, knocking over the mountain of bags in the back seat. The Nespresso machine next to me also toppled to the floor. MapQuest indicated the house was the last one on the lane. The gravel ground under my tires and I made out the wide lawn anchoring the front of the property, bringing me back to that crisp fall day when Rob and his friends had played a raucous game of touch football there. Christine had cheered him on like a teenager, leaping and doing cartwheels to distract the other guys. It seemed like another era; we had been so brash and full of optimism. Whatever I aspired to back then, I do know that I never imagined I would return, depleted and demoralized.

The cottage was set further back from the front yard and its stone façade appeared like a mirage in the darkness. Next to it stood an odd little structure, a roof with no sides, very much like a child's simple drawing of a house. Stopping, I put the car into park and took a deep breath before getting out. Why was everything so damn dark? Kevin had insisted I personally hand over the keys to the apartment so we could go over any last minute details—and at eighteen grand a month, who was I to protest?—but his private jet from LA had taken off three hours late. As a result, I got on the road much later than I planned, arriving at the cottage in much more darkness than I was comfortable with. City darkness was kinetic; noises and street lamps, cars zipping past at all hours of the night. Country darkness was so quiet and ominous. Anything could be lurking in the shadows.

"You'd better get used to it," I mumbled, feeling blindly in the cup holder for my Blackberry and the house keys Christine had FedExed.

I stepped gingerly out of the car, but the stinging cold numbed my cheeks. At seventy miles north, Overlook was about ten degrees cooler than the city. I darted from the Escape to the front door faster than a bunch of shoppers waiting for the Black Friday sale at Wal-Mart. With every step, motion sensors activated the lights on the roof and entry way. I fiddled clumsily with the key, my hands shaking as though someone were chasing me. But when the locks finally turned, I rushed inside and pinned my back against the door, chest thumping. Just when I started to calm down, I remembered that Christine had given me a special code to turn off the alarm. I found the light switch and, above it, the small box with a keypad. Was it OFF plus code? Or code plus OFF? I tried both and finally heard the two beeps she said would signal that the alarm had been deactivated.

Home. Sweet. Home.

But I still had to go back outside and get all my stuff from the car.

I slept through my first night in Overlook with the bedroom lights on and my BlackBerry under the pillow. I had expected to feel disoriented and anxious, waking up in this strange, new place I would call home for the next year, but a sense of mellow acceptance enveloped me. After brushing my teeth in the white-tiled bathroom, I called Christine.

"I'm still alive!" I told her once she answered the phone. "An ax murderer didn't come in the middle of the night and attack me."

Laughing, she replied, "I said you wouldn't have anything to worry about. Overlook is so safe, it's practically boring."

"Mmm . . . boring sounds good these days."

"And thank you for the beautiful flowers." She paused. "You didn't have to."

"Yes, I did. How can I ever thank you enough for helping me out like this?"

"Because we're like family. You'd do the same for us."

"In a heartbeat! I'm just not used to feeling this helpless and dependent."

"You're not. You never could be. You have to stop thinking you're too tough or proud to accept help. You've been wired like that since the first day I met you."

"And look how much good that did me!"

"Now's the time to let go. Don't be afraid to see where it takes you."

"Yes, Dr. Hughes."

She laughed. "Okay, I'll stop with my pop psychology.

What are you going to do today?"

"I was thinking I'd go out for breakfast and check things out."

"Rob told me to tell you that Overlook Avenue is the main street, with all the best stores and restaurants."

"Like Woolworths and the country diner?"

"Hey, Woolworths was the shit back in the day!"

"Ha ha. My bad."

"Have fun."

"I will—sending you guys all my love."

"The same to you, my friend. The same to you."

The daytime drive from the cottage to Overlook Avenue was much more agreeable than last night's journey in the dead of night. Pittsfield Way was one of the main roads that led back to the center of town. It was populated with all sorts of homes: unpretentious cottages like Rob's; stately old mansions; and new, family-friendly colonials. The lots must have been at least two acres and I drove at a leisurely speed, enjoying the unexpected detour. My mother would have loved to live in one of the small Tudor houses I passed, with the sloping roofs and half-timbered mahogany exterior. They were straight out of *Inspector Morse*, the English mystery series we watched together on PBS. Foul play at these dark, stately homes always had an air of elegance and refinement. Completely unannounced, tears ran down my face. My mother died at forty-five and, if I reached her age, I would have been without her for more than half my life.

There was no room for melancholy as more practical matters greeted me on Overlook Avenue; it was impossible to find a parking spot. It seemed like a caravan of SUVs had overtaken the strip. After driving the length of the avenue and waiting patiently for a mother to load her two children and stroller into the back of a Lexus, I finally found a spot in front of the CVS pharmacy. All parking was metered, a quarter for thirty minutes. I had exactly one quarter, just enough to buy time and find a bank. I walked all the way down the Avenue and nearly passed the white frame house that was actually a Chase branch. It had probably been there since the 1950s, when bank offices moved out to the suburbs and wanted to mirror their communities. I went in and exchanged twenty dollars for the two rolls of quarters I planned to keep in my car.

Once the parking logistics had been taken care of, I craved food and a cup of coffee. I hadn't seen a Starbucks anywhere, which suited me just fine. Starbucks symbolized "work," that lunchtime latte or afternoon espresso I always got to keep my engines running. I was in the mood for atmosphere, a place that would give me a window into the soul of Overlook. The pungent combination of onions and grilling hamburgers charred the air around the Overlook Family Diner. I smiled inwardly; every town had a diner. Across the street, a black and white striped awning caught my eye: "Cupcake de Ville Bakery & Café." Certain words enchanted me and "cupcake" was one of them. I used to go Magnolia Bakery in the West Village about once a month for the best cupcakes in the city. I'd buy half a dozen, take them home and stuff myself like a five year-old in one sitting.

Cupcake de Ville was bustling inside. Every table was

packed and the order line snaked into the seating area. *Good choice, Mia,* I thought, but was too hungry—and charmed—by the café's interior to leave. Metal chairs surrounded wooden tables and rows of nickel pendant lamps hung from the ceiling. Vintage black and white photographs recalled the Parisian nostalgia I had idealized as a kid; chic women in white gloves sashaying along the Champs-Élysées or lovers stealing a kiss by the River Seine. The only splashes of color came from the cupcakes themselves, whimsical creations crowned in lavender, mint green or pink icing.

Taking a spot behind a woman in yoga pants, I checked if there was a place for me to sit. A high marble ledge was attached to the front window, allowing customers to eat standing up and look out onto the avenue, but that didn't seem very comfortable. There was an empty chair wedged in the corner at a table for two. A man in a baseball cap sat with his back to the room, reading a newspaper. Would it be too forward to ask if I could share the table with him?

My turn arrived and I asked for a latte, croque monsieur and carrot cupcake.

"The croque monsieur will be about five minutes," the cashier said. "You can find a table and we'll bring it to you." He smiled weakly, knowing full well that was a remote possibility.

I considered the lone seat in the corner. It was still empty, so I decided to go for it. Balancing the hot latte and small plate with the cupcake in my hands, I navigated through all the chairs and shopping bags towards the back table. As I got closer, I saw the man lift his espresso cup and realized, to my surprise, that he was about a shade darker than I was. On the one hand, I was pleased. I hadn't thought to ask Christine about how diverse Overlook was. It really didn't matter to me. I was used to being the only black girl in my neighborhood growing up, or one of a few at school and at work, but I couldn't deny that my curiosity grew when I saw another person of color in a room. I had once heard a psychologist refer to this as fictive kinship, where we assumed to have more in common with each other simply because we shared the same phenotype. More often than not, there would be some point of connection—a similar experience, a mutual friend or even a tacit understanding that, apart from race, we actually had *nothing* in common and needn't form any sort of relationship at all.

His profile became clearer as I neared the table. He seemed to be in his late thirties, stubble on his cheeks, slightly upturned nose, nice cable-knit cashmere sweater. His attractiveness made me leery. I had perceived, both through dating and observation, that good-looking black men tend to be fawned over by women of all colors, shapes and sizes. As a result, they got used to—and began to expect—a certain level of attention. I had seen it all the time with David. The sales assistants or junior attorneys who always smiled a little wider in his presence, regardless of whether or not I was by his side. Here I was, not only a woman, but the only other black person in the café, and I had to pick this guy's table. He would probably think I was trying to hit on him.

I soon reached the point of no return and said, "Ahem. Excuse me."

No reaction.

Thinking he hadn't heard me, I tried again. "Excuse me?"

He finally looked up. "Yes?"

"Is that seat empty? Do you mind if I sit down?"

"Oh, of course. Go right ahead." He put his paper down and stood, making room for me to pass.

"Thanks," I said and smiled.

He nodded and smiled back without showing any teeth.

"No problem," he said and resumed reading the Sports Section of the *Times*.

I put a packet of Sugar in the Raw in my latte and tried to stir it inside my mug as quietly as possible, all the while staring at my over-the-top cupcake with cream cheese frosting, candied walnuts and fresh carrot shavings. Since I was still waiting for my croque monsieur, I didn't want to start eating it first and look like a total pig. I also didn't have anything to read that would have made me look busy. It was actually much worse sharing a table with a good-looking stranger than sitting alone. I became ill-at-ease, aware of every movement I made. These could only be the thoughts of a single black female in her mid-thirties because my mystery companion seemed totally oblivious to my presence. In the end, I hid behind my BlackBerry and went on the *Times* website to check out the headlines.

A waitress appeared a few minutes later.

"Croque monsieur?" she asked, seesawing the plate and looking from me to the guy across the table.

I raised an index finger. "Mine."

She set it down and said, "Bon appétit!"

"Thank you," I replied and took a bite of the toasted sandwich, showering a cascade of crumbs on my scarf. Sweeping them away, I tried to eat more delicately as I read Charles Blow's latest Opinion piece.

I heard the rustle of newspaper across the table, but didn't look up.

"Enjoy your cupcake," the stranger said.

I lifted my head and smiled, not daring to speak in case I had some food stuck on my teeth.

"The carrot's my son's favorite," he added before putting on a thick, hooded parka and walking away.

I took a sip of my latte, perturbed. He obviously wasn't as oblivious as I'd thought, but why'd he bring up that bit about his son? He *must* have thought I'd been scoping him out and wanted to make sure I knew he was unavailable. *As if.* I stabbed the cream cheese frosting with an index finger and let its sour sweetness melt in my mouth. The arrogance of some men really knew no bounds.

13.

The four-bedroom cottage was decorated in that shabby-chic style I disliked—distressed wood furniture, white slip-covered sofas, signs with quotes like "Live, laugh, love"—and was in dire need of a design intervention. With Christine's blessing, I spent the first few days going through the entire contents of the house and basement. Out went chipped plates and rusty cutlery, threadbare towels and yellowing sheets. It took six garbage bags for the cottage to feel less cluttered, freeing up space for a thorough dusting and disinfection. Every room smelled like fresh lemons by the time I finished and made me feel, in some small way, that I was earning my keep.

After all the cleaning and purging, I needed to buy new sheets and towels and remembered passing a linens store near Cupcake de Ville. I got on the avenue a few minutes before the stores opened at ten o'clock and found a good parking spot near the top. I put in enough quarters for two hours and a felt a ripple of anticipation about my little outing. The white clapboard houses, old stone churches and Federal-style buildings imparted Overlook with an authenticity I found appealing. A book I found in the cottage described how Overlook's early settlers had engaged in the fur trade along the Hudson's banks, transforming this territory into a prosperous nineteenth-century village. The port had also functioned as a transport hub for ships to ferry goods up and down the river. The Hudson was viewable from the avenue, linking me to the life I had left behind in Battery Park, but its contours had changed. The rolling hills in the far distance had replaced the skyscrapers and barges that defined the Hudson's urban identity.

I grew up in a place called Spring Valley, a suburb in Rockland County about thirty-five miles north of Manhattan. David once told me that "Spring Valley" sounded like a name I had made up. For a Brooklyn boy who rarely left the five boroughs, it sounded so perfect that it couldn't possibly be real. In a way, I did spend my youth in an artificially constructed haven. Our town hall was the big shopping mall where all the kids hung out. We passed time in pizzerias, not coffee houses, listened to Top 40 radio, and did everything to blend in with each other. My parents moved to Spring Valley when my father got a job as an engineer for the American division of a Swiss chemical company. A few months after my third birthday, he died in a fire at their plant and I have no evidence of him beyond the early pictures of us together. Scenes where he carries me on his shoulders, or when we ride a carousel together, seem painfully staged, as though I've been photo-shopped into a world I have no recollection of. My father's carefree smile and his youthful, strong frame all the more tragic since he would never grow old or get to see me grow up.

Rockland County, with its good schools and well-kept homes, was a stable place to raise a family. Had ours prevailed and grown, I might have better understood my mother's reasons for staying there, but she worked in retail and was much more sophisticated and outward-looking than the other parents I knew. She was the mom who showed up at PTA meetings in a wrap dress or double-breasted jacket with gold buttons, overshadowing the other moms in jeans and pullovers. On her weekends off, she took me to the city for museum visits and the ballet. She even eschewed the local public high school and made me apply to Sacred Heart, a private, all-girls academy in nearby New Jersey. We may have lived in Spring Valley, but were never really *of* it. Maybe that's why I avoided the suburbs. They reminded me of our broken family and the oppressive awareness that I never really fit in. Only as an adult did I finally find the place where I belonged: New York City.

Overlook Avenue was undoubtedly the center of town and timeworn storefronts (Overlook Hardware) maintained a quiet dignity next to modish upstarts (J. Crew). No other clothing chains had muscled in and I spotted an Arne Jacobsen leather "Egg" chair—one of my favorite mid-century designs—in a clustered window display of vintage suitcases and cameras. The antique store went by the name Eclectibles and although I had no money, old habits die hard and I went inside to inquire about the price. Expecting more modern gems, my disappointment thickened as I passed shelf after shelf overrun with the silver tchotchke, seashells and coral one amassed on exotic trips.

"Are you looking for anything in particular?" asked a voice from behind.

Startled, I turned and collided with a large peacock atop a stand, its blue, green and gold plumage reaching down to the floor. "Oh!" I cried.

"Don't worry. Everyone reacts that way," said the sales assistant.

"Is it . . . real?"

She nodded, petting one of the two, dark braids grazing her shoulders. "Taxidermied. From India. Peacocks are sacred there. Symbolizing kindness, goodness and patience. Do you want to touch it?"

Whoever had snuffed that poor peacock wasn't kind or good.

"No, thank you!"

"He won't bite!" she added. "Kidding! Bad joke."

The store was filled with other oddities too: shark jaw sculptures and ostrich egg ornaments. I knew it was popular to decorate like that these days, but I preferred shiny and contemporary.

"Unfortunately, I'm in a hurry. I have to buy some sheets," I babbled, explaining far more than I needed to.

"Are you new in town?" she asked, striking me as one of those people who would keep you on the phone forever, even if you told her you had to go.

"Just visiting for a little while," I said and began to walk towards the front door.

"Well, I hope you can pay us another visit when you have more time," she trilled.

"I will!"

Outside on the sidewalk, I realized I had never asked her about the chair.

I had better luck at Bed, Bath & Table. I've always been a sucker for a luxurious bed or a beautifully set table, and the store was brimming with Egyptian cotton sheets, Turkish towels and embellished Italian linens that could take me through every holiday and season. Budget-conscious, I asked to see their moderate-priced line of white hotel bedding embroidered in different colored stitching. I chose azure, sage, sand and tangerine for the cottage's four bedrooms; coordinated with matching bathroom towels; and threw in some linen tissue box holders and Diptyque candles. These would be another one of my small contributions for living rent-free at the cottage.

After sprucing up the house, the novelty of small-town living abated and my next couple of weeks settled into a stale predictability: breakfast, morning shows, online surfing, errands, window-shopping, checking out books at the Overlook library. I tried to work out, but couldn't find the inspiration to go running in below zero temps. I knew I was languishing with no stimulation, friends or meaningful contact with anyone else in the community. The cottage was also cloistered in the backwoods, making it unlikely someone would pay me a spontaneous visit.

Frustrated, I called Mannheimer. How had my lawyer become my only friend in New York?

"Mr. Mannheimer, it's Mia Lewis. Please tell me you're making some progress with my case," I said as soon as he answered the phone.

"Mia! I was just about to call you."

"Hmph . . . Really?"

"I wanted to let you know that we're undergoing the discovery process now."

"Discovery?"

"I'm gathering more information. I also plan on interrogating people from your old firm . . ."

"Like who?"

"Tripp, Peter—"

"Right. But who else?"

"The other guys who reported to you."

This made me nervous. I didn't trust any of my former colleagues. They knew which side their bread was buttered on and would do anything to save their asses.

"What are the odds of them being fair and objective?"

"Don't know. We'll have to see. But there's something else I've been meaning to ask you . . ."

"Yes?"

"I don't have any work-related material from you like your job offer letter or performance reviews."

"I can get those to you right away."

"Great. What about stuff concerning the trade you and Tripp argued about?"

"All of that was proprietary information. I couldn't take any of it with me. All correspondence was through my Atlas email account."

"Mmm . . . So you have nothing to back up your statement that you two only differed on strategy about that particular trade? That you weren't 'out to get him,' as he claims?"

"I'm afraid not. The only thing we've got is that bleary video with me screaming at him for what looks like no apparent reason."

"Please write down your version of events." Mannheimer sighed. "I guess I'll have to subpoena the records about those trades."

Subpoena! That word scared me. By compelling Atlas to turn that information over, Mannheimer would signal that we were ready to play hardball. Could I really go toe-to-toe with a better-financed, better-connected opponent like Peter?

"Will they let you do that?" I asked.

Mannheimer chuckled. "Don't worry. I love a good fight."

We hung up and I went upstairs to retrieve the large container from the master bedroom closet that stored the relics of my Wall Street career. Among them were newspaper and magazine articles where I was quoted. I had saved them all, foolishly thinking that one day my future children might be interested. My ID card from Atlas Capital was stuck between the pages of a program from last year's Sherwood Forest Foundation gala. I tried to bend the stiff plastic, but it popped back in place; impenetrable, just as I thought my job at Atlas had been. The picture was even worse than the one in my passport. My eyes stared blankly at the camera, my lips pouted impatiently. It seemed like I had far more important things to do than pose for my work ID (which, at the time, I probably did). The folder with my employment contract and performance reviews was at the very bottom. I read through the evaluations, trying to reconnect with the woman they described as "savvy, diligent and committed." My areas for improvement included "learning how to delegate more" and "setting realistic expectations;" humdrum critiques that never had a negative impact on my promotions or bonuses. So what the hell had gone wrong? I played by the rules my whole life and look where it had gotten me.

I collated the papers and snapped the lid shut on the container. My finance career might be on hold, but there were still a host of things I could do. Someone, somewhere in Overlook could benefit from the skills I had to offer. I needed to be around people and feel useful again. I needed to escape this lonely cottage before I started talking to the walls.

Tomorrow, I would walk the avenue again, but this time in search of a job.

14.

My first stop the next morning was Kinko's. I photocopied my employment contract and performance reviews and FedExed those documents, along with my summary of the Touchnology trades, to Mannheimer. Once that was done, I marshalled my courage and descended on the avenue for my job search. I had printed out a list of all the businesses from the Overlook community website, highlighting the stores that sounded most interesting. I had purposely not brought my resume with me and still wasn't sure how I would sell myself to a potential employer, given my now less-than-stellar Wall Street career, but I hoped my positive attitude and professional demeanor would outweigh any drawbacks.

I went into J.Crew first since it was a retail chain and accustomed to people coming in off the street and asking for a job.

"Good morning!" greeted a peppy blond with a top-knot bun as soon as I stepped over the threshold.

"Hi!"

"Can I help you?"

"Yes, I was interested in filling out a job application."

Her smile dimmed just a bit, seeing that I wouldn't be a paying customer, and she pointed to check-out. "My manager, Emily, will be able to help you with that."

Emily's back was to me, folding tee-shirts. "Excuse me," I said.

She pirouetted and smiled. "No, excuse *me*! What can I help you with?"

"I wanted to fill out a job application."

She squinched her eyes, clearly not expecting me to be someone seeking work. Were the wool coat, skinny jeans and black knee boots I wore too boring? Was I too old?

"Part-time? Full-time?" she asked.

"Either. I'm really flexible."

"Great. Well, let me get you an application." She reached under the register and handed it to me with a pen. "You can stand to the side and fill it out."

I wrote my name, address and telephone number, but paused when I reached the section that asked about my employment history. I had to state my three most recent employers, assignments or volunteer activities; my job title; immediate supervisor; and reason for leaving. After a few crazy seconds of seriously contemplating the unthinkable, I put down the truth: Trader, Atlas Capital; Leadership Council, Sherwood Forest Foundation; and finished with my first job at Morgan Stanley.

I proofread the application and handed it back to Emily. She was probably around twenty-five and a walking advertisement for geek-chic style: a grey and green striped sweater; cropped, checked pants; and some oxfords with no socks. I would have never thought to put those two clashing patterns together, but could certainly learn if J.Crew hired me.

After a few minutes, she said, "I see you don't have any retail experience."

"But I'm an experienced shopper," I joked, trying to break the ice.

"At the moment, we can only consider applicants with retail experience." Her mouth turned down in pity. "You're seriously overqualified to work in a store. Why don't you apply for something at our corporate office? I think it'd be a better fit for you."

Stumped by Emily's millennial audacity, I finally beckoned my best off-hand voice and replied, "I'm actually on sabbatical, taking a break from the corporate rat race, and was just looking for something fun and interesting to do for a few hours a day. But thank you so much for your consideration."

"Oh! My apologies," Emily stammered. "I didn't mean to imply . . ."

I simulated the stop signal with my hand. "No apology necessary."

"Well, thank you for wanting to work here—and good luck."

"You too," I couldn't resist saying. Emily was still young, but life would eventually throw her a curveball too.

It was the same story at every business I approached. Most of them were family-run and didn't even bother going through the formality of an application, so their reasons were painfully blunt. *Business is slow. Who knows when the economy will pick up again? We can't afford to have another person on payroll.* My last stop was a children's boutique, Pipsqueak Chic. The space was large, with separate sections for clothes, shoes and toys, and I recognized many of the trendy, European brands that Christine preferred for her kids. An older woman sat on a stool by the cash register, munching on animal crackers. She seemed unusually relaxed, so I pegged her as the owner. The only other person in the store was a woman comparing sweaters on a table.

"If I get the size twelve, it'll fit him perfectly now, but a size fourteen will be too big," the customer remarked.

"I'd buy the larger size; he can grow into it for next year. Just fold the sleeves over," the older woman suggested.

"You're right. But what color?" the customer wondered and resumed her deliberations.

"What can I help you with, my dear?" the owner asked when I walked up to the check-out counter.

"This might sound like a really stupid question, but I was wondering if you were looking for some extra help?" I asked.

She laughed. "I would have *loved* some extra help, but the store will close next month."

"Oh! I'm sorry to hear that."

"Don't be. After twenty-five years, it's time."

"But this store is so cute! There isn't another one like it on the avenue. Where else will people go to buy children's clothes?"

"Thank you, but I'm sure they won't mind the new Apple store that's taking my place."

"Seriously?"

"They wanted this location so badly; they paid me a small fortune to leave. Florida, here I come!"

"I'm sure you deserve it," I said, laughing.

"Times have been tough for most of us here on the avenue. It's getting harder and harder to stay in business. We're so dependent on the weekend visitors and they're spending less. I got lucky and my kids told me to take the money and run," she explained.

"They're right. Cash is king in times like these."

She smiled. "I'm sorry I have nothing available, my dear. I think we would have worked well together."

"Now that's the *nicest* rejection I've gotten all day!"

I actually left Pipsqueak Chic in a much better mood than when I started my job search. I'd tried, but a paying job in

Overlook wasn't in the cards. I'd sit tight and help Mannheimer build my case against Atlas. It was the only way I could restore my reputation and resurrect my Wall Street career. In the meantime, I'd put together a list of not-for-profit organizations in town and offer to volunteer a few days a week. I could lend a hand with bookkeeping, telemarketing, driving ... I had to make sure the rest of the year didn't become a total waste.

Rejection had made me ravenous, so I went back to Cupcake de Ville for a latte and a French vanilla cupcake with chocolate ganache icing. Mid-afternoon, the café wasn't as crowded and I had plenty of tables to choose from. As I headed towards one with a prime vista of the display cases and all the jazzy cupcakes, I felt a tap on my shoulder.

"Excuse me, but I couldn't help overhearing your conversation with Fran at Pipsqueak Chic," said a woman, bedecked in a black winter hat with furry ear flaps.

I thought back to the store and remembered the customer by the boys' sweaters. "Yes?" I replied, my guard up.

"Are you still looking for some extra work?"

"I might be ..."

"Well, then maybe we should talk." She held up her cup of coffee. "Do you want to share a table?"

And so, in spite of my qualms, mental fatigue and the need for a little solitude after a string of rejections, I said, "Sure."

I installed myself at the table and waited patiently for the other woman to put down her coffee, untwist her handbag and take off the kooky hat.

Smoothing down strands of fly-away blonde hair, she sat down and offered her hand. "I should probably introduce myself first. Elizabeth Jansing. Everyone calls me Liz."

"Mia Lewis," I said, returning her handshake.

She took a quick sip of her coffee. "I own an antique shop further up the avenue and I'm looking for another person to help me out in the store."

"Which store?" I asked, stripping the baking wrapper from my cupcake.

"Eclectibles."

"With the peacock?" I blurted out.

She perked up. "You know it? You've been inside?"

I cut a forkful of cupcake and made a point of chewing and nodding at the same time. How on earth would I get myself out of this one?

"I basically work full-time, but can't always be on-site, so I have a person who helps, Amaryllis," Liz explained. "She must have been working when you came in."

"I think so."

"Well, Amaryllis is going to be taking a lighting design course in the city a couple of times a week. I'm all for it, of course. I don't believe in holding people back, but I'll need someone to cover her hours."

"Interesting," I said, waffling.

"It'd be like a part-time gig," Liz added.

"How many hours are you talking about?"

"Maybe twenty? Twenty-five?"

I certainly had the time to spare, but did I want to spend it in a dreary antique shop? Liz must have read the doubt on my face because she hooted with laughter.

"I'm sorry. You don't know me from Adam and I practically attacked you in the middle of a cupcake café!"

It did sound a bit bizarre, so I laughed along with her.

"I probably seem a little desperate," she said.

"Frankly, I've heard 'not interested' so many times today that I'm just a little surprised."

"What brings you to Overlook?" she asked, changing the subject. "I've lived here for twenty years. I would've noticed you before."

I wasn't put off by her question. In spite of all the visitors streaming in and out of Overlook, the local community was probably still very clannish.

"I'm borrowing my best friends' cottage for the rest of the year. The Hughes Family—do you know them?"

"I know of them. They've been in Overlook for generations, but have been renting out their place for quite some time now, right?"

I nodded. "Rob and Christine live in Chicago; his sister's in LA; their parents are in Arizona. Family's so spread out, but they still want to hold on to the place."

"How do you like it here?"

"I like it a lot. Everything is really charming."

"Did you move from the city?"

"I did."

"Be honest. Things must seem really small and slow."

"I wouldn't say that. Just different."

"Overlook's lovely on weekends and in the summertime. There's lots of local culture—theater, galleries, fairs, good restaurants. All the visitors and chic New Yorkers add some much-needed flavor. But the rest of the time, it's just a pretty, little place to raise a family. I have four kids and can open my back door and let them run wild here."

"How old are your kids?"

"Sixteen, thirteen, eleven and seven."

I tried to guess Liz's age. Mid-forties? That would have made her only a few years older than me when she had her last one. "You must have your hands full."

"I do and I'm not ashamed to admit it! That's why I don't know how I'm going to manage the store without Amaryllis," she said and sighed theatrically, working the sob story to great effect.

"I've never worked in a store before," I cautioned.

"What's there to know? You have to be sharp, responsible, customer-service oriented. Being able to close the register at the end of the day would be a plus." She paused. "What'd you do before you moved here?"

"I worked on Wall Street. I was a trader."

"Perfect! You're good with numbers." Liz strummed the lid of the coffee cup with her thumb. "So I guess with all the bailouts and downsizing, you're in transition?"

Right then and there, she gave me an unexpected opening and, without so much as an afterthought, I took it. "Yes. That's right."

"I think it's really brave of you to move out here and dive into something completely different."

I didn't really have much of a choice, did I?

"I'm taking a break to see if I want to go back to that life." Why was I playing along with her benign assumptions? But what else could I tell her? She was a complete stranger and not entitled to know anything more specific about my personal life.

"In the meantime, would you consider my little store?"

I did a quick mental check and saw only a tide of listless, empty days ahead of me. I really had nothing to lose by working in her store. The stuffed peacock still freaked me out, but I'd deal with it.

"When do you want me to start?"

15.

Liz said she needed the extra help right away, so we agreed to meet at Eclectibles two days later. But when I appeared at a quarter to ten Thursday morning, it was Amaryllis who unlocked the front door.

"You're back!" she said.

"Yes! But I'll be working here now," I explained.

"I know. Liz said you'd be covering for me. Amaryllis Reynolds," she said, extending her hand. Her black hair was put up in messy, half-braided pigtails this time, and they dangled against her pale skin like tassels. "But I'm sure you already knew that."

"I did, but it's nice to meet you properly." Returning her handshake, I felt faintly guilty since Liz had told me a lot more about Amaryllis than just her name. She came from an established Overlook family and had a degree in interior design, procuring a job directly after graduation with a famous New York decorator. But while the decorator was charming to clients, he was abusive to his staff, calling at all hours of the night and insulting them in public. After a year, Amaryllis had a breakdown and returned to Overlook, fragile and seeking refuge with her parents, friends of Liz and her husband, Philip. With this new class at Parsons, Amaryllis was dipping her toe back in the design world. I gave her credit for trying, since I knew much more about terrible bosses and professional reinvention than I was willing to let on.

Amaryllis turned on the lights and the sales floor shimmered like an old film set in all its cluttered glory. I followed her down the aisle, sneaking worried glances at the jammed display shelves, étagères and tables, reminding myself to keep an open mind.

"Where does Liz find all her merchandise?" I asked.

"From all over: travels, gift shows, estate sales, auctions, relationships with local craftsman . . ." She pointed to a colony of resin insects on a marble-topped sideboard. "Liz got these from a natural history store in Chinatown that was going out of business. She bought their stock of bugs, replica skulls and fossils for a song."

Only a true believer would consider that a coup.

"Does the stuff sell?" I asked.

"Oh, yeah! The skulls are among our best sellers. A little touch of evolution makes people feel good. I think it's a reaction to all the technology and the fast-paced world we live in."

Skulls, fossils, and elk antlers were interspersed among traditional gifts like bowls, paperweights and trays, most of them with a natural evolution motif.

"What happened to that Jacobsen Egg chair that was in a window?" I asked.

"Ah! So you do know something about design!"

"A little."

"That was a random find for Liz and it sold right away."

"Hmm, that's too bad. How long has she had the store?" I asked.

"She opened when her firstborn started preschool, so that would make it about thirteen years now."

"Who's your clientele?"

"Some locals are really into this stuff, but mostly designers and decorators from outside of Overlook. Liz has built a reputation for having really unique pieces. We can get people who buy up a whole stock, like coral for a beach house."

"I would have never guessed. The store seems so unassuming from the outside."

"Well, Liz hasn't changed things much over the years," Amaryllis said. Her statement was ambiguous; it could have been neutral or some sort of critique.

"When is she coming in?"

"She didn't call and tell you?"

"Tell me what? She gave me her business card, but never asked for my number."

"Her youngest daughter is home sick today and she couldn't get a sitter, so she won't be in."

"I see."

"Don't worry," Amaryllis said. "I'll bring you up to speed."

I smiled, masking my irritation. "What would you like me to do first?"

"We dust all the merchandise every morning and that'll give me the perfect chance to tell you about everything."

Amaryllis opened a door at the far end of the store. We walked down a flight of iron stairs to the stockroom, equipped with a small kitchen and a glass-enclosed office. She took out two dust brushes from a cabinet underneath the sink and handed one to me. Gazing at the rainbow-colored whiskers, I realized I had done more cleaning in the last month than in the past ten years.

"Let me open the store and then we'll get started," Amaryllis said.

Following her back up the stairs, I asked, "Are you usually busy in the morning?"

"Not really. That's why it's a good time to clean up, unpack merchandise and get organized."

"What's your busiest time?"

"Usually from about noon to three. And then the weekends, of course." Amaryllis turned to me. "You know we open Saturdays and Sundays, right?"

I nodded. "Liz told me I'd be working every other weekend."

Amaryllis looked relieved. "You and I will alternate. And we only open from noon to four on Sundays."

"That's good," I replied. Forget Wall Street. You signed your life away by working in retail. But I had nothing else going on and wanted to be so active that my "sabbatical" in Overlook would fly by and I could begin my real life again. This was nothing more than a welcome diversion and I'd play the role of the dutiful shop girl until then.

For the next hour, I shadowed Amaryllis, listening to her descriptions of the products and learning there was actually a method to the jumbled displays. Each section had a theme—land, sea and air—and Liz had categorized the merchandise accordingly. Framed butterflies? Air. Decorative coral? Sea.

"Corals are endangered, so remember to tell customers that these are just resin impressions, so they don't think we're profiting from ruining the ecosystem. Same thing with these ivory boxes. *Faux*," she explained. "And the elks shed their antlers every year."

Even the display furniture was for sale. I admired a $1500 brass twig table with a mirrored top.

"It must be a pain when you sell a shelf or cabinet from the floor and then have to find another place for all the stuff inside," I said.

Amaryllis grinned, a gummy smile that lightened the severity of her charcoal hair. "We always have something else in the stockroom we can use. We actually have more stuff than we have room for on the floor."

I thought back to the boxes I had glimpsed downstairs. "Of course you do."

At one o'clock, Amaryllis announced she was going on a thirty-minute lunch break. Not one person had come in the store all morning.

"What'll I do while you're gone?" I asked, worried.

"If someone comes in, I'm sure you'll be able to help them."

"But what if they want to pay? You haven't shown me how to use the register or swipe a credit card."

"Just put their stuff aside and ask them to come back."

"Are you sure they will?"

Amaryllis giggled. "Whoever's buying anything here on a Thursday afternoon has time to kill, trust me."

After only three hours on the job, I was mystified by how Liz ran her business. She had an interesting eye and had cultivated an insider's market for her wares, but the whole organization seemed unstructured. I was really curious about her daily sales figures and how many people on average visited the store each week. Did she even have a Website? I went to the desktop next to the register (there had to be some way to integrate them both into one system) and Googled Eclectibles + Overlook. Bingo! She had a Website, but when I clicked on the link, a message flashed on the screen: *Site under reconstruction. Please visit us again soon.* I shook my head in dismay. This message had probably been up for quite some time. I walked to the rear of the store and stared at the peacock. It really was a beautiful creature, so regal and majestic, but its vacant eyes seemed to ask: *What now? What other indignity do you have in mind for me?* Why was it sequestered in the back of the shop? The peacock was a statement piece and needed to be front and center. I extracted it from the stand and placed it on the check-out counter. If I moved the peacock near the entryway, someone might knock it down. Squarely in the middle of the shop, it would hide the merchandise in the center aisle. My eyes traveled to the storefront window. It wasn't too wide, yet accommodated a desk with multiple compartments; a wood and straw African mask; wicker baskets; and a full-size, human medical skeleton. Not exactly a window at Bergdorf's, but I could work with it.

I snuck into the display window and began removing objects from the desk: candles, magnifying glasses, fraying books. Several minutes later, I heard banging against the glass. Taken aback, I twisted my torso and there stood Amaryllis—kohl-penciled eyebrows hiked up in alarm—holding takeout coffee.

She barged inside and shrieked, "What are you doing?"

"Cleaning up the window display," I chanced, holding up a candlestick.

"That's Liz's job! No one else is allowed to do that. She comes in every Thursday to change the displays for the weekend."

I shrugged. "Well, today's Thursday and she's not here to do it."

"It doesn't matter! We're just not supposed to do it."

"Has Liz said that to you explicitly?"

"Well, no . . ."

"Have you ever asked her if you could do the windows one week?"

"No . . ."

"Well, she might appreciate someone else taking that load off her shoulders with her daughter home sick today." I paused. "Do you want to call her and ask?"

"I think we should just put everything back," Amaryllis said, stomping to the check-out counter.

Immobilized, I waited for the reaction that would come next.

"You. Moved. The. Peacock!" she howled.

I wriggled out of the store window and hurried over.

"Listen, Amaryllis, I had a flash of inspiration while you were gone. The peacock is, like, the store's mascot. I don't think it should be hiding, scaring people all the way in the back. It's so beautiful and should be in the store window."

Amaryllis considered this as she smoothed the peacock's blue-green back. "Mmm . . . I never thought of it that way . . ."

"Don't you think we can dress the window a little differently this week? Simplify it a bit and put out a few strong, statement objects instead of—of—a mish-mash of stuff?"

"Liz always said piling things together made it look like you could find bargains."

I gestured around the sales floor. "I haven't seen any bargains yet. Maybe a box of vintage cards for twenty bucks, but Liz is selling to a sophisticated clientele. I think the windows should reflect that."

"You've got a point."

"You've been working here for years *and* have a design

degree. You've got skills! I bet you Liz wouldn't mind if we tweaked the window a bit. Should we call her and ask?"

Amaryllis stayed quiet and then looked up brightly.

"Why don't we just surprise her?" she suggested. "Plus I have tomorrow off, so you'll have to deal with it, Mia!"

When I got to Eclectibles the next day, I found Liz standing outside, staring at the window display.

"Good morning!" I said.

"Hello there!"

"So, what do you think?" I asked.

She grinned and I felt a wave of relief.

"I can't get over how great this looks. I would have never thought to put the peacock in the window or to do this whole gypsy traveler theme that's going on here—the silver, the beads, the pillows ..."

"You can thank Amaryllis for that. She's immensely talented."

Liz narrowed her eyes. "You must have given her the idea."

"She only needed a little encouragement—and confidence."

"Well, thank you both! It's the best window we've ever had."

"Is your daughter feeling better?" I asked.

"She didn't have a high temperature this morning, so I hope she'll get through the day," Liz said, crossing her fingers. "I'm sorry I wasn't in yesterday, but I knew you could handle it. And we probably wouldn't have had this beautiful window display!"

At that moment, I concluded it would be difficult to stay irritated with Liz. Although she came off like a frazzled shopkeeper with eccentric tastes, she also took things in stride and wasn't afraid of getting extra help from someone she barely knew.

"No worries, but I'll give you my number for the next time."

She laughed. "That's probably a good idea. It's supposed to be unseasonably warm this weekend, so we might have a lot of customers."

"That would be wonderful!" I said, excited at the prospect of a shop filled with people.

Liz gave me a crash course on how to use the cash register and by Friday afternoon, the first crop of weekend visitors arrived. They were mostly creative types from the city who seemed to know exactly what they were looking for. I spent most of my time ringing up and wrapping decorative items that would be given as hostess gifts. Saturday brought more locals; collectors who shared Liz's love of natural history. I noticed that taking a customer "downstairs" to the jam-packed basement was actually quite a compliment, only reserved for true enthusiasts and the big spenders. A decorator from the city spent three hours in the shop on Sunday, purchasing two bureaus, a couple of paintings and a fully-stocked étagère for a client who wanted to her new country house to look like it had been there forever.

I went to bed Sunday night with an achy back and a little bit of stress over how I would package the paintings and organize delivery of the furniture the decorator had bought. My eyes closed as soon as my head hit the pillow, without red wine or Nyquil. I think I had a smile on my face as I fell asleep.

16.

The weekend rush gave way to quieter hours the following week. Liz and I spent most of Wednesday afternoon unpacking boxes of new merchandise from two artisans she had discovered at the New York International Gift Fair, a major industry event I learned takes place every January and August. One designer worked with polished metals and his cutting-edge pieces would stand out in the store; while the other repurposed vintage images to create one-of-a-kind decoupage objects.

"Liz, these will be a huge hit for you," I said, admiring a sculptural, nickelplated bowl.

"I hope so," she remarked, without looking up from the packing list she was cross-referencing. "That order cost me enough."

"Maybe you should have a party to introduce the new stuff?" I suggested. "Some wine, a few hors d'oeuvres, a ten percent discount ..."

Liz dropped her papers and clapped her hands together. "That's such a great idea! I haven't had a little 'happening' in ages."

I thought back to all the launch parties and trunk shows I had been to in the city, invitation-only events where I meant to only "drop by" for a little while, but got caught up in the flurry of free drinks and mingling with designers. I ended up spending money for no good reason other than I was too insecure to leave empty-handed.

"I'd love to help," I offered.

"Let's start brainstorming," Liz said and grabbed a note-book and pen from the counter. "First of all, when should we have it?"

"Thursdays are always a good night for cocktails, but if we want to get the weekenders, maybe a Friday from five to eight would be better?"

"Agreed. What about invites. Snail mail or email?"

"I still think it's nice to get a paper invitation, but if you don't have an address, we can scan the invitation and email it." At that instant, I had a eureka moment and blurted out, "Why don't we use the peacock as your logo? We can incorporate it on everything: the invites, your business cards, napkins ..."

Liz closed her eyes and did not move, causing me to worry if I was being too pushy. I really had to stop volunteering my two-cents about everything. Eclectibles was *her* store—practically her fifth child—but I saw so much potential in it, it was almost painful for me to stay quiet.

"Mia?"

"Yes?" I whispered, ready for my smack-down.

She exhaled and said, "I'm picturing it all in my head and am absolutely blown away by your ideas. I've wanted to shake things up, make this store vibrant again, but didn't know how. I guess I needed a new set of eyes to give me a kick in the—" Her cell phone rang and she took it out of the little leather case hanging around her neck. "Excuse me, it's my husband."

"Hi, Philip!" she answered brightly and walked a few feet away for more privacy. I had never met her husband, but he ran an IT consulting firm. Liz told me he worked a lot, joking they had conceived their four kids on the few nights he was actually home for dinner. At the end of their conversation, she walked back to the counter, wringing her hands.

"Is everything all right?" I asked.

She laughed grudgingly. "Oh, I should be used to it by now. Philip and I had planned a date night, but he has to stay in the city and take a potential client out to dinner." She shrugged. "I can't fault him; times are tough. He has to fight for every deal."

"Still, I'm sorry to hear that."

"I have the babysitter coming, the restaurant's booked . . ."

"It's a shame it has to go to waste, but I'm sure he'll make it up to you."

Liz watched me for a few seconds and asked, "What are *you* doing tonight?"

"My usual," I said and paused. "Nothing."

"Then let's go out together!"

"I'd make a poor substitute for a romantic date."

"It wasn't going to be anything fancy. We were going to a wine tasting first at The Bishops's Cellar—you know the wine shop off of the avenue?"

Since I hadn't allowed myself a drop of wine in Overlook, it was unfamiliar. In those haphazard weeks after Atlas, I could easily open a bottle of cheap red in the afternoon and drink glass after glass throughout the day, emptying the bottle and letting the gauzy high lull me to sleep. Until I got fired, my whole life had been about strict self-disclipline—avoiding destructive behaviors that could interfere with work—but I began to see how addictive his new habit could get, how my morose mood could justify another glass. Moving to Overlook had been an inflection point and I stopped cold turkey, but I couldn't explain my true reasons to Liz.

Instead I replied, "You know, I'm not much of a wine connoisseur."

"Neither am I, but it's really interesting. And Oliver, who owns the shop, is brilliant."

"I don't think I should be drinking when I have to drive home on those dark roads."

"You won't get drunk! Take small sips or spit it out. Dinner afterwards at Catalonia. My treat. Have you ever been there?"

I shook my head.

"It's this great tapas bar. I know it's not Manhattan, but Overlook's trying. Mia, you've got to get out more! Consider it a working dinner or something. I *insist*."

I had only planned to eat a boring salad and finish up Season 2 of *Mad Men*. "Okay, you're probably right." I looked down at my jeans and beige cardigan. "I'm not exactly dressed for a night out on the town."

"Remember: I said this wasn't Manhattan. Just put on some lipstick and you'll be fine."

The Bishop's Cellar was a free-standing, one-story brick building located on an outgrowth of Overlook Avenue, providing it with a highly coveted parking lot. Its trimming and archway were painted a glossy hunter green, popping in color and standing out against the red stone. The logotype, written in old-fashioned gold leaf on a wooden plank above the glass door, reminded me of an Irish pub. Rather than dotting the 'i', a bishop's pointy mitre floated above it.

"This is the best wine shop in Overlook," Liz said, parking her car in front of the store.

"Really? How long has it been around?"

"About five years. Before this, we only had one liquor store, a little place owned by an old man who actually had some decent wines, but was so rude, it seemed like he didn't want to sell anything! But we had no choice, so everyone shopped there anyway."

I laughed. "Is he still in business?"

"Yes. Some people think Oliver's too expensive."

"That's not so good."

"But you get service, knowledge and atmosphere when you shop here, so it's worth it."

Liz pushed open the front door and a shop assistant, who had been restocking shelves, told us that everyone was in the back, waiting in the private tasting room. We hurried and I noticed nothing beyond the blur of bottles whizzing by.

Once we entered the tasting room, a few faces eyeballed us impatiently, but Liz seemed unruffled.

"Hello, everyone," she said. "Sorry we're late."

I smiled apologetically and offered a little wave. We each removed a stool from underneath the long mahogany table and sat down. Lacquered to a high gloss with straight lines and sharp edges, a thin, white platform ran down the middle of the table and seemed to glow from within. I had expected much stuffier surroundings, but the setting was funky with red velvet curtains, spotlights and small potted orchids. Little clear bowls with cut salami, parmesan chunks and slices of bread were artfully arranged along the center platform. Each place-setting had six Riedel glasses, filled to a third with red wine; a pencil; and a small brochure describing the tasting: "Red Wines of the

Rhône Valley." Just looking at all the glasses made me woozy and I shivered, wondering if it was too early to help myself to a snack.

"The wine cellar is behind you," Liz whispered. "That's why it feels chilly."

I swung around and saw two pulled-back curtains, exposing industrial-sized windows and the cavernous vault inside. The shelves were loaded with mounds of bottles and unopened wooden cases. The whole set-up smelled of money. Fine wines were a another status symbol and opportunity for one-upmanship on Wall Street, but I had never gotten into it. Peter always made such a big show of choosing wines whenever we took clients out to dinner. He would study the wine list and ask the sommelier things that sounded like questions—but were really statements demonstrating his own knowledge—and then pick something insanely expensive that I felt obliged to like and praise. I could also count on Peter to rehash the story about how he was out-bid on a rare bottle of Château d'Yquem at Sotheby's. Although it had been part of the job, I always silently rebelled against the theater and snobbery of fine wines.

My head became lost in thoughts of Peter and my old life, until a deep, booming voice from somewhere at the other end of the table transported me back to the present.

"Welcome, everyone!" he said.

What I didn't expect—in the few seconds it took me to redirect my body and brain to the purpose of the evening—was seeing the one person in Overlook who had inexplicably piqued my curiosity: the mysteriously handsome guy I shared a table with at Cupcake de Ville. Could he be *the* Oliver Bishop? Unintentionally, my mouth opened wide. I immediately sealed it shut.

"I'm so happy you took the time out this evening to share in some of my favorite wines from one of the world's most famous wine regions, the Rhône River Valley in Southeastern France," he said with a smile. He was clean-shaven tonight and more broad-shouldered than I remembered from our brief encounter. He managed to look both cool and proper in a white button-down under a light grey, v-neck sweater.

"The Rhône stretches from Lyon in the North to Avignon in the South," he continued. "While the region produces both red and white wines, it's best known for its spectacular reds, great value wines that match well with all kinds of food: beef, lamb, stews, pasta . . . Tonight we'll just focus on reds, varietals made from grapes like Syrah, Grenache, Cinsault and Mouvèdre."

He didn't shy away from using the correct French pronunciations either, putting his accents in all the right places.

A dark-haired woman with pretty blue eyes lifted her hand, displaying a wrist stacked with silver bangles. Smiling, Oliver nodded in her direction.

"Now, I always get confused about this: Is the Syrah grape the same as Shiraz?" she asked.

"Good question! There's actually no genetic difference between the grapes; it's really a question of location. What we refer to as the New World in winemaking—Australia, New Zealand and even some parts of the US—Syrah is called *Shiraz*," he explained. "There's always been a lot of debate about where the grape originated. Some DNA testing proved that it came from the Rhône region itself, while others still insist the Greeks brought it from the Persian city of Shiraz. But there is a small difference: Australian Shiraz is cultivated in the south, in the Barossa Valley which is warmer than the Rhône, so they tend to be riper and fuller, less peppery and acidic than Syrah."

I assumed I'd feel intimidated, but Oliver's enthusiasm was infectious, demystifying the six glasses of wine before me, infusing them with lineage and tradition. Even if he hadn't been so good-looking, it would have been difficult not to give him my full attention.

"Rhône wines can be divided into two sub-regions with their very own wine traditions, the Northern Rhône and the Southern Rhône," he went on. "The climate in the Northern Rhône is very similar to what we have here in New York—with our harsh winters and warm summers—but it's also heavily influenced by the Mistral winds that whip through the valley at speeds of up to eighty-five miles an hour, bringing colder air."

"Oh, I remember renting a house in Provence one year," inserted an older gentleman with round, horn-rimmed glasses. He was the only other man in the room besides Oliver. Liz's husband would have made it three. We ladies numbered ten. "The Mistral was brutal, but once it blew away, we had clear blue skies as far as the eye could see."

Oliver grinned. "That's the beauty of the Mistral. It accounts for the three hundred days of sunshine a year in Provence, shaping the vegetation of the region. So the cooler, semi-continental climate in the North produces wine that are known for their elegance and finesse. The steep landscape and granite soil are perfect for growing Syrah. Syrah can also be mixed with some white varietals like Viognier, Marsanne and Roussanne for added complexity."

The group took careful notes in their small brochures.

Could they even *spell* the grapes he was talking about? I jotted down a few words for good measure.

"What are some of the leading vineyards in the region?" asked the man.

"Hermitage, Côte Rôtie, Cornas and Saint-Joseph. They have lower yields and tend to be quite pricey."

Oliver often used his hands to illustrate a point and I couldn't help but notice he didn't wear a wedding band. Hadn't he mentioned a son during our ten-second exchange? I began speculating about the status of his personal life. Was he married, but didn't believe in wearing a ring? Divorced? Same-sex relationship with an adopted child? Should I ask Liz? I ruled that one out. Too obvious.

"Will we be tasting anything from Hermitage?" asked a blonde woman of a certain age. She was shrouded in greige cashmere, with unusually full lips and a smooth forehead.

"I wouldn't think of giving you anything less, Barbara," Oliver said.

Did he just flirt with that grande dame? She beamed and reached for a piece of salami.

"Now the Southern Rhône has a much more Mediterranean climate with milder winters and hot summers, so their wines tend to be rounder and full-bodied. Many are easy-drinking table wines and the majority are blended with different grape varieties," Oliver said.

"Do they blend different reds together?" Liz asked.

"Absolutely. The Southern Rhône's most famous red wine, Châteauneuf-du-Pape, can contain up to thirteen varieties of grapes, eight red and five white," he replied.

Murmurs of surprise were followed by more notetaking.

"The Southern Rhône is fascinating for a lot of reasons, but what I've always found really fascinating is how rocky and rugged the landscape is." He balled one hand into a fist. "There are these stones at the base of the vine that absorb the heat of the sun during the day and reflect that heat at night, keeping the vines warm. The rains also run through the stones, keeping the vines dry. So the wines produced there are very earthy, fruity and spicy."

I was confused about how something could be both fruity and spicy.

"Now, enough talk! It's time to drink," he said, eliciting laughter from the group. "I think most of you liked the blind tasting we did last time when we tried to match the wines with their descriptions?"

Everyone, except me, nodded in recognition and began recounting how well or poorly they had done.

"It's not a contest, so don't worry so much about getting everything right," Oliver advised. "Focus on a couple of basic things: Is it light or dark in color? What does it smell like? Is it spicy or sweet? Does it feel like milk or cream in your mouth? Remember these descriptions are just guidelines. I uncorked the bottles about three hours ago, so they've had time to breath and evolve. Their characteristics change over time, so it's by no means set in stone."

I looked down and analyzed the first page of my brochure. The left hand column listed the wines from one to six, corresponding to the glasses that were arranged at my place setting. The right hand column contained the six different, randomly ordered vignettes we were supposed to match with a glass. I read the first description:

"Exhibiting a dense ruby/purple hue, this broad, dense, tannic wine features touches of licorice, earth, smoke and tapenade."

I didn't even know what "tannic" meant. And tapenade? Should the wine smell like olives? Furthermore, each glass of wine was colored a deep red. How on earth would I be able to tell the difference? I went on to the next one:

"Grenache dominates in this medium-bodied blend with notes of lavender, black currants, sweet cherry jam, licorice and a hint of Provençal herbs."

What was up with all the licorice? It barely qualified as a candy in my opinion and had no business whatsoever being in wine.

I glanced at Liz. She had put on her drugstore reading glasses and looked very concentrated, but hadn't yet matched anything.

"Liz, are you getting this?" I whispered.

"Not yet. Let's try to figure it out together."

"I've never done this before."

"I've done it a few times, but I'm not any good. Just watch what I'm doing."

Liz picked up the first glass and tipped it in front of the illuminated white platform in the middle of the table. Against it, the gradations of red became easier to identify. This one was actually paler at the top before cascading into a deeper hue at the bottom.

"This probably has lots of red fruits, like cherries and strawberries." She swirled the glass a couple of times, brought it to her nose and inhaled.

"What does it smell like?" I asked.

"Uh, alcohol?"

"Liz, I'm serious!"

"*You* smell it and tell me what you think!"

Before picking up my glass, I surveyed the rest of the group. They were all in the throes of seeing, swirling, smelling and sipping. The older gentleman seemed the most at ease. He held a glass in front of his nose and twirled it in the air, unencumbered by small matters like droplets falling onto the table. Oliver watched us, front and center at the opposite end, and his eyes met mine before I could look down again. He pointed at me questioningly and I must have looked baffled, because he quickly rounded the table and stood behind me before I could gather my thoughts.

"How're you doing?" he asked

"Fine!" I piped.

"Oh, Oliver, thank goodness you're here," Liz said, jumping in. "We need help. This is my friend, Mia. She's my date for the evening. Philip couldn't make it after all."

"Pleased to meet you, Mia," he replied. "Is this your first wine tasting?"

"You can tell?" I asked.

"No, not at all. I was just guessing since I haven't seen you here before."

He clearly didn't remember our meeting at Cupcake de Ville. But, then again, why would he? It was a forgettable, non-event that had nevertheless left an impression on me.

"Well, I do enjoy wines," I admitted, "but I don't know much about them."

"It's never too late to start and I guarantee you'll enjoy them so much more. So, what are you ladies wondering about?"

"I'm curious about this one: 'Aged in small oak barrels, this blend of Grenache, Syrah, Mourvèdre and Cinsault bursts with rich black cherry and black currant fruit as well as hints of tobacco, pepper and spice box,'" Liz said.

"That's a good one. It actually has lots of clues. All the different grape varieties tell you that the wine comes from—"

"The Southern Rhône!" I shouted, and a few of the others grimaced in my direction.

Oliver nodded. "Exactly. So is it going to be a full or medium-bodied wine?"

"Medium?" guessed Liz.

"Correct. And the color?"

"Pretty dark?" I said.

"Now you're getting the hang of this. Let's go around and look at each glass against the white surface," he said, slanting my first glass towards the center platform.

"Pretty cool table, by the way," I said.

"Thanks! I designed it myself so you could judge the wine's color better. Does this one look dark enough to you?"

Beside the lighted surface, the first wine looked more burgundy than black cherry. "Mmm ... not really."

We repeated the same procedure with the other five glasses until we were left with three possibilities. "Now, time to swirl," he said.

Liz and I picked up the fourth glass among our six. She spun her wrist in the air, took a brief sniff and then a big sip. Winking at me, she declared: "I've been waiting all night to do that!"

Oliver laughed. "Before you tell us what you really think, Liz, I want Mia to give it a try."

"I don't think I can swirl it without spilling," I said.

"You don't have to hold your glass in the air. Keep it on the table, hold the stem firmly and just give it a little spin."

I moved the glass from side to side, but there was a lot more sloshing than spinning. Liz giggled and I kicked her chair.

"You can do it with a little more gusto. Let me show you." Oliver arched over, capped my hand with his and spun so quickly, a whirlpool formed in my glass. His closeness was pleasing; his touch warm and reassuring. When he removed his hand, I felt silly for reacting so strongly to his presence.

I had to stay focused and not let myself get too distracted by Oliver. I sniffed the wine, trying hard to distinguish the fruits, spices and minerals in its composition. I then sipped— waiting for the flavors to settle in my mouth—and caught Dark Hair/Blue Eyes spying on Oliver across the table. I obviously wasn't the only one who found him attractive. His good looks and charisma probably accounted for the fact that ninety percent of the people here were female. I wondered if Oliver knew this, if he turned on the charm to win customers. Well, I wasn't going to be another groupie.

"What does it taste like?" he asked.

I straightened up in my stool and said in a more business-like voice, "Lighter, fruitier. I'm picking up a bit of strawberry."

"Very perceptive, but does that sound like the wine we're looking for?"

"Not really."

"Just go on like that, smelling, tasting and testing the wines against each other and you'll be fine."

Assuming that was his cue to end our little tutorial, I said,

"Thanks."

Oliver walked around the table, checking in on the others; fielding questions; and offering tips. Once it was time to reveal the correct answers, they all became animated, coloring their commentary with grandiose winespeak, which made me want to roll my eyes. The older gentleman claimed to have gotten everything right, while Liz was satisfied with her two. Since I had guessed incorrectly for all six, I stayed silent. I tried to convince myself it didn't matter, but I was competitive and it would have been nice to have something to show for the evening. When it was all over, I threw the marked-up brochure in my bag and finished the glass of water to steady myself.

Liz took a final sip of Glass #3 and said, "I think that one was my favorite: the Cabrières Châteauneuf-du-Pape. I want to buy a couple of bottles for Philip. Do you mind waiting a few minutes?"

"No, not at all."

"I just want say goodbye to Oliver first."

I smiled. "Sure! No problem."

Oliver stood with two other women who hadn't said much during the tasting, but now seemed intent on plying him with questions. Liz and I waited at the edge of their little triangle and, after about a minute, Oliver motioned for us to join in.

"Thank you so much for such a lovely evening," Liz said. "The wines literally took me back to Provence and I'm going to buy a few bottles to get me through the rest of the winter."

"I'm glad you enjoyed it. Tell Philip he was missed, but I have a new bottle of whisky here that I think he'd enjoy," Oliver said.

Liz laughed. "I'm sure he would."

She and the others glanced at me expectantly. How odd I must have looked, standing there silently, with nothing amusing to contribute to the conversation. Thinking fast, I added, "Yes, thank you. It was very interesting."

"Did you have any favorites?" Oliver asked.

"The Hermitage was, uh, very smooth."

"Yes, that's a nice one," he agreed.

"If we had to buy one bottle tonight, Oliver," cut in one of the other ladies with her high-pitched voice, "which one would you recommend?"

"I've always been partial to a good Châteauneuf-du-Pape," he said.

"That's the one I plan on buying!" Liz exclaimed. "See— my taste isn't that bad after all."

"I think I'll get a case of that too," said the woman who had posed the question and her friend nodded.

"Mia, I'll see you out front," Liz said and rushed out. Not to be outdone, the other two ladies dashed behind her.

Oliver and I had been following the whole spectacle and broke into laughter at the same time.

"You've got women fighting over your wine!" I joked and instantly regretted my *double entendre*.

He smiled. "Well, I hope you'll stop by the shop again."

"And I better get more right next time!"

"I'm sure you will." He paused. "Have a good night."

"Thanks. You too."

Outside, as I helped Liz rearrange things in the back of her SUV to make room for the new case of wine, she said, "That Oliver Bishop is something. He opens a few bottles, we taste them, get a little tipsy and *voilà*! I end up spending a king's ransom!"

"He seems really savvy."

"He's like a Renaissance Man: smart, has style, knows about food and wine, is a great dad—"

"He has kids?" I asked, pretending I had no clue. "Is he married?"

Liz stopped tinkering in her trunk and sighed before speaking. "There was someone . . ."

Pause.

" . . . but she walked out on him and their child, a son. The cutest little boy you've ever seen."

Her news floored me. *That* scenario had never entered my imagination. "When did this happen?"

"A few years ago. No one really knows the full story."

I felt my heart soften in empathy. "That's so sad."

Liz puckered her lips in distaste. "I think it's beyond the pale. Mothers don't just leave—no matter how crazy your kids drive you."

"I don't understand it either," I said, reflecting on how cancer had stolen my own mother from me. It was a natural loss, but the scars endured. How, then, could a child overcome his mother's abandonment?

"Oliver does a fantastic job keeping it all together, considering the circumstances," said Liz.

"He certainly does," I responded, seeing him in an entirely new light.

Liz pushed down the trunk door and we climbed into the SUV, both of us lost in our own thoughts.

"Listen, I really want to go through with your party idea for the store," she said finally, turning her key in the ignition. "I think it would really raise our profile."

"Tell me what I can do to help."

"Let's finalize the date and invitations."

I nodded.

"The store needs a total overhaul and I'll have to come up with some new displays. Would you mind taking care of the food and drinks?"

"Not at all."

"Why don't you meet with Oliver for some wine recommendations? Nothing super-expensive, but a nice red and white. And some bubbly, of course."

"Sure."

Turned out I would be going back to The Bishop's Cellar much sooner than I'd planned.

17.

Liz wanted to throw the cocktail party in two weeks, so the pressure was on to get the invitations out, plan the event and revamp the store. Therefore, I couldn't apply my preferred strategy of contacting Oliver two or three days after the wine-tasting. Liz asked me to speak to him the *very next day*. Powerless to resist, I breezed into The Bishop's Cellar less than twenty-four hours later, shortly before lunchtime.

The same sales assistant from the previous evening manned the register. "Hi!" he said. "What can I help you with?"

"My name is Mia Lewis and I work at Eclectibles with Liz Jansing. We were here last night for the wine-tasting," I explained.

He creased his brows together, jogging his memory. "Oh, yes! Do you want to buy the wines from the tasting? Unfortunately we only have a few bottles left of the L'Obrieu and the Tardieu-Laurent. Everything else sold out."

"Mmm," I murmured. "I actually wanted to speak to Oliver."

He sized me up incredulously. I was definitely getting the "all-the-housewives-have-a-crush-on-Oliver" vibe from him, but didn't look away since I wasn't a frustrated, flirty housewife and had a legitimate reason for being there. Granted, I had taken a little bit of extra care with my appearance—wearing shoes instead of Uggs as well as some make-up—but I always tried to look well-groomed for business meetings (which, technically, this was).

"I can help you with anything you need," said the gatekeeper finally.

"Oh, I'm sure you can, but I need help with a special order for a cocktail party Liz is throwing at Eclectibles. She specifically asked for Oliver's help in selecting the wine. *We're talking several cases here.* I'm sure you understand."

I was exaggerating the potential of this sale; the whole event budget couldn't exceed a thousand dollars. We only had five hundred dollars for alcohol—peanuts considering the wines in Oliver's back room cellar—but his little helper didn't need to know that. To keep costs down, we planned on emailing the peacock-themed invitations and Liz knew a caterer who could give her a good deal on appetizers. Amaryllis had also volunteered to create floral arrangements using fresh blooms from Whole Foods.

He sighed. "Let me see if he's in his office."

In the meantime, I browsed through the French wines section. There *was* something to be said about a beautiful bottle of wine, the color and curve of its shape; the elegant labels that conjured up images of abundant vineyards and magnificent estates. I held up a bottle of Château Latour 2008, recognizing the famous appellation from my fine restaurant forays with Peter, but balked at the price: $795.00! I had spent that much on a pair of shoes once upon a time, but now all I felt was sticker shock-induced nausea.

I heard the sound of brisk footsteps and looked up. Oliver came towards me with one outstretched arm. I smiled and tendered my own, feeling relieved that he at least *seemed* happy to see me again.

"Mia! You're back!" he said.

"I am!"

"Josh tells me that Liz would like some help with wines for a cocktail party at her store?"

"Yes, she's planning a launch party for two new lines that have come in."

"That's as good a reason as any to celebrate! What did you guys have in mind? Just wine? Champagne?"

"We wanted to serve a little bit of everything," I replied, anticipating his next question.

"What's your budget?"

I giggled nervously. "About five hundred dollars. Can you work with that?"

He looked aghast for a moment and then smiled. "Of course I can! People will be happy to drink anything if it's free."

"Well, we think it'll be a great way to get more buzz and store traffic."

"Absolutely." He pointed to the bottles of Latour. "But we should probably stay away from this aisle. Latour can put you in debt."

"I've noticed!"

"I'd recommend some domestic wines," he said, leading the way to the top of the aisle and turning left. He was dressed in another slim v-neck sweater and black jeans. A white tee shirt stuck out from underneath the heather blue wool. I wondered if those sweaters were his uniform, freeing him from having to think about what he would wear everyday, allowing him to focus on his son and the store. They also accentuated his muscular upper body. I couldn't deny that Oliver's studied casualness was sexy, reducing me to an adolescent with a fluttery stomach.

"California?" I asked.

"Or even Oregon. They have some great Pinot Noirs."

"That could be a possibility."

"Are you planning on serving anything?"

"Just some light hors d'oeuvres. We're thinking proscuitto with melon, tomato bruschetta, mini quiches."

"If you're going for an Italian theme, I'd definitely recommend Prosecco instead of champagne. It'll be delicious and cost you a fraction of the price."

"That sounds interesting . . ."

He guided me to the sparkling wines and removed a black bottle with a large gold "Z" on the label. "This one is nice: Zardetto Conegliano. Dry and peachy with a clean finish. Goes for about sixteen dollars a bottle."

"And champagne would be?" I asked, still a bit unsure.

"That's the price for a half bottle of"—he searched the rows—"Piper-Heidsieck, which is fine, but not as kicky as a nice Prosecco. Americans are always surprised by how tasty Prosecco is. Besides Liz never shies away from being a little different."

I smiled. "She certainly doesn't."

"How long have you known her?"

"Not long at all. I moved to town in January."

"From where?"

"The city."

"Did you just buy a place?"

"No, I'm borrowing a friend's house on Meadow Lane."

"You're in the boondocks!"

"Tell me about it. I have to sleep with all the lights on."

He laughed. "So how'd you start working for Liz?"

"I was getting a little restless and wanted something to

do. She offered me a job to help her out in the store, so here I am."

"Are you enjoying it?"

"I am. It's fun meeting all the customers and getting to know the town better."

He nodded. "Things sure have changed since I was a kid."

"You grew up here?" I asked, surprised. Why did I assume he had grown up in a big city, a product of liberal parents who might have let him take his first sip of wine at fourteen?

"I did. By the train station, before they redeveloped and it became cool to live in that neighborhood. Now it's packed with all the commuters who don't have to worry about a second car or a parking permit."

He said this with no resentment; these people were probably his best customers.

"Have you been here the whole time?"

He hesitated and it seemed like a shadow fell over his face. "No. I went away to school and then worked in the city." He paused. "I came back around five years ago. Thought it would be a nice place to raise a family."

With Liz's information about Oliver, his ex and their son, it was difficult not to fixate on that painful asterisk in his bio. I couldn't tell if he suspected how much I already knew, so I replied, "Overlook seems like a geat place for kids."

His expression brightened again. "Do you have any of your own?"

I shook my head. "Three godchildren though."

He nodded slowly, appearing to methodically take in the nuggets of information I had fed him. "So you left an exciting life in the city for the quiet charms of Overlook?"

"I don't know if it was that exciting, but change is good."

A guarded silence followed my comment as Oliver and I interpreted each other's responses. Parties and wine had detoured to kids and life. Maybe we both sensed there was more to our stories than we were willing to share.

"Well, do you want to go for some Oregon wine?" he asked, smoothly bringing us back on-topic.

"I think the Prosecco is as far out-of-the-box as I'm willing to go. Would you mind just showing me some 'good value' Californian wines?"

Oliver bowed his head a little. "Of course."

"But no Merlot," I added, implicitly referring to the hit movie *Sideways* and the main character's strict aversion to Merlot.

He laughed, catching on to my joke. "Merlot is actually making a comeback."

We spent the next ten minutes going through the main wineries in Napa Valley and, in the end, I chose a Ravens Wood Zinfandel and a Robert Mondavi Sauvignon Blanc. I gave Oliver extra points for not handing me off to Josh, the shop assistant, when we were through. He walked me back to the check-out counter and wrote out the order himself.

"So, when is the party again?" he asked, filling out my name along with Liz's on the order form. He wrote rapidly, using uppercase print letters throughout.

"March nineteenth," I replied. "That's a Friday."

"From what time?"

"Five to eight PM."

"Mmm ... maybe I should stay open late to get your stragglers."

"Maybe you should."

"How many people do you expect?"

"It's hard to say. We're sending around 150 invitations, maybe half will come. Maybe fifty. Maybe no one ..."

"Don't say that. They'll come. Since you're not sure, get a case of everything. That's thirty-six bottles of alcohol, giving you some wiggle room. Just return whatever you guys don't open and I'll bill you after the event."

"That's *so* nice of you to do that."

"It's a professional courtesy, along with the twenty pro-cent discount."

"Thank you! Liz will really appreciate this." We would now be under budget for the alcohol and could use the extra funds to upgrade the food and flowers.

"Should I list you as the contact person?"

"Uh, sure. I guess so."

"Phone number in case we need to reach you?"

"Well, you can find me at the store: 638-3808."

"Cell?"

"Umm, I only have my personal cell."

"That works too."

I realized how presumptuous I sounded and tried to blunt my social goofiness with a terse enumeration of my digits, "917-219-3677."

"E-mail?"

"It's mialewis@gmail.com."

Coordinates duly recorded, he put down the pen. "We'll deliver the bottles that afternoon at 4:00. We'll keep the Prosecco and Sauvignon Blanc chilled and you guys will be all set."

"Perfect!" I paused. "Thanks again for all your help."

"My pleasure. And don't worry, you'll have a great party."

"Well, stop by if you need a tray or some other random object," I said and could have kicked myself. Why did I add another angle to a perfectly innocent business exchange? *He must think I'm flirting with him. That I'm no different from those bored housewives.*

"I will definitely keep that in mind," he remarked, but I wasn't convinced.

There wasn't much else for me to say except, "Take care. Have a nice day."

"Thanks. You too."

I negotiated the small distance to the front door, wondering if Oliver was still at the check-out counter watching me leave, or if he had already dismissed our little encounter and was halfway down the store back to his office. An irrational pang of disappointment hit me when I realized I wouldn't have an excuse to see him again for another two weeks.

18.

Pouring equal amounts of Prosecco into the fluted glasses we had rented for the party, my eyes beheld a scene I would have never thought possible two weeks ago. Eclectibles had risen from her slumber, restored and reinvigorated, but with signature touches—peacock and all—intact. The new metal trays and bowls stood on the old stone and iron garden table in the center of the room. Decorative plates and paperweights, imprinted with bygone images of flowers, animals, letters and skulls, enlivened a lackluster bookcase. Liz's caterer had elevated finger quiches, deli meats, cheeses and crackers from Costco by serving them on blue and white earthenware. Garnished with rosemary sprigs, nuts, olives and dried fruit, I dared anyone to guess their provenance.

The last glass filled, I wiped the front of the bottle and threw the damp cloth into the empty Prosecco box. I had spent the whole day waiting for the alcohol to be delivered from The Bishop's Cellar, hoping Oliver would come by and I could impress him further with my capacity for small talk. Instead, Liz had opened the back door and Josh swooped in, carrying three cases. He deposited them on the floor and was gone in less than a minute. In a way, I should have been relieved. My flighty, arbitrary thoughts about Oliver confounded me and I may have made a fool of myself.

This was the problem: I couldn't quite read him. I was normally a very good judge of character, used to rating people I wanted to hire or do business with, but I couldn't decide if Oliver was genuinely nice or a really good salesman. He was friendly and I sometimes sensed a subtext to our banter, but just as quickly, he would revert to casual-polite mode again. And, to my dismay, I found that I actually *cared* about what kind of impression I made on him.

Banishing these foolish thoughts, I checked my watch. Ten minutes to go until the first of the sixty customers who had responded "yes" would arrive. Amaryllis hovered over a pedestal stand by the entrance, adjusting the tall flower arrangement that would welcome everyone when they entered the store. She straightened a snapdragon in one spot, cut a brownish leaf from a tiger lily in another.

"The flowers look great," I told her. "You don't have to fix them anymore."

She cocked her head to the side. "I think I should have added more eucalyptus."

Mimicking her movement, I replied, "No, I don't think so. You're just a perfectionist. No one else would think that except you."

She half-smiled, revealing an insecurity that manifested itself whenever she dared to show her own talents.

"Thank you, Mia. You've done a great job with everything too."

"Girls! Come here!" Liz called to us from the register.

We joined her as she doled out Prosecco in three glasses, the bubbly overflowing onto the counter.

"Let's have a toast before showtime," she suggested. The sequins on her magenta top glittered in the light, matching the radiant smile on her face. "Thank you so much for doing such a fantastic job. I haven't felt this excited about the store in years."

Amaryllis and I tilted our glasses, but stopped mid-air

when Liz exclaimed, "Wait a second! Mia, I think Amaryllis would agree with me in saying that Eclectibles has you to thank for shaking things up. When I asked you to work here and you told me that you left some fancy job on Wall Street, I thought, 'Oh no! She'll probably be so bored.' But you've shown me how much you care about Eclectibles. You've challenged me to get out of my comfort zone and I can't thank you enough for that." She tipped her Prosecco in my direction. "So cheers to Mia."

"Mia! Mia!" Amaryllis chanted.

"Thank you!" I replied. "I just hope this evening is a success."

"Look at this place," Liz said, looping her free arm around the room. "How could it not be?"

We banged the sides of our glasses as one, yelping as suds dribbled onto our hands, uniting us in this endeavor that was Eclectibles.

Emotions swelled in my chest. I could have never imagined how Eclectibles would become more than a time-killer. I had *latched* on to it. Liz's eccentric little shop had become my savior. If she knew my real reasons for being in Overlook she might not be so complimentary, but it felt so rewarding to be a part of a team again, to have a purpose, to be appreciated.

We finished our Prosecco and spread out. Liz tended the front; Amaryllis stationed herself by the appetizer buffet; I took care of the center with the new merchandise. The first to arrive was an Asian couple I had never seen in the shop before, but Liz hugged them like long-lost friends and led them towards the Gustavian sideboard with the drinks. More people streamed in, creating an atmosphere of lively chatter and bonhomie.

Watching Liz in action, I came to appreciate just how much she had the gift for retail. My mother had embodied it too; that passion for the product, a desire to get close to the customer. Liz didn't live by the "profit and loss" calculation—both in work and personal relationships—that had defined my years on Wall Street. Warmth and authenticity were her calling cards. Her eyes would enlarge when she recognized an old customer and she could rhapsodize about an antique without ever letting a customer feel intimidated. She kept me busy, ferrying people my way until we sold out of many key items. Since the crowd skewed middle-aged and up, I took instant notice of the pretty, black-clad teenage girl who came in with a man in a quilted green jacket. Spotting Liz, she rushed over and hugged her. Liz held on for a few beats longer than usual and gave the man a peck on the lips. I assumed the pair was her husband and eldest daughter. He gesticulated and seemed to be paying Liz a compliment. She pointed to me and I gave her the thumbs-up sign. Minutes later, all three traversed the store to where I stood.

"So this is the famous Mia I've been hearing about!" said her husband. Liz told me they had met in college and twenty-five years later, he was completely white-haired, from his head right down to his short, boxed mustache and beard.

Liz nodded. "Mia, please meet my husband Philip and daughter Clementine."

There was a lot of hand-shaking and praise, which I quickly tried to downplay.

Clementine was almost as tall as her father, but she owed her green eyes and wavy blond hair to Liz. Tugging at Liz's arm, she said, "Mom, where are those skull and cross bone things you were going to show me?"

"Oh right! Please excuse us."

Clementine smiled at me again before leaving. "It was nice meeting you."

"You too!" Her politeness—and the fact that I appreciated it so much—made me feel ancient.

Philip smiled at me, clasping his palms together. "So, Mia, Liz told me you used to work on Wall Street."

I gulped. "Yes, I did."

"For what firm?"

Shrugging dismissively, I replied, "It's a really small one. You've probably never heard of it."

"Oh, I do a lot of consulting with financial services to get their systems in place, especially with all the compliance regulations these days, so I'm familiar with most of them."

For the life of me, I could not get myself to say "Atlas Capital." Those two words stuck in my throat like a lump of coal. Philip's question wasn't outrageous. He was being friendly, trying to find common ground. If I had nothing to hide, then my response should have been automatic, but my blinkers went up. If I said Atlas, what if he went back home and Googled me? He'd discover my disgrace, inform Liz and then she'd fire me for misleading her. I'd be right back to where I started five months ago: humiliated and unemployed. But did Philip and Liz really look like the type who went around Googling people? Their hands were full managing two jobs and shuttling four kids around. Had Liz Googled me, I certainly wouldn't be standing here, chatting up her husband. To deflect, I employed a classic parlor trick and swung the conversation back to Philip.

"I think banks will spend at least fifty percent of their time on compliance issues going forward," I said.

Philip nodded approvingly, sensing he had an ally. "Management doesn't like all the extra work, says it takes away from their money-making operations, but it's for their own protection. How did your old firm—what was the name of it again—handle it?"

He wouldn't let it go! Maybe he was fishing for a contact name to pitch his business.

"Well, we had a really good compliance officer and, um, he used to, um," I stammered; stalling for time, a fairy godmother, anything. Miraculously, my BlackBerry vibrated in my back pocket and I brought it out as a diversionary tactic. "I'm sorry, but someone's calling me."

Philip looked at me curiously. "Do you need to take that?"

It was Mannheimer. My lawyer. Talk about bad timing.

I put the phone away. "No, it's nothing important, but I should really be getting back to work. We've been doing so much business tonight and I don't want to miss anyone."

"Of course! And here I am, taking up your time!"

"Not at all. It was so nice to finally meet you," I said. "Hope we can catch up again some other time."

"Me too. I better go and check out that tasty buffet before it's all gone!"

We parted ways and I converged on two male decorators testing a pair of brocade chairs. They peppered me with questions, but I couldn't focus. My heart galloped; I had made a narrow escape and wondered if I would be so lucky the next time.

When I got back to the cottage, it was almost 10:00PM

and Mannheimer had called four times. I had sensed it was important, but couldn't answer or call him back with all the people milling about at Eclectibles. Redialing, I waited for him to pick up.

"Mia! I've been trying to reach you for the past three hours."

"I know. Sorry. It was a busy night. I was working."

"*Working?* Where?"

"At a store. You told me to keep busy. I couldn't sit around and do nothing!"

"Point taken. Listen, I've uncovered something really interesting."

"Go on."

"You told me that Peter didn't know Tripp before he hired him at Atlas?"

"I didn't mean that *literally*. Peter had heard of Tripp professionally. I guess they met before at a conference or something."

"The connection goes deeper than that." Mannheimer paused. "Are you ready?"

I sighed. He could be so dramatic. "Yes."

"Peter's half-sister, Isabelle, is married to Tripp's younger brother, Scott."

I thought back to what I knew of Peter's family life. "I didn't even know he had a half-sister. He always talked about his older brother, Mark."

"Mark is from Peter's father's first marriage to his mother. They divorced when Peter was in college. His father remarried a few years later and had two more children, Adam and Isabelle."

I quickly did the math. "Then that would make Adam and Isabelle at least twenty years younger than Peter. That's probably why he never talked about them."

"He was already out on his own when Isabelle was born, so they probably only saw each other during the holidays, maybe the summer, or on special occasions like weddings. *Especially Isabelle's wedding to Scott two years ago on Turks & Caicos.* Do you remember Peter going to Turks & Caicos?"

"He traveled a lot. It's possible he could have mentioned a wedding on Turks & Caicos, but I don't remember."

"Well, I have the guest register from Parrot Cay, the weekend of February fifteenth to eighteenth 2008, and among them are Mr. & Mrs. Peter Branco and one Tripp Armsden."

I think I finally understood what it meant to have one's blood boil. "They played me."

"Big time, I'm sorry to say."

"But what does that prove?"

"It proves a prior connection! Something you weren't privy to. Don't you think that's strange?"

"Yes."

"And you have to ask yourself: Why would Peter keep you in the dark about something like that?"

"Maybe he didn't want me to accuse him of nepotism even though, technically, he and Tripp aren't even really related."

"We can still claim that there's a strong family connection, making him more willing to throw you under the bus."

"How did you find this out?"

Mannheimer chuckled. "That's my job."

"Seriously."

"I've always thought it was strange how quickly and completely your relationship with Peter changed. You'd always been his loyal right hand. Why was he so willing to let you go? It couldn't be incompetence. You kept everything functional during the worst days of the financial crisis. Insubordination? You're tough, but in this case you were looking out for the firm's best interests. Then why? Maybe it wasn't only professional, so I dug around, checked out their family histories and this is where I ended up." Mannheimer chortled. "It was even better than I'd hoped for."

This bombshell left me utterly confused, wondering what else Peter had hidden from me. Did anyone else at Atlas know that Peter and Tripp were related by marriage? Suddenly, the months leading up to my downfall began to make perfect sense. Tripp's familial bond explained his lack of respect towards me, his belief that the rules didn't apply to him.

"Why would Peter do this?" I asked.

"Mia, that's what I intend to find out."

19.

Mannheimer's news about Tripp and Peter was nothing less than a thunderbolt; it upended my entire worldview. They had clearly seen me as clueless and expendable, supremely confident that their family connection would escape my knowledge. Sunday was my first day off in two weeks and, without the store to distract me, I grew more and more incensed thinking about their deception. On top of this, as I slathered lotion on my legs, I noticed that dimples had formed on my once-even, firm thighs. I was also a little short of breath going up the stairs. I hadn't exercised in months. Winter and Overlook's dark roads had given me a convenient excuse not to go running, but I needed to let off steam as well as get back in shape. After a breakfast of black coffee and one hard-boiled egg, I squeezed into a pair of tights and dug in the hallway closet for my sneakers. Grabbing my iPod, water bottle, keys and BlackBerry, I revved up the Ford and drove through the back roads—even lovelier now in the early spring light—towards town.

Overlook High School had a regulation track about a quarter of a mile long. Twelve times around the track would give me three miles, a decent distance for someone as out-of-shape as I was. It wouldn't be the most scenic jog, but I didn't know my way around the parks and wooded areas and the last thing I needed was to get lost. I warmed up near the bleachers, trying not to get intimidated by the reed-thin woman circling the inside lane. I began running at a brisk speed and the first two laps were easy. I slowed down for the third and fourth;

struggled in the fifth; and got a knife-edged abdominal cramp at the start of the sixth lap. I kept on going, but my movements were like baby steps; the more I ran, the longer the track seemed. Panting, I hobbled back to the bleachers and grabbed my water bottle, slurping as water slobbered down my chin onto my sport top.

I couldn't produce another six laps and ambled off the track, taking a shortcut through the bushes that separated it from the baseball diamond. Even the school grounds in Overlook were substantial; boasting three tennis courts, a football turf and two soccer fields. By the time I reached the soccer playing area, I had finally regained my breath and could walk at a normal pace. Further ahead, I saw two people kicking a ball by the goal net. At the halfway line, I realized it was an adult and a child. Once I got a clearer view of them, it was too late to turn back. I trudged on, eyes fixed on a tree, hoping to go unnoticed. But the soccer ball flew in the air and landed a few feet to my left. When Oliver jogged up to retrieve it—his young son in tow—it was impossible for us not to say hello.

"Hey, Mia!" he called out. "Out for a run?"

I stopped walking and smiled. "Just finished! What are you guys up to?"

Oliver scooped up the ball, wedging it between his arm and hip, while his son hid behind his legs. His face had the healthy glow of fresh air and exercise. He also seemed more laid-back in Adidas soccer pants, cleats and an NYU sweatshirt.

"Just practicing with Balthazar," he said, wriggling around to wheedle his son out of hiding. "Hey, Balthazar, don't be shy. Come out and say hi to one of my customers. She's really nice. I promise."

A small head peeped out from behind Oliver's knee. Brown eyes the color of dark chocolate watched me with some trepidation. I waved; Balthazar hid behind Oliver again and we both laughed.

"Sorry," he said, as Balthazar clutched his leg more tightly.

"Please, no need to apologize. One of my godchildren wouldn't come near me until she was three years old!"

"I find that hard to believe!" He paused. "How did the party go?"

"It turned out really well. We sold out of almost all our new stuff, everyone raved about the food and wine. And you were right; the Prosecco was a big hit. We only have a few bottles of white left over. We couldn't have asked for a better evening."

"I'm so happy to hear that!"

Balthazar had slowly been edging his way out from behind Oliver's legs and Liz's words rang true: He *was* beautiful. His skin glistened, as satiny and unblemished as a new penny; long eyelashes fringed his dark eyes like a baby giraffe's; and his shy smile—when it finally materialized—unveiled a row of perfect small white teeth. You didn't get that cute from just one good-looking parent. Balthazar's mother must also be a beauty. I bent down to meet his line of sight.

"Hi, Balthazar, I'm Mia. It's really nice to meet you." I pointed to his shirt. "I really like your soccer jersey. Barcelona's the best team in the world. Whose number are you wearing? Is that Messi's?"

Balthazar took a few steps forward and turned around, showing off the famed maroon and blue striped *Futbol Club Barcelona* jersey. The number ten on his back was indeed Lionel Messi's, Barcelona's star player.

"Very cool," I complimented.

I hoisted myself back up and Oliver scrunched his brows together in surprise.

"Are you a big soccer fan?" he asked.

"I like it. It's fun to watch the World Cup. I used to work with a bunch of guys who were *huge* fans, like a step away from being hooligans!" I said, thinking of Nick Vamvakis and a few other junior traders at Atlas. "They were obsessed with Barcelona, Manchester United, Réal Madrid, Chelsea ... I guess some of it rubbed off."

He chuckled. "They sound hard core."

"Oh, they definitely were." *In more ways than one,* I thought.

"So what was this place that employed a bunch of soccer hooligans?"

"I traded stocks for a small firm in the city."

He slanted sideways to get a better look at me. I hoped the water spots on my shirt had dried off.

"I would have never guessed," he said finally.

Folding my arms across my chest, I pretended to be outraged. "What's that supposed to mean?!"

He shrugged. "You just seem so calm. I've got some Wall Street friends and they are one intense bunch."

"I could be pretty intense too," I quipped and we both laughed.

"So why'd you leave?" he asked.

"Well, with all the changes and everything, it seemed like a good time for me to reassess what I wanted to do with the rest of my life." I did it again, with no hesitation. The obfuscations flowing out of my mouth were becoming second-nature.

He nodded. "I can definitely relate to that. That's why I moved back to Overlook."

"What'd *you* do before you opened the wine shop?"

"I worked in advertising for a long time, specialized in urban branding. You know, marketing products to the hip-hop generation."

"That sounds like fun."

"It was for a while." He looked down at Balthazar and ruffled his dark curls. "And then it wasn't."

Balthazar began to get antsy, hooking one ankle in front of the other.

"I should be going," I said.

"Oh, sure. It's been a busy weekend for you."

"Between the cocktail party and this run, I'm wiped out!"

He gave the soccer ball to Balthazar. "Little man, take the ball back to the net and I'll be right over."

Balthazar snatched the ball and took off.

"Balthazar!" Oliver called, but his son kept on running. "Sorry. He forgot to say goodbye."

"He's adorable," I said.

Oliver smiled. "Thank you."

"How old is he?"

"He's five, a bit restless, but a great kid." He paused. "Listen, I meant to come by the store Friday night, but I had to get home. My babysitter was leaving early . . ."

"No worries! I totally understand. You were a big help, so thank you."

"Dad!" Balthazar shouted from the goalpost.

"I better go," Oliver said, jogging backwards. "And Mia?"

"Yes?"

"It's really nice that you moved to town," he added and turned around, picking up speed to rejoin Balthazar.

I walked back to the school parking lot, thinking Oliver had been more than just cordial-friendly this time. I couldn't set my finger on what it was. Curiosity? Boredom? If we became friends, would I ever talk about my past in full? I sighed. Everything was just too complicated—my lawsuit, pitiful finances, cellulite on my thighs . . .

It was best to leave things as they were.

Later that night, after a three-episode *Mad Men* marathon, I logged on to my Gmail. There was nothing personal, only notices from Net-a-Porter, Saks and Amazon. I hadn't spoken to Christine in over a week and sent her a quick note: What's up? I'd probably be asleep by the time she answered and went to the bathroom to perform my nightly face and hair ritual. A new email awaited me when I got under the covers, but it wasn't from Christine. The sender was Oliver Bishop. There was nothing on the subject line so, nervously, I clicked.

> Mia,
> Great running into you today. Would you like to go out
> for dinner on Saturday?
> Best,
> Oliver

I read his email a couple of times and couldn't stop smiling. Delirious, elated, dizzy—I hadn't felt this excited since my early days with David. I didn't fuss over a coy answer or the "appropriate" amount of time before responding. I replied right away:

> Oliver,
> I'd love to.
> Best,
> Mia

> Mia,
> Great! I'll pick you up at seven.
> Best,
> Oliver

For good measure I added: Looking forward to it!
And waited.
His reply was swift: So am I.
Good night, I typed back.
Good night.

I closed my eyes and had my best night's sleep in six months.

20.

"How's it going?" Christine asked when she called me back on Tuesday night.

"Guess what?! I have a date!"

"Ahh!" she screamed and then stopped. "With whom?"

"A hot guy who owns the wine shop in town."

"A local! What's his name?"

"Oliver Bishop. And get this: His store is called The Bishop's Cellar!"

She screamed again. "Love it!"

"Have you and Rob ever been there?"

"I don't think Rob's ever bought a bottle of fine wine in Overlook!" she said, laughing. "But, just a sec, I'm in front of my computer. I'll Google him."

"No!" I screeched. "Please don't do that."

"Why?"

"I want to maintain an air of mystery. I want to get to know him on my own, not through words and images on the Internet."

"Mia, this sounds serious! You've always done background checks on every guy you've dated."

I sighed. "I know, but this feels different."

"How?"

"I don't know! It's silly. I barely know him but—"

"But what?"

"I just don't feel as in control and it's nice to be surprised for a change, to look forward to something."

"In other words, it's exciting."

I giggled. "Yes."

"He must be really hot."

"He's kind-of-actually really hot. I'm surprised he even asked me out. Can't say I've been lookin' my best here in Overlook."

"Oh, stop! I'm sure you look fine."

"I'm in jeans and Uggs all day at the store!"

"I'm sure it was your dazzling personality that did it. What are you guys doing?"

"He's taking me out to dinner."

"So adult and sexy! I wanna go on a first date again. Nothing beats that feeling."

"I know."

Our date was all I could think about. The anticipation; I wanted to capture it and keep it with me for when I felt tired or anxious or had trouble sleeping. It gave me renewed hope that, maybe, I wasn't such a basket case after all. It was such a relief to finally open up to someone. I didn't dare say anything to Liz at work. Sharing romantic details about my personal life would be awkward, no matter how easygoing she seemed. *By the way, I've got a date with your wine merchant!* Such a confession would inevitably lead to more detailed questions about my feelings. Then, what about the follow-up? I'd have to debrief Liz about our date and, if the whole thing blew up in my face, I'd have to share that with her too. It was so much easier to dish with Christine, who was not only my best friend, but a convenient eight hundred miles away.

"So, what are you wearing?" Christine asked.

"That's the problem. I have nothing to wear. I sold all my good stuff to raise cash."

"All of it?"

"Basically."

"Your Lanvin blouses?"

"I kept all of those for when I get a new job, a real one that requires me to look professional again."

"Your Dolce & Gabbana dresses?"

There were risks in oversharing with your best friend. In bountiful times, Christine and I had discussed our purchases in great detail. My budget and impulses had been greater, but she knew my closet, especially when she came to New York for our annual girls' weekend.

"I may still have a few of them left . . ." I said, hedging.

She chuckled. "It sounds like you've got plenty of stuff to choose from."

"I kept them because a) I'll never be able to afford them again and b) I can't go around naked!"

"Where's he taking you?" she asked.

"He didn't say."

"Is it in town? There aren't that many great places on the avenue, not first date places anyway."

"We're probably going to the local pizzeria."

"I doubt it." She paused. "Oliver looks too smooth for that. *Chardonnay, anyone?*" she asked in an exaggerated, suave voice.

"Christine! Are you Googling him?"

"You knew I would!"

"Anything interesting?" I couldn't refrain from asking.

"Just some pictures from the store's Website and a couple of articles where he's quoted. He seems to be quite the wine expert."

"Is he alone in the pictures or"— I spoke quickly before I could regret it—"is he with anyone who could be his wife?"

"*He's married?!*" she howled.

I imagined her face at that moment: eyes popping, mouth agape.

"I don't think so," I murmured.

"You don't think so?!"

"I mean no," I added quickly. "But he has a son. He's a single dad. I think it's complicated."

"You'd better find out fast before you get too involved."

"Listen, everybody our age has some baggage. I've got it under control." I hadn't seen a ring on Oliver's finger. No ring, no wife. He had an ex, someone who had run out on him and Balthazar, but it was too much information to share with Christine at this stage. I wasn't ready for her reality check, whatever that might be.

"Moving right along," I continued. "What do you think I should wear?"

I hadn't been this primped and polished since the week prior to my getting fired at Atlas, the last time I could afford a weekly beauty regimen. On the eve of my date with Oliver, I spent hours in the bathroom, exfoliating from top to toe, tweezing my eyebrows and blowing out my hair. I only indulged in a mani-pedi at the nail bar in town. It had huge windows facing Overlook Avenue and I sat in fear that Oliver would pass by and see me getting all gussied up . . . for him. I admitted this with no shame or feminist/career-woman ambivalence. I hadn't been on a date for two years. There was nothing unusual about wanting to feel good about my appearance *and* look good for him, but I was careful not to overdo it. My goal was to look like I wasn't trying too hard. By employing covert beautification tactics—natural make-up, subtle polish, soft fragrance— Oliver probably wouldn't even notice (he had, after all, asked me out in spite of my plain Overlook style), but the combined effect gave me self-confidence, eliminating the worry lines on my forehead and the dark circles under my eyes. I didn't want to jinx it, but I almost looked like my old, successful, bad-ass self again.

Date night, I was ready fifteen minutes before seven and puttered around the cottage, fluffing pillows and straightening books and knick-knacks. I didn't want to sit down and wrinkle the cropped black pants and a draped crepe top I had excavated from shopping in my closet. The weather was mild and a pair of YSL platform sandals, a light leather jacket and a Balenciaga clutch (another item I had decided not to sell) gave the ensemble some edge and stopped it from looking too suburban. It was frightening enough that I found those damn Uggs so comfortable.

The drinks trolley, parked below an oil painting of birds in the living room, was stocked with half-full bottles of Jack Daniels, Johnny Walker and Absolut, along with some psychedelic flasks of Aperol and Chartreuse. I unscrewed the cap of the lime-green Chartreuse and inhaled. Whew! How long had this stuff been in the house? The bottles could have been decades old for all I knew. Should I offer Oliver a drink before we went out? No, that wouldn't do. He was driving. I realized how unschooled I was in the "I'll-pick-you-up" date protocol.

In the city, I always met my dates at the mutually agreed upon spot, always a few minutes late, so I wouldn't be the one kept waiting. We then either parted company at the spot or shared a cab ride home—and sometimes a little more, depending on my mood. I had already decided, despite my makeover, that I wouldn't get intimate with Oliver tonight. I might have been dateless-for-two-years, fired and broke, but I still had a modicum of self-respect left. Plus, I didn't think Oliver seemed like the type. I sensed something cautious beneath his professional charm, an inkling he kept the eager women at his wine tastings at arm's length. This made our date even more special and I didn't want to ruin it by throwing myself at him.

The doorbell rang at five minutes to seven and I came to a halt. I wasn't ready! I had planned a final check in the bathroom mirror. What if I had lipstick on my teeth? But it was too late for second-guessing and, walking on the balls of my feet, I opened the front door.

"Hi!" I said, trying to keep my voice as natural as possible.

Oliver smiled. "Hi. Sorry, I'm a little early. It didn't take me as long as I'd thought to get here."

"Please, come in! I'm glad you didn't get lost."

"I have a lot of clients in backcountry, but nothing has brought me to Meadow Lane before," he answered, stepping into the modest hallway.

He filled the space in a way I hadn't expected, his immediacy both thrilling and unnerving. I tried to quell the butterflies in my stomach, leading Oliver into the living room while simultaneously taking note of the slight cleft in his chin and how much taller he seemed inside the cottage. His classic, well-tailored clothes were simple and unfussy: dark jeans, white button-down, navy blazer. But I was most touched by the rim of polka-dotted silk jutting out of his breast pocket. I dared to think he had chosen the pocket square with care, wanting to make a good impression on me as well.

He glanced around the room. "Nice place. Not bad for a rental."

"Thanks, it's cozy." I gestured to the drinks cart. "Can I offer you anything?"

He checked his watch. "Our reservation is at 7:30. It's a little further away, so we should probably leave now to be safe, if that's okay with you."

"Sounds mysterious!"

"Did you really think I'd take you out on the avenue?"

"It wouldn't have made a difference," I assured him, collecting my jacket from the armchair. I slipped it on, took the clutch in my hand and added, "All set!"

He must have been watching me because our eyes met as soon as I faced him again.

"You look great," he said.

I was tempted to return the compliment, or make a witty comment, but chose instead to savor the moment. "Thank you."

"How large is this property?" Oliver asked as we walked towards his car, a black Audi SUV that mirrored the cool yet domesticated image of him I had built up in my mind.

"About an acre and a half."

"It's rare to find such a level piece of land, without rocks or trees in the back. I'm surprised a developer hasn't made an offer to buy it off of your friends and build three houses on it."

I had always considered the cottage a shabby shack, but maybe Rob's family was sitting on a goldmine. "You think?

They probably don't realize how much it's really worth."

"Or they might just be sentimental about the place?" Oliver asked, opening the passenger door for me.

After we both got settled in the car, seatbelts on, background music at a comfortable volume, I said, "I think they might be sentimental out of habit. Too attached to sell, but not attached enough to live in it."

"And that's where you came in."

"Better me than letting it stand empty."

"They must be really good friends."

"They are. I consider them family," I said, ignoring Christine's cautious words about Oliver. "Christine and I met at our first job right out of college, at Morgan Stanley. I'm also Godmother to her and Rob's three kids."

"Where'd you go to school?" he asked.

"Wellesley and then Wharton. Did you go to NYU?" I asked, remembering the sweatshirt he wore the day I met him on the soccer field.

"I did, though I'm definitely not the math whiz you are."

My botched finances tell another story, I thought.

"I'm hardly a math quiz. I knew enough to do my job. What did you study?"

"Do you want the long or short version?" he asked, putting the car in reverse.

"If this ride's going to be as long as you say," I teased, "you might as well give me the long version."

"Well, I was always a bit of a lazy student," he began, in a way that seemed to indicate he regretted it now. "I played football in high school; we practiced all the time. Why study for an A, when I could do the bare minimum and still get a C, maybe a B if I was lucky? It drove my parents crazy. Then I tore my ACL at the beginning of the season senior year and I'd had enough. I wasn't in the mood to get thrown around anymore, or give up my youth to play college ball and end up with some kind of traumatic head injury. My parents were relieved, but I also gave up a chance at getting a football scholarship to a decent school and there was no way I was going to get a regular scholarship based on my grades. But my guidance counselor told me that NYU had a General Studies program for kids whose grades didn't really reflect their potential, so I applied and got in."

"NYU's a great school."

"It is, but in the late '80s, it didn't seem as competitive as it is now. There were lots of different kids running around, doing their thing, trying to find themselves. Downtown was still underground-cool back then, not commercial-cool like it is today."

"And how'd a former jock like you fit in?"

"I grew dreads and tried to pass for Lenny Kravitz."

"Really?" I asked, picturing a halo of locks around Oliver's face. By now we had turned left onto Pittsfield Way, heading into the depths of backcountry and the sprawling parcels of farmland I had heard about. The journey was getting more and more curious.

"No, I'm kidding! I lived in student housing the first year, right next to Washington Square Park, and it was the best thing that ever happened to me. The vibe, the artists in the park, the clubs, the bars—I was in my element, but it was expensive as hell. So my sophomore year, I started working at a wine store."

"Is this how you became a wine aficionado?"

"But I started working for Hanley's Wine & Spirits before I was even legally old enough to drink. Tim Hanley, the owner, needed help in the stockroom. I guess I looked strong from all my years of playing football. Then I started helping customers. Tim let me meet some of his importers and before long I was learning how to swirl, sniff and sip."

"You had time to do all this between classes and studying?"

"Mia, with that comment alone, I can tell you were the model student."

"Sorry! I was stressed in college. I felt like I was studying all the time."

"I probably should have been too, but I worked every day after school and on Friday and Saturday nights. It was tough, but I was younger, needed less sleep. And I was having a great time."

"What is it about the world of wine that you found so intriguing?"

"Hmm . . . that's a good question. My parents didn't drink wine. We didn't even keep beer in the refrigerator. And it's not because they were opposed to alcohol or anything like that. I think it was a control thing for them. My father was the Overlook fire chief. My mom worked for the Board of Ed."

"Are your parents still in town?"

"They're retired and moved to North Carolina. They couldn't handle these winters anymore. I think they felt they had to set an example when we were growing up, be upstanding citizens. I also have a younger sister who's now a doctor. She was Miss Perfect."

"And you?"

Chuckling, he said, "I experimented a little. But back to your question: Hanley's shop introduced me to a whole new world. It was fascinating, the history of the vineyards, the geography, nuances in taste, the interesting people who came into his store. Lots of celebrities and business people, but I couldn't afford to make a career of it. I had all these student loans, so I majored in marketing to get a good job after graduation and pay it all back. And I ended up being pretty good at the marketing thing."

"That sounds all too familiar."

"Which part?"

"Choosing a career for the money and security."

"Is that what you did?"

"When I fell into trading, I definitely had those reasons in the back of my mind. I wanted to be successful and financially independent, but I also wasn't passionate about anything else. And once I became entrenched in the system, there was no reason to change."

"Did you grow up in one of those super high-achieving families?"

"We were a really small family, just my mom and me. My dad died when I was three."

"Oh, I'm really sorry to hear that."

"It's okay. I don't really remember him, just some photographs."

"And your mother never remarried?"

"No, she never did. She was a young widow too, only twenty-seven when he died, but she threw all her energy into raising me, supporting us. I guess that's where I get my work ethic from. She was very driven, worked her way up the ladder until she was general manager of our local department store."

"Where did you grow up?"

"Rockland County."

"I know where that is. I've passed it on the thruway."

"That's been about the extent of my return to Rockland."

"Why's that?"

"My mom died my senior year of college and there wasn't any reason for me to go back."

Taking his eyes off the road, he asked, "You've lost both your parents?"

His tone had assumed that thorny mixture of shock and sympathy. I laughed lightly, to make him feel better. "Yes. It happens, you know."

"So you must have been only twenty-one when your mom passed away?"

I nodded.

"That's a lot to deal with at that age."

"It was."

"Was it cancer?" he asked.

"How'd you guess?"

"Breast cancer?"

"No. This might sound crazy, but I remember wishing it was breast cancer. At least that's more common, and researchers have made so many strides, but it was pancreatic cancer. It came out of nowhere and she was gone within three months."

I wouldn't tell Oliver that my mother had kept her illness from me until it was too late and she was so far along, there was absolutely nothing the doctors could do. She had let me live out my senior year in oblivion, prioritizing friends and job interviews, chasing the last parties until we all went our separate ways. As I called home less and less, she visited one doctor after another, on her own, until she got the devastating verdict. Later, she said it had been for my own good. She wanted to protect me and didn't want me to lose my focus and blow off my degree, but my own guilt threatened to consume me after she died.

"I didn't mean to bring up painful memories," he said.

"You're not. It's a part of my life. I've learned to accept it."

He switched off the music. It had been playing softly and didn't bother me, but Oliver seemed to find the noise disturbing after all my talk of death. He drove in silence for the next few minutes and I looked out the window, seeing the gray silhouettes of trees and farmhouses in the night. I preferred not to talk about my parents. Describing my own emptiness—and the belief that life had shortchanged them—never accomplished anything beyond sowing more anger and bitterness. Yet I was doing it with Oliver on our first date.

I felt a hand over mine. Surprised, I shifted my head and found Oliver's concerned gaze.

"Are you okay?" he asked.

"I'm fine," I said, thinking that this time I really meant it.

Soon after, Oliver veered the car up a lighted path and parked opposite a large red house with white trim.

"What is this place?" I asked, as he held open the passenger door.

"Have you ever heard of Hudson Barn?"

I shook my head and took cautious steps forward in my platforms. The pointy heels poked holes in the soft ground. I hoped the mushiness was mud and not manure.

"It's a restaurant run by an old buddy of mine, a Swede

I met during my party days in New York. He opened it a few years ago and uses only local products, seasonal ingredients, things he's grown on this farm." Oliver chuckled and said, "He's like this new culinary phenomenon! People have even started to make *pilgrimages* here. I thought you might enjoy something different."

"I'm always up for something different."

We entered the barn and were greeted by a melodic gaggle of voices that hung over the pleasant discord of plates and glasses. Oliver gave his name to the maître d' and we were seated at a table secluded enough to feel private, but with an expansive view of the room. Fairy lights were strung around the exposed beams and pillars, adding texture to the unpainted barn walls. Raw linen cloths swathed tables adorned with rustic porcelain and brass lanterns. A handful of wild flowers sprouted from a Mason jar in the center. The crowd was a mixture of relaxed locals in jeans and a more formal contingent, people like me and Oliver, who seemed to be marking a special occasion.

I also noticed that the maître d' hadn't given us our menus, but she disappeared and was soon replaced by a husky man about Oliver's age in chef's whites.

"Mats!" Oliver said as he pushed back his chair and stood up. He and Mats shared a man-hug, clapping each other on the back. When they separated, Oliver swung his head from me to Mats. "Mats, please meet Mia. Mia, Mats Gustavsson, owner and executive chef at Hudson Barn."

Lowering his chin, Mats offered his hand. "Welcome! So nice to meet you."

Mats' soft-spoken English bore little traces of a Swedish

accent, but his sky-blue eyes, longish blond hair and scraggly beard hinted at his Nordic roots.

"It's not often that I get my old friend to dine here," he added.

"I like your spring menu better," Oliver said, smiling.

Mats shaped his hands into a pyramid and said, "Tonight we're serving Hudson Valley foie gras; Lynnhaven goat cheese with caramelized beets; Arctic char with new potatoes; and chocolate cake with Smith Farms raspberries."

"Sounds delicious," I said.

"But first, let me first bring you both a glass of champagne. Pol Roger, right?"

"My favorite," Oliver replied.

"Would you also like to choose the wines with the meal?" Mats asked.

Oliver waved his hand. "Go ahead. I trust you."

"I have a pretty good wine merchant," Mats said.

Oliver laughed. "So I've heard."

Mats then vanished as quietly as he'd arrived.

"He seems really nice," I said. "Very low-key, almost like a monk when he was talking about the food."

"Don't be fooled. He's a nut! He was a bartender at one of the clubs I used to go to all the time, went to culinary school on the side, and now this. As you can see, there's no menu. Mats puts together the dishes based on what's seasonal—"

"Or what he feels like eating . . ."

"Or what he has too much of and wants to get rid of!"

For some odd reason, we found this train of thought extremely funny and began to outdo each other with images of poor Mats in the kitchen, drenched in a sea of mushrooms or parsnips. We finally composed ourselves when the waitress brought our glasses of champagne.

Oliver lifted his glass. "Should we make a toast?"

"Sure. To what?"

"New friends?"

I raised my glass. "Yes. To new friends."

It's as though Mats had heard my taunts and wanted to prove me wrong because he prepared the best meal I'd ever had. Everything tasted richer, layered in intensity.

Was it because I knew that his team had harvested the potatoes themselves? Or that the foie gras came from a nearby farm where the ducks roamed cage-free? I took my time with dessert, swirling the last raspberry around my plate, coating it with velvety sauce from the molten chocolate cake, as Oliver and I talked about living in New York City. We had overlapped there for a number of years, but our paths never crossed.

"And why is that?" Oliver asked.

"We traveled in different circles."

"Didn't you go out? Or were you working all the time?"

"I went out, just not to where you hung out."

"I was an equal-opportunity partier. I went everywhere."

I thought back to the mostly uptown, after-work places I had frequented with clients and other traders. Strip clubs had been out of the question for obvious reasons, as were the super-hip spots that required clothes far cooler than what I normally wore to the office. "Your New York days were flashier than mine."

"I think high finance sounds pretty exciting."

I took a final sip of the vintage port Mats had selected. Sweet upon sweet, it should have been too much, but it went down perfectly. I had, in fact, imbibed all the alcohol Hudson Barn put before me. *I* even knew better than to say no to a bottle of Montrachet. Oliver drank sparingly and ended his meal with an espresso.

"Yeah, but it wasn't that much *fun*. Besides—" I started to say, but then caught myself and popped the raspberry in my mouth.

"Besides what?"

Too much champagne and wine had made less inhibited, so I let my words tumble with no restrictions. "I wouldn't have been your type anyway."

Oliver threw back his head and laughed.

"What makes you so sure?" he asked.

"I was a neurotic workaholic."

"I can see the workaholic part. I was one too. But neurotic?" His hand etched a line in the air, from my face right down to the empty wine glasses in front of me. "I don't think so."

"I could be really stiff," I insisted.

"I *do* think if I had offered to buy you a drink, you would've just given me a dirty look."

I dabbed the napkin around my lips. "That's entirely possible."

He laughed again and then looked straight at me. "Sometimes you have to leave the city to get more clarity."

I had an opening here; a chance to ask him about Balthazar, his ex and what had happened between them, but the restaurant had emptied out. It was as though we had spent the last couple of hours in a cocoon, shut off from the commotion around us. Why bring up the other woman at a time like this?

I leaned forward and said, "Thank you for taking me here tonight and not to some minimalistic Japanese restaurant where I would have struggled with the chopsticks, eating one rice kernel at a time ..."

"Now that would've been funny, but I'm glad you liked it here." Oliver scanned the room. "It looks like we've closed the place."

"What time is it?"

"Eleven-thirty. That's late for this neck of the woods."

"You should probably be getting back to Balthazar anyway."

"Yeah, I should. He's got soccer practice at nine tomorrow morning."

"Who's watching him tonight?" I asked.

"My weekend sitter. She helps me out on Saturdays when I'm working." He sighed. "I'm sure she's exhausted by now."

Mats came out of the kitchen again before we left and we thanked—and lauded—him for the great meal. The car ride back to the cottage was lively, a far cry from the heaviness that had seeped into the beginning of our evening. I listened to Oliver talk about Balthazar's burgeoning soccer skills and how he, Oliver, had to be removed from the field after disputing a bad call that left Balthazar in tears.

"I obviously don't have the temperament to be a coach," he said.

"You can't make a scene when everyone in town knows who you are!"

"I realized that afterwards. Now I'm on my best behavior."

We reached the cottage far quicker than I'd hoped. It was past midnight and I knew Oliver's evening would take on a different tenor, transforming from my dapper date to responsible dad, and I found the contrast endearing. He walked me to the front door and we stood, bathed in the golden light of the exterior lamps, as that awkward post-date silence ensued.

"I had a great time," Oliver said finally.

"Me, too. Thank you for a wonderful evening."

I reached up and hugged him, burying my face in his neck. I closed my eyes, inhaling the lemony essence on his skin, and felt his arms tighten around my back.

"Goodnight," he said, separating from our embrace.

"Goodnight."

He waited for me to go inside the cottage. I sat in darkness on a hallway chair, tearing off my shoes. My feet pulsated, but I didn't care. After hearing Oliver's car leave the driveway, I padded to the kitchen and downed a glass of ice water.

I definitely wanted more than what I had let on.

And, just maybe, Oliver did too.

21.

I didn't hear from Oliver again until the Thursday after our date. He sent me a text message asking if we could meet for a walk in Overlook Park the next morning. It arrived just as I was restyling a shelf at Eclectibles and Liz caught me glaring at my phone.

"Is everything OK?" she asked.

I clicked back to the main screen and stashed the phone in my pocket. "Everything's fine. I can take care of that later."

I spent the next few hours calibrating my response, peevish as I replayed the high points of our date in my mind. I certainly hadn't expected a call the day after, but some sort of acknowledgement a bit sooner would have been nice. Of course I could have made the first move, but I was still old-fashioned in those situations. By the time I got home, however, I wondered if I was being self-important and delusional. Hadn't I learned by now not to expect too much? However, I finished dinner before typing out a response: A walk in Overlook Park works tomorrow morning.

To which he wrote back within minutes: How about 8:15 by the Gargoyle?

I had no idea where the Gargoyle was, but I'd find out.

The Gargoyle turned out to be a bronze statue at the base of the parking lot. It was pudgy, more cherubic than grotesque and, according to Overlook's website, a hit with all the kids who'd been climbing it for decades. Oliver had parked his Audi rear-in and came out with two takeaway cups of coffee when he saw me wheel into the lot.

"I wasn't sure what you liked, so it's either a latte with one packet of sugar," he offered, raising his right hand, "or black, straight up."

"I'll have the latte, please," I said and took the cup from him, putting my keys and BlackBerry in the pocket of my fleece jacket. I had thrown on a pair of jeans and sneakers, purposely not making much of an effort, but Oliver was attired in a stylish nylon windbreaker and brown suede shoes. He looked neat, starched and ready for work.

"How've you been?" he asked, walking towards the craggy path that led to the park grounds. A peanut-shaped pond divided the tract into two sections: a level walking trail on our side and more rugged, wooded terrain across the water.

I opened the mouthpiece of the coffee lid and took a sip before answering. The latte was still warm enough to have a satisfying effect. "Fine, thanks."

"Are things busy at the store?"

"It's actually been a pretty slow week. And you?"

"Same here."

Then you obviously weren't too busy to call.

Frustrated by all the mixed signals, I looked up at the cloudless sky and said, "What a beautiful day!"

"It is, but that's not why I asked you to come for a walk."

"Oh."

Switching the coffee cup from one hand to the other, he said, "I've thought a lot about last Saturday."

"Oh," I said again. "That's nice."

"It *was* really nice."

I felt the ice thawing within me. "Yes, it was."

"I thought that I really wanted to see you again."

"Well . . . here we are."

"And that if we were to see each other again, there were some things I needed to tell you."

Surprised, I coughed somewhat. "Okay."

"Overlook's small," he began. "Maybe you've heard some things about my situation with Balthazar?"

I sighed. There was no point hiding what I knew. "Liz told me something once."

He nodded. "I figured as much."

"But she wasn't gossiping!" I clarified. "She just commented on what a great job you were doing with, um, *everything*."

"I don't know if it's such a great job, but I try."

We walked for a few more feet until I finally asked, "What happened?"

Oliver took a large gulp of coffee and then dumped the surplus onto a heap of dead branches. A green metal trash can stood conveniently ahead of us, next to a park bench. He threw the empty cup away and sat down. I was now too edgy to drink my latte and could have easily gotten rid of it too, but holding it keep me occupied while I waited for Oliver to continue. He signalled for me to take the space next to him.

"Where do I begin?" he said, running a hand across his face. "I met Sophie when I was still working for the ad agency in the city. She wanted to be a writer, but was working as a waitress at Raoul's. I was a regular there and we eventually started dating. We were together for two years when she became pregnant with Balthazar."

"Oh! Was it planned?"

"No. We were both surprised, but obviously shouldn't have been."

"How did you feel about it?"

"I was actually really happy. She was thirty. I was thirty-three. I had a successful career. We were supposed to be in love. It seemed like the pregnancy was meant to be."

"And Sophie?"

"She was less sure about it. She's French-Moroccan, grew up in a Paris suburb and had absolutely no family here. She was also working on a book. She'd been working on that book since the day I met her and it wasn't really going anywhere. She had a hard time staying disciplined and was worried about what a child would do to her creativity. I told her I'd give her the support she needed. I even asked her to marry me."

I finally set the coffee cup down next to my feet. There's something surreal about listening to a man you're deeply interested in talk about his ex; the woman he obviously loved very much, the mother of his child, no less. I felt like I should make the appropriate sounds of sympathy, but in my mind, I was already competing with the absentee Sophie. What did she look like? What had made her so special? The words "Raoul's," "writer" and "French-Moroccan" had already painted a picture of an exotically beautiful, free spirit who had charmed Oliver in one of Soho's coziest bistros.

"Did you get married?" I asked.

"No. She asked if we could wait until after the baby was born."

I was reaching now, but this filled me with some relief.

"What happened next?"

"Halfway through the pregnancy, my parents announced they had bought a place in North Carolina and were putting their Overlook house on the market. I liked growing up here and thought it would be good for our child, so I told them I would buy their house and move out here with Sophie and the baby full-time."

Call it female intuition, but the pieces of Oliver and Sophie's complicated puzzle were falling into place and I began to assess their dilemma as though it were my own—and it foreshadowed impending disaster. "What did Sophie say about that?"

"I hadn't discussed it with her. She wasn't thrilled."

"That's not so strange."

"Not at all, but I had convinced myself she wanted the same things I did."

"But you guys moved out here in the end, right?"

"Yeah, we did. I persuaded her it would be great for her and the baby. We'd have more room. She'd have peace and quiet, more time to write. We'd get a nanny to help out . . ."

I tried to put all of the events on a timeline. "And when did you open The Bishop's Cellar?"

"I signed the lease for the store around the same time."

"A baby, a move and a new business all at once?" I asked, my voice rising a notch.

"There was also an extensive renovation of my parent's house."

"Oh, Oliver."

"I know—it was too much at the same time. But I thought we might as well go all in. A few months of stress and then everything would be fine." He stooped over, pinching the bridge of his nose. "We were unpacking moving boxes when Sophie went into labor."

I groaned, but said nothing.

Oliver turned to me. "I sound like the bad guy now, right?"

"No," I said, trying to console him. "More like someone who thought he was doing the right thing."

"I take a lot of blame for what happened afterwards because I had put so much pressure on Sophie to accept all these changes. I kept telling her what was for her own good, what was for the baby's best and she basically rebelled. She wasn't ready to be a mother and play house."

"But she was already thirty years old," I remarked, thinking of Christine and Rob, who had their first child at twenty-seven and thirty respectively.

"But a young thirty. She thought she had all the time in the world to settle down."

"Weren't you guys already settled anyway? You said you had been together for two years when she became pregnant."

"I think for Sophie there was still something exciting about being together in Manhattan with no kids. She considered not being married liberating. There's still an out, your options aren't dead. Sophie liked having that option, that independence." He paused. "When I finally realized that, it was too late."

"And Balthazar?" I asked, daring to verbalize their innocent son's name. "How were things with him?"

He sighed. "She couldn't really bond with him after he was born."

"Did she have a difficult delivery?"

He nodded. "Her labor was long and she ended up having

a C-section. Afterwards, she was exhausted and couldn't nurse. I think she was in some sort of mental shock."

"I don't think that sounds so unusual. Every woman reacts differently to childbirth. It's not all sweetness and light," I said, recalling the conversations I had with Christine. She confessed that giving birth for the first time had left her traumatized. Aside from the physical effects, the awareness that once this new life came into the world, hers would never be the same again, had left her completely overwhelmed. But she also believed, with every fiber of her being, that motherhood had made her a better person.

"I understand that," Oliver agreed. "But we had this beautiful, healthy son and Sophie couldn't connect with him. He cried a lot in her arms. I think he could sense her anxiety."

"How was he with you?"

"Calm. I wish there hadn't been such a huge difference."

"Maybe Sophie was suffering from post-partum depression?"

"From what I've read about it, I think she was. We had become a family, but she said she had never felt more alone in her life. Then there were the mood swings. If Balthazar wasn't fussy, she had a good day. But if he kept us up at night, it was torture for her. I never realized how lethal sleep-deprivation could be until I had a newborn."

"My friend Christine said the same thing."

"I kept hoping it would get better. But our relationship just got more and more volatile. I was working six days a week and we argued all the time. Any conversation was a list of complaints—about Overlook, her weight, how lonely she felt in the house when I was at the store. And she couldn't write anymore. She said Balthazar had sucked everything out of her and she resented him for it."

This wasn't supposed to happen, but the rawness of Sophie's struggles seized me—unannounced—and began to touch a familiar chord. Was it because I could understand her need to forge her own identity and make something of herself? Hadn't I let David go because I wouldn't submerge my own dreams for his? But an image of Balthazar—sweet, blameless Balthazar—slapped me back to reality. Self and motherhood did not have to be mutually exclusive. There had to be another, better way.

"Did she consider counseling or medication?" I asked.

"Sophie wouldn't have it. We got a full-time nanny instead and when Balthazar was almost a year old, it looked like she was finally getting out of that black hole. She became more affectionate and started to write again. She still complained about Overlook, so I encouraged her to go into the city more often. She signed up for a writing class once-a-week and it really looked like things were going in the right direction. Getting away for a little while actually made her more present when she was at home, if you get what I mean?"

I nodded. "This must have all been very hard on you too."

"It was, but I didn't know what else to do." He shrugged. "Once-a-week in the city became twice-a-week and then one night she didn't come home at all. She didn't answer her phone. I called everyone she knew, but no one had seen her. I was worried sick. Maybe she was passed out or lying dead somewhere. But she came back the next night and said she needed to get away. She wanted some time on her own and would be going back to Paris for a few weeks ... by herself. When she came back, she told me it was over. Not just us, but everything."

"Everything?" I repeated.

"She threw it all back in my face. I had pushed her to have the baby. She had never been ready. She wasn't capable of giving Balthazar what he needed. He would be better off with just me. I was the parent he always turned to anyway. She needed to be free to write, to think, to live!" Oliver took a deep breath and shook his head. "It was such a bunch of selfish bullshit, but Sophie really believed that what she was doing would be better for everyone."

"Did you try to make her stay?"

"No. I'd had enough. I was done begging. By then, I was so disgusted and disappointed. This was the person I had fallen in love with? And she was Balthazar's mother? I had no one but myself to blame."

"Don't be so hard on yourself . . ."

"All that happened three years ago," he added.

My jaw dropped. "She hasn't seen Balthazar in three years?"

"In the beginning, she cut off all contact, like she wanted to make a clean break. But she hasn't completely disappeared and sends him presents for his birthday and Christmas."

"At least she does that."

"I even took him to see her once when she passed through New York, but he wouldn't go near her. He started crying and screaming. I had never seen him so upset before and decided, right then and there, that he was better off having no relationship with Sophie whatsoever, no matter how little it was."

"But is that fair to him?"

"I don't know. All I know is that it's taken me three years

to get to a point where I feel like our family life is finally stable. I'm proud of Balthazar and our relationship. He's thriving. He doesn't ask about her anymore. He knows it's just me and him."

I nodded in recognition. "My mother and I also had that kind of relationship, sort of like us against the world."

"Exactly!" He paused. "It's been all about him for the last three years and, suddenly, I find myself thinking about someone else too."

It took me a few seconds to realize he was referring to me. "Well, you're not alone."

We stared straight ahead, determined to maintain a casual façade on the park bench, but I grappled with everything Oliver had confided and the ease with which I had admitted my own feelings.

"You came into town and changed everything!"

I touched his knee. "Thank you for sharing all of this with me."

"I haven't scared you off?"

"No." Yes, there was Balthazar and so many other unknown variables, but Oliver had awoken something in me I did not want to lose.

"I have a hell of a lot of baggage."

"Everyone does," I said, thinking once again of all the things I was too embarrassed to talk about.

Oliver put his arm around my shoulders and I leaned in, sighing softly.

Yes, it was definitely worth giving this a chance.

22.

Sitting in bed, I searched for recipes on the Internet. I had invited Oliver over for dinner the following Saturday and couldn't decide what to cook. There were tons of choices, but many seemed so elaborate, requiring marination and esoteric spices like truffle salt and cardamom. What had possessed me to suggest dinner at my place? I hadn't made a proper meal in years and instead of starting off slowly, I wanted to outdo myself with three courses. It was already Wednesday night and I needed to make a decision. Oliver was bringing the wine— something special from his own personal collection—and I had to tell him if it should be red or white.

I closed my laptop on the Barefoot Contessa, lazed back on a pillow and closed my eyes, contented. Oliver and I hadn't seen each other since that revelatory morning in the park. His weekend had been filled with work, a private wine tasting event and, of course, Balthazar, but we spoke on the phone every evening after he put Balthazar to bed. Our conversations were long, interesting and funny; we talked about everything from our crazy customers to current events. I constantly replayed them in my head and couldn't wait until "bedtime" when he would call again. Although we worked only a few streets away from each other, we never met up, as though our exploration merited careful nurturing, away from the town's prying eyes.

I tried to pinpoint what made him so different. Of course his outward smoothness was sexy and had kept me guessing, but being a single dad gave him a deeper dimension. Here was a man who valued fatherhood and didn't shirk from his responsibility. Balthazar was his first priority and I wouldn't dream of placing myself between them, but it moved me, knowing that Oliver was capable of such a commitment. His stories about Balthazar's obsession with Star Wars and Lego, or his antics on the soccer field, were hilarious, bringing out Oliver's own playful side. I sounded too straight-laced in comparison and had decided—privately—to show him a more passionate side of myself. Maybe that's why I had suggested dinner *chez moi*.

Such naughty thoughts, but the sensual effect Oliver had on me was maddening. Although our chats never crossed into anything suggestive, he aroused me—it had been two years since David after all—and I fell asleep imagining what it would be like to lay with him, side-by-side, on my bed. Then I would wake up, shaking off the sheets in embarrassment.

When my phone rang, I answered without looking at the screen, certain it was Oliver.

"Hello," I whispered.

"Mia? Is that you?" asked a throaty voice, thick with traces of New York and the good fight.

"Mr. Mannheimer?" I asked, springing up from my pillow.

"Oh, Mia! It is you! You sounded funny there for a minute. Is everything Okay?"

"Yes, I'm doing fine," I replied, over-articulating. "I was just about to go to bed. How are you?"

"Sorry for disturbing," he answered, ignoring my question, "but we need to meet."

"Something specific about my case? Has Atlas agreed to settle?"

"Not yet. I might be on to something, but I need your input, your expertise, if you will."

"Can you *please* be a little more specific?"

"Patience, my dear, patience. Come by my office at 2:00PM on Friday and we can talk all about it then."

"*This* Friday?" Going into Manhattan was the last thing I wanted to do.

"Yeees," Mannheimer drawled. "Is there a problem, because I didn't think anything was more important than your case?"

Actually, Mr. Mannheimer, Friday is my day off and I planned on cleaning this place; shopping at Whole Foods; trying on outfits from my pathetic wardrobe; and beautifying myself for a hot date on Saturday night BECAUSE I HAVE TO WORK ALL DAY SATURDAY AND WON'T BE ABLE TO GET ANYTHING DONE!

I changed course and said haughtily, "Of course not! I'll see you on Friday afternoon."

The train from Overlook to Grand Central Terminal bobbed through picturesque Hudson Valley towns for a grueling ninety minutes. I was fine on long journeys, but relatively short ones drove me to a level of restlessness rivaling a three-year old child's. I used to feel sorry for people who commuted to the city. In fact, I used to feel sorry for people who couldn't walk to work in ten minutes like I did. Imagine wasting all that time in transit! Verdant trees and tidy houses passed by in one endless streak, but my mind focused on all the other things I could have been doing at home. The morning had been hectic, giving me just enough time to shop at Whole Foods. After

Mannheimer's mysterious meeting, I'd clean the cottage and set the table.

Once the train squeaked into Grand Central, I walked across town from 42nd and Vanderbilt to Mannheimer's office on 35th and 9th. It was my first time back in the city since moving to Overlook, and the past six months of driving had clearly left me at a disadvantage; my gait was slower. Members of my old tribe, in their dark suits and pencil skirts, cruised past. After Fifth, the distance between avenues grew longer and the leather straps of my sandals indented my tired, swollen feet. *Just what did Mannheimer want to talk to me about?* I wondered, riding the rickety elevator up to his office. He opened the door dressed in a yellow, short-sleeved shirt and skinny tie, a throwback to IBM circa 1964.

"Mia, please sit down," he instructed, walking behind his desk. Two manila folders were on it and he passed one to me.

"What's this?" I asked.

"Open it."

Flummoxed, I did as he requested and fanned through the pages. It was a printout of Touchnology's daily stock price from October, the month I got fired, right up until yesterday's closing bell.

I shrugged. "So?"

"Have you been following Touchnology at all?"

"No. That stock got me fired."

"So you haven't heard any news about the company?"

I shook my head. "I've been in a self-imposed financial blackout."

He waved his manila folder in the air. "Get in your best Wall Street-state-of-mind, Mia, and read this carefully."

Using my index finger to slide down the page, I analyzed the numbers. At the time of my dismissal, Touchnology was trading at fifty-two dollars per share, down from Tripp's over-blown sixty-five dollar position, and below the fifty-six dollar stop-limit where I had told him to dump it. The stock had continued to plummet, and traded on average forty-nine dollars per share in November; forty-four in December; and a dismal thirty-nine dollars per share in January. The losses would have been egregious enough for Peter to realize that my premonition had been right all along.

I looked up triumphantly. "This stock was a loser, just as I'd suspected!"

"Keep going," Mannheimer said.

By February, Touchnology had gone up to fifty dollars per share.

"That's strange," I remarked, looking ahead to the subsequent pages. "Touchnology's price went up almost forty percent in a month and then closed yesterday at sixty-seven."

"So you think it's a bit strange, too?"

"Yeah, I do."

"What could cause such a dramatic upswing?"

"Hmm, a couple of things: a new technological innovation, a huge order, phenomenal sales ... But none of these factors seemed to be on the horizon when I analyzed the company."

"How about an acquisition?"

"Companies' stock prices usually go down when they announce an acquisition."

"But what if Touchnology was the company being acquired?"

"Then its stock price could go up pretty significantly."

"Well, that's exactly what happened." Mannheimer rifled through his file. "Read the press release at the end."

TOKYO, March 27, 2010/PRNewswire

Nihontek Corp. (TSE: 7109, NYSE: NHTK) today announced that it had entered into a definitive agreement to acquire Touchnology Systems Inc., (NASDAQ: TUCH), a developer, manufacturer and marketer of touch screen products with diverse applications in smartphones, video games, electronic readers and satellite navigation systems based in La Jolla, California, for approximately US$550 million. The acquisition will significantly augment Nihontek's capabilities in the rapidly expanding smartphone and tablet market.

Dr. Taki Fujiyama, Nihontek's President and Chief Executive Officer, said, "Today's consumer wants a hand-held device that can accomplish all of their telecommunication needs with the touch of a screen. By acquiring Touchnology Systems, we will have the ability to bring cutting-edge innovation in-house. We are confident that Touchnology will continue to drive new design and functionality to maximize the user experience."

Bailey Perkins, Founder and CEO of Touchnology Systems, said, "This transaction offers significant value for Touchnology stockholders and provides

exciting new opportunities for our employees, customers and partners."

Upon closing the transaction, Touchnology will
become a wholly owned subsidiary of Nihontek. The
transaction is subject to certain regulatory approvals
and customary closing conditions.

About Nihontek Corp.
Nihontek is a leading Japanese telecommunication
and wireless equipment company best known for the
Kanji mobile phone. With annual revenue of US$13.6
billion, Nihontek has R&D institutes in Japan, the
United States, Germany, Sweden and India.

I evened out the documents and put the manila folder back on
Mannheimer's desk.

"The folks at Touchnology Systems sure hit the jackpot,"
I mocked. "From a technological standpoint, the company was
obviously very exciting. But from a pure P&L trading perspective, based on the data I had in October, I still stand by my
assessment."

"Do you think it was a good deal?"

"Sounds a bit overvalued to me. The CEO, this Bailey
guy, might leave the company after a year or two and take a
bunch of talent with him. Nihontek's taking a chance, but in
their industry, you've got to move fast."

"Let's try to imagine how Atlas could have fared from all
of this. What if Tripp doubled the position, even as it continued its huge slide, what would those shares be worth now?"

"600,000 shares at sixty-seven"—I did a mental calculation—"they'd be worth about forty million dollars as of yesterday's close."

Mannheimer whistled. "That's a lot of money."

"It is, but the firm's profit depends on what price he bought them at. In order for them to make serious money, Tripp would have had to buy more stocks on the low-end."

"For argument's sake, what percentage of the profit would go to Tripp at year-end?"

"I have no idea what his compensation structure is, but it could go as high as seven figures."

"Would you say, then, that it would have been worth the risk to hold on to that stock, to keep buying, because of the potential reward?"

"But you can't know that! You can only go by the information, the knowledge about a given stock or industry that you have at a given time. It's still a guessing game, but any experienced trader would tell you that it would have been better for Tripp to get out of that trade early and take his losses. I had given him a stop-limit; he ignored it. On paper, he lost a hell of a lot of money for Atlas. He got lucky if he still owned the stock when the company was acquired."

"But was it really luck?"

"What do you mean?"

"Did Tripp really get lucky or did he have a certain kind of edge? Black edge? Information that no one else had which he acquired through questionable or illegal means?"

I clenched and unclenched my fists; buttressing my fury, processing the enormity of his theory until I could finally put it into words. "Do you think Tripp was involved in insider trading?"

Mannheimer's black eyes bored into mine. "I don't know. Do you?"

Tripp was a cunning bastard—ambitious and competitive—but would he knowingly cross the line and make trades based on material, non-public information? I sighed, overcome by the alleged treachery. "Mr. Mannheimer, I can't vouch for anyone. I feel like I don't know anything anymore. The longer I'm away from Wall Street, the more I begin to wonder if I can ever go back. There's so much shady stuff that goes on—and I'm not even talking about anything that's illegal."

"I understand, but before you go tackling those existential questions, we've got to get to the bottom of this and prosecute your case. Are you with me?"

Mannheimer had been an activist long before my birth, fighting injustice and taking on cases that no one else would touch. He never hid his contempt for the "fat-cats" on Wall Street and was willing to go all the way for me, but I needed to be steadfast. I had to be ready to bring Tripp down and, by proxy, Atlas too.

I swallowed. "Yes. I'm with you."

"Good!" He began pacing back and forth. "There are several things we need to figure out: What did Tripp know? When did he know it?"

"That's what's so hard to prove about insider trading! It's a slippery slope, a gray zone. When does information go from being good research and analysis to being black edge?"

"*But*"—Mannheimer pointed his finger up in the air— "what if Tripp had a contact inside Touchnology or at Nihontek who tipped him off about the impending acquisition?"

"That information would have been passed along over

several months before the actual acquisition. I don't believe Peter would have let Tripp hold on to such a losing stock, for that long, without thinking it was strange and making him dump it."

"Unless—" Mannheimer began.

"Unless what?"

Mannheimer stopped in his tracks and peered at me. "Unless Peter was in on it, too."

His suggestion sounded far-fetched and completely outside my realm of probability.

"Tripp I could see, but Peter? No, no, no—that would've never happened!" I argued. "Peter would've never sanctioned such a thing! He's always had the highest integrity and ethical standards."

"Then why did he fire you when you wanted to dump the stock?"

"I—I don't know."

"Why did he pick Tripp over you?" he continued, unrelenting.

I covered my face. Crying in front of Mannheimer was not an option, but the world was quaking from under me again. I didn't have the energy to contemplate Peter's morality—or lack thereof—and the possibility he could be a twenty-first-century Gordon Gekko. All I had wanted to do today was plan for my date with Oliver. Was that so much to ask for?

"Well, there's more to your dismissal than poor execution and insubordination. What if *you* were the only thing standing in the way of Atlas making millions of dollars in profit on Touchnology?" Mannheimer asked.

"And you think I was?"

He nodded. "I do."

"But how are you going to prove that? Beyond a reasonable doubt?"

He circled back to his chair and sat down. "That'll be the tough part. We need witnesses, documentation, a timeline of their trades . . ."

"You keep opening up a can of worms, but what has that led to in the past six months? If anything, it just proves how much smarter Peter and Tripp have been all along."

"I know. These guys have the money and the Wall Street lawyers to mount a vigorous defense. I can't accuse them of anything until I have incontrovertible evidence of wrongdoing." Mannheimer took off his glasses and wiped them with the bottom of his tie. He put them back on and said gravely, "And I'm sorry, Mia, I just don't have that right now."

23.

After work the next day, I rushed back to the cottage to freshen up and change into a chiffon slip dress and sandals, pausing at my reflection in the mirror. Something had changed; something deeper than just blush and lipstick. I looked happy. I *felt* happy, even after Mannheimer's dark conspiracy theories. Consigning his allegations to the back of my mind, I was determined not to let Tripp or Peter encroach upon my evening with Oliver. The havoc they spawned was always skulking in the background, casting a shadow over this fragile peace I had found in Overlook. Mannheimer would have to nose around Atlas by himself—and go on what could very well be a wild goose chase—because, for the first time in my life, I was focusing on romance instead of my career and it felt wonderfully liberating.

Back downstairs, I donned the old apron hanging in the pantry closet and got busy with last minute preparations; arranging potato wedges in a roasting pan and chopping the ends off asparagus spears that would join the rack of lamb *Provençale*. I hadn't expected to find cooking so therapeutic, but digging into a recipe provided a satisfying break from my problems and I almost dropped a spoon when the doorbell rang. Throwing the stained apron back in the closet, I opened the front door with a huge smile on my face.

Oliver's grin was equally wide and I melted, thinking: *I'm not imagining this.*

"Finally!" he exclaimed. "Feels like I haven't seen you in ages!"

We hugged like old friends, but then Oliver pressed me closer, my chest fusing with his, the weight of his hands crinkling the feathery threads of my dress. I felt exposed and light-headed, torn between blind faith and my customary caution. When we detached, I noticed a large shopping bag from The Bishop's Cellar on the entry mat.

"What have you got in there?" I asked, lifting it up. "Ooh, it's heavy! We won't be able to drink it all, unless you plan on getting me hopelessly drunk . . ."

"Not so fast," he teased, taking the bag from me. "Are you going to let me in or what?"

"Ummm," I said, pretending to mull it over before throwing the door open. "Yes!"

Oliver stepped inside and pointed to the bag. "Where can I put these?"

"Follow me," I said, heading to the small dining room, my most beloved part of the house. The dark oak French country table, china cabinet and wrought-iron chandelier were Hughes family heirlooms. They added a rare personal touch, bringing patina to a place that had seen so many people come and go.

"What have you done here?" he asked, pointing to the peonies in small bud vases and the flickering votive candles I had scattered along the table. It sat eight and, rather than put myself and Oliver at each end, I seated us in the middle, across from each other. I had gotten over my conundrum that it might look corny. This was supposed to be an intimate dinner after all. Calling it by any other name would be denying the romantic tension that had been building up since our morning in the park. The wine glasses and plates were more casual than I would have liked and made me wish—momentarily—for the elegant Hermès porcelain and Cristofle flatware stowed away in my apartment, but I don't think I would have appreciated the end result as much.

"I wanted everything to look . . . nice."

He placed the shopping bag on a chair. "Well, it looks great." He turned to me. "*You* look great."

I wanted to say: *Thank you. Thank you for noticing. For making me feel special and desired.* But that might scare him off, so I swished my hand as though I didn't take him seriously.

"These are for you," he said, delivering a billowy package from the bag.

I unfastened the florist's paper and let loose a bouquet of purple blooms—hydrangeas, lilacs and irises—speckled with white gardenias. Bringing it my nose, I inhaled the heady fragrance.

"They're beautiful," I said. "Thank you."

We fell silent. It would have been the ideal moment for our first kiss. I heard it on the phone in all the things we left unsaid. I felt it between us now, too, a longing that was difficult to ignore. I could have tilted my chin upwards, or touched Oliver's lips, giving him clear signs that I was ready. But it had been so long since I'd opened myself to someone and I still felt unsteady, wary of diving in too soon.

"I better put these in water," I said, moving back.

"Right," Oliver said. "And I'd better unpack this bag."

I found a cylinder vase in the pantry and waited for it to fill up with water. Soaking in the honeyed scent of nectar and the petals' kaleidoscopic shades of violet made me giddy. I dunked the hand-tied stems in the vase, splattering pellets of water on the counter. Moments later, I heard a few soft knocks from the swinging door that connected the kitchen and dining room.

"Yes?" I called out.

"Is it safe to come in?" Oliver asked.

The kitchen didn't quite look like a disaster area, but the sink bulged with mixing bowls and pots camouflaged the stovetop.

"Sure, but it's a bit of a mess in here," I warned.

Oliver pushed through the door with his foot, hands full of different liquor bottles. "Thought I could make us cocktails before dinner."

I laughed. "You're full of surprises tonight."

"Have you ever had a Boulevardier?" he asked, arranging the bottles on the little prep island in the middle of the kitchen.

"No, but it sounds tempting when you say it with that nice French accent."

"It's made with bourbon, vermouth and Campari. Kind of sweet, but very tasty."

"I'd love one."

"Then I'll get started!" he said, uncapping bottles and measuring ingredients into his own cocktail shaker. "We'll also need some ice."

After getting an ice tray from the freezer, I carried the bouquet back to the dining room, placing the vase on the window ledge. Oliver was busy opening and closing cabinets when I came back to the kitchen.

"Any martini glasses?" he asked.

"I haven't seen any, but take these," I said, reaching for two tumblers in the cupboard above the refrigerator.

He decanted from the cocktail shaker, mindful that we both got equal amounts. I didn't want to be a wimp, so I took a big first sip. It started out cold and sugary, but finished with a kick from the bourbon. It took great effort not to make a face.

"What do you think?" Oliver asked.

I swallowed again to dilute the aftertaste. "I think you're a man of many talents."

He laughed. "Take another sip. It'll go down much easier. I promise."

And so we stood in that cramped kitchen, guzzling strong cocktails, our chatter growing louder with each sip. I don't know why I had imagined him sitting patiently in another room while I made—and served—dinner, but quickly saw how outlandish that image was. It felt oddly natural when Oliver insisted on helping me put the meal together, urging me to shed my manic need for perfection and getting me to just relax. We moved comfortably around each other; he blanched the asparagus while I stirred the carrot ginger soup and, when we finally sat down for dinner, it felt like we had bonded over the basic act of cooking.

"I'm stuffed," Oliver announced after eating the last morsel of food on his plate.

"Me, too," I said, placing my knife and fork together over small chunks of potato.

"It was delicious," he added.

I had been so nervous, but the meal exceeded my expectations. The natural sweetness of the carrots balanced the spicy ginger in the soup and the lamb was juicy, oozing the perfect reddish-pink when I cut it between the bones. "I love the wine you brought."

Oliver held up the bottle like a rare artifact. "'89 Gaja Barbaresco—probably the best red of the decade."

"Ooh, I'm honored."

"Cheers!" he said, draining the last drops.

"Cheers!" I echoed. "Do you have room for dessert?"

"I always have room for dessert."

"Why don't you go into the living room? We can have it there."

"Let me help you clean up."

"It's okay," I said, reaching for his plate before he could stop me. "I can manage."

I stacked the plates and utensils together and cleared space for them in the sink. I'd load the dishwasher later. Baking wasn't my forte, so I had cheated and purchased two squares of *dulce de leche* cheesecake from Whole Foods. I'd make them look fancier by swirling caramel syrup onto our dessert plates, but realized I had forgotten to offer Oliver coffee or tea. I made my way to the living room where he sat on the couch, reading a back issue of *New York* magazine.

"Espresso or tea?" I asked, standing directly in front of him.

Oliver looked up at me and slowly closed the magazine. With one nimble motion, he grabbed my hand and pulled me forward. I landed in his lap, the left strap of my dress slipping from my shoulder. He fondled the thin strip and put it back in place. Staring into my eyes, he asked in a low voice, "When are you going to stay in one spot long enough for me to kiss you?"

I didn't squirm or look away, but a current, which had started in the center of my body, expanded, emboldening me. I lowered my head and took Oliver's face in my hands. Our lips met and I stayed there for several seconds with my eyes shut, freezing those first moments of intimacy. I drew back and Oliver smiled, caressing under my ribcage, warming me to the core. I sprinkled small kisses around his face, savoring how the stubble on his cheeks stung my mouth. When I grazed his lips again, his tongue slipped inside and I drank in the taste of wine and mint and lust before both straps of my dress hung down and every nerve ending tingled. Our mouths found a rhythm, swaying and whirling till we both had to come up for air. Oliver lifted me by the hips and we stretched out on the couch, his pelvis between my thighs. I bent my knees and untucked his shirt, combing his back with my nails; his smooth skin growing hot and sticky as our breathing got heavier. Oliver's hand slid underneath my dress, but when he caught the waistband of my panties, I let out a small moan.

He stopped. "I'm sorry. Guess I got a little carried away."

I put my finger to his lips. "Shhh," I said, "let's go upstairs."

"Are you sure?"

I smothered his question with a kiss, muzzling any ambiguity about what I meant. We shed our shoes and stumbled up the stairs. My bedroom was dark, but the full moon emitted an iridescent shaft of light. Oliver unzipped the back of my dress. I eased out of it and let it drop, a halo of silk puddling around my feet, leaving me in the strapless black lace bra and matching panties I had chosen with care, hoping for precisely this moment.

"Let me look at you," he said, leaning back, our hands linked. "You're so beautiful."

Burning, I huddled closer; unbuttoning Oliver's shirt,

trailing my hands from the lines of his ribs to the tautness of his stomach. He led us to my bed and unclipped my bra; kneading and nibbling my breasts until I purred, floating into the unknown. Every inch of me existed in the moment and I unbuckled his jeans, peeling them and his briefs off simultaneously. In this fervor, my panties also disappeared and we were both completely naked. Skin on skin, our movements switched from gradual and tender to urgent and clawing. My hands slithered around his head; his hardness scraped my stomach, my navel, my thatch of hair; and a delicious chill engulfed me. I reached under the pillow for a condom and he entered effortlessly; our bodies merging and moving together. Oliver's eyes captured mine the whole time, deepening our connection, and only closed towards the end, when trembling, he dissolved onto my chest. I was swooning, electrified that I could still give pleasure after two years of singleness and celibacy. Lying still, the only exertion was the rising and falling of our stomachs, but Oliver's fingers found their way to my center and he rubbed and kissed; teasing my senses until, arching my back, I finally submitted.

We eventually fell asleep, but I woke up with a start in the middle of the night and checked the clock.

"Oliver, it's 1:30," I said, shaking him by the shoulder.

"Mmm," he mumbled, eyes closed, cuddling close to me again. "What is it?"

"It's late. Shouldn't you be getting back home to Balthazar?" I said.

"I asked the sitter to stay the night," he murmured.

"What?"

Oliver opened his eyes. "She's staying over. We have until

eight o'clock tomorrow morning."

"Are you serious?"

"It's bad of me, right? It looks like this was premeditated, like I planned to get you in bed, even though I *did* want you very badly, but I would've been perfectly fine and gone home if you didn't want to. Nothing would have changed." He paused. "I'm rambling."

I started laughing.

"What is it?" he asked.

"Look underneath my pillow."

Oliver reached over and groped around in the darkness. "It's a bunch of condoms! One, two, three, four ... Four of them!"

"So does that make us even?"

He was on top of me again, fully awake.

"Why ..." he began, lips nuzzling my ear.

"Do you have ..." he continued, tickling my collarbone.

"So many condoms?" he asked, sliding his tongue across my breasts, setting off that stirring sensation in my stomach again.

"Because," I breathed, remembering how I had buried them under a basket of toiletries at CVS. "I haven't stopped thinking about sleeping with you since our first date."

"Good," Oliver said, working his way down my abdomen. "Because neither have I."

He made us omelets for breakfast with the *herbs de Provence* and then we ate the cheesecake for dessert. The night seemed like a fog, dreamy and long in its own way, but we had been on borrowed time, trying to make the most of the hours before he had to leave.

"I wish I could stay," he told me.

"Me, too, but then you'd have one very disappointed little boy at soccer practice."

"Let me put it this way: I wish I could be in two places at once," he said, taking a sip of coffee. "Are you working today?"

I nodded. "But we're closed on Mondays, so I'll have tomorrow off."

"When can we see each other again? Do you want to have lunch this week?"

Lunch could be nice, but it was so public and confining. "Why don't you come over tomorrow morning?"

"I have to drive Balthazar to school and then the shop opens at eleven."

"I know." I paused. "Come after you drop him off. For coffee."

Oliver chuckled. He got up and walked around the table, bending down by my chair. "I think I'm catching on." He kissed my hand. "You're very sneaky."

I smiled. "You don't know the half of it."

24.

The next day, I answered the front door in only my bathrobe. Oliver and I barely made it to my bedroom before he had untied the belt and I shimmied out of it. We stared at each other—smiling conspiratorially in Monday's unforgiving daylight as I ripped off his shirt and jeans—relishing our shared moment of rebellion, like cutting class or playing hooky from work. He came back every morning that first week, sometimes staying for only an hour, and we would steadily migrate from my bed to the shower. I don't know how I spent the next eight hours in Liz's shop without giving myself away. I still felt Oliver all over me, even after he'd gone.

"Do you think this is normal?" I asked him, halfway into Week Two of our coffee mornings. He was propped up on pillows against the headboard and I snuggled closer, my head in the crook of his neck. The official start of summer was a few weeks away, but humidity was high. The dense mist of flowers and grass wafted from the open windows.

"What do you mean by 'this'?"

"Please don't make me spell it out."

"Okay, then I'd say that coffee in the morning is perfectly normal."

"Seriously!" I cried, swatting his chest.

"Ow!" he shrieked, snatching my wrist. "That almost hurt."

"This is definitely crazy." I sighed. "I only wish we could have more time together."

He stroked my hair, but said anything.

"Sorry," I said, filling the silence. "That sounded whiny. Forget I said it."

"So you think we're having too much sex?" he asked finally.

"I didn't say that." I paused. "I don't know."

"Because if you think I've come back every day just to sleep with you, you're dead wrong."

I wanted to be that carefree woman who fulfilled her needs and fantasies with no doubts or apologies, but I was also aware that I was making it incredibly convenient for Oliver and it had started to trouble me. Trying to hold my new spate of insecurity at bay, I said softly, "I hope that's true."

We both stayed in our original positions. I closed my eyes, analyzing the last week and a half. Internally, I had gone through all the reasons about why we couldn't be a conventional couple. We both worked long hours—requiring most weekends and some holidays. As his own boss, Oliver had more flexibility than I did, but it didn't feel right to ask Liz to reschedule my hours, not when the store was running so smoothly. Hence, the "morning coffees" crammed in before work. It was also a given that Oliver's evenings belonged to Balthazar. He didn't need to explain; I accepted it as sacred. With advance planning and a sitter, we might get one Saturday night every other week, but that also depended on whether Oliver had other work commitments. I also assumed that meeting at Oliver's place was a no-no and I'd wondered, many times over, if he had erased all traces of Sophie from his house. Maybe photos with her and Balthazar as a baby remained?

We had also never discussed the subject of my getting together with *both* him and Balthazar. Our intimate relationship was too new and another woman would surely confuse the five-year old. It was undeniably the right decision and did it really matter where and when we saw each other? Wasn't it enough that we stole these precious moments when we could? And what was my endgame in all of this anyway? My stint in Overlook was supposed to be temporary, just until I recouped my professional reputation and landed a new job. Romance had never been on my agenda, but Oliver—and Mannheimer's suspicions about Tripp and Peter—had thrown my carefully plotted comeback into question.

"Are you free Saturday night?" he asked suddenly.

"Yes. Why?"

"Why don't we go to dinner and a movie?"

I refrained from laughing out loud—a chaste movie date after hours of salacious activity. "Sure, that sounds great."

"Good. Then I'll see you Saturday," he said, rolling off the bed onto his feet.

"Saturday?" I repeated, fixing the tousled sheets to cover my chest. "That's three days away."

Oliver turned back to look at me. "I'll have to wean myself off of you, but I don't want you to have any doubts as to why I'm here."

Unable to stop myself, I asked, "Why are you here?"

He sat on the bed and peered down at me. I thought he might be annoyed and waited for him to tell me not to ruin the fun we were having.

"Because I feel things when I'm with you that I thought were gone and never coming back."

That sentence came out in a lower octave, as though he wasn't sure if it was safe to say out loud. It feed my hunger for validation, but it also filled me with a yearning to take away his pain, to unscramble the wreckage someone else had caused. I lifted the sheets, inviting him back in. We lay together, fore-heads touching. Oliver closed his eyes and our legs melded under the duvet. I kissed him; gently parting his lips, unleash-ing pinpricks of desire as I felt him harden against my thigh.

Then he disentangled.

"You can't keep doing that," he told me, laughing.

"I can't help it."

"It's going to be a long next couple of days." He pecked me on the nose and scooted off before I could stop him.

On Saturday we went for dinner at Paparazzi, the little Italian restaurant on Overlook Avenue. Oliver said hello or nodded to about half the people in the restaurant while I smiled and tried to look somewhere in the middle distance, avoiding the curi-ous glances that first placed me at Eclectibles and then now at Oliver's side.

"You're like the mayor here," I joked when we sat down.

"If they're not customers, then they knew my parents. I can't escape them."

"Must be a burden sometimes too," I said, opening my menu.

"It can be. Especially after Sophie left. Everyone seemed to know what happened. I only told my parents and sister, but word got around. I think it might have been the babysitter who helped us. Who knows? It didn't really matter in the end. I had to learn to get over the stigma and embarrassment of it all."

I stopped turning the pages of the menu. Any mention of

their past together disarmed me. "I wish that had never happened to Balthazar—and you too, of course—but then—" I wavered, realizing what I was about to say.

"We probably wouldn't be here right now," Oliver said, finishing my sentence.

"Isn't it terrible of me to think that?"

"I've thought about that too."

I searched for signs of guilt on his face, but then our waiter arrived.

"What are you having?" Oliver asked, looking down at his menu.

"Ummm ... Probably the beef carpaccio and then the *pasta frutti di mare*."

"I can recommend them both," said the waiter and then turned to Oliver. "You, sir?"

"I'll start with the antipasto and then have the *tagliatelle al ragu*."

"And wine?" asked the waiter.

Oliver pointed to me.

"The house Chianti is fine," I said, grateful that he never made our dinners out into a big wine production.

"So how'd you spend the rest of the week?" Oliver asked once the waiter left us alone.

"Well, let's see," I began, trying to trick him into believing he had missed out on something special. "I worked all day and then went running. Then I watched some TV and tried to read a book, but I fell asleep after a couple of pages ... "

"Sounds nice."

"And you?"

"I had a wine tasting course on Thursday night."

"What'd you treat the lovely ladies of Overlook to this time?"

"Since it was the last course before the summer, we explored the wonderful world of rosé."

"My favorite! Sorry I missed it."

"I don't know what it is with women and rosé," he mused. "These ladies drank it like it was juice. I was about to call a cab for a few of them! But I'm completely sold out of Domaines Ott, so I guess I shouldn't complain."

I laughed. "Do you know why we women love rosé so much?"

"No, why?"

"It's young and fun and sexy," I explained, recalling holidays in South Beach and St. Barth. "It's pure escape. People *never* drink rosé when they're depressed!"

"You might have a good point."

"I think I do."

"Maybe I should include your comments in my wine notes the next time I do the course."

"Be my guest. You have my permission."

We continued talking in this light-hearted vein and even switched entrées halfway through the dinner. I appreciated this ordinariness; it tempered my doubts about the last time we had been together. Dinner ran late, forcing us to rush out of the restaurant, race to the bottom of the avenue and sneak into the art house movie theater right before the doors closed.

We ducked into our seats just as Michael Douglas appeared on-screen, conversing with his doctor. The film was called *Solitary Man*. Oliver had chosen it and I knew nothing about the plot. Douglas was a master at playing urbane, morally-flawed characters and this one was no exception. However, his portrayal of Ben Kalman, an aging auto tycoon disgraced in a business scandal, was excruciating to watch. Granted, Ben hits rock-bottom by continuously making the same dumb mistakes—cheating and chasing much younger women—but I could have ended up as the female version of Ben: alone, evicted, begging for money and jobs. I even covered my eyes during one scene when Ben suffers total humiliation, prompting Oliver to ask if I was okay. Where would I be if Christine hadn't stepped in to help me? Oliver had no idea how my life had been hanging by a thread and I was afraid the time was coming for me to tell him my whole story. He had been so open about his flaws, his shame after Sophie. What was my problem?

I was scared if Oliver knew The Whole Truth he would think less of me.

That realization shook me up so much I excused myself to go to the bathroom during the closing credits. I blotted water on my eyes and put on a fresh coat of lip gloss, hoping to look more alert. My features still looked ashen, but I hoped Oliver wouldn't notice in the theater's dim lighting. When I got out of the bathroom, I saw him by the snack bar immersed in conversation with Liz and her husband Philip!

Straightening up, I strode over to them. Oliver curled his arm casually around my waist and Liz's green eyes flew from me to Oliver and back again.

"Liz! Philip! What a surprise!" I blathered, suppressing my angst.

"It's a surprise seeing you guys here too!" Liz answered, flapping her hands in the air.

Philip seemed totally unaware and prattled on, praising Michael Douglas' acting prowess. "He's just such a screen presence and not afraid to play someone disagreeable, like in *Falling Down*. Now there's a character I could relate to—all that pent-up anger about everyday day life . . ." He turned to me. "Did you like the movie, Mia?"

"Well, there were some cringe-worthy scenes," I said and we all laughed.

"I thought I was going to die when he slept with his girlfriend's eighteen-year old daughter!" Liz cried.

"That was pretty bad," I agreed.

Oliver shook his head. "Yeah, some parts of the movie were pretty depressing."

"The ladies love him, even in real-life," Philip continued. "He's got a much younger wife . . . What's her name again? She played Velma in *Chicago* . . ."

"Catherine Zeta-Jones!" I said.

He snapped his fingers in recognition. "That's right!"

We stood in silence for the next several seconds, having exhausted the film topic and not sure where to segue from there.

"What are you guys doing after this?" Oliver asked.

"I actually think we'd better go," Philip said, taking Liz's arm. "It's a late night for us and we don't want to hold you guys up."

"Yes, Phil's right. Good night. Have fun," Liz said, giving us a final, inscrutable glance.

Did she approve? Did she feel slighted that I hadn't told her? I wondered what she would say to Philip when they got back outside.

"Bye!" Oliver and I crooned.

"Did Liz know about us?" he asked, as we walked back to The Bishop's Cellar's lot where our cars were parked.

"No, she didn't," I admitted, noting his use of "us," rather than just "me."

"I could tell by her expression." He paused. "I thought you guys were friends."

"She's great, but things have never really gotten personal."

"Have you told anyone about us?"

"Just Christine. How about you?"

"My sister, Gwen."

"Why do you ask?"

"I was just curious."

We walked for another block and I asked, "Would you mind if I had talked to other people around here about you?"

"No. Why would I mind?"

I shrugged. "I don't know. You seem so private. In any case, I have no friends here anyway, so you're saved."

We reached our cars. My faded Ford and his sleek Audi were the only ones left, parked next to each other like an odd couple. Oliver took out his key and the Audi beeped and blinked, signaling we would soon have to go our separate ways.

He leaned against the driver's side door. "Sometimes it does feel like we're hiding something. I don't know why."

I knew what I was hiding from him. I was weighed down by key elements of my past, and the closer we grew, the harder it was becoming for me to conceal.

"Isn't it better to be discreet?" I asked, stepping closer, filling the space between us. "Balthazar won't get confused or upset by seeing you with me. We don't have to explain ourselves to anyone—although that might change now with Liz . . . "

Oliver sighed deeply and wrapped his arms around my shoulders. My head fit neatly in the nook underneath his chin.

"I'm sorry this is becoming so complicated," he said.

"Don't be. I'm happy with the way things are," I said. It wasn't exactly the truth, but I knew how limited our options were.

"He's never seen me with someone else."

"I know it's a big step. I understand. Truly, I do."

"I wish I could take you back to my place right now and wake up with you tomorrow morning without having to watch the time. You know what I really miss?"

"What?"

"Lingering in bed. I never linger in bed anymore."

I laughed. "You're a dad. You're not allowed to linger."

"I promise you we'll get a chance to linger in bed."

"It's okay," I assured him. "I'd rather have a few hours with you than nothing at all."

"No. It's decided. I'll make it happen."

"Promise?" I asked, warming up to the possibility. I really didn't want the evening to end. I didn't want to go back to that quiet little house in backcountry by myself. It was getting harder to say goodbye to Oliver each time.

"Promise."

25.

"So, how long have you and Oliver been seeing each other?" Liz asked the next morning. We were setting up at the store and she had waited a full fifteen minutes to spring the question on me.

"Oh, not long," I replied, spraying Windex onto a tattered cloth. I had already rehearsed my answer and added, "That was only our third date."

"Really? You guys seemed really close."

"You think?" I asked, ignoring my vow of caution, keen as I was to hear her opinion.

She nodded. "Oliver seemed really relaxed and happy. I haven't seen him out and about in years."

"Well, we *do* enjoy each other's company," I said, trying to play down the significance of her words.

Liz giggled. "I never saw it coming, but I guess I shouldn't have been surprised!"

"Really? Why's that?"

"You're both single and attractive. You work in the same neighborhood. You were bound to notice each other." She removed a bracelet from a pile of muslin bags on the check-out counter and tried it on, fingering the twinkling beads on her wrist. "You're also not an Overlook mouse. He's had his share of local offers, believe me, but he didn't go for them."

"Mmm . . . I've kind of wondered about that."

"I don't know if that reflects positively on Oliver or just says that the women in this town aren't that tempting. And it's usually those who don't stand a chance that try!"

I laughed. "You're too much!"

She continued emptying bracelets into a wooden bowl and said, "There was this sort of quiet sympathy for Oliver after what happened. He kind of kept everyone at a distance, which wasn't surprising. I think he didn't want people to feel sorry for Balthazar and treat him differently."

"Did you ever meet her?" I asked, wandering over to the counter.

"Sophie?" Liz asked, knowing exactly whom I meant. "A few times."

"Did she shop here?"

"This was definitely not her type of store! But she came in once when Balthazar was still an infant. She carried him in a Baby Björn and they looked like they had stepped out of an ad or something; that kid was so cute. She was also striking, with lots of dark hair and the kind of skin that's always tan, even in the depths of winter. And she was skinny. So shallow of me, but I noticed that right away because Balthazar couldn't have been more than six months old and it looked like she had already lost her pregnancy weight." Liz patted her stomach. "As you can see, I've given up."

I picked at the edge of the Windex label with my nail. "Liz, your description of her is, like, confirming my worst nightmare."

"She was nice, but—"

"But what?"

"In that I'm-too-good-for-this-place kind of way. She didn't try to get to know anyone or to be a part of the community, which would have been the smart thing to do since her husband owned a business here."

"They weren't married," I corrected.

"Yes. Right. Well, in everyone's eyes, they might as well have been married since they had a child together."

"Oliver told me that she didn't like it here."

"That was pretty obvious."

"I guess you weren't a fan."

"No, I never was and, when she picked up sticks and left, I saw no reason to be tactful anymore."

"Did you ever ask Oliver what happened?"

"No! It was really none of my business, but I told him to call us if he needed any extra help with Balthazar. I think he knew what I meant, but he never took me up on it." She paused. "You know, it would have been so much cleaner if they'd been married and just gotten a divorce. That would have been *normal* and Balthazar could've still had a relationship with her. I never understood why she had to abandon him."

"Usch—abandon is such a harsh word."

Liz shrugged. "But that's exactly what she did."

I had wanted information—maybe even some gossip—but it felt more uncomfortable talking about Sophie than I'd expected. Liz was entitled to her opinions, but I was reluctant to participate in a deeper analysis about Sophie's state of mind or her motives. Her rapid weight loss and aloofness could have reflected the post-partum depression Oliver had talked about rather than any sort of pretension. Perhaps it was a sense of loyalty to Oliver that stopped me from skewering Sophie as heartily as Liz did. I felt a strange obligation not only to protect his privacy, but to protect his choices—even if that choice was the woman who had walked out on him.

Liz joined me by the display case, clutching the wooden

bowl that was now studded with beaded bracelets. "Do you mind if I ask you something? It's, uh, a little personal."

"Shoot," I replied, hoping it wouldn't be another inquisition about my Wall Street job.

"Do you want kids?"

Her question caught me off-guard; most people no longer dared to ask. As a young analyst, I had never mentioned children since I was so concerned The Mommy Track could derail my "promising career." But the older I got, the issue simply became taboo. Most of the men I'd dated feared the topic of children would lead to that other c-word—commitment—so they avoided it with a ten-foot pole. Within my circle of women friends, the subject was too emotionally fraught. Maybe I had tried, but was physically incapable of getting pregnant. I could have also suffered the heartbreak of a miscarriage. And, what if I actually didn't want kids? It was almost offensive to assume this desire factored in every woman's life. Not wanting children wasn't an all-encompassing statement about a woman's character. The maternal instinct didn't automatically equate with virtue or selflessness—as Sophie proved.

However, kids were something I'd been thinking a lot about lately.

"Yes, I'd like to have children someday."

"So what's stopping you?"

I smiled wanly. "It's never been the right time or the right person."

"And now?"

"I don't know," I said, jacking up my shoulders like they were a big question mark. "Women don't really need the 'right person' anymore, do we? We have all sorts of options these days: adoption, sperm banks, a gay best friend . . ."

"How old are you, Mia?"

"Thirty-five."

"It's not too late, you know. I had my last one at thirty-nine."

It lasted only a few seconds, but that look passed on her face. The one married women—mothers—gave to women like me: the sympathetic gaze, the wistful slant of the chin. *I hope you meet the right person. I hope you get a chance to experience motherhood, too. There's so much more to life than just work.*

"Whew—I still have time!" I joked, placing a hand to my forehead.

Liz smiled and squeezed my arm. I smiled back and watched her sturdy frame, the one with the soft stomach that had carried four babies, waddle down the aisle in search of a free spot for the wooden bowl.

26.

Mannheimer had summoned me back to his office. It was another scorching Friday in the city, underscoring how weary New York made me these days. Being there knowing I had roots—memories, an apartment and possessions—but unable to access them, only exacerbated the disconnection. I was also frustrated by Mannheimer's slow progress, his fondness for roping me in with oblique phone calls.

"Mia, I realized we needed someone on the inside to help us with this case," he said after I sunk into the green Chesterfield chair opposite his desk. I'd worn a shorter dress this time and the back of my thighs stuck to the leather.

"You know as well as I do that no one at Atlas will help me. Not one of them has called or emailed since I was fired."

"Well, someone has come forward!" Mannheimer announced victoriously.

"Who?" I asked, stunned.

"Someone well-positioned to watch the comings and goings at the firm."

Mannheimer's cryptic statements were trying, but I speculated on possible candidates anyway. Jack Wong? He never went out for drinks with the other traders, which might make him more objective. Tom Schultz? The old-timer, who was so balanced and wise? Tom and I had seen eye-to-eye on most matters and his self-made ethos might not have squared with Tripp's sense of entitlement.

"Is it Tom Schultz?" I asked.

Mannheimer shook his head.

"Is it someone from my team?"

"No."

Lifting my tote bag from the floor, I said, "Mr. Mannheimer, I don't have time for guessing games."

"It's Clifton!"

"Clifton? Clifton who?"

"Clifton Johnson!"

"Clifton Johnson?" I repeated, confused. "Who the hell is Clifton Johnson?"

"The security guard who's worked at Atlas for the past four years!"

"*You mean CJ?!*" I exclaimed, thinking of the man who had escorted me out of the building.

No wonder Mannheimer had been so evasive. My fate relied on the security guard at Atlas? CJ had always been professional, but what did he know about trading or the machinations between Peter and Tripp? He spent most of his day *outside* in the reception area, not inside the office where all the action took place.

"Don't discount what he has to offer," Mannheimer reproached, as though he could read my mind.

"And what, exactly, does CJ have to offer?"

"I don't know yet, but he's coming to my office"— Mannheimer checked his watch— "in five minutes."

"In five minutes?!" I shrieked, my forbearance all but gone.

Mannheimer raised his fluffy eyebrows and looked contrite for the first time. "Let me go to reception and wait for him," he said, hastening to the door. "I'll leave you to your thoughts."

Mannheimer was grasping at straws and I seriously began to question choosing him as my lawyer. Atlas would have an army of shrewd, expensive attorneys from a top Midtown firm, but I was stuck with a doddering activist from the garment district. I couldn't see a way out of my dilemma and tried to calm down before Mannheimer returned with CJ. I heard the door open and the sound of their voices behind my chair. Knowing I had to go through this drill no matter what, I got up, turned and smiled, determined to eradicate the humiliated woman from last October.

It was strange seeing CJ out of context. He wasn't wearing the navy blue security guard pants and jacket, but jeans and a white polo shirt. Statuesque next to the shorter, stouter Mannheimer, they looked downright comical standing next to each other.

"Mia, you remember Clifton Johnson?" Mannheimer asked.

"Of course I do. Thank you so much for coming here today, CJ."

CJ smiled shyly. "I was always sorry about how things turned out."

"And how is your daughter doing?" I asked.

Pride lit up every corner of his face. "She's doing great. On her way to Northwestern this fall."

"That's wonderful! You must be so proud."

"We are," he said. "You really inspired her, you know."

Strangely, a lump formed in my throat. CJ was still the same kind, sympathetic man he'd always been. I thought of his sweet daughter, on the cusp of her exciting new journey, and my heart caved in. *I* had been that girl at once. What happened? How could I have let things go so wrong?

I felt Mannheimer's eyes on me and nodded, unable to formulate any words.

"Clifton, please sit down and we can get started," Mannheimer said and waited for CJ to occupy the armchair next to mine.

"You can call me CJ," he told Mannheimer. "Everybody does."

"CJ it is then!" Mannheimer then transferred his attention to me. "Mia, let me begin by saying that CJ is here of his own accord and that he has nothing to gain by helping us."

I had regained my bearings, but was still skeptical about this new collaboration. "Mr. Mannheimer, how did you get in contact with CJ?"

"I'd been scouting the premises and CJ noticed," Mannheimer said.

"He looked kind of suspicious," CJ added.

"But when I mentioned you, Mia, and explained why I was there, CJ became much more amenable, right?" Mannheimer said.

CJ nodded.

They sat still, waiting for my reaction, and I finally responded, "Okay."

Relieved, Mannheimer turned to CJ. "What can you tell us about the firm since Mia was let go?"

"That guy Tripp took over Mia's job."

This was nothing new, but Mannheimer placed an index finger on his cheek, deep in thought, as though hearing it for the first time. "And how has that turned out?" he inquired.

"I don't work in the office, so I don't have any specifics, but from what I see, things have gotten really stressful."

"Why's that?"

"Maybe they're losing money?" CJ asked, glancing at me.

I shrugged. "Your guess is as good as mine."

"But how are things between Peter and Tripp?" Mannheimer asked.

"They seem tight," CJ said.

"What makes you think that?"

"They've both been in the office really early for the past couple of weeks, before everyone else gets in."

"How early?"

"I get there at seven and sometimes they've been there before me."

CJ's comment seemed to give credence to our theory that Peter and Tripp were involved in something suspicious.

"Did you have the chance to overhear anything they were talking about?" Mannheimer grilled.

"Mr. Mannheimer, I told you that I wasn't going to spy on anyone," CJ said. "That would be violating my job."

My eyes threw daggers in Mannheimer's direction. Didn't he realize he was going too far?

CJ faced me and continued, "I only wanted Mia to know that I always felt badly about how things went down that day. I really hope you get the compensation you deserve."

"Thank you," I said softly.

"I hope so too," Mannheimer said. "Is there anything else you'd like to add, CJ?"

The man never let up!

"Not really," CJ replied.

I leapt to my feet. "CJ, you've done more than enough. Please excuse Mr. Mannheimer. He can be a bit aggressive at times."

Chuckling, CJ rose from his chair. "It's okay. You want a pit bull as your lawyer."

I glowered at Mannheimer, but he watched us, untroubled. "I guess I do."

"I really hope things work out. The office hasn't been the same since you left."

"That's nice of you to say, but nobody's indispensable."

"Sad, but true." He offered his hand again. "You take care."

"You, too," I said, taking it with both of my palms. "And please give Erica my best wishes," I said, remembering his daughter's name.

"I will."

We walked to the door together, but halfway there, he asked, "Do you remember Nick Vamvakis?"

"Sure. We sat next to each other for a long time."

"He left Atlas in January."

"Did he?"

"Yeah, he got a job at another firm in Stamford, not far from his house."

"Good for him. I knew he wasn't crazy about the commute."

"He and Tripp hung out for a while."

"I remember; they used to go out for drinks."

CJ paused by the door, his hand on the knob. "He might know something," he said in a near-whisper.

"Nick?" I asked, astonished.

"Just sayin'," CJ said and, before I could press him further, he was out the door.

"What were you guys talking about?" Mannheimer asked

when I came back.

"CJ just mentioned a former colleague."

"Who?"

"A guy: Nick Vamvakis."

"That name doesn't sound familiar."

"He wasn't on my team. Nick's a bond trader."

"Were you friends?"

I thought about our work relationship. "We were *friendly*. He helped the day go by faster."

"Can he help you?"

"I don't know. CJ said he might be able to. Nick and Tripp were drinking buddies."

Mannheimer grabbed a pen. "Spell his name and give me his number so I can call him."

"I don't have his number. He left Atlas in January for some firm in Stamford."

He whacked his pen across the pad. "Don't worry. I'll find him."

"I won't get my hopes up."

"Mia, you have to admit that meeting CJ today wasn't a total waste of time."

I sighed, exasperated. "Somehow, Mr. Mannheimer, you always manage to redeem yourself."

He smiled. "Thank goodness because I don't think I could handle your wrath."

I caught the 6:10 train to Overlook, which meant that I wouldn't get back to the cottage until eight o'clock. I bought two magazines and a bowl of mango slices for the journey, but sloped back my head and closed my eyes as soon as I found a seat. After Mannheimer's office, I had loitered around midtown, walking up to 59th Street and then back down again towards Grand Central via Fifth Avenue, and grew depressed. A half-day Friday for many, the streets and stores were eerily quiet. I had a strange sense that everyone was busy—at work or at play—and I had been left behind.

My phone rang five minutes after the train left the station and, seeing it was Oliver, my mood brightened.

"What are you up to?" he asked.

"I'm on the train back to Overlook from the city."

"Oh, I didn't know you were going in. What'd you do?"

"Oh . . . just some . . . errands."

"'Errands' used to be my mother's code word for shopping."

"No shopping for me today—too hot and too tired."

"Are you okay?"

"I'm fine," I reassured him.

"I have a little surprise for you."

"What?"

"I booked a hotel for us to spend next weekend together."

"You did? Oh, Oliver, that's wonderful!" I said. It was the best news of the day, but after a mental check of my work schedule, my excitement fell. "I have to work next Saturday."

"I took care of that too."

"How?"

"I asked Liz if you could have the weekend off."

I stayed quiet.

"Are you upset?" he was quick to ask. "I wanted to surprise

you and Liz is cool. I've known her for a long time."

"No, I'm not upset," I said slowly, resisting my natural tendency for discretion. Who cared if Liz knew what I'd be up to next week? "I'm really, really glad you did. I might have been too embarrassed to ask her myself! Where are we going?"

"Gwen is going to watch Balthazar for the weekend, so I didn't want to go too far away . . ."

"Of course!"

" . . . and I thought you might enjoy a nice weekend in the city because I didn't think you had been there in a while, but you were just there now, so I don't know . . ."

"No! I'd love to spend the weekend in the city."

"I don't mind changing it if you'd like. We could go somewhere else. Maybe the Hamptons?"

"You don't have to change anything," I said, looking at the New York skyline outside the window. "The city with you sounds absolutely perfect."

27.

Oliver and I left for the city right after work on Friday evening, but traffic was light and we crossed the George Washington Bridge in a little over an hour. As he merged onto the West Side Highway, I finally asked the question that had bedeviled me all week. "*Where* are you taking us?"

"Don't worry. I know where I'm going."

"Seriously—*what* are we doing this weekend?"

"It's driving you crazy, right? Not knowing."

"I just want to make sure I packed the right things," I said, thinking about my black carry-on stowed away in the trunk. My downsized closet hadn't automatically transformed me into a light packer, but I didn't want to seem high-maintenance and stuck to a strict script of one casual and one dressy outfit a day.

Oliver took his eyes off the road for a second and smiled. "You'll look great, regardless."

"Thank you, but flattery won't work! If you're taking the West Side Highway, we must be going around here somewhere," I surmised. "The Mandarin Oriental?"

Oliver shook his head.

"Am I at least in the right neighborhood?"

Oliver sighed. "No."

"Okay." I stayed silent until the Frank Gehry-designed IAC building, a mammoth glass-encased beehive of a structure on West 18th Street, came into view. "Now I get it . . . we're probably going someplace downtown."

"Stop!" Oliver begged, laughing. "You're impossible."

"Ah, so I'm getting close!"

"Please stop guessing. *Stop thinking.* Just sit back, relax and enjoy the ride. You'll find out soon enough."

"You're right. Sorry. I'm just a little nervous."

"Don't be. I hope you won't be disappointed."

I smiled. "I'm sure I won't."

I took his advice and reclined my seat, stretching out my legs. What a difference it made to come into the city with Oliver and rekindle those old sensations of excitement and adventure. I was so afraid my relationship to New York had been damaged beyond repair, associating it as I did with my spectacular fall from grace. The lonely train rides to meet Mannheimer also sapped the life out of me since he rarely had anything promising to report. With so many questions revolving around Atlas, Oliver's surprise couldn't have come at a better time. We were going to have a full two days together—with no work, time constraints, or family obligations.

Oliver drove further downtown, turning just behind Broadway and Prince onto Crosby Street, a quieter thoroughfare in the center of SoHo. He guided the car to the front of a handsome brick building with iron-trimmed windows. Its utilitarian design paid tribute to SoHo's industrial past, but the glass and red stone were less weather-beaten than the other buildings on the block. Oliver shut off the ignition and a doorman dashed around the hood to open the passenger door.

"Good evening!" he said, helping me out. "Welcome to the Crosby Street Hotel!"

"Thank you!" I replied, landing gently on the cobblestone street.

A porter inquired about our luggage and Oliver pointed

to the trunk. He hauled our bags out and vanished through the glass doors, leaving me and Oliver on the sidewalk. Chastened, I began to comprehend how my insatiable curiosity could have ruined his careful planning.

"I'm sorry I was so nosy in the car."

Oliver laughed away my apology. "Don't worry about it. Have you ever been here before?"

"No."

"Then I managed to surprise you."

I stroked his cheek. "You didn't have to do this, you know."

He moved my hand to his lips and planted a small kiss. "I wanted to. Why don't you go inside? We can check in after I've parked the car."

I strode through the buzzing lobby where the chairs and sofas—upholstered in off-beat stripes, colors and patterns—reflected my ebullient mood. A big, white steel sculpture of a human head, formed from letters of the alphabet, dominated the space. Guests in the adjacent drawing room lounged in velvet couches, nursing cocktails or quietly escaping into their iPads. How I missed this slice of New York! The unexpected beauty of places like this hotel; the patchwork quilt of people the city attracted; the promise and possibility it espoused, not the ruthlessness that had discarded me. Positive energy seemed to crackle from the purple-painted walls and I devoured it, making up for lost time, until a hand pressed the small of my back.

"There you are," Oliver murmured.

I angled my head towards him and smiled. "I was exploring and got stuck in here."

"Our room's ready. Do you want to go up?"

I had tried not to read too much into our weekend away. We were both mature adults, veterans of bad relationships, and spending forty-eight hours together shouldn't make or break us. But it *was* a big deal—otherwise Oliver wouldn't have left Balthazar for the weekend.

He seemed to notice my apprehension. "Or we can go get a bite to eat."

"Let's do that," I said. "I'm starving after the car ride."

We strolled arm in arm for a few blocks and ended up on Kenmare Street, outside a Mexican restaurant called La Esquina that I had also never been to. It looked like a hole in the wall from the outside, with a tacky neon sign that read "The Corner Deli," but we sat upstairs in the casual café, a room filled with shelves of books and vintage record albums. Suffice it to say that with a DJ playing a clever mix of music, scrumptious tacos in my belly and a few choice glasses of tequila down my throat, I couldn't wait to go back to the hotel.

It was only when I woke up the next morning—ensconced in a cloud of soft sheets and pillows—that I felt relaxed, yesterday's doubts a distant memory. Oliver had nestled his chest against my back and I felt him move.

"What time is it?" he asked.

I looked at my watch. "It's about eleven."

"I can't remember the last time I slept until eleven. Balthazar's usually in my room by seven."

Interlocking his hand with mine, I asked, "Does this qualify as 'lingering'?"

"Definitely."

"I'm glad."

"So what do you want to do today?"

"I'm not sure. We can just stay in the room if you want."

"As tempting as that sounds, I really want to make this weekend special for you, so you decide."

"I'm at a loss. I haven't been following what's happening in the city so much."

"How did you usually spend your Saturdays when you lived here?"

"I usually went for a run in the morning."

"Can't do that—didn't bring my running shoes."

"Then I would eat brunch."

"By yourself?"

"Usually."

"Awwww . . . that's not right. A big brunch is definitely in order. And then what else?"

I thought about my old Saturday routine. It had seemed so indulgent at the time, but I hadn't really done anything special. With David out of the picture and work-related stress, I had gotten lost in my own company, convincing myself that I wasn't lonely.

"I did a little shopping; walked around the city; went to galleries . . ."

"Do you want to do that today?"

"You won't think it's boring?"

"Why would I think it's boring?"

I let out a small laugh. "Because I think you're much more adventurous than I am."

"Me? I'm just a suburban dad," he said, slinking his fingers down my thigh. "And nothing about you is ever boring."

We made it down to brunch around one o'clock and sat outside in the full courtyard, among all the other guests who had also decided to sleep in. Conversation was light and unhurried and we were famished by the time our food arrived.

"I think the best part of staying at a hotel is the breakfast," I said, twisting fresh pepper onto my sundried tomato, feta and spinach frittata. "I love seeing everything served up and having a great cup of coffee that I didn't have to make myself."

"Me too," he agreed.

"And bacon," I continued, looking down at the strips on my plate. "Eating as many as I want."

Oliver laughed. "Balthazar's also a bacon freak. He says the same thing when we go on vacation."

"Do you guys travel together a lot?"

"Not as much as I'd like. It's hard with the store, but I close for two weeks in August and I'm taking him to Barcelona. We'll do a little sight-seeing, hang out at the beach, go to a soccer match—which is what he's really looking forward to."

"Barcelona's great. I was in college the last time I was there, but I still remember the architecture, late dinners, dancing 'til dawn ..."

He winked. "This trip will be the kid-friendly version."

"Where else have you guys been?"

"North Carolina to see my parents, Martha's Vineyard and Florida."

"Disneyworld?"

"Cliché I know, but he loved it."

"Lucky him. I've never been to Disneyworld."

"Really? Barcelona, but never Disney?"

"My mother never took me."

"Did you ever ask her?"

"I did once, in fifth grade, after a bunch of friends had been there for spring break, but she told me Disney was terrible. She was very high-brow and made going to the Met sound much more sophisticated."

"That's funny."

"I've probably been deprived in some way!"

"What was your mom like?"

"Oh, she was wonderful! Beautiful, funny, smart, cultured . . ."

"Like mother, like daughter."

"She was very special. She had high expectations, high standards and was very strong, right to the end."

"You don't talk about her much."

"That's because if I talk about her, I remember how much I love her. How much I miss her." I looked down briefly. "And it makes me sad."

He sighed and shook his head. "I've done it again, haven't I? I have this knack for bringing her up at the oddest moments. Sorry."

"Don't be. I'm so not sad right now!" I paused, my finger charting a circle around the rim of the orange juice glass. "I just think you'll always need your mother, no matter how old you are."

His eyes never left my face as I spoke, but I didn't withdraw. Suppressing my most difficult emotions had become second nature, but with Oliver's probing, these fragments of my history had become something I wanted to cherish, not forget.

"What do you think she would have thought of me?" he asked at last, cutting through his Eggs Benedict.

I was moved that he would care and entranced by the thought—no matter how fanciful—that my mother was still alive to share in my newfound happiness.

"I think she would have loved you."

He smiled. "I hope she would've too."

We must have walked for miles that day—through the quaint streets of SoHo, checking out novelty shops; to the congested quarter of West Broadway filled with tourists; and then on to the circus of Washington Square Park. We bought gelatos to cool off and watched the hodgepodge of street performers, dawdling by a man performing tricks on a unicycle, applauding and yelling loudly when he finished.

"Nothing's changed here in twenty years," Oliver remarked, bending down to place a ten dollar bill into the man's felt hat.

"You know what I want to do?" I asked.

"What?"

"See the wine shop where you worked in college."

"Hanley's?"

I nodded.

"It could be fun to go back," he said, as though he had never considered the idea before. "We're not too far away, so let's go!"

Hanley's Wine & Spirits was located on Seventh Avenue South, on the corner of Charles Street in the West Village. It was on the ground level of a stone building, adjacent to a pizzeria and drugstore. Apartments took up the top floors, their windows and tiny terraces spilling over with colorful potted plants. Oliver nudged the door open, setting off a tinkle of bells.

"Oh, I forgot about those," he said, grinning.

I noticed the floor first, a vivid mosaic pattern of small octagonal tiles. The white pieces had become gray with age, but they—along with the aged wood shelves and plastic vines spiraling the wall—gave the shop an Old World Mediterranean atmosphere.

"I didn't expect it to look like this," I told Oliver, as we walked up an aisle filled with Spanish wines. "I thought it would look more like your shop does—clean, minimalistic, intimidating . . ."

"This shop is like a tired bottle of wine; dusty on the outside, but when you uncork it and take that first sip, it's the best thing you've ever tasted."

Hooking my arm with his, I said, "Did I ever tell you that I could listen to you talk about wine for hours?"

"Well, anything that's worth knowing, I learned here."

"Whatever happened to Mr. Hanley?"

"He retired and bought a vineyard in Chile."

"Who runs this place now?"

"It's gone through several different owners, so I'm not sure anymore."

"Do you regret not taking it over?"

"No, not at all. This place closes at midnight six days a week!"

We continued to meander around the store, perusing different vintages, but when we reached the shelf that sold sake, Oliver got excited.

"Wait a minute. I've got to show you something," he said, moving a few bottles away and peeking further inside. "Ah! It's still there."

"What is it?"

"Come and see."

I poked my head in and saw two initials, "OB," coupled with a peace sign, written in black marker on the wood.

"A peace sign? In the sake section?"

"What can I say? I was really into sake in college."

"Can I help you with anything?" asked a voice behind us.

Oliver and I swerved like two greedy kids caught with our hands in the cookie jar. A middle-aged man with a receding hairline and thin ponytail tapped his foot and raised an eyebrow, eyeing us suspiciously.

"I thought I wanted some sake," Oliver explained, "but I've changed my mind."

"Is there anything else I can suggest?" he asked.

"No, thank you. I think we're fine for now."

"Very well then," said the salesman with a cold stare.

We had no choice but to hightail it out of the shop, exploding with laughter once we reached the safety of the sidewalk.

"Why didn't you just tell him you used to work there twenty years ago? He might have found it interesting, funny even," I said.

"Did that guy look like he had a sense of humor?"

"Not really," I answered, sending us both into another fit of giggles.

"So now that you've seen some of my past," Oliver said, scratching his chin, "it's your turn to show me something."

"What do you want to see?" I asked, still feeling a bit nutty from the scene at Hanley's.

"Your place."

"My place?"

"Your old neighborhood."

"My old neighborhood?"

"Didn't you live in Battery Park City?"

I bit my lip and nodded.

"Let's go check it out! I haven't been down there in years."

"It's too far for us to walk," I said, hoping to discourage him.

"No problem. We can cab it," he said, lifting his arm to hail a taxi.

"But it's so hot."

"Too hot? Do you want to go back to the hotel?" he asked, concerned.

Right then, I knew that my moment of reckoning had come. Battery Park or the hotel—it no longer mattered. Putting on a brave smile, I said, "Not at all! I'll be fine. Let's go."

Oliver flagged down a yellow cab and we stepped inside.

"Battery Park City," I told the cabbie.

The driver mumbled something that sounded like a yes; although it could have also been a response to the person on the other end of his earphones. The air conditioner was turned off and it was steaming hot in the back seat, but the cab had a built-in TV monitor and I watched a clip from a previous episode of the "Today" show. The cabbie careened past the other cars and, with the open windows and faulty latch, I was afraid the door would fly open. Readjusting my seatbelt, I concentrated on Al Roker's cheerful voice.

When the sign for West Thames Park came into view, I told the cabbie, "You can just drop us off here."

"Okay, miss," he replied and the cab came to a screeching halt.

I paid the fare and opened my door before Oliver had a chance to unlock his seatbelt. I had to escape the stifling heat and annoying television; the half-truths and the shame of my past. Storming out of the cab and down the grassy knoll, I heard Oliver call out my name, but kept going, past the bikeway and promenade, weaving my way through all the people lounging and playing in the park. He finally caught up and grabbed my arm so tightly, I was forced to look at him.

"Mia! What the hell is going on with you?"

Confusion was ingrained on his face and I imagined what he must have been thinking. I was flipping out—just like Sophie—and there was nothing I could do to stop it. Hell, I'd been melting down for the past eight months and Oliver was finally seeing the real me.

I wrested my arm away. "You see that building over there?" I cried, pointing to the third high rise behind the park. "That's where my apartment is. That's where I lived. Are you satisfied?"

Oliver glanced perfunctorily at the building and then switched his eyes to me. "Okay, I see it," he said calmly. "Can you please explain what's making you so upset?"

I collapsed onto the grass, plagued by the weight of my predicament and the simplicity of Oliver's decency. If I wanted any chance of going forward with him, I had to tell him everything. He knelt down and put his arm around my shoulders.

Turning, I sobbed into his chest.

Smoothing down my hair, he said, "Mia, it's alright. There's no need to cry. Please tell me what's wrong. I want to help you—if I can."

I pulled back and dried the tears with my hand. "I'm not who you think I am."

"That sounds very serious," he said. "Are you a spy or something?"

"It's serious enough—for me." I paused. "Do you know the real reason why I moved to Overlook?"

"I thought you were taking a career sabbatical."

"I'm not a Wall Street dropout who's taking a 'break'." I paused. "I got fired from my job."

"But getting fired isn't the end of the world!"

"I know, but it happened in a very public and humiliating way. Everybody in the business shunned me and it was impossible for me to get another one."

"What happened?"

Holding nothing back, I told him about Atlas, my relationship with Peter and how threatened I felt when Tripp entered the picture. I also went into detail about the Touchnology trade and how Peter had demoted me.

"So Peter wanted you to report to someone who you thought was less qualified?" he asked.

"Yes, but I also did something really stupid and totally sabotaged my career."

"What could you have possibly done that was so bad?"

My head pounded as the agonizing memory resurfaced. "I threw a cup of water in Tripp's face."

Oliver began laughing. "That's the funniest thing I've ever

heard! I can't even imagine you doing something like that unless he deserved it!"

"It gets worse. Our whole confrontation was recorded on a cell phone—not the water-throwing part—but our argument on the trading floor and it was posted on the Internet . . ."

He winced, all humor gone. "Are you serious?"

I nodded. "I became a laughingstock. Didn't you ever Google me?"

"Of course not! I only Google people I'm thinking of doing business with." He paused. "Did you ever Google me?"

"No. You were too special to Google."

He took my hand. "What you've just told me doesn't change anything, you know."

"Oh, Oliver, there's so much more!"

Now he looked worried. "Like what?"

I pointed back to my apartment building. "I'm renting out my apartment to some big Hollywood producer because I'm broke, flat-out broke. I spent practically everything I ever made and when I lost my job, I could barely pay my bills. Christine offered to let me stay at her house in Overlook rent-free; otherwise, I'd probably be out on the street."

He recoiled at my turn of phrase and who could blame him? I was a woman in crisis and this unfiltered version of my life was so different from the one I had led him to believe.

"Mia, I'm so sorry," he said, after some time.

"I'm sorry, too! I'm sorry I gave you this impression that I was better off than I actually am. *My shit is not together.* I can't pretend anymore."

"Do you think I care that you got fired or that you're in the middle of a rough patch?"

"Maybe you should. I'm a basket case, a total failure."

"My God, Mia, please don't say that about yourself!"

"Why not? That's how I feel."

"Even when you're with me?"

"No! Never when I'm with you, but now that I've told you the truth, you're probably going to see me differently and I wouldn't blame you."

"Do you really think I'm that shallow?"

"I would understand since I haven't been completely up front with you. Not in the same way that you've been up front with me about Sophie and I'm so sorry . . . I just couldn't do it."

He reached out and cupped my face. "Mia, please look at me."

I closed my eyes and the teardrops wormed their way down my cheeks.

"Please," he repeated.

Shame gnawed at me, but I steeled myself to do as he asked.

"In case you haven't noticed," he began, "I've fallen for you. And the woman I've fallen for is funny, smart, beautiful and brave. Other people might have given up, but you picked yourself up and got on with it. Don't start selling yourself short now."

I took in his words, slowly interpreting their significance. Oliver had fallen in love with the Mia I thought was a lesser version of myself.

"I was so embarrassed and ashamed," I whispered. "That's why I never told you the whole story."

"I can understand that, but you don't have to feel that way anymore."

I edged closer to him. "Do you think I would have gotten this worked up about my past if I hadn't already fallen for you, too?"

He grabbed me by the waist and the familiarity of his touch made me feel safe. Our faces met and we kissed, right there in the middle of the park—among all the playing children, runners and picnickers—and I finally felt free from the mental discord of the past eight months. Afterwards, we sat in silence, watching the sky transform from orange to pink to blue-violet, as the sun receded into the horizon.

"So what happens now?" he asked.

I sighed. "I have a lawyer and we've filed a wrongful termination suit, but it'll be tough to prove since I undermined myself by going ballistic on Tripp. He has a new strategy now, though. He thinks insider trading may have played a role in all of this."

"Aha. That would explain their strange behavior. Has your lawyer turned up anything yet?"

"No. And I'm not sure he will."

"What if he does?"

"Hopefully I'll get to clear my name and regain my reputation."

"Does that also mean you'll get a new job and move back to the city?"

I watched the boats sailing along the Hudson River. Such a familiar sight, one of the many cityscapes I had longed to see again.

"I don't know, Oliver. I still have to support myself and trading is the only way I know how."

Neither of us moved. Maybe we were thinking the same

thing: Love and honesty had not granted clarity.

"Well, I hope things will work out in your favor," he said after a while.

"Let's not think about that now." I caught a glimpse of my watch. "My goodness—it's already 8:30! What should we do for dinner?"

"We already missed dinner."

"Did we have a reservation somewhere?"

"Eight o'clock at Eleven Madison Park."

I groaned. It was one of the most-talked about restaurants in the city, with notoriously difficult reservations. I had been dying to go there for years.

"It's my fault. I'm so sorry."

"I'd rather be here with you than sit through a four-hour tasting menu."

"You're just saying that to make me feel better! I promise to make it up to you. We can go there another time."

"Please make the reservation in your name since I'm probably blacklisted for not showing up."

"You planned everything so well. How can I ever thank you for understanding and not judging me too harshly?"

"I would never do that. Let's go back to the hotel," he said, offering his hand.

Taking it, I eased myself up off the ground.

We called for room service and changed into comfy clothes, slipping into bed as soon as we finished eating. Oliver suggested a movie and ordered a creepy thriller with Leonardo

DiCaprio called *Shutter Island.* I tried to stay awake, but the turmoil of the day caught up with me and I drifted into a semi-sleep, albeit with enough consciousness to feel Oliver's kisses on my forehead. I think I also smiled as he traced outlines on my arm. Gradually, the light pecks and tickling grew more insistent. Our clothes came off and we made love in the true sense of the word, but also with a new intensity, an eagerness to explore and release any inhibitions. When we finally fell asleep—sweaty, our tangled limbs partially concealed by the sheets—it was as though we had become intoxicated. That's probably why we didn't hear the phone at first when it rang. It took several seconds for us to figure out it was Oliver's cell and he lunged for it frantically.

"It's Gwen," he said, worry marking each little word. His sister was close to Balthazar. She knew his schedule, habits and preferences as well as Oliver; she wouldn't be calling unless something serious had happened.

He sat up in bed and said straightaway, "Gwen, what's wrong?"

The fear in Oliver's voice was palpable and I tried to console him by massaging his arm.

After several minutes, he exhaled and said, "Okay, I will. Bye."

"Oliver, what happened?" I asked after he hung up.

"It's Sophie."

"What about Sophie?"

"She's back."

"Back where?"

"At my house. She showed up this morning and wants to see Balthazar."

"Oh my God! When was the last time she saw him?"

"A little over a year ago."

"She's done this before?"

"Never without contacting me first."

"Wasn't Balthazar upset the last time he saw her?"

Oliver nodded. "That's why I need to get back home. I'm sorry."

I waved for him leave. "Don't worry about me. You have to be there."

"How will you get back home?"

"I'll ask the hotel to arrange a car."

"You don't have to rush back. Stay in the city longer; enjoy the day."

"I'll try."

It felt like goodbye and we clung to each other. He kissed me hard, bringing his weight down on me, coaxing me onto the bed again. I should have been distraught—this wasn't the time for sex—yet I welcomed him with a willingness that overpowered me.

It was over quickly.

"I love you," he whispered afterwards.

"I love you, too."

Then he rose from the bed and walked to the bathroom. I heard the door shut and swaddled the comforter around me, hoping I would doze off and block out—if only for a few hours—what awaited Oliver back in Overlook.

28.

The hotel ordered an Escalade to drive me back home and once the driver dropped me off, I headed straight to the dining room table where I kept my laptop. After months of silent speculation, I was finally ready. Clicking onto Goggle, I began typing, stringing together words, determined to find details about the mystery woman hanging over Oliver's head just as potently as professional disgrace had been hanging over mine. Since I didn't know Sophie's last name, I tried several different combinations: Sophie + Oliver Bishop; Sophie + French + Morrocan + writer; Sophie + Overlook; Sophie + Raoul's.

The results seemed endless; things that sounded like a perfect match were merely perfect studies in coincidence. There was a Sophie Bishop from Dublin, a crimson-haired woman who kept a weekly blog about life with her three children and two dogs in the Irish countryside. A Dr. Sophie Sommerville turned up as head of the Overlook Oncology Center in Summit, New Jersey. The word "Sophie" attached to anything with "French" unearthed articles for the beautiful French actress, Sophie Marceau. I also came across a photo of a younger Oliver at his old advertising firm, parsing every word of the seven-year old press release announcing he had been promoted to Senior Vice President. The young ad exec in a tieless suit impressed, but the self-assured stance he assumed—hands in pockets, thumbs out—bared scant resemblance to the sensitive man I'd been with hours before. I then viewed every page of The Bishop Cellar's website, searching for pictures of Sophie, but they never materialized.

This irrational exercise continued for nearly two hours. Oliver's Sophie seemed not to have left a digital footprint at all, at least not one that I could track. What were her reasons for showing up now? Coming back into Oliver's life when he finally seemed ready to move on?

I stopped searching when my stomach growled. There wasn't much in the fridge since I had planned on spending the entire weekend with Oliver in the city, but I cobbled together a salad from leftover arugula, tomato and quinoa. Nine hours had passed since Gwen's call, but my weekend with Oliver already seemed faraway, ephemeral. Sophie's reappearance had unsettled me and I closed my eyes to remember his tenderness, his words of assurance. I needed a clue about the state of things and texted a message:

> Got home safely! Thank you for a very special
> weekend. Hope everything is Okay... Love, Mia

I was tempted to resume Googling, but stopped myself, realizing I verged on the obsessive. *But I am obsessed.* I was fully engrossed with thoughts of this woman who had walked out on her son and then waltzed back in when the moment suited her. What was going on at Oliver's house right now? I checked my phone for what seemed like the hundredth time. Three hours after my text, I still had no response. I promised Christine a phone call when I returned from the city and had been putting it off, hoping I'd have better news to report as the evening progressed. But this manic Sophie Derangement Syndrome was threatening my psyche, so I rang her anyway.

"It's about time!" Christine exclaimed once I got her on

the line. "I've been walking around with my cell phone all afternoon."

"Sorry. It's been a long day."

"How was the weekend?"

"I told him everything."

"And what did he say?" she asked, her chipper tone suddenly serious.

"He was very supportive. He said that I had nothing to be ashamed of."

"I've told you the same thing."

"I know, but you're my best friend! I was afraid Oliver would think less of me if he knew the whole story."

"Then he wouldn't be worth your time. You're much more than a high-powered job and fancy apartment!"

"So I'm learning."

"What did you guys end up doing over the weekend?"

"We had a great Mexican dinner on Friday night and spent Saturday walking around downtown. After I dropped the bomb on him, it got late and we missed our dinner reservation, so we hung out in our hotel room."

"That doesn't sound too bad."

"It wasn't." I paused. "He told me he loved me."

"Oh, Mia! What did you say?"

"I actually told him that I loved him back."

"I'm so happy for you! But are you sure about him? In light of everything, are you sure this is what you want?"

"Everything is a leap of faith anyway, isn't it? But yes, I'm in love with him. I've been holding back because of my problems, but he handled it beautifully. This might sound strange, but I feel like we're these two lost souls who found each other . . ."

"It *is* pretty amazing how your paths crossed."

I twirled a loose string from the duvet cover around my forefinger. "But there's a slight problem."

"What kind of problem?"

"His ex showed up on his doorstep this morning while we were still in the city, so we had to cut the weekend short."

"You're kidding, right?!"

"I wish I were."

"She showed up—just like that?"

"She's done it before, about a year ago. It's very disturbing for their son—"

"To say the least! How old is he again?"

"Balthazar's five."

"Umm . . . that's a very delicate age. He's still young, but starting to become more aware of things." She paused. "Have you spoken to Oliver yet?"

"I texted him earlier, but haven't heard back. I feel like I'm in limbo."

"I bet! But I guess there's not much you can do, is there?"

"I feel paralyzed—just waiting and thinking."

"If I were you, I'd just lay low for the moment. Since she just blindsided him, he probably needs some space to deal with it. The last thing he needs is you texting and calling all the time."

"I know," I said.

"Even if, deep-down, that's what you really feel like doing!"

"I'm pathetic, right?"

"No," Christine said. "Just a woman in love."

"Then why does it feel like someone's raining on my parade?"

"Oh, sweetie, I'm sorry. Just hang tight. Do you still want me to come and visit in August?"

"Of course! Nothing will change our annual girls' weekend—it'll just be the low-budget variety."

"Good, because if I don't have some 'me time' soon, I think I'll go nuts!"

After we hung up, I thought about Christine's advice for some time. It would be prudent to step back and let Oliver handle the situation, with no interference from me. Balthazar, an innocent child, would be the one most affected by Sophie's visit. I was an outsider, a grown woman better-equipped to deal with life's surprises. Calmer, I puffed up my pillows and turned off the bedside lamp. After all the tumult, sleep should come if I allowed it.

My eyes opened as soon as I heard the sound of the text message alert on my BlackBerry. I had placed the phone next to me on the bed and it lit up like a beacon.

> Thanks for your message. Sorry, but it's been a long day. Everything's upside down right now, but I'll let you know as soon as things get better. Love, Oliver

I read the message several times, trying to quell my jitters. Christine was right; Oliver's life had been turned inside out. I needed to show patience and give him support, just as he had shown me. I typed back:

> Totally understand. Take the time you need.

I put the phone face-down on the table and lay on my back, knowing full well I was in for a long night.

29.

"Mia! How are you?"

Liz uttered those words on Tuesday morning, more of an order than a polite inquiry. She had charged into the store, inflamed and breathless, which could only mean one thing: *She knew.* Liz knew Sophie was back.

Sorting through papers behind the counter, I put on my armor, the plastered smile that had become like a bad habit in the last year. "I'm fine, thanks. And you?"

"Things could be better."

"It's amazing how much junk mail you get," I remarked, throwing a catalogue away in the recycling bin.

Liz folded her arms across her chest and watched me, gnarling her lips in displeasure.

"It's okay to be pissed," she said. "I sure as hell would be."

"I don't have the right to be pissed."

"And why is that?"

"Sophie was before my time," I said, keeping my voice neutral. "I knew what I was getting myself into, that she wasn't completely gone from their lives. There's nothing I can do."

"Do you want to know how I found out she was back?" Liz asked. "She came to the last-day-of-school assembly! Walked right in with Balthazar as though she had never left."

I tensed up. "Oh . . . *that's* surprising."

"And bold."

"How did she look?" I asked. It was silly to focus on the superficial, but I couldn't help myself.

Liz smirked, satisfied she had finally gotten to me.

"She managed to look like every other mom running around with kids."

"How did the other parents react when they saw her?"

"They're too well-bred to be rude."

"I guess that's a good thing, right? For Bathalzar's sake?"

"No! She's a deadbeat mom!" Liz thundered. "She can't just come back and think everything will be normal again. There are consequences."

"Liz, why are you taking this so personally?" I asked, rocked by the depth of her anger.

"Because what she did was unconscionable! If you—" she began and then stopped.

"If I what?"

She put up her hands in surrender. "Nothing. You're right. I should stay out of this."

"Liz, what were you about to say?" I asked, staring her down.

"If you had children of your own," she whispered, "then you'd understand why I find that woman so offensive."

"That's what I thought you were going to say."

"I'm sorry. It was wrong of me to think that. I shouldn't have brought any of this up," she confessed, shame-faced.

I didn't doubt the sincerity of her apology and said, "Well, I see I'm not the only one with Sophie Derangement Syndrome,"

"What'd you call it?"

"Sophie Derangement Syndrome. She doesn't bring out the best in us."

"Ha! You're taking this a lot better than I thought you would."

"Trust me, I'm not."

"You don't have to be so stoic all the time, Mia."

I shrugged. "What else can I do? I haven't spoken to Oliver since Sophie came back to town. Aside from one text message, I have no idea what's going on. I'm trying to be the bigger person and not just think about myself because there's a child involved. I don't have to be a parent to understand how heavy and potentially damaging this all is. That's why I'm trying to step back and stay calm, even though what I really want to do is run down the street to ask him what the hell's going on!"

"So why don't you?" Liz asked.

"Because I promised to give him time to sort things out."

"That's generous of you."

"I'm not just doing this for him. It's for Balthazar."

Liz joined me behind the counter and put an arm around my shoulder. "Oliver's lucky. You're a better person than I am."

Squeezing her hand, I said, "No—you're the better person for caring so much."

For the rest of the week, as I stood in the store or sat at home, waiting for Oliver to call, I pondered what kept me from reaching out to him. It's not as though I was the other woman. I hadn't started an affair with Oliver while he and Sophie were together, nor had I lured him away from his son and home. Yet I was behaving like the mistress, walking guardedly on Overlook Avenue while also searching for signs of Oliver. I was also petrified of running into Sophie. I still didn't know what she looked like, but what if she had already identified and taken measure of me? This possibility, of course, was predicated on the assumption that Oliver had told her about us. As another weekend approached, I began to feel more vulnerable, finding it increasingly difficult to justify Oliver's silence. He must have known that I had questions and, even if I had *only* been a friend, my concern would have been a logical extension of our friendship.

Oliver finally texted on Sunday morning—it was the Fourth of July and a full week after we last communicated—asking if we could meet that evening. The thought of finally seeing him again ignited a deluge of relief and elation, affirming just how hard I had fallen for him. My pledge to give him space had been genuine, but a week of no contact had resurrected my post-Atlas malaise and it took all my strength not to regress to that empty place again.

It was just getting dark when Oliver arrived and a few firecrackers rocketed across the backcountry sky, bursting into red, white and blue stars.

"Hey," I said, wrapping my arms around his neck. When his body encircled mine, the hollowness of the past week subsided. "How are you?"

He held onto my hand as we walked to the living room couch. "I'm okay."

"Did you do anything special today? It being the Fourth of July and all . . ."

"Just the park," he replied in a bland voice.

"Is there anything I can do to help?"

"No, I feel so badly as it is, bringing you into this . . ."

"You shouldn't," I reassured him. "Would you like some wine?" I asked, pointing to the open bottle of Pinot Noir on the table. Oliver had given me a case for the summer, anticipating al fresco dinners in the garden.

He shook his head. "I'm sorry I haven't called."

"It's all right. How's Balthazar?"

Rubbing the nape of his neck, he said, "Maybe I will have some wine. Do you want one too?"

"Sure."

He filled our glasses and took a mouthful.

"Are you sure you're okay?" I asked, placing a hand on his knee.

He closed his eyes briefly. "Not really."

"Do you want to talk about it?"

He nodded, but made no move to speak.

"What happened when you got home last Sunday?" I prodded.

"They were all in the back yard, watching Balthazar ride his bike."

"Really? That doesn't sound so bad."

"I know. I was expecting worse, but Gwen told me that she'd had it out with Sophie, tried to get her to leave—at least until I came back—but Balthazar was already awake and came to the front door. When Sophie saw him, she refused to go and Gwen didn't want to make a bigger scene, so she let Sophie come in. That's when I got the call."

Did you tell Sophie where you'd been? I wanted to ask. Did you tell her about us?

"What happened next?"

"After I got back to Overlook, Gwen left and I asked Sophie why she'd come."

"What did she say?"

"She said she missed her son."

It was a vapid statement and I could finally comprehend Liz's distaste for Sophie. "I'm sorry, Oliver, but she can't just choose to parent when it suits her."

"I know. I said as much to her, but Balthazar—"

"How did he take her coming back this time?" I interjected. "She's putting him through an emotional rollercoaster."

"But that's the thing: He didn't seem traumatized by her visit this time. There was no crying or holding on to me. He was"—Oliver paused— "*curious*. He seemed more curious about her than anything else."

"Is that why you let her take him to school?" I blurted out.

He nodded, expressing no surprise that I knew.

"Then *why* did she come back?" I demanded. "Did she explain why she came back now?"

He stared into his glass, as though the answer waded in the depths of the red liquid. "She said she wanted to be a part of Balthazar's life again."

"And what did you say?"

He finally looked at me again, giving the barest of shrugs. "What could I say?"

I shrugged back in response. "I don't know. What did you tell her?"

"I told her it was going to take time. She couldn't undo three years just like that. He was so young when she left and I'd have to feel that I could trust her. So, she and Balthazar have been getting reacquainted with each other this past week."

"Has she been staying at your house?"

"Yes, in the guest room."

"I guess that explains why you didn't call."

"I wanted to, but things have been so chaotic . . ."

"Did you tell her about us?" I asked.

"Yes."

"What did you say?"

"I told her that I'd met someone else."

Something in his voice—a certain frailty—made me inch away. He didn't say "I've fallen in love with a woman named Mia." He had reduced our relationship to two words: *someone else*. I had become undefined, a generalization. I thought my reaction was imperceptible, but Oliver noticed. Putting down his wine glass, he looked at me with pained expression.

"Mia—"

My lower lip began to quiver uncontrollably. "What?"

"I love you," he said. "Don't ever doubt that I love you."

I held up my hand. "Just tell me. What do you want to say?"

"Sophie," he began, lowering his head. "Sophie and I have decided to try being a family again."

Shock closed in like a noose around my throat and I wasn't sure I could breathe, let alone speak. Oliver's words were from left field; they belonged to someone else. He couldn't possibly go back to her, not after last weekend.

"I don't understand . . ." I said, giving him a reprieve, a chance to disavow that last sentence.

"We're going to try again," Oliver whispered.

"Was last weekend just a game for you?" I asked, my voice rising. "Because I feel like a fool!"

"Please don't say that."

"What else am I supposed to think? I know it would have been unrealistic for me to assume that Sophie wouldn't be a part of Balthazar's life again at some point, but this—*this!* How can I not think you turned to me out of convenience and the minute Sophie reappeared, you went running back to her!"

"I swear to you it didn't happen like that!"

"Then give me a better explanation."

"Balthazar wants her back. He wants to have a mother again. If you saw them together again, you'd understand—"

I gasped in shock. "How can you even say that to me?"

"The part of me that loves you, that wants to be with you, doesn't want to do this. But Balthazar's never been so responsive to Sophie before—not even when he was a baby. And she's changed. She seems more at peace, less selfish. My son wants her to stay. He wants to have a normal family. I've always thought that I was enough, that I could be both mom and dad, but after all he's been through, I can't *not* give this a chance. I don't think I could forgive myself if I didn't try."

"Are you only doing this for Balthazar?"

His gaze dipped to the floor.

"Oliver, is Balthazar the only reason you're letting her stay?"

"I don't know." Pause. "Maybe there's still something there."

I sprang from the couch and stopped in front of the oil painting by the drinks trolley. "All last week," I began, gazing at the bluebirds in the picture, "I thought about you and Balthazar, feeling horrible for the way your lives had been disrupted again. I didn't call, didn't nag because I trusted you. I believed everything you told me. It never once occurred to me that you would take her back!"

Oliver walked over to where I stood. "Mia, please listen

to me. After last weekend, all I wanted to think about was us."

"I could kick myself for believing your feelings for me were strong enough."

"Everything I said was true."

"Then why are you walking away from it?" I asked, voice breaking.

"You told me once that you never stop needing your mother. If I don't do this now, if I don't do this for Balthazar—before you and I get any deeper—then it'll be harder for me. I don't think I'd be able to give you up. And I don't know if I could live with that guilt."

He was choosing his son over me. It was the natural thing to do, the noble thing to do.

"Please leave," I said.

"Mia—"

"You're ending this, so let's make it clean," I said, trying to push him away.

He stayed rooted in place. "If I said I wished things had turned out differently, would you believe me?"

"It really doesn't matter now, does it? You want Balthazar to have a normal family. I can't compete with that."

"And you shouldn't have to," he murmured. "I'm so sorry that I put you through this."

I refused to look at him and heard the front door close seconds later. That's when I splintered into pieces, each shard a reminder of the pain and disappointments.

"Not again," I sobbed. "Not again."

30.

It was a small blessing the shop was closed the next morning. My head was clogged with grief and I couldn't bear Liz's well-meaning questions. I'd sat on the couch for hours after Oliver left, emptying that bottle of Pinot Noir, and trying to piece together a chronology of what had transpired between us. At what point did Oliver realize he was still into his ex? Before or after he'd slept with her again? I wasn't stupid; reconciliation wouldn't have happened without intimacy and that thought, after our own transformative weekend, gutted me. I finally made a cup of tea and called Christine.

"It's over," I said, when she picked up.

"Your case?" she asked and then, after a cautious hesitation I did not try to fill, "Is it Oliver?"

"Yes," I whispered.

"Oh, sweetie, what happened?"

"He ended it last night."

"Because of Sophie?"

"She wants them to be a family again and he agreed."

"Whoa . . . I'm in shock."

"So am I."

"How can he go back to her after what she did?"

"Balthazar wants his mommy back." It came out like a contemptuous nursery chant.

"But there must be some other way, some compromise or shared custody . . ."

"Unless Oliver isn't completely over her."

"He said that?"

"'Maybe there's still something there.' I think those were his words."

"Damn, Mia, that's just about the most screwed up thing I've ever heard!"

"I agree, but maybe I'm incapable of understanding this overarching sense of parental responsibility Oliver has," I said, moving from the kitchen to an armchair. "He wants to give Balthazar a normal family. *He* wants to be a normal family."

"I'm a parent and would never take Rob back if he walked out on us!"

"But what if he had an affair and wanted you to forgive him?"

"That's different."

"Is it? Wouldn't you put your hurt and anger aside for your children's sake? To keep your family together?"

Christine was silent for several seconds and then sighed. "Maybe I would—if Rob was genuinely sorry and promised never to do it again."

"Maybe that's what Sophie said."

"Why are you making excuses for her? For them?"

"I'm trying to understand his thought process, because none of it makes sense after our weekend in the city. The park, our nights in the hotel—it feels like my heart's been split open."

"Oh, Mia, I'm so sorry!"

"Remember David?" I asked her. "We seemed so perfect together, but when it ended, I had my job, so it was easier to move on. With Oliver, I was stripped down, freed from whomever I was trying to be all those years, and I started to believe that all the missteps—Atlas and my moving here—were fate, as though everything happened to bring us together."

"I thought you guys really had a connection too . . . I just don't get it."

"Maybe we were just two lost souls who had great sex." I paused. "Can I ask you something?"

"Of course!"

"Which is worse: a deadbeat mom or a disgraced trader?"

"Do you even have to ask?! Do you think he ended things because of what you told him last weekend?"

"I'm trying to figure out why things changed and wonder if that might be the reason."

"He's damaged; there's nothing you could do to fix that."

"Then I guess we were doomed to fail."

"Not if she hadn't come back. It would have worked if she hadn't come back."

"For a while maybe, but then she would have showed up at his doorstep sooner or later."

"Or *your* doorstep. You guys might have been living to-gether by then."

"Oh, Christine, I never thought that far ahead!"

"Really? The thought never entered your mind?"

I massaged my temples for a few seconds, a silly attempt to cleanse my brain of what I was about to confess. "I did think about a future with Oliver. I thought about what it would be like to be a step-mom. I even thought about us having kids of our own."

"Oh, Mia!"

"Do you see why I feel like such a fool?"

"You could never be a fool. It's his loss, believe me!"

"I feel like we both lost out."

"Listen, I don't think you should be alone right now. I can

probably find a sitter to watch the kids for a few days and get to New York by Wednesday at the latest."

"Seriously, Christine, you don't have to come now. I'm done falling apart. I've got to focus on getting my life back on track. This whole thing with Oliver has already taken too much time and energy. I must be doing something wrong. My job, relationships . . ."

"You've done nothing wrong, especially not with Oliver. It's other people. We can't predict how they'll behave. That's the risk of getting close."

"Well, I'm finished with all that."

"What will you do now?"

"The first thing I want to do is get the hell out of Over-look." Saying the words out loud gave me a purpose, a sense that I still had some control over my life. "I'm so grateful for this beautiful cottage and everything you've done for me, Christine, but I can't stay in this town anymore. I can't be here when he's with *her*."

"I don't blame you, but where will you go? What will you do?"

"I don't know yet. I really don't know."

"Oh, Mia, I was just about to call you," Mannheimer told me when he answered the phone.

"You're always 'just about to call' whenever I call you first. What have you got to report?"

"I tracked down Nick Vamvakis."

"Where is he?"

"He's working for a new firm called Rittenhouse Square Asset Management."

"Rittenhouse Square?"

"Have you heard of it?"

"No, but I'll bet a hundred bucks the founder went to Wharton. Rittenhouse Square is a neighborhood in Philly."

"Ummm . . . let me check my notes," Mannheimer paused. "Firm's been around since 2001, started by a Neil Connors, '93 Wharton MBA, so you were right! Rittenhouse is one of those macro funds where they take bets on the market as a whole . . ."

"I know what a macro fund is," I said through gritted teeth.

"Sorry. Anyway, Nick is one of their portfolio managers and they're based out of Washington Boulevard in Stamford. Not far from his house in Greenwich."

"He was never thrilled with the commute."

"I don't think he left just because of the commute."

"What do you mean?"

"I spoke to Vamvakis."

"You actually got a hold of him and now you're telling me?!"

"I only spoke to him last night. Believe me, I *was* about to call you."

"What did Nick say?" I asked impatiently.

"He wasn't exactly in the mood to talk."

"Did you call him on his cell or at work?"

"I don't have his cell, so I had to call him at Rittenhouse."

"Then of course he wasn't in the mood to talk! First CJ and now Nick; you have to stop ambushing people at their places of business. What did you ask him?"

"Standard questions: How well did he know you? Did he know why you got fired? How well did he know Tripp and Peter? And, did he suspect any funny business at the firm?"

"That last question couldn't have gone over so well."

"He was cagey with all his answers, sounded like he barely knew you."

"That's ridiculous! We sat across from each other for two years. I knew the name of his kids, for God's sake!"

"Well, the only thing he would say is that he knew you professionally, but never reported to you."

"I can't believe he's still following the company line."

"He said a confidentiality agreement prevented him from discussing the activities at his old firm. And that if he did say anything that could possibly cast a negative light on Atlas, not only could he be sued, he would also be putting his current job in jeopardy."

"Well, I guess that's it then. He's got a family and all that . . ." *Family* seemed to be the word of the day.

"I still think he was trying to tell me something," Mannheimer said.

"I thought he was vague."

"But he used an interesting choice of words: *cast a negative light on Atlas.*" Mannheimer made a clucking sound. "My gut tells me there's something fishy with your old firm."

"Mine does too, but if Nick isn't willing to help us, then we'll probably never find out. He was our last hope."

"Don't say that. There's always hope. As my friend Rev. Jackson says, 'Keep hope alive.'"

"Really, Mr. Mannheimer?"

"Mia, please be patient—"

"All I've been is patient! But the more time that goes by, the more my case weakens and I've reached my limit. This is my life we're talking about and"—I took a deep breath—"my career's all I've got. If you don't come up with something concrete in the next couple of weeks, I'll have to look for a new lawyer."

With that, I muted Mannheimer before he could rattle off more inane phrases of reassurance.

31.

I called in sick on Tuesday with a curt text message to avoid any direct interaction, but Liz mollified me with her sympathetic response: Feel better and focus on yourself. Let me know if I can do anything! Her tone seemed to imply knowledge about the demise of my relationship with Oliver. Maybe she had seen him and Sophie running errands at Overlook Commons; or noticed Sophie playing with Balthazar in the park. My foolishness and naïveté, the easy way I had let down my defenses haunted me. But even as I berated myself, I knew why I fell in love with Oliver. I had recognized a kindred spirit; someone who had suffered loss, but soldiered on. I still couldn't fathom how things had changed so quickly and the mental upheaval was making it difficult to function. I think that's what prompted my spontaneous decision to drive out to Stamford and confront Nick Vamvakis. I couldn't stay home feeling sorry for myself. I needed to act.

I reached Exit 6 on the Connecticut Turnpike at about three in the afternoon. I'd been to Stamford only a handful of times, but dialing the 203-area code had been a constant in my former life. Tax breaks had lured hedge funds, private equity, and trading firms to the area, turning it into one of the country's largest financial districts outside of New York City. It also didn't hurt that a large swath of these high-flyers lived in the grand, multi-million dollar homes gracing the nearby towns of Greenwich and Darien.

Rittenhouse Square Asset Management was located on Washington Boulevard, inside an office park with a security guard booth and one of those beam barriers that go up and down. I decreased speed and began to lose my nerve. What if the guard would only let me through if I had an appointment? I definitely couldn't announce myself and ask for Nick. He would refuse to see me, might even ask the guard to eject me from the premises. No, I had to be sly about it.

"Hello!" I said cheerily, sliding down my window. It was like an oven outside and the thick heat infiltrated my car. Temperatures had soared to 103 degrees; power outages and malfunctioning traffic lights were causing havoc throughout the region.

"Can I help you, Ma'm?" asked the guard wearily, a tan, dark-haired guy with the name Hector on his brass chest tag.

I could see flecks of perspiration under his arms and sweat trickled from his brow, in spite of the small fan on the control panel. A large sign in front of me contained a list of businesses in the complex. I skimmed through it and found an alibi worth trying.

"I have an appointment with Long Ridge Mammography," I fibbed.

"Sure, go right in," the guard said, pressing an orange button to raise the barrier. He knew better than to question a woman and her mammogram.

"Thank you," I replied, with a sliver of guilt.

The front lot was packed with cars, but I zigzagged a few times until a blue Mercedes backed out of a space in the last row. I parked, nose-out. It was a good spot; far enough from the gate for me not to be seen, yet affording a good view of the people entering and exiting the building. I glanced at my watch: 3:24. Nick could theoretically come out any time between now and 7:00PM. I sighed, switched the station from music to NPR and hunkered down to wait.

Two hours passed without a Nick sighting and then the automatic sounds of car doors unlocking signaled that people were heading home *en masse*. I sunk lower in the driver's seat, observing the exodus. The usual suspects in polo shirts and fleece vests (in this heatwave!) trooped down the walkway to their cars, but Nick wasn't among them. A group of young women had also congregated by a fountain in front of the building. I could tell they were summer interns by their sensible Ann Taylor suits. A few had already shed their pumps for flip-flops. One even had the gall to smoke. I couldn't stop gawking at them. These would be the women applying for Wall Street jobs in the fall. Women who thought they would be the ones to break the glass ceiling; be taken seriously by their male colleagues; and successfully balance career, marriage and family. I felt like marching over and shaking every one of them. "Run," I would say. "It'll only be a matter of time before they screw you over."

Nick finally surfaced at 6:30, but he wasn't alone and chatted to a shorter guy with a crew-cut. *Please don't let them get into the car together,* I thought. I had no desire to stake out Rittenhouse Square again. They parted company when Crew Cut got into a Prius and Nick continued towards the opposite end of the lot from where I had parked. I tailed him, undetected, until he stopped at a silver BMW. I turned off the ignition and got out, gently shoving the door so it closed without making any noise. Nick had gotten sidetracked and was checking something on his BlackBerry, so I advanced slowly, standing several inches behind him.

"Nick," I said, tapping him on the back.

He twisted his head and cried, "Jesus, Mia! You scared the shit out of me!"

"Sorry." He was leaner and browner from a summer tan, but I saw veins protruding on his temples. "How've you been?"

He glanced from left to right, as though he didn't want anyone to see us talking. "I already told your lawyer that I have nothing to say."

"I know."

"Then why are you here? *In Stamford?* At my job?"

"I'm not stalking you! But I was afraid you wouldn't want to talk to me if I called."

"I don't know what happened between you and Atlas, but I don't want to get involved."

"Nick, I'm not asking you to get involved. I just want to talk. I feel like they pushed me out and I still don't understand why. It wasn't fair—not after all the years I put in. Not after all the money I made for that firm. I was good at my job. Tripp undermined me and should've been the one out the door. Not me."

"Mia, I was there. I saw the video. I also heard you threw water in his face!"

"He provoked me!"

"Yeah," Nick sneered, "he could be a provocative jackass at times."

"What's that supposed to mean?"

He shrugged. "Nothing."

"Nick, why'd you leave Atlas?"

He checked over his shoulder. "Listen, we can't talk here."

"So you *are* willing to talk to me."

"I'm willing to *listen* to you, but we have to go someplace else."

"Just tell me where and I'll go."

He lifted the door handle of his BMW. "Follow me in your car."

I tailgated him from the gentrified, commercial streets of downtown Stamford to a dodgier strip, where a daycare center shared the same block as a bodega and laundromat. These two parts of town were only a few miles away, but the socio-economic disparity was total. Nick was taking me to the hood; the only place no one he knew would see us. He turned left into a KFC and, if I wasn't so desperate, I would have been pissed.

"Is this your way of slumming it?" I asked once I met up with him inside the restaurant. It was air-conditioned, but the scent of chicken and grease was rampant and I knew it would stick to our clothes.

Nick ignored me and ordered a Diet Coke. Just to spite him, I ordered a 3-piece meal with mashed potatoes and cole-slaw. I joined him at a table in the back, close to the restrooms and away from the main entrance. He sat, hunched over, sipping his drink.

"Nick, you don't have to look so uncomfortable. I'm not gonna bite. You were one of the people at Atlas I really liked and respected. You weren't an asshole then, so please stop acting like one now."

He let go of the straw and exhaled. "You're right. I'm sorry. This is just a little weird for me."

"Being at KFC?"

"No! I come here all the time with my kids after soccer practice."

I opened the box with my extra-crispy chicken. "How are they?"

His expression untightened for the first time. "Great, growing up way too fast."

"Your family must love having you so close by now."

He nodded. "My quality of life has increased tenfold. I can drop them off at school a couple of mornings a week; step out for an hour or two if there's a performance; and then get back to work. I could never do that at Atlas. I realized I was missing so much of their childhood and you can never get that back."

"Is that the only reason you left Atlas?" I asked.

"Hey, I left them on good terms," he emphasized. "Peter gave me an excellent reference."

"I can't really say the same."

"Listen, did I think it was weird that Peter let you go like that? Of course I did. We all did! Everyone knew how far back you went, so you must have done something pretty drastic for him to cut you off like that."

"I don't regret throwing water in Tripp's face for one second, if that's what you mean."

Nick chuckled. "I would've paid to see that."

"Weren't you and Tripp good friends? You guys hung out a lot."

"We only went out for drinks."

"So you weren't close?"

"We're very different."

"Can you be more specific?"

"Mia, you sound like you're interrogating me!"

"Sorry," I said, dipping a crunchy piece of white meat in

barbecue sauce. "You don't have to answer that if you don't want to."

"I think the answer's pretty obvious. I'm married with three kids and live in the suburbs. Tripp's a party guy. He doesn't have a wife and kids to answer to, so late nights, alcohol, girls . . . I couldn't do that shit." He shrugged. "I didn't want to either."

I remembered the occasions when Tripp didn't show up for our morning meetings. "Do you think it affected his work?"

"I don't know."

"Nick, you're a stand-up guy; you must have had some opinion about it."

"I left him a couple of times when he was pretty wasted. I think it's hard to do your job effectively after a late night of drinking and there's a lot of money at stake, but Tripp wasn't worried. He said he could handle it."

"Did you know why Tripp and I locked horns?"

Nick shook his head.

"It was over a specific trade, a massive position on a company called Touchnology Systems."

"Weren't they recently acquired by a Japanese tech giant?"

I nodded. "But last fall, we were sitting on almost twenty million dollars' worth of shares."

"Damn—that was some bet."

"It was our biggest position and I had my doubts about Touchnology, so I wanted Tripp to get out, but he didn't follow the stop-limit. He was so sure of himself—even when the stock went in the other direction—and he managed to convince Peter too."

"I guess he made a good call, given the acquisition," Nick

said.

I looked at Nick without blinking. "But was it just a good call?"

"If this is going where I think it is, you can count me out," he said and started to get up.

"Nick, wait!" I pleaded, grabbing his hand. "Just tell me if you think Tripp was capable of insider trading."

"Are you wearing a wire, Mia?" he asked, eyes blazing with anger. "Because I'm not going down with this."

"Of course not!" I assured him. "But if you know anything about what happened, it could really help me."

He slouched into the seat again. "I hope you're being up front with me, because I respect you too. I think Atlas robbed you, so I'm putting everything on the line with what I'm about to tell you." He paused. "But if anything happens to me or my career because of this, you will have hell to pay."

"You can trust me."

"Putnam Dixon." His lips barely moved; the words came from somewhere in the back of his teeth.

"What?" I asked. "Who's that?"

"Putnam Dixon," he repeated. "That's the last time I'm gonna say it."

I took a pen from my bag and wrote it down on a napkin.

Nick got up again and this time I could tell it was for good. "I wish you well, Mia. I really mean that."

He left KFC from the side entrance, but I stayed at the table, finishing up my meal. Nick's caginess had made me paranoid, so I waited until I was in my car to Google Putnam Dixon on my BlackBerry. I had expected a posh law firm, but the only hit that made sense was the Putnam Dixon Group, an expert network firm that connected investors with industry experts. *Some of the very same experts that worked for the companies a trader might be looking to invest in.* Of course I was familiar with the practice of using these expert networks as part of the investment due diligence process, but I had never retained one, and didn't think Peter had either during my time at Atlas. These networks were an unchecked domain where the potential for conflict—or corruption—was rife. Was Putnam Dixon Tripp's black edge? I dialed Mannheimer's number and it went straight to voice mail. He was probably avoiding me after last night's tongue-lashing, but I decided to leave him a message anyway, if only to prove how effective I could be acting alone.

"Mr. Mannheimer, it's Mia. I just met with Nick Vamvakis and he gave me a lead. Something called the Putnam Dixon Group. They're one of those expert network firms that investors use when they want to get more insight about a specific company or industry. I think Tripp used them and we need to look into it." Just to be nice, I added, "Thanks."

32.

Nick's clue made it impossible for me to go to bed when I got home. Armed with a cup of tea and a bag of biscotti, I sat at the dining room table with my laptop and immediately went on the Putnam Dixon Group's website. Seeing it properly now, in its entirety and not in the limited format on my small Black-Berry screen, sent my mind into overdrive. I was convinced the truth—about Tripp, his plan, why I was fired—was hidden somewhere in that Website. Biting into a biscuit, I began at the most logical place: "About."

> Wouldn't you want to have as much information as possible in order to make an informed decision? Putnam Dixon is a leading research firm linking corporations, investors, consultancies and nonprofits with relevant expertise in a wide range of industries. Through our extensive network of industry experts, we provide access to top-tier professionals who can supply knowledge and insight critical to helping shape your business and achieving the best possible outcomes.
>
> Our experts are industry-focused, domestic and international executives, physicians, scientists, engineers, attorneys, policy analysts and market researchers who share their knowledge with decision-makers through telephone consultations, surveys, seminars, and face-to-face meetings. Putnam Dixon

adheres to a rigorous compliance policy and every
interaction between our clients and experts must
conform to the rules of proper engagement.

It was a persuasive spiel. Each section—solutions, experts,
practice areas and research—was cloaked in impressive gener-
alities, but with just enough meat to entice potential clients. An
equity trading firm interested in the tech industry would only
have to connect with one of Putnam's experts to gain valuable
intelligence on trends and price targets, which could inform an
investor's decision to long or short the stock. The very nature of
this expert/client relationship relied on non-public information to gain a competitive edge, but as long as no *material, non-
public* information was disclosed, like secret revenue numbers
or earnings per share, why wouldn't an investment firm hire a
Putnam Dixon expert?

Yet I couldn't shake my skepticism. These expert network
firms flew under the radar. I doubted many people outside
of Wall Street had ever heard of them. They also charged a
pretty penny, anything from $250-$1000 an hour for expert
consultations. It was a small price to pay if those consultations enabled a firm to profit from a trade or, at the very least,
avoid a loss. Atlas had received many calls from similar expert
network firms that we turned away because Peter and I considered them a waste of time and money. If they were calling on
Atlas, then they were soliciting business from our competitors
as well. What leverage would we have gained from an expert's
boilerplate analysis if we didn't have access to more detailed,
confidential information? The type of information that vio-
lated insider trading laws.

Even if Tripp had used an expert network firm in an un-scrupulous way, had Peter known about it? More importantly, had he sanctioned it? This whole day had spooked me; staking out Nick, our secret meeting, that cryptic tip about Putnam Dixon ... The whole thing reeked of dealings that, even if not technically illegal, raised questions about the ethics at Atlas. David Warren would not have been surprised. He always be-lieved the way we made money was morally reprehensible, even if it was legal and followed protocol. It had been a sore spot in our relationship, but I always found coverage in the legality of our business transactions.

My cell buzzed. It was Mannheimer and I answered mid-ring.

"I guessed you'd still be up," he said.

"I've been on the Putnam Dixon Website since I got home."

"Well, I never made it home. I'm still at the office. I've been researching expert network firms for hours."

"It's almost midnight!"

"I know, but I'm riveted, riveted that this is all legal!"

His voice was full of passionate, anti-Wall Street indigna-tion, so I tried to add a dose of objectivity. "But if used prop-erly, these firms can provide a valuable service—"

"Oh, Mia, stop being so damn diplomatic! Something's rotten in Denmark and you know it as well as I do!" He paused. "Do you how firms like Putnam Dixon came into being? Do you remember Regulation Fair Disclosure back in 2000?"

"Reg FD? Absolutely. It required all publicly traded com-panies to disclose material information to all investors at the same time."

"As opposed to the selective information they were disclosing before."

"Yes, companies played favorites and the big institutional investors often got market-moving information before individual, private ones."

"Main Street investors, people like me. Maybe I'm crazy, but shouldn't the concept behind Reg FD been a given?"

"It defied logic, I agree."

"It was another way for them to rig the system in their favor; that's all."

Mr. Mannheimer's "them" always sounded so sinister. Sometimes I think he forgot I was technically a part of "them" and that he was working to bring me back into "their" club.

"But Regulation FD put an end to that," I argued. "It brought more transparency and leveled the playing field for all investors."

"What do you think about Global Settlement that followed three years later?"

"Another plus. It put a Chinese wall between research and investment banking."

"Again—maybe I'm stupid—but how did investment bankers get away with pressuring research analysts to put a positive spin on the stock recommendations they were pitching?"

"It was a clear conflict of interest, no doubt."

"But you know what those regulations left?"

I considered the repercussions of both rules and replied, "A void."

"Exactly! Wall Street's knowledge base was significantly reduced, so they needed other sources of information."

"And the expert networks filled that void. But they're legal, Mr. Mannheimer," I reminded him. "The SEC hasn't shut them down."

"But they could be the lynchpin to God knows how many insider trading cases!"

"I only care about one."

"So do I! And I think Nick has given us the lead we need. Good work, Mia, even if I think it was unwise of you, as the plaintiff in this suit, to confront him directly like that."

"I know. It was a rash decision."

"Tripp must have had a contact at Putnam! He must have persuaded someone to pass along confidential information to him about Touchnology or the Japanese company that would eventually acquire it."

"But the experts at these firms are given strict guidelines as to what would constitute a breach of duty. Let's see here," I said, clicking on Terms and Conditions. "They can't discuss confidential information like earnings forecasts, corporate strategies, new product developments, unpublished clinical trials, proposed mergers and acquisitions . . . The list goes on and on. And this is on top of the confidentiality agreements they've already signed with their primary employers. Putnam is even so blunt as to say that when in doubt, shut down the discussion and notify them immediately."

"That's all well and good, but I'm not condemning the firm. I'm saying that someone—an *individual* there—must have been on the take. These are strange times we're living in. We're still in the middle of the worst financial crisis since the Great Depression: people's savings have depreciated; unemployment could hit ten percent; the housing market is still weak ... I don't think these experts are doing as well as they did five or six years ago, when everything was so gung-ho! Why wouldn't someone be tempted to cross the line and give up a little bit of information in exchange for money or gifts?"

"It's just such a big risk to take—on both sides!"

"Not if you think you won't get caught. Not if you've been grooming that contact for a long time, befriended them, gained their trust."

"I still don't believe Peter would have approved."

"Mia, let me ask you something and please don't get your feathers all ruffled." Mannheimer paused. "How well did you really know Peter?"

"I worked with the man for fifteen years!"

"Fair enough, but how stable were his finances?"

I thought of Peter's weekend sanctuary, his love of art, wine and travel. "He seemed ... *rich*." The label sounded incredibly juvenile, but there was no need to understate it. Peter lived the good life on a grand scale.

"Like you?" Mannheimer asked.

I bristled at the comment, but I understood Mannheimer's intent.

"Are you implying Peter might have been overleveraged?"

"Do you know how many hedge fund managers have had to file for bankruptcy? Women who've had to sell their gold jewelry for cash?"

"Everything isn't as rosy as it seems. I can certainly attest to that," I said, my own Ebay fire sale coming to mind.

"And you don't really know a man until you check his debts."

"In other words, if Peter was carrying too much debt, he

might have been persuadable."

"Exactly."

"I feel duped," I said, thinking about all the people I'd trusted who weren't what they claimed to be. "I should be found guilty of stupidity."

"It's not your fault! They ran circles around you with their lies, but you're not like them. You'll feel better when we get to the bottom of this mess."

"Where do we begin? Putnam Dixon has"—I looked at my screen—"almost fifty full-time employees and can tap into a network of one thousand experts. How will we ever find who Tripp was talking to? It's like looking for a needle in a haystack."

"We'll just have to narrow the list of possibilities. First of all, Tripp must have used a tech expert."

I clicked on the tab with Putnam Dixon's practice areas. "They have two hundred and eighteen experts in technology, media and telecom."

"That's better than having to look through a thousand. Can you tighten the search even more?"

"It was probably someone with expertise in hardware."

"That narrows it down further."

"And maybe even experience in Asia," I said, filtering my search by regional expertise.

"How many does that leave you with?"

"Thirty-six possibilities."

"We can start with them."

"How can you possibly get in touch with all these people?"

"Leave that to me. I have a couple of investigators that I've used on other things."

"I don't have the money to pay for outside investigators!"

"We can sort that out later. I don't want to back down. I just want to get those scumbags."

"Thirty-six 'experts'," I repeated. "Can I help you contact them?"

"No. I don't want you involved."

"But it's my life! I can't just sit and wait. I have to do something!"

"Mia, that's exactly my point. You're too emotionally invested in this. It can lead to mistakes. You might scare someone off, make them suspicious."

Mannheimer was right. In order to track down and interview thirty-six people, one had to be cold and methodical. I couldn't be truthful about my identity or present the real reason for my inquiry. I didn't know what kind of questions to ask. I was even uncomfortable telling white lies. This stealth operation required a level of deception I didn't possess.

"Mia?"

"Yes."

"Just leave this to me, okay?"

I sighed. "Okay."

"And I meant what I said: Good job."

"Thank you," I whispered and hung up. I closed down my laptop and cleaned up the tea and biscuits from the table. It was no surprise that Nick hadn't wanted to speak to anyone. If this thing with Tripp really went as deep as we suspected, more livelihoods were at stake than I had bargained for. What if I brought down Atlas to save myself? Could I have that on my conscience?

It was almost one in the morning and I wished I could

talk to someone about my ambivalence, the vacillating guilt about my relentless pursuit of Atlas. Except the person I most wanted to speak to was home with his family.

33.

"Mia, do you realize you've been wiping that bowl for the past five minutes?"

Liz's voice interrupted my trance. The heat wave brought in fewer customers, so we had taken on the tedious task of cleaning out all the shelves and display cases. I appreciated the robotic chore—lift, wipe, replace—since it enabled me to escape into the mysterious world of network experts.

"Um, thanks for letting me know."

"I think we need a break." She walked to the front door, locked it shut and turned the sign over from "Open" to "Closed."

"Sorry, Liz, but it's too hot to go outside."

"Who said anything about going outside?" she asked, heading towards the back staircase.

I dropped the dust cloth and followed Liz downstairs, where she plucked a bottle of rosé, slab of Gruyère cheese and a carton of red grapes from the mini-refrigerator. She poured rosé into disposable cups and we availed ourselves of the heat with a few hearty gulps.

"That was good," I said, smacking my lips. "When it's that cold, almost makes you forget there's alcohol in it."

"Which would be defeating the purpose."

I grinned. "Exactly."

Liz pulled two large grapes from the pack. "Have you seen or talked to Oliver since—"

"He ended it?" I finished. "No."

"I thought you might have left the door open . . ."

"Liz, Sophie's back. He wants to be with her. I can't torture myself about it anymore."

"I don't understand how he can take her back after everything that happened!"

"I don't even think I *want* to understand. He tried explaining it to me—how he wants to try being a family again, how it's for Balthazar's sake—but it doesn't matter anymore. I'm trying to block him out."

"Is it working?"

I shrugged. "Not really. Sleeping together was okay. I just wasn't supposed to fall in love."

"He fell in love with you too! Don't ever doubt that. I saw the way he looked at you that night at the movies. Maybe you couldn't tell, but I've known Oliver for years and I saw it."

"The bottom line is I should have never gotten so deeply involved with him. He was a single dad, for God's sake, with a—"

"Crazy ex!"

"Even to me, it sounds ridiculous! I should have run in the other direction, but so much happened before I moved here. I was vulnerable . . . I wasn't thinking straight . . ." I actually didn't think I was thinking straight now. Why was I being so forthcoming? It was the damn wine. And the heat.

"What happened before you came to Overlook?" Liz asked. "I'm sorry, but I've always wondered why a single, successful woman like you would end up here."

I chiseled off a chunk of Guyère with a cheese knife and considered my options. Here was my chance to finally tell Liz the truth. I had known her long enough and she seemed to genuinely care about my well-being. She was the closest thing to a friend I had in this town—my *only* friend at the moment.

Should I begin by telling her about getting fired from Atlas and how Overlook was my chance to regroup? Was I willing to tell her how broke I was? Or how my former boss might be implicated in an insider trading scandal? She would never be able to keep that information from her husband—who also had contacts on Wall Street. Only Oliver knew the cold, hard truth and he had turned his back on me. No, confiding in Liz would only breed suspicion. She trusted me, had misguidedly placed me on some sort of pedestal, and I was too scared for it to come crashing down. It would be better, for both me and Liz, to maintain whatever illusions we had created.

"Before Oliver, I was involved in a relationship with someone who wanted me to give up my career and marry him."

"Did you?"

"No. I felt like he was trying to change me into something I wasn't. He didn't respect my career and my career was every-thing to me. I *loved* what I did. I didn't want to give it up, so we went our separate ways."

"What happened to him?"

"He married someone else four months later," I said, eliminating the details of David's Congressional seat. "She's the exact opposite of me."

Shaking her head, Liz said, "Men can be so stupid some-times, but you're tough, Mia, and I admire that. I noticed it by the not-so-subtle ways you got me to remake the store."

I chuckled. "Sorry if I was too pushy."

"I'm sorry my store was so lame before you got here!" She paused. "You know, I've been thinking a lot about Sophie."

"You're getting to be as bad as I am, Liz!"

"It's like she has this strange hold on Oliver, coming in

and out of his life like that. She won't let him go."

"That's because he lets her! I won't get wrapped up in a messy triangle, no matter how much I care about him."

"Oliver is literally down the street from us, *as we speak*. How will you avoid him?"

"I have to try, Liz. I can't match up to his and Sophie's shared history."

"Or their mistakes," she added.

I thought about my own unforced errors and wondered if we, as mere mortals, could ever really outrun them.

We stayed in the back room finishing the entire bottle of rosé, unconcerned as its chill diminished. Oliver and Sophie were also cast aside as talk turned to Liz's family and their upcoming trip to Nantucket.

Afterwards, as I rounded up the empty wine bottle and cups, Liz looked at her watch and said, "It doesn't make any sense to open the store for only twenty minutes does it?"

"I don't think so. We might even be a little drunk."

"Then let's call it a day," she decided, throwing the barren grape stalks and cheese rind into the trash. We grabbed our bags and walked out through the back door.

Locking up, she asked, "Do you want to come over for dinner?"

I think she felt badly about letting me go home to an empty house, but I had those thirty-six Putnam Dixon names I wanted to Google. "Thank you, but I feel like I need to take a cold shower."

"Are you sure? We're grilling steaks. And we have a pool."

I laughed. "I'd love a rain-check, if that's okay."

"Next time, I won't take no for an answer."

We got into our cars; mine felt like a pressure cooker. I turned on the AC, but knew it would take several minutes to take effect. The wine had made me queasy and, with the heat, sluggish. I drove to Overlook Commons and went inside Dunkin' Donuts for an iced latte. There were four other people ahead of me and only one person working. I fanned myself and stared out the glass windows. Soon, I saw a little boy, smiling and walking backwards, pass by. It was Balthazar, dressed in swim trunks, flip-flops and a Lycra rash guard. I knew I should turn away, but I couldn't move, praying Oliver wouldn't appear behind him. Seconds later, a woman jogged by; black, cork-screw curls, a set of tan limbs in cut-off shorts and a gray tank top. She had to be Sophie. *He could still show up*, I thought, but no one else appeared except for an elderly couple. Just to be safe, I waited inside Dunkin' Donuts for a few extra minutes after getting my latte.

I tried to interpret this picture of Balthazar with Sophie. They were spending time alone together. They had gone swimming. He looked happy. She seemed attentive and, from the little I could see, *pretty*. I flipped down the sun visor, but only saw half my face in the narrow mirror. My eyes were red and haggard from lack of sleep and the front of my hair was frizzy, thanks to the humidity. I should have accepted Liz's invitation to dinner and spared myself this glimpse of Sophie's rehabilitation campaign.

And, from what I could tell, she was succeeding.

34.

By the end of the week, I had Googled everyone on the list. Since these expert network consultants were also salesman marketing their industry knowledge, their names and photographs appeared in numerous trade publications and news articles. I printed out all the relevant data and made separate files for each one, categorizing them into different groups.

Some interesting facts emerged:

- fifteen out of the thirty-six worked for external companies,
- seven were self-employed or ran their own consulting firms,
- one was a professor at Caltech,
- two worked for a business research and consulting firm called Foley & Blake,
- five worked for a Tokyo-based media and telecommunications consultancy called Bold Ideas International, and
- six were women.

I emailed my findings to Mannheimer, but when we spoke, his reaction wasn't as positive as I'd hoped.

"Mia, I told you to stop digging around. Leave this to me," he admonished.

"I'm not digging! I'm doing research to help my case."

"I've already got my investigators analyzing those profiles."

"Have they gotten in touch with any of them?"

"Not yet. This type of work requires finesse so it doesn't look like we're attacking them all at once. We don't want them talking to each other or, worse yet, informing Putnam Dixon. That could shut down our investigation before we even get started."

"Can you at least hear me out? I've got a few theories."

Mannheimer sighed. "Okay. Proceed."

I referred to my notes on the dining room table. "I think someone working on their own is more likely to be a tipper than someone associated with an external company. Being self-employed is unstable; there's no steady income. Making extra money on the side would be tempting, so those freelancers look more suspicious to me."

"But would Tripp really want to hire a consultant who was an outside contractor? I think someone affiliated with a real company has more current insight on trends and issues."

"Point taken. I also noticed that certain companies keep coming up. For example, two people work for Foley & Black and five work for Bold Ideas International. I think that's kind of fishy. Maybe they heard expert consulting could be lucrative if they colored outside the lines a bit?"

"That also came to my attention and I agree it's worth pursuing."

"Bold Ideas is also based in Tokyo, just like the company that acquired Touchnology Systems, and one of their specialties is human interface technology. That's just a fancy way for saying touchscreen! Tripp's mole must have come from Bold Ideas. I think we should start with them first," I said, pleased by my powers of deduction.

"We're looking into that one, but it seems almost *too* obvious, which brings us to my main theory."

"Oh? You have one? That's nice to know," I said, irritated he had knocked down all of my ideas.

"Look at your list again."

In an instant, the answer became painfully obvious. "The women."

"Bingo! I think Tripp wined and dined one of these female expert consultants and got her to spill the beans."

"That analysis is offensive on so many levels."

"Excuse me?"

"Why are we always using women as scapegoats when something goes wrong? These are intelligent, accomplished women who wouldn't be gullible enough to fall for a few gifts and tricks. I can't believe that you, a civil rights activist, would make such a sexist assumption!"

"Full equality means that women should be allowed to screw up as badly as men do. They shouldn't be given a pass because we think they're not capable of being corrupted. *That* would be most sexist thing I've ever heard!"

"I'm still not buying it."

"Why? Because they're not that attractive?"

"Mr. Mannheimer, I'm going to hang up soon!"

"You have to admit they don't seem like Tripp's type."

"And what's to say he's their type?!"

"Well, he could have charmed one of these women and she never knew what hit her."

Despite my objection to Mannheimer's theory, I thought of Tripp's clean-cut looks, his preppy mannerisms, and quickly began flipping through the women's files. The first one was Lara Albrecht, Ph.D.: short, white-blonde hair; an elongated nose; square rimless glasses; and lips that were no thicker than a slit. She looked stern, like the evil scientist in a Bond movie. Next up was Ms. Debra Caruso. Her face was full and unlined, but her chin-length hair was entirely gray. She could be thirty or fifty years old; it was difficult to tell. Tripp might have been a cad, but I didn't see him with either Lara or Debra.

"Mia, are you still there?" asked Mannheimer.

"I'm checking these women out again."

"I'll save you time. Go directly to Divya Thakur."

Divya was the last one in the pile. She was born and raised in Bangalore, India, but had attended Stanford University. Her career was a mix of start-up and household name tech companies, but her expertise was smartphones. Her current job was as Director of Strategic Development for a company that sourced the raw materials required to manufacture them, focusing on environmental sustainability. It was a far-sighted position, combining technology with eco-minded solutions. Smiling, with bright red lipstick and a middle-parted low ponytail, Divya had wisely avoided the unforgiving close-up chosen by the previous two. Sitting a bit back from the camera, she displayed nicely toned arms in a sleeveless red dress.

"Divya's definitely the most attractive of the bunch," I conceded. "But she seems ambitious, not naïve. Her resume is a recruiter's dream. Why would she jeopardize her own career to help Tripp?"

"She and Tripp know each other," Mannheimer announced. "They worked at the same start-up a few years ago."

I studied Divya's prim photo, trying to imagine clandestine meetings with Tripp in bars or bedrooms where she shared secret information. "Are you sure?"

"We cross-referenced each expert with Tripp and Peter to see if there was any prior history. This is what we found."

"It didn't occur to me to do that."

"Mia, it's *my* job to think of those things."

"Divya looks like a nice girl, not a calculating accomplice!"

"She may not have done it intentionally. A slip here or there, something said in confidence that Tripp jumped on . . ."

"So, what will you do? Confront her directly?"

"I'm sending someone to California to do some more digging."

I considered Mannheimer's escalating expenses and began to perspire. When—no—*if* this was over, there would barely be any money left for me to live on.

"You *still* don't know if she's the one."

"No, I don't." He paused. "But she's the best lead we have so far."

Mannheimer stated, in no uncertain terms, that I was to cease flying solo. He and his team of investigators would take over; my continued involvement would only yield diminishing returns. I had no counterargument. He had schooled me by uncovering that hidden connection between Tripp and Divya.

The record-breaking heat wave continued and when I wasn't at Eclectibles, I was in the cottage's back yard, evading my woes with a book or eating dinner at the old cast iron table. It was part of an ornate patio set, the iron grooved into the intricate loops and floral patterns of another era, but it had suffered through years of harsh winters and neglect. In my overwrought state of mind, I began picking at its flaking white paint and couldn't stop, grating all the way down to the metal. The veneer probably wouldn't last one more snowy winter and, on a whim, I decided to repaint it.

With a little help from YouTube and Overlook Hardware, I bought a dozen cans of spray paint, a dust mask, rubber gloves and safety goggles. The first night of my new project, I power-washed the furniture with a garden hose and sanded the surfaces to remove loose flakes of paint and rust. I then placed the table on top of old newspapers, meticulously spraying white gloss until the sun went down and the table glimmered with new life.

The following evening, I turned my attention to the eight chairs, but as I adjusted the goggles on my face, my cell phone rang. Annoyed by the interruption, I dragged them off and fished for the phone in the back pocket of my jeans. It was a blocked number. No one I knew had a blocked number, but curiosity always got the better of me.

"Hello," I said warily.

"Mia?"

I stopped breathing, my ears adjusting to the voice at the other end. I'd heard my name addressed like that for years, but had relegated it so far to the past, it no longer seemed real.

"Peter?"

"Yes." His tone was flat, as though he didn't consider this an unusual call at all.

"How—how did you find me?"

"I stopped by your old building. The doorman told me that you had moved upstate and rented your apartment to someone else. He wouldn't give me any forwarding information, so I just dialed 411. You weren't that hard to track down."

No, I hadn't exactly obliterated my existence from public records, despite my attempt to disappear in Overlook.

"Why are you calling me now?" I needed to sit down, but the patio chairs were in disarray. I trotted to the kitchen and found a stool to regain my moorings.

"Listen, can we meet somewhere and talk?" he asked.

"I don't think that would be a good idea."

"Why not?"

"Anything you want to say has to go through my lawyer, Eric Mannheimer. I think you may have heard of him?"

"Yes, I have, along with that ridiculous lawsuit you're bringing against me."

"It's not ridiculous. You fired me for unjust cause and ruined my reputation. After fifteen years of working by your side, I deserved better. The time for us to meet and talk passed long ago."

"Can you just hear me out? Just the two of us. As former colleagues. Old friends?"

"No, Peter, we were never friends. That was the problem. You were my boss, my *mentor*, but I turned you into some sort of father-figure," I said. Putting words—for the first time—on the dynamic of our relationship both saddened and empowered me. "I only wanted to please you and that blinded me to how callous you really are. You didn't care what happened after you fired me and made sure I became an outcast on Wall Street. You ruined my life."

"I never wanted you to end up like this! I thought you would bounce back."

"In this economy? Without a reference from you?"

"Mia, I had the firm to protect. Things aren't easy these days—regulators, compliance. We have to work twice as hard to make half the money."

"If you want my sympathy, you're not going to get it."

"But that's why I couldn't risk the tension between you and Tripp."

"Then I guess you made the right choice. Touchnology turned out to be a winner."

"Look, I didn't call to re-litigate the past. I want to discuss the future."

"Future? My future is up in the air at the moment."

"It doesn't have to be. We can settle this. That's why I'm calling."

I registered his use of one single word. "What do you mean by *settle?*"

"I'm ready to offer you a settlement that will give you a severance and some financial security. I'll also sign a confidentiality agreement to never discuss what happened between you and Tripp and provide you with a positive reference when you look for a new job."

I thought back to all the sleepless nights I'd endured, struggling to construct a solution for my financial problems. Peter's proposal was everything I wanted, but he had made me wait nine, harrowing months for it. I still couldn't forget my public humiliation and how everything I worked for had been discredited in one fell swoop.

"Peter, it's too late," I said, seething. "All the negative comments and speculation on the Internet—you can't fix that. If you had released a statement backing me up or settled with me earlier, that would have cleared my name. But now everyone thinks I'm unstable. You know damn well that's not true, but you never did anything to change it!"

"Wall Street has a short memory. Nobody will dwell on that if you list me as a reference. If things ended so badly, why would I endorse you?"

"To save your ass."

He chuckled. "Mia, I really have missed your colorful language. I don't have to save my ass. The choice is yours: We can prolong this for another year and my lawyers will fight your little attorney, tooth and nail, or we can agree on a number and you drop your flimsy lawsuit."

"It's not a flimsy lawsuit and you know it."

"What jury would award you damages once your histrionics are paraded out in court?" he asked, raising his voice. "Listen, I don't want this to devolve into a shouting match. I'm calling because I care about you."

"Well, you've had a funny way of showing it."

"You shouldn't be toiling away in some small town, stressed about money, worried about your next job. *You* were my protégé, the heir apparent. I wanted to make you COO, but you changed after Tripp joined the firm and, frankly, Mia, I lost confidence in you."

"It felt like you were pitting me and Tripp against each other."

"I wasn't, I swear."

"If you had your doubts, you should have said something. I would have fixed it." Peter was the source of all my problems yet, at that moment, I still sought his approval, inexplicably reverting to our pseudo father-daughter dynamic.

"It can still be fixed. I've wanted to contact you for months;

my lawyers advised me against it, but I think it's time to put this all behind us."

Toiling away in some small town. Peter was absolutely right. What the hell was I doing here, in this old kitchen, dressed in crappy clothes, painting garden furniture? I'd been primed for bigger things. Necessity had made me weak and acquiescent, but I could end that right now.

"What kind of settlement are we talking about?" I asked.

"Say your number. What do you want—need—to feel whole again?"

My last pre-financial crisis salary and bonus at Atlas had been in the neighborhood of one and a half million dollars. If I took that amount in lost pay and added another year as a buffer while I looked for another job, I'd be asking for three million. But then I'd have to give Mannheimer a third of that in fees.

"Five million," I replied. "Five would go a long way towards repairing the damage that's been done."

"That's a steep number, Mia."

"I don't think so, not after the killing you made with Touchnology. Maybe you should thank me for that. With me gone, Tripp got free rein with that stock."

"Four. I'll give you four."

I suspected he would decrease it to four, just as he knew I would ask for a sum he had no intention of giving. We had to play games before reaching a truce. "I could live with four, but let me talk to my lawyer first."

"I fully expect you to."

"Good," I said, rising from the kitchen stool. "I noticed this is a blocked number. How can I get in touch with you?"

"I'm at the same number. I blocked it because I was afraid

you wouldn't answer if you saw it was me."

I opened the refrigerator door and let the cool air blanket my face. "Peter, I think you know I would've answered."

"Maybe," he replied, and I could almost see him smiling. "Maybe I do."

I phoned Mannheimer to tell him the news. *Peter called me and wants to settle.* He listened quietly, never once interrupting. I was breathless by the end, as though I had run several miles uphill and finally reached the finish line.

"What do you want to do?" he asked.

"What do you think I should do?"

"Before I give you my opinion, what does your gut tell you?"

"I want to settle," I said, with more conviction than my response to Peter had indicated. "I want the four million dollars so I can get my life in order."

Mannheimer cleared his throat. "I think you'd be making a big mistake."

"Why?"

"Peter wants to settle because he has dirt on his hands. He knows how messy a court case could get. He'd be eviscerated in the press, just another Wall Street fat cat with no clue. His personal life would also be fair game and who knows what skeletons are hiding in his closet. He's trying to avoid that by making it look like he's doing you a favor when, in fact, you'd be doing him one."

"And how do you think I'd be portrayed by the press?

Even if we ignore the video of me telling Tripp off, I'd still be vilified. I'm just as much a product of the system as Peter is. My fall from riches to rags would also be a nice cautionary tale and I'm not sure there'd be a lot of sympathy for me out there."

"I think you'd be a sympathetic plaintiff."

"I stand to lose more if we move forward with this. It'd be so much easier to just—"

"Take the money and run?"

"No! That's not what I meant."

"What about our theory regarding the possibility of insider trading at Atlas?"

"That's a long-shot."

"You didn't seem to think so a week ago, when you stayed up all night Googling those expert network consultants. We're close to finding a connection there; I can feel it."

"Mr. Mannheimer, are you doing this for me or because you want to make a statement by bringing down a Wall Street firm?"

"For you, of course! If Atlas goes down in the process, so be it."

"But there's no guarantee this will work out in my favor. I think Peter's offer is the best possible outcome for me, given the circumstances." I paused. "Why are you so resistant? You would end up with over a million in fees."

"The money has never motivated me. I *believe* in your case. I think you were wronged, that you were provoked. Peter, Tripp and that parasitical firm are guilty of screwing you and probably a whole lot more."

"But, Mr. Mannheimer, the money means something to *me*. I assume you've saved up, provided a nice nest egg for your retirement. I haven't. I'm a heartbeat away from bankruptcy. This is my opportunity for a fresh start."

"Trust me, Mia, I do understand. But I think you could still win a big settlement if we stick to our strategy."

"How long would that take, with the investigation, the subpoenas, the despositions . . . A year? Two? I can't stay here, withering away, for that long." Seeing Sophie and Balthazar the other day had been the final straw. It had only been at a distance, but how long would that last? Overlook was small. Sooner or later, we'd have to face each other.

"I don't know," Mannheimer admitted.

"And if you do uncover something illegal at Atlas, then I get nothing. Isn't that what they call a Pyrrhic victory?"

"It wouldn't be 'nothing.' You could still be proud."

"No, Mr. Mannheimer, I couldn't. I've made up my mind. I'm going to settle."

"Mia, please! Wait—"

"No, I'm done waiting. Done."

"Can you think it through over the weekend?"

"There's nothing for me to think through! I've decided."

"Please. Can you just do me that favor?"

Tomorrow was Friday. Not much would get accomplished in the coming days. I'd give Mannheimer the weekend as an expression of gratitude for his belief in my case.

"But *if* I still want to settle," I said, qualifying my words to be fair, "will you call Peter's lawyers and get the ball rolling?"

It was dead silent on the other end.

"Yes," Mannheimer said finally. "I will."

I did just as I promised. I thought about it over the week-end—while the hours lagged at the store and I had to listen to Amaryllis's long-winded anecdotes; while I finished spray-painting the garden furniture; and while I spent another lonely evening with a bottle of wine. On Monday morning, I woke up in a sweat, drained from all the stress and heartbreak, and sent Mannheimer an email: I want to settle.

35.

Mannheimer was no longer speaking to me. We only communicated via e-mail, but I didn't care since his latest one telegraphed the news I'd been waiting for: Atlas agrees to terms of settlement. Drawing up paperwork this week for your signature. I wrote back to thank him for his efforts, but stopped short of apologizing for selling out. Mannheimer and Peter, two men on opposite ends of the moral spectrum; foes who had the power to elicit a sense of guilt from me, a self-perception that I'd disappointed them in some way.

There was no hesitation as I planned for my Post-Settlement Life. I had already begun checking the real estate section of the *Times* for a rental and wanted to move back to the city as soon as possible, but it was the beginning of August and Liz would soon leave for two weeks in Nantucket with her family. I would manage the store with Amaryllis, but when Liz returned, I'd take her out to dinner and explain *everything*: my dire circumstances; why working for her had been a godsend; and how this settlement would be my chance for a new beginning.

Kevin Stackdale's contract on my Battery Park apartment ran until mid-January. Once he moved out, I'd put it up for sale, forfeiting the biggest trophy of my old Wall Street life. It didn't matter if I only broke even; I had to get rid of it. The final, most important component would be finding a new job. Peter claimed Wall Street had a short memory, so I was counting on his positive reference to make the difference.

Christine was coming to visit at the end of the month

and the settlement would give me extra money to treat her for a night in the city and a few nice meals—a drop in the bucket for living rent-free at the cottage. I knew she didn't care, but *I* cared. She was my oldest friend and I was still ashamed by the mess I'd made out of things. That's what Mannheimer refused to understand; without this settlement, my life was in shambles, no matter how much I tried to put my best foot forward. This settlement was my lifeline. I couldn't afford to screw up a second time.

Planning for the future, counting the days until I left Overlook, dominated my thoughts, but I still struggled with Oliver's absence, our transformation from intimacy to nothingness. He continued to be part of the air I breathed, the couch and bedsheets in the cottage, the park in town; places and memories that connected us. It was harder to lose Oliver in the calm environs of Overlook than it had been to forget David in the hustle and bustle of Manhattan life. Settling with Atlas had been the decisive moment. Now I could put Oliver in my past.

"Have you told Oliver your plans?" Christine asked during one of our nightly conversations.

"Why would I?" I answered, surprised by her question. "It's none of his business."

"I'm sure he must still think about you."

"Mmm ... I'm not so sure," I said, remembering how it had taken him days to call me after our first date. "He's really good at compartmentalizing."

"Maybe you should call and tell him about the settlement."

"Absolutely not!"

"Why? He was supportive when you told him about your situation."

"*Was* being the operative word and then he left."

"That wasn't the reason why."

"Maybe not. But I showed my weak spot and it was a mistake."

"Mia, you just won a four million dollar settlement with your dignity intact! I'd say that was far from weak."

"I don't want to brag about 'winning' a lawsuit."

"It's not bragging," she said, exasperated. "It's about keeping him updated about your life since you'll be leaving town next month."

"Exactly. So whether he knows or not won't make a difference."

"But won't you get a little satisfaction by showing him you're moving on? Reminding him that you're the complete opposite of flaky Sophie?"

"That's a devious way of looking at it."

"So you plan on leaving town without telling him?"

"What's there to tell? I never planned on staying here forever."

"Well, out of courtesy, I think you should tell him your plans," she said piously. "Otherwise you'll look bitter."

"I'm not bitter! I'm just looking ahead."

"Which is why telling him about the settlement and your move would give this whole affair closure."

"Hmph," I replied, unconvinced. "Don't you have to put some kids to bed?"

Although I would never admit it to Christine, she *had* succeeded in planting a seed of doubt in my mind. When I'd exposed my humiliating secret to Oliver, he'd been a friend, first and foremost. Surely he'd be happy to hear that I'd landed on my feet again.

Instead of calling, it was much safer to send a text. I could control the tone and wouldn't write anything personal suggesting our past relationship. I also wouldn't have to hear that uncomfortable modification of his voice if Sophie was close by. Searching for something cheery but impersonal, I hatched this message:

> Good news! I've reached an amicable settlement with Atlas and will be moving back to the city. Thank you for your support! Best wishes, Mia

I sounded effusive, but wanted to wash away the broken woman he'd said goodbye to that evening in July. I purposely left my phone in the kitchen when I went to bed so I wouldn't check it all night, waiting for his reply.

The first thing I did the next morning, before brushing my teeth or turning on the news, was race downstairs to my phone. My heart drummed as I brought up the message icon and found ... nothing. I scrolled through the list, illogically thinking Oliver's response got lost between earlier texts. Eight hours had passed and he still hadn't responded. Wide-eyed and hot-faced, I was jarred that an acknowledgment from him still mattered so much. I became more obsessed as the day wore on and kept the phone close to me at the store, taking it out several times an hour, hoping for some sign of life from Oliver.

Fourteen hours later, I faced the truth: Oliver had willfully left me hanging. He was someone who always had his phone nearby, who promptly answered emails and texts. Given our history, I had expected a minimum level of courtesy, but he was letting me know that he didn't appreciate my intrusion into his new life. Why had Christine talked me into contacting him when he obviously didn't care? *This whole ordeal will be over soon,* I thought. Knowing I had one foot out the door was the only thing that kept me going.

Shortly before closing, the phone vibrated in my back pocket, but it was only Mannheimer. I sighed, weirdly comforted. He could be a grouch, but he hadn't abandoned me yet.

"Mr. Mannheimer! I'm so glad you finally called!"

"Mia, are you at home?" he asked, his tone grave.

"No. I'm at the store."

"Are you alone?"

"I'm with Amaryllis. We'll be closing in about half an hour."

"Go someplace where we can speak in private."

"Mr. Mannheimer, you're making me nervous! Please tell me what's going on."

"Mia, for once, please just do what I say."

Dread silenced me. It was the same sort of fear I had felt listening to the doctor explain my mother's illness; a sixth sense that foretold of something horrible, something completely beyond my control.

"Okay," I whispered and rushed downstairs to the stockroom. I sat in the chair by Liz's desk. "I'm alone now. What is it?"

"The FBI raided Atlas's office today."

"No!" I shrieked. "When?"

"Today. At the crack of dawn. They've taken files, computers, phones—you name it."

My mind reeled. "Do you know why?"

"Suspicion of insider trading." He paused. "It's all over CNBC, Bloomberg. . . ."

I thought back to my day, listlessly waiting for a message from Oliver. "I haven't listened to the news."

"The Feds and the SEC have been investigating Atlas for months now. They were way ahead of us."

"I guess our suspicions were right then," I said, with no satisfaction. "Who are they after?"

"Sources tell me that Peter and Tripp were brought in for questioning."

"Do you think this has something to do with Touchnology?" I asked as the ramifications of this raid sunk in. My settlement. If Atlas closed down, if Peter was indicted, there would be no settlement. I was finished; all hope was well and truly gone. The only thing left for Mannheimer to say was "I told you so."

"It must be because—" Mannheimer began and paused. "My source told me the FBI wants to question you too."

I dropped the phone and it struck the wooden floor.

"Mia?" Mannheimer called, his voice ricocheting by my feet. "Are you still there?"

Shuddering, I put the phone to my ear again. "What does the FBI want with me? I haven't done anything."

"I don't know. That's what I'm trying to find out."

"I have nothing to do with any of this! I haven't been there for almost a year."

"I know."

"I was only doing my job ..."

"Mia, listen to me. As hard as this may sound, I want you to calm down. I'm on the Thruway and should be at your house in fifteen minutes. Make some excuse to leave work right now and meet me there. Don't do anything foolish. Don't drive off someplace else because you're scared. I'm going to help you get through this."

How was an aging hippie like Mannheimer going to help me with the mighty FBI? But my options were limited, perhaps non-existent. "Okay."

I went to the bathroom and doused water on my face, drying my eyes with a coarse towel. Back on the sales floor, I mumbled an excuse to Amaryllis about some sort of emergency that required me to leave right away.

I drove home, discombobulated, but with enough sense to obey the speed limit. A white Volvo station wagon was already parked outside and I maneuvered my car next to it. Mannheimer and I got out, exchanged a long glance, but said nothing. We entered the cottage and I threw the house keys in a bowl on the hallway table.

"Why don't you sit down, Mia?" Mannheimer suggested, pointing to the couch.

I complied and watched him move to the drinks trolley. His plump arms lifted different bottles of liquor, uncapping them, smelling their contents. I fell back onto the headrest and shut my eyes, but visions of FBI agents pillaging my old workplace were stamped on my lids. When I opened them again, Mannheimer sat beside me, proffering a crystal tumbler.

"Drink this," he said.

"Thanks," I said. "Scotch?"

Mannheimer nodded.

I took a nip of the amber liquid and wrinkled my nose. "Damn, that's strong! I haven't had a thing from that cart since I moved here."

"Now's a good time to start," he replied and downed his glass in a single gulp. "Should I put on the TV?"

"Sure." I handed him the remote and he flicked through the channels until CNBC appeared. We watched a few talking heads analyze the markets before they cut to another reporter, Hannah Gilmore, for the latest business news. I didn't recognize her; she was young and blonde, with feathered hair reaching past her shoulders, and must have started during my ban on CNBC. Her segment began with a bare-bones recitation of the latest financial malfeasance:

"Insider trading investigations heat up and Wall Street was rattled today when news broke that the FBI raided the New York headquarters of Atlas Capital this morning, a boutique investment firm with $1.5 billion of assets under management. Led by Morgan Stanley alum, Peter Branco, Atlas has been a quiet player in the tech sector, making large bets on up-and-coming companies."

An old photo of Peter flashed on the screen. He was smiling and looked exceptionally smug, a man shrouded in wealth and status.

"An FBI vehicle was seen outside the building and several men with badges emerged carrying boxes and computers. It's still unclear what the specific charges are, but a spokesman for Atlas said that they are cooperating fully with the FBI and that the firm is still operational."

"That's bullshit, you know," I interjected, shaking my head. "Atlas can't recover from this."

"The big question now is: How many more firms will be implicated?" Hannah asked.

The camera panned to a man sitting across from her in a navy suit and striped tie.

"With me to discuss the impact of this raid at Atlas Capital—and on the industry as a whole—is Benjamin Riley. Benjamin has been on both sides of the aisle, as a lawyer suing and defending investment firms. What's your read on what happened today?"

Riley's lips were glossy and the shine extended above his lip line.

"Thanks for having me here, Hannah. The FBI has been engaged in an extensive investigation of insider trading for years and uncovered that the contagion was even more widespread than they previously thought, so Atlas and this new round of scrutiny may just be the tip of the iceberg."

"Atlas hasn't been formally accused of any wrongdoing, but what kind of evidence might the FBI have that could have warranted this raid?" Hannah asked.

"Let's just say the FBI wouldn't have executed those search warrants if they didn't have probable cause. I'm talking informants, wire taps, maybe even people with a relationship to Atlas that the FBI was able to turn into cooperating witnesses."

"Such tactics have all been a part of the FBI's strategy to treat white-collar crime as aggressively as mob activity, am I right?"

Riley nodded.

"They've proved very effective in identifying the most egregious offenders and serving as a deterrent for others who might entertain the thought of trading on inside information," he replied.

"What's the near-term impact for the industry as a result of these insider trading investigations?" Hannah asked.

"Well, market confidence is still weak. Investor confidence is low and they're steering clear of equities, turning to bonds. Financial stocks were down today when word of the Atlas raid became public. Accusations of suspicious activity hurt the market, hurt the ordinary investor. They no longer trust it's a level playing field."

Hannah tilted her head sideways, looking pensive.

"Benjamin, many of these people accused of obtaining inside information are already among the most privileged people in the industry, in this country! So why do they do it? Why do they risk it all?"

"My philosophical answer would be that sometimes too much is never enough, but practically speaking, people are under pressure in this down economy to show results, so they cut corners. It's as simple as that."

The camera zeroed in on Hannah again.

"That's it, folks, the last word from Benjamin Riley, partner at Riley & Gold. Thank you for stopping by. CNBC will continue to follow this developing story."

Mannheimer turned off the television and asked if I wanted more scotch.

I looked inside my glass. Mesmerized, I had been watching and drinking and it was almost empty. "No thanks. One's enough."

"What'd you think of the story?"

"What is it she said? 'Using mob tactics to catch white collar criminals?'"

"You know how insular Wall Street is. Insider trading cases are very difficult to prove without concrete evidence, so the FBI was able to get the courts to authorize the use of wiretaps."

"And with all the financial bogeymen out there, I guess it wasn't too hard,"

"There's a lot of motivation to go after these guys and they keep digging their own graves."

"I'm up shit's creek, right?!" I said, putting down my glass. "Just when I thought I'd get some justice, the FBI suspects that I'm involved in Peter's illegal activity? What the hell did I do to deserve this?"

"Mia, getting yourself all worked up isn't going to change anything."

"This is so far from anything I'm capable of doing!" I lay a hand on my heart. "*I* am an ethical person. I play by the rules. I don't cut corners!"

The tears began trickling again, but I was past losing face in front of Mannheimer. He reached into his pocket for a handkerchief and passed it to me. I wiped my eyes and smiled weakly. "I'm sorry that I'm such a difficult client."

"You're my least boring client," he said. "Keeps me young."

"What do you think the FBI wants?"

"My guess is they think you know something valuable about Peter and Tripp or that you might have been involved in their scheme."

"We don't even know for sure what that scheme is!"

"But if *we* think there might be some expert network collusion, you can be sure the FBI does too."

"You believe me, don't you?" I asked, unable to control my rising hysteria. "I had nothing to do with expert networks or secret alliances or inside tips. I just wanted Tripp to get out of that stupid trade! If he had just listened to me, none of us would be in this mess. I'd still have my job. Atlas wouldn't be in jeopardy—"

Mannheimer put a hand on my wrist. "Mia, I think Atlas may have been involved in shady activity for some time, possibly while you were still there."

I stared at him, stupefied. "How could it have gone on without my knowing? I was in charge of the equities desk."

Mannheimer looked solemn. "I think that's what the FBI wants to find out."

"I'm screwed, right? Screwed."

"Mia, listen to what I'm about to tell you and listen good. I want you to go back and think about everything surrounding the Touchnology trade, from the time Tripp placed the order to the day you were fired. Make a timeline, write everything down: prices, stop-limits, your instructions to Tripp ... That's going to be your defense if they try to pin anything on you."

I nodded. "What am I supposed to do after that?"

"I want you to go about your life, business as usual."

"That'll be impossible if the FBI is on my tail!"

"That's exactly why you shouldn't change anything. Go to work, go to the gym, go to Starbucks. You have nothing to hide, right?"

After months of half-truths, I almost didn't trust myself anymore. Peter had played with my head so completely, I was afraid my memory was no longer reliable. But the one thing I was still certain of was my innocence.

I met Mannheimer's eyes and declared, "I have absolutely nothing to hide."

36.

Heeding Mannheimer's advice, I reported for work as scheduled on Friday, but couldn't muster a phony façade or blunt the sharp nerves pricking my stomach. Amaryllis tried to engage, but I rebuffed her. By the time we closed up on Saturday afternoon, my paranoia had reached fever-pitch. Leaving my house had made things worse. I felt besieged, eyes darting left and right, searching for a black, unmarked sedan and a dark-suited man who would lead me away. I finally came to the conclusion that not eating or sleeping, waiting for the FBI to surface, wouldn't put me in a better frame of mind to withstand their questioning. Hysterics would only project guilt. I had to find my reservoir of strength, however faint that might be.

Balance would begin with a decent meal and I drove to Whole Foods, positioning my car into a spot with no other vehicle to the right or left. Grabbing a cart, I wheeled up and down the aisles, choosing fresh greens; plum tomatoes; sweet corn on the cob; ripe avocadoes; luscious strawberries; white potatoes; skirt steak; yellow fin tuna . . . I'd eat my way through this crisis. When I came back to the car with four bags of groceries, my Escape was sandwiched between a Chevy Suburban and a Porsche Cayenne. Sighing, I opened the trunk, wondering how I would wiggle into the driver's side.

"Ma'am, do you need help with anything?" asked a voice behind me.

I whipped my head around and faced a guy sporting a Mets baseball cap, who couldn't have been more than a few years out of college.

"I think I can manage, but thanks," I told him.

"Hey, I don't mind. It's the least I can do for parking so close to you," he insisted, pointing to the Suburban.

"Uh, okay."

He bent over and retrieved the other bags, placing them in the trunk.

"Thanks again for your help," I said, wanting nothing more than for him to get inside his Suburban and drive away.

"No problem at all," he said, smiling. Crow's feet rimmed his eyes and I realized he was older than I had assumed. I began to feel nervous, but didn't want to show it. Mercifully, it was still light outside and the parking lot was milling with people.

"Well, I should really be going . . ." I said, reminding him that he had promised to move his SUV so I could get into my car.

However, his feet stayed put. "Mia," he said, as though it were the most natural thing in the world.

"How do you know my name?" I asked, but no sooner had I spoken those words than *I knew*. The boyish man in front of me was FBI. *FBI*. I had been searching for men in black suits and sunglasses—silly of me not to realize they came in different varieties. How long had he been tailing me? How could I have missed him in the supermarket?

"I'm Special Agent Forrester from the FBI, but please don't panic. We only want to talk to you."

"How can I be sure you are who you say?" I hissed, trying to sound tough. "Someone could have sent you to scare me."

"I can show you my badge, but not here."

"I won't talk unless I see it."

Forrester lowered his cap and produced a black wallet from his pocket. As clear as day, I saw everything: the blue FBI lettering, the seal, his picture, the gold badge and, finally, his full name, *Special Agent Ryan Forrester*.

Swallowing, I said. "Where do you want to talk?"

He stepped back. "You can follow me inside the Suburban."

I closed the trunk, locked all the doors and took out the BlackBerry from my handbag. "I think I should call my lawyer first."

"You're perfectly free to do so."

Mannheimer's number went immediately into voicemail, but I texted as quickly as possible: Mtg w/ Ryan Forrester from FBI as well as the Suburban's license plate number. Forrester had already opened one of the back seat doors and I got inside. Unexpectedly, there was another man sitting behind the steering wheel.

"This is my colleague, Special Agent Umesh Singh," Forrester said from the passenger side, buckling his seatbelt. "We're part of the FBI's securities and commodities fraud unit."

Singh turned around. His tawny skin was set off by jet black hair and eyebrows, but his eyes were hazel, softening the aquiline features. "Thanks for agreeing to meet with us."

"I didn't think I had a choice," I replied.

"Oh, we all have a choice," Forrester said.

"Where are you taking me?" I asked.

"Don't worry. We're going someplace where we can have more privacy."

The navy-blue Suburban felt like a tank with its funereal interior and tinted windows; in hindsight telltale signs of a federal law-enforcement vehicle. Forrester and Singh had bided their time wisely, waiting until I was addled to pounce. Their approach, an ordinary afternoon at Whole Foods was brilliant, almost comically so. I had imagined they would come to my house or the store, but the whole point was to catch me flat-footed, wasn't it? I glanced down at the phone in my lap. Mannheimer was still missing-in-action, but it wouldn't have made a difference. There was no dodging the FBI.

Singh's greenish-gold eyes checked on me every so often from the front mirror. The penetrating looks were brief but disconcerting, and I finally slanted my head towards the window. The sun had disappeared under a cluster of darkening clouds; a summer thunderstorm was imminent. About ten minutes later, Singh came to a familiar bend in the road and I saw the sign for Meadow Lane. The FBI must have been in the shadows for some time now. They were privy to my habits, my schedule, the twists and curves of remote backcountry roads. This fact chilled me more than their approach at Whole Foods had.

"Why are you going to my place?" I asked.

"We thought you'd be more comfortable there," Forrester said.

"And we don't want to draw attention to ourselves," Singh added.

Once he parked the Suburban in front of the cottage, I hopped out. Inside, I went directly to the dining room and sat down. Forrester came in first. He no longer appeared boyish; the Mets cap was off, laying bare a thinning hairline. Prepped to be indistinct, the ordinary Joe at every American mall or gas station. Singh was more imposing, broad-shouldered and decked out in a suit and tie despite the day's heat. Both agents commandeered chairs across from me and folded their hands on the table.

"So, Mia," Forrester began. "I'll bet you're wondering why we're here."

"I'm not stupid," I said. "I watch the news. I know you raided the firm I used to work for."

They both nodded, but Singh spoke, "Listen, Mia, we know you used to be incredibly close to Peter Branco. He was your mentor, even a father-figure if you will."

I couldn't stop blinking. In less than a minute, they had already come too close for comfort.

"We also know that Peter fired you under strange circumstances and that's what led you here," Forrester said.

"More importantly, we suspect that Peter and William 'Tripp' Armsden were engaged in insider trading," Singh added, "and that you might have also been involved."

I squeezed my eyes shut to stop the twitching. Mannheimer's theory was spot-on.

"I had nothing to do with their illegal activity! I haven't been at Atlas in almost a year."

"When we questioned Peter after the raid, he said you were fired because he was afraid *you* were involved in suspicious activity," Singh said.

"So the bastard's blaming me now?!" I crowed. "Are any of the suspicious trades related to Touchnology Systems?"

Blank-faced, Singh responded, "Why do you ask?"

"Those trades were the source of conflict between me and Tripp. I wanted him to dump them, but he refused."

"Listen, Mia, we're going to be frank with you. Peter ran an incredibly successful outfit, producing impressive returns even in a recession. Some of it was skill, some of it was luck. Was any of it based on inside information?" Forrester shrugged, hands facing upwards.

I cut in. "Not from me. Never!"

"I'm not really concerned about the past. What I want to solve—and prosecute—is what happened once Tripp joined the firm."

"Had you ever heard of Tripp before?" Singh asked.

"No. He seemed to come out of nowhere, but he and Peter have a family connection."

"Yeah, Tripp's younger brother and Peter's half-sister are married," Singh said. "What does that make them, Ryan?"

Forrester chuckled. "Co-conspirators."

"Tripp may not have been known to you, but he was certainly known to us," Singh added.

"About five years ago, before he left for that California start-up, he was suspected of trading on an inside tip he received from an old college buddy," Forrester explained. "This buddy worked at a semiconductor company and passed along information regarding a quarterly earnings report before it was made public. Earnings were slated to drop, but Tripp dumped the stock before the announcement and saved his firm a loss of over three million dollars."

"How did you find that out?" I asked.

"The semiconductor company began to suspect that one of its own was selling secrets and brought it to the attention of the FBI."

"Was Tripp ever convicted?"

"No, his buddy wasn't a very reliable witness. He was hooked on Vicodin, had a slew of debt . . . .. Tripp's lawyer convinced the judge that the money Tripp had given him was a charitable loan, not payment for the tip. The case was eventually dismissed for lack of evidence."

"Why is there no public record of this?" I probed, fuming.

"The semiconductor company didn't want any bad publicity, so they went to great pains to keep things quiet," Singh said.

"So Tripp got away with it," I said.

"Yes and no. He got a slap on the wrist and was barred from working in the securities industry for a year. That's when he went to that tech start-up."

"Peter must have known about that," I concluded.

"There's no way he *couldn't* have known, given their prior connection," Singh said.

"Maybe Peter thought Tripp was reformed," I said.

"Ha! Guys like Tripp think they're invincible," Forrester said. "He'd gotten away with it once, so maybe he could do it again. But what he didn't realize is that the SEC keeps a close eye on individuals who've already been suspected of wrongdoing."

"If the SEC had already raised a red flag about Tripp, then this has nothing to do with me," I said. "I only wanted him to get out of that trade."

"But that's not what the records show," Singh said.

"Excuse me?"

"You know that search warrant executed at Atlas?" Singh asked. "We confiscated documents, emails, computers, etc . . . "

"And we found an email sent from your account showing you pushed for acquiring more Touchnology shares," Forrester finished.

"That's impossible!" I exclaimed. "I never sent such an email!"

Singh removed a smart phone from his breast pocket, tapped the screen a few times and read: "Tripp, I have a good feeling about Touchnology. Keep buying on the downside. Regards, Mia."

"That's—that's not mine," I said, pulse rising.

"It was sent from your account at 2:49PM on October seventeenth," Singh said.

"That was the day Peter fired me. Tripp and I were arguing about his buys. I wanted him to get out. Why would I send him an email telling him to do the exact opposite?"

"Maybe because you had inside information about the eventual sale of Touchnology to that Japanese company," Forrester said.

I leapt from the chair. "I'm not continuing this conversation without my lawyer."

"Mia, please sit down," Singh said.

"No! I want to speak to my lawyer." I said, moving to the window.

"Mia, we know that Peter and Tripp fabricated evidence," Singh said.

I stared icily at him. "Are you saying that so I can make some kind of self-incriminating statement? I'm not going to fall for it."

"That's not our intention. Please just listen," he said.

Could I trust them? Forrester was combative and played the bigmouth, but Singh seemed more restrained, so I decided to hear him out. "Okay."

"When you were escorted out the door on October seventeenth, did you have the chance to log out of your computer?" Singh asked.

"No! Everything happened so quickly. I didn't even have time to get my personal items. They were sent to me."

"Did anyone have your passwords?"

"I don't think so, but it wouldn't have been hard to breach. And when Tripp took over my position, he would have needed access to my book of trades anyway."

"Do you remember what time you left the building?" Forrester asked.

"It was sometime after lunch, I think," I said. The time line was foggy. Only the sharp verbal exchanges were crystal-clear.

"I think Peter and Tripp realized they would have to cover themselves in some way and since you were out of the picture, the easiest thing for them to do was gain access to your email and send a bogus message. You *were* at work that day, so chances are no one would question the time or origin of that email," Singh said.

My shoulders sagged as the enormity of Peter and Tripp's deception set in. "We didn't punch in or out, only logging on or off of our computers and since I never logged off . . . Well, I guess they could have written anything."

"They certainly tried, but as I mentioned earlier, the email was sent at 2:49PM," Singh said. "But we have a security video showing you being escorted out of the building by the guard, Clifton Johnson, at 2:34PM." He paused. "And there's no visual of you coming back into the building. So—"

"I couldn't have sent that email."

"Exactly," Forrester concurred.

I scrutinized the agents sitting solemnly at the dining room table for several seconds. After years of working with two-faced guys on the trading floor, I could sense that something was amiss.

"If you already knew that I had no part in Peter's scheme, why'd put me through this?" I asked.

"We knew," Forrester said.

"But we had to be *sure*," Singh added.

"Now that I've passed that test," I seethed, "what do you want from me?"

"We want you to help us get Peter," Singh said.

"How the hell do you expect me to do that?"

"We'd like you get in touch with him and ask how he's doing. Say you're worried about the firm and all the false accusations. Don't act like you know he's trying to set you up. Tell him you always thought Tripp was bad news and that you want to help in any way you can."

"Why would he talk to me?"

"Because he's got his back to the wall! He doesn't know how much we know. He can't be sure Tripp won't cut a deal and rat him out. His whole life is on the line right now. He stands to lose everything," Singh said

"He needs an ally—any ally—and that could be you right now," Forrester said. "The 'prodigal daughter' returning to the fold."

I chafed at his use of that expression. "In order for me to do this, I'd have to wear a wire, right?"

Singh and Forrester shared a shifty sideways glance.

"Well, yes, that would be the only way we'd be able to obtain irrefutable evidence," Forrester said, sounding less cocky for the first time all afternoon.

"But couldn't that also be seen as entrapment?" I asked.

"We'd be with you every step of the way," Singh said. "Wherever you decide to talk, on the phone or in person, we'd have your back."

I looked out the window, past the raindrops coating the glass, to the blue and purple hydrangeas in the garden. I had been oblivious to the downpour that had come and gone while I spoke to Singh and Forrester.

Turning back, I said, "I won't do it."

"Why—Why not?" Singh stammered.

"Because I don't have to," I said. "I've done nothing wrong, you've said so as well, and I just want to put this all behind me."

"What about your sense of right and wrong? Your commitment to justice?" Forrester asked, his face reddening.

"Justice for whom? Certainly not for me. Peter ruined my life and my wearing a wire and baiting him won't change that." I shrugged. "Sorry, guys, but I can't help you."

"How about helping yourself?" Forrester asked.

"Ha! I'm beyond help. The damage has already been done. Atlas is finished. My career is over. Nothing I do or say can change that."

Suddenly, the palm of Singh's hand struck the tabletop and I flinched.

"Mia, why are you willing to give up so easily?" he yelled. "Peter and Tripp screwed you over *royally*. Do you want them to get away with that?"

"Of course not!"

"Do you like living like this—no money, no job, no credibility?" he needled. "Is this what you've worked so hard for?"

"No!" I screamed.

"Then why won't you help us bring them down?"

"Because everyone I've trusted has betrayed me! You're right; I'm ready to give up because I'm sick and tired of losing!"

My rage—part confessional, part tantrum—pummeled the air and Forrester looked away, but Singh had the spine not cower.

"When Peter and Tripp go down, I promise you *will* get your self-respect back; you'll repair the damage to your reputation," he said. "You'll see, once and for all, that it wasn't about you. It was about them and their insatiable greed. There was nothing you could have done differently."

"In fact, be happy you got the hell out of there when you did," Forrester added. "Otherwise you could've been further implicated in this mess and no amount of explaining would have helped."

"Mia, I'm sure today has been overwhelming," Singh said, taking a more conciliatory tack. "We don't expect you to make a snap decision, but we don't have a lot of time. Please give our proposal some thought." He dug in his pocket for a business card. "Call me if you change your mind."

I took it, sketching my fingers over the text. Singh was right. All I had left was my reputation.

"Okay," I said, badgered by memories of humiliation and despair. "I'll do it."

37.

I drove to an FBI field office in Westchester on Monday morning and was escorted to a small room with no windows. Forrester, Singh and I sat around a table equipped with recording paraphernalia and three glasses of water.

"Here's the latest: Although Atlas has been raided, no charges have been filed yet. Peter and Tripp are still free. The firm is still, for all intents and purposes, operational. But the evidence supporting the insider trading accusation is mounting and if you can help us get an admission or any whiff of a misdeed from Peter, it could be the final nail in the coffin," Singh explained.

"Mia, let me see your cell phone," Forrester said kindly, Saturday's prickly demeanor absent. "You're going to initiate the call from there since that's the number Peter recognizes and responds to."

I nodded and placed my BlackBerry on the table.

"This is a mobile telephone recording lead," he said, holding up a single earphone attached to a long thin black cord. "It looks just like a regular in-ear headphone, but it has a tiny mic built in, so we'll be able to record both sides of the conversation. Put it in your receiving ear."

"Receiving ear?" I asked, as he gave me the cord.

"The side where you usually hold your phone," Forrester said.

"Oh," I replied, carefully adjusting the microphone so it fit snugly into my right ear.

"How does it feel?" asked Forrester. "Do you need another

size?"

"No, this one is fine."

"I'm going to plug the cable into the microphone socket of this digital voice recorder," Forrester said, connecting the cord to the pocket-sized device on the table. After a small click, he smiled. "We're ready. All you have to do is start talking normally on your cell. We'll be able to hear your dialogue and everything will be recorded. You won't even notice the difference."

Singh slid a manila folder across the table. "Now, let's go over the script."

"Script?" I repeated, opening it to find a one page document, two paragraphs long. I lifted the paper and began reading silently.

"Would you mind reading it out loud?" asked Singh.

After taking a deep breath, I began:

"'Hi, Peter, it's Mia. How are you? I'm so sorry to hear about this terrible mess. Of course I don't believe any of it. You would never get involved with insider trading—'" I paused. "These lines sound totally contrived."

"They are contrived," Forrester said tightly.

"But I would never speak in such a monotone; the flow is weird."

"We're trying to deliver dialogue that'll work for a number of different scenarios," Singh said. "Please continue."

"'I just want you to know that I'm here to vouch for you and think that Tripp is trying to throw you under the bus. Why don't we meet somewhere to discuss how we can clear the firm's good name?'" Laughing, I threw the paper back in the folder. "*'Clear the firm's good name?'*"

"What's so funny?" Forrester asked.

"I could give a shit about clearing Atlas's good name and Peter knows that." I said, passing the folder back to Singh. "I can't say this script."

After some hesitation, he took it and crossed his hands neatly on top. "Well, what would you like to say instead?"

"I don't know exactly, but I would need to feel it out, be spontaneous, otherwise Peter will see right through me."

"This isn't an audition!" Forrester cried. "We have one chance to do this and we need to get it right."

"You're asking me to do something I'm already uncomfortable with and"—I pointed to the paper—"that lame script will only make it worse."

"And what kind of expertise do you have to make that judgment?" Forrester asked.

"I *know* Peter and have a gut feeling—"

"Call him now and say whatever you think feels right," Singh said, cutting me off.

Forrester's eyes bugged out. "Umesh, she can't go off-script! We have too much riding on this case."

"I know," conceded Singh, "but she's not totally off-base."

After a few moments, Forrester threw his pen on the table and said, "Fine."

"But make no mistake, Mia, Ryan is right," Singh cautioned. "Everything depends on this phone call you're about to make. We're putting our trust in you, so please: *Don't fuck it up*."

"Don't worry. I won't."

I brought up Peter's cell phone number from my contact list and Singh switched on the recorder as soon as the phone began ringing. It rang once, twice, three times—each pause seemed to deepen between signals. I made eye contact with Singh and raised my eyebrows as if to say: *Should I hang up?*

Both agents shook their heads no. By the sixth ring, I began to feel jittery, but Singh had fixed his gaze on me. Abandoning the call without his approval was out of the question. By about the tenth ring, I heard static in the background and the sounds of huffing and puffing.

"Hello," a man answered in a raspy voice.

"Peter?"

"Mia," he wheezed. "I knew I'd be hearing from you sooner or later."

That statement only accelerated the nervous throbbing on the right-side of my neck and I glanced at Singh again for help. He scribbled a few words on the folder: STAY CALM.

"Why do you say that?" I asked.

"Don't play games with me."

"Hold on there, Peter," I said, finding my fire. "I'm not the one who's been playing games."

After a few seconds, he said, "Things have changed since we last spoke."

"You should've been speaking to me all along instead of Tripp. Then you wouldn't have been sucked into this mess."

"It's a shitshow. You can't imagine the half of it."

Hearing some vulnerability, I plowed on. "I don't believe the things they're saying in the press. This is all Tripp's doing, right?"

Several moments passed, but nothing came. I debated saying Peter's name again, but decided to hold out. In this room, I had all the time in the world.

"You're probably wondering about your settlement," he

said finally. "I can't come up with the money right now."

His announcement didn't surprise me; I had already re-moved that money from my mind.

"That's not the reason I called," I said. "I wanted to give you my support. In spite of everything that's happened, I still love Atlas. I feel like I helped you build that firm and don't want to see it go down in flames. It's been your whole life—and mine too."

"Everything I've worked for is at risk," he whispered.

"I know."

He made a guttural noise. "I think we should meet."

"Tell me when and where."

"Tomorrow. 3:00PM at the lake. You remember that spot where we all went kayaking?"

He was referring to a firm-wide retreat in better days, a hilarious kayak race on Lake Waramaug where seven out of ten kayaks had capsized. "Yes, I remember."

"Meet me there. And Mia—"

"Yes?"

"Thank you for calling."

"You're welcome." I waited for him to hang up first before turning off the phone and taking the mic out of my ear. Only then did Singh stop recording.

Forrester's grin took up half his face.

"Good job!" he said, raising his hand to give me a high-five.

Now he was singing my praises. I merely grazed his palm, denying him an enthusiastic slap.

"How do you feel, Mia?" Singh asked.

"Okay, I guess."

"Do you feel guilty about misleading Peter or about what

you're going to do when you meet him tomorrow?"

"No, I don't feel guilty. I feel sad. Just sad," I admitted. Not everything I'd said was a lie. Atlas had been my world for over a decade. It had defined me, dictated every decision I'd made. In a way, I would have loved to turn back the clock and relive those days when I was Peter's trusted deputy. Now I was plotting to wear a wire and bring him down.

"That's understandable. He was like a father-figure to you."

I nodded. "Yes, he was."

"But don't feel sorry for him!" Forrester chimed in. "Keep in mind how he threw you to the curb with no job, no salary, not even a decent reference. Peter brought this upon himself."

"I know he did. He betrayed me, the firm, everyone who works there . . . What's going to happen to them?" I asked.

"That's not your problem. Peter bears complete responsibility for jeopardizing their livelihoods," Forrester said.

"I know," I said, taking a sip of water from the glass in front of me. "This feels worse than when I was fired."

"Why? Because Peter has finally shown you that he's a paper tiger? An emperor with no clothes?" Singh asked.

"Something like that."

"Are you sure you're up to the task tomorrow?" asked Forrester.

"I think so."

"We'll come by your house at about eleven to fit you with the wire and go through how this will go down," Forrester said.

"I'll have to make up some excuse about not coming in to work," I mumbled.

"Call in sick and don't worry; we'll be driving behind you at a safe distance. We're familiar with Lake Waramaug. We've followed Peter there a couple of times. Try not to be nervous or afraid."

The room suddenly felt cold. "This whole thing has gotten really creepy. I just want to get it over with," I said, rubbing my arms.

"By tomorrow night it will be," Singh said reassuringly.

38.

I tossed and turned the whole night before my meeting with Peter. With Liz in Nantucket, I had called Amaryllis earlier in the evening to say I felt ill, complaining of vomiting and intense stomach pains. It might as well have been the truth; I had no appetite and an excruciating headache made it impossible to sleep, but I knew it was anxiety over my mission. Quite simply: I was terrified. What if Peter suspected I was helping the FBI? What if he searched me and found the wire? And my ultimate fear: What if he got violent? Thoughts of being strangled or gunned down in the woods paralyzed me. I seriously considered calling Singh to tell him I couldn't go through with it, but he would only try to convince me otherwise. Backing out now would raise Peter's suspicion and the FBI would blame me for botching their investigation. My fate sealed, I clambered out of bed at around 4:00AM, took two Nyquils and fell asleep within minutes.

It felt like the toll of a death-bell when my BlackBerry pealed at 10:02AM and I wasn't surprised to see Singh's name on the caller ID.

"Hello," I whispered.

"Mia! Did you just wake up?"

"Yes. I had a really bad night."

"So you haven't turned on your television."

"No, I haven't. Why?"

"Because you're all over the fucking news!" he shrieked.

"What are you talking about?"

"CNBC, Bloomberg, Fox Business, MSNBC, CNN—all

the cable channels have picked up on it . . . "

"Picked up on what?"

"They've identified you as the 'mystery woman' behind Atlas Capital!"

His rantings were nonsensical, so I tore my head from the pillow. "What? How?"

"Turn on CNBC. They're running the piece again and you'll hear it for yourself."

I rummaged through the night stand drawer for the remote control and flipped through the channels until CNBC appeared. An image of my face was plastered on the screen, right next to the reporter's talking head.

"Are you watching?" asked Singh.

"Y-yes," I replied, fazed by the old picture from a Sherwood Forest Foundation gala. Instead of looking mousy and capable—which would have been my preference—I looked aloof and glamorous, having had my hair and make-up done for the event.

"All of Wall Street is wondering who the mystery woman is behind Atlas Capital. Sources say that Mia Lewis, former head of equities at the boutique investment firm, hasn't been seen for almost a year and that her departure coincided with some suspicious trading activity at the firm," said the female reporter.

Those damning words came from Patricia Martinez, a veteran at the network who gave instant gravitas to any story.

"Lewis had been Peter Branco's right hand and his rumored successor. Soon after her hasty departure, a heated video of her upbraiding William 'Tripp' Armsden emerged on the Internet, causing speculation that there had been tension at the firm."

A grainy still of the video appeared, but fortunately there was no sound or close-up.

"Armsden and Branco were both brought in for questioning last week after the FBI raided Atlas's headquarters. But where is Lewis? Sources say that the FBI has fingered her as a 'person of interest.' CNBC reporter Colin Fuchs has been following this developing story. Colin, what's the word on the street?"

The screen changed to a man standing outside somewhere in Manhattan. He was hemmed in by trees and park benches to the left, lampposts and the Hudson River to the right. Squinting, I recognized the greenery and waterfront promenade. As if on cue, Fuchs's voice blared from the television:

"Patricia, I'm here in Battery Park City, the affluent downtown neighborhood Mia Lewis called home before she did a professional disappearing act. In the male-dominated world of finance, Lewis was a rising star, responsible for Atlas Capital's largest trading portfolio and a team of about ten traders. But who is Mia Lewis?" he asked, inserting a dramatic pause. "She grew up in Rockland County and attended the exclusive Convent of Sacred Heart School. Smart and ambitious, she graduated summa cum laude from Wellesley and quickly found work as an analyst at Morgan Stanley where she reported directly to Peter Branco. A Wharton MBA, she joined Branco soon after he launched Atlas Capital which, as previously reported, is now the subject of an FBI investigation . . ."

Slack-jawed, I watched it all, transfixed. Fuchs spiced up his reportage with images of the bucolic Sacred Heart campus, my big-haired high school yearbook headshot, even a photo of me and Peter from a Morgan Stanly recruiting brochure. Where had they gotten all of this material?

"Lewis had forged a successful career with a million-dollar paycheck, exclusive Manhattan address—even a personal shopper at Saks. She was also involved in a long-term relationship with former Manhattan Assistant District Attorney and current United States Representative, David Warren. Ironically, during his tenure in the DA's office, Congressman Warren was Chief in the Investigation Division, the department investigating financial crimes."

Flash to a smiling picture of me and David in full black-tie regalia. I felt nauseated. David would be mortified at being associated with me again, the woman in the center of a financial scandal.

"But somewhere along the way, it all went wrong and Lewis vanished from the spotlight," Fuchs said.

The television screen split, with Patricia Martinez on one side in the studio; Colin Fuchs in Battery Park on the other.

"Do you have any idea why the FBI is interested in Lewis?" Martinez asked.

"Various theories abound, Patricia. I've heard some speculation that Lewis could have information about the specific trades in question. She might also hold damaging evidence against Branco and Armsden, which could also explain why she went underground."

"But is there any talk of her direct involvement with trading on inside information?" Martinez prodded.

"No," Colin said soberly. "But things could change very quickly."

"Thank you, Colin. I'm sure we'll be hearing more about

this intriguing story," Martinez said.

I would have found it all intriguing too—a woman, Wall Street, men, money—had it not been for the fact that *I* was the woman in question.

"Mia?" Singh's voice called out from the phone that I had been holding in a death grip. "Are you still there?"

Bringing it back to my ear, I whispered, "Yes, I'm here."

"I'm sorry you had to see that."

"Some of that information wasn't even true! I'm not under suspicion for anything. The FBI's not looking for me. *I'm working with you guys, for God's sake!*"

"Whoever tipped them wants to harm your credibility."

"Peter? He sounded pathetic yesterday, not like someone planning a counter-attack."

"Well, whoever did this has been accumulating information about you and waited until the most critical moment to release it."

"Tripp and his lawyers must have been plotting this. But aside from maligning me, what does he have to gain?"

"He's broadening the ring of suspicion, deflecting some of the attention away from himself," Singh said.

"So he thinks he can scare me by trashing my name in the media?"

"You'll just have to ride this out. August is a sleepy news month, everyone's on vacation—"

"Really? I can't remember the last time I took a vacation in August. My last couple of Augusts were pretty busy: the liquidity crunch in '07, the subprime mortgage mess in '08 . . ."

"At this moment, the media are chomping at the bit for a sexy news story and yours—well, yours is a doozy."

"I barely recognized the person they were talking about. I came off like a total bitch who didn't care about anything except getting ahead and making money."

I expected a sympathetic remark from Singh, but it was quiet on the other end.

"Singh?"

"Mia, brace yourself: Things will get worse before they get better."

"Can you guys do anything to stop it? Can't you release a statement touting my innocence?"

"Unfortunately we can't at this juncture since we're in the middle of an ongoing investigation."

Pretty damn quick, Singh had stopped being human and reverted to an FBI drone.

"What about my meeting with Peter? Do you still want me to go through with it?" I asked.

"I don't think that would be a good idea."

"Should I phone him and call it off?"

"No, we'll take care of it."

"So this is it? You guys are just gonna leave me out in the cold? What am I supposed to do in the meantime?"

"Stay in your house and lay low. I'll be in touch soon," Singh said and hung up.

Mannheimer called me soon after and added insult to injury by agreeing with Singh. "I'll also work some of my contacts and try to get to the bottom of this," he said.

Trapped, there was nothing else for me to do except stay in bed and watch television. CNBC had the story on a continuous hourly loop. By the closing bell, Colin Fuchs was no longer reporting live from Battery Park, so they ran a recorded version of his piece. I took that as a hopeful sign he had nothing new to report. MSNBC was more interested in my past with David, stating he had declined to comment or sit for an interview. In his place, two little-known policy makers hammered away about the need financial reform. Predictably, they condemned "greedy traders" like me and called for stricter insider trading penalties.

With those words, I turned off the television completely. So much of what the networks reported were either outright lies or snippets of truth that had been tailored to fit a particular storyline; one that portrayed me as the culprit for Atlas's troubles. I debated taken two Nyquils when my cell hummed. Since my new number was public, unknowns had been calling since the story broke, but this time it was Christine.

"Let me guess: You called to swap beauty tips," I said.

"You know that's not why," she answered.

"I'm actually surprised it took you this long to call."

"That's because I've been traveling all day."

"Where to?"

"To you. I'm downstairs. The back door. Please come down and open it."

When I unlocked the door and saw Christine's face—big blue eyes, strawberry blonde hair scraped back in a messy ponytail, lines of concern across her shiny forehead—I welled up within seconds and we hugged for what seemed like an eternity. She stepped into the kitchen and closed the door behind her.

"Don't you have any luggage?" I asked.

She shook her head. "Just this tote bag. I booked a flight as soon as I saw that report on CNBC."

"You didn't have to drop everything and rush over! Please sit down," I said. "Who's watching the kids? You should've called me."

"That's precisely why I *didn't* call. I knew you'd try to discourage me."

I slumped into a chair. "You're right. I can't be alone anymore."

"How are holding up?"

"Well, I've gotten over the initial shock of seeing my face on TV."

Christine plopped into the chair next to me. "At least it was a good picture! I said to Rob 'Thank God they found one where her hair is blown out and she's not wearing glasses.'"

"That picture's too flashy. Who would take me seriously in a strapless dress?"

"I think you look like you've been kickin' ass and takin' names!"

"Only you could find something positive with this situation!"

"What's the story with FBI? That's what has me most worried."

I briefed her on their surprise visit at Whole Foods and the plan for me to wear a wire and trap Peter. With each installment, her eyes expanded like discs; her mouth into an oval.

After adjusting her distorted facial expression, she exclaimed, "Mia, this is some serious stuff you've gotten into!"

"I didn't want to do it, but they got me all riled up about how badly I had been treated."

"I'm glad you didn't go. I don't think you could have trusted him."

"Neither do I, but I had no choice."

"Have you eaten?" asked Christine.

"No. I haven't even left the house."

"Then let me make dinner. We can open a bottle of wine and talk about everything but this. Atlas has been hounding you for too long now."

"I know. I just want to be free of that place, once and for all."

Christine threw together a tuna salad from my Whole Foods provisions (Forrester had driven my car back from the parking lot.) and brought me up-to-date on her kids, my lovely godchildren whom I saw far too seldom. We reminisced about our glory days in Manhattan too, laughing over bad dates and our first apartment together. Atlas—and Oliver—were deliberately not mentioned and, by the time we emptied the second bottle of wine, my eyelids were drooping.

"Christine, this is just what I needed. Thank you," I said, slurring my words.

She smiled. "You need to go to bed."

"I should help you clean up. Plus you just got here."

"No, I got here"—she looked at her watch—"about seven hours ago. It's almost midnight and you need to rest up."

"Okay, okay," I said, lugging myself from the chair. "Let me show you to the guest room."

"Don't worry. I think I remember where it is."

"Right. Of course you do. Goodnight," I said. She was still sitting down, so I kissed the top of her head.

"Goodnight. Sleep well."

Holding tightly to the bannister, I lumbered up the stairs to my room. The unmade bed looked so warm and cozy; I flopped down and closed my eyes. I did have a thought about the shitstorm I was in, but it faded quickly as everything turned blissfully black.

39.

After two Alka-Seltzers and a long, hot shower, I followed the aroma of fresh coffee into the kitchen and found Christine beating eggs in a bowl, the table set for breakfast.

"Good morning!" she crooned. "Did you sleep well?"

"I did, thank you. Knowing you were here made a big difference," I said. "Can I help with anything?"

She shook her head. "I'm making scrambled eggs. Would you like some?"

"Yes, please. What time did you wake up?"

"About seven o'clock."

"What have you been doing in the two hours it's taken me to make an appearance?"

"I called Rob, checked my emails, snooped around the house ..." she said, ladling the egg mixture into a frying pan. "I just love what you've done with this place. It was so crowded before, but now it's easy-breezy chic."

I smiled. "It makes me so happy to hear that."

"See? I knew you'd make the perfect tenant."

I poured a cup of coffee and said, "Christine, that's something I've wanted to talk to you about. With Peter's settlement off the table, I can't afford to move back to the city as quickly as I'd planned. Would it be possible to stay here longer? Maybe until year-end? I'll put Battery Park on the market in the meantime."

"You can stay as long as you need. It's not a problem."

"Are you sure? I thought you might have already been looking for a paying tenant since I was pretty firm about my imminent departure a few weeks ago . . . "

"Nope."

Placated by her reaction—and a generosity that continued to amaze—I added, "Someday I'll make this up to you and Rob. I promise."

"That's not necessary; that's what friends are for."

"I've been on my own for so long, I think I forgot what it was like to ask for—and receive—help."

"Given your family history, that's not so strange. It's been a defensive mechanism, but it is okay to let go."

"You're right. I know that now."

"Should we put on CNBC?" Christine asked. "I'm curious to see if your story still has legs."

"Well, it can't be any worse than yesterday."

I turned on the small, flip-down television that was nailed to the bottom of a cabinet while Christine dished out the scrambled eggs. We ate and watched the "Squawk on the Street" panel discuss the pros and cons of investing in gold. Following that segment, one of the "Squawk" anchors, a British man by the name of Trevor Smith, spoke directly to the camera:

"Let's turn over to our colleague, Colin Fuchs, who has a new development in the Mia Lewis story. Lewis, the former top trader at beleaguered investment firm, Atlas Capital, has been dubbed the 'Mystery Woman of Wall Street' since leaving her post there last year."

I stopped chewing my toast and, whatever I had already swallowed, lodged in my throat. The screen panned to Colin Fuchs, who was grinning like the cat who ate the canary.

"Thank you, Trevor. The trail in search of Mia Lewis has

led us to the small town of Overlook in upstate New York. This place has been her home since January, after leaving Atlas Capital under what can best be described as dubious circumstances. Reliable sources tell me that Lewis was, in fact, terminated from her job. As I mentioned in earlier reports, speculation is rife over the cause and whether it has anything to do with the FBI's ongoing insider trading probe at Atlas. However, Lewis seems to have turned her back on Wall Street all together and has been working at the local antique store, Eclectibles, for several months."

The camera zoomed in on the Eclectibles storefront and its distinctive peacock. My safe haven in Overlook had been compromised.

"With me is Amaryllis Reynolds, who works with Ms. Lewis at Eclectibles. Ms. Reynolds, what was your impression of her?"

Amaryllis had her classic "deer in headlights" expression and when Fuchs aimed the microphone at her, she gasped in horror.

"Well, uh, Mia seemed kind of aggressive at first, but she's, uh, nice and a really good worker," she stammered.

"Did she ever tell you about her past?"

"Um, no. She just said she was taking a break from Wall Street."

"Did that seem strange to you?"

Amaryllis shrugged. "Tons of people get fired from Wall Street every day."

"Did she ever go into detail about her firm or the people she worked with?"

"No."

"Have you seen or spoken to Ms. Lewis, since the news broke about her association with Atlas Capital?"

"No, I haven't."

Fuchs smiled awkwardly back at the camera. "Thank you, Ms. Reynolds, for your time."

The "Squawk on the Street" studio reappeared and Christine abruptly shut off the TV, flipping up the screen to its original position.

"That's not going to make it go away," I told her.

"I'm just as shocked as you are, but Amaryllis wasn't that bad."

"She did more harm than good!"

"Let's come up with a game plan."

"What 'game plan?' Singh said this would get worse before it got better and he was right! How the hell did they find me?"

"It was inevitable. Someone in town must have seen yesterday's report and recognized you from the store."

"Why would they snitch? I'm not bothering anyone here."

"Mia, Atlas is under a cloud of suspicion and you suddenly pop up as a 'person of interest!' People think bankers and traders are a bunch of crooks anyway, so if you're hiding out in Overlook, you must've done something wrong. You better believe someone was going to rat on you. They probably considered it their civic duty."

"I'm only hiding out because I'm broke and humiliated. I wish someone would see this from my perspective for a change!"

"I see it from your perspective! So do Mannheimer and even the FBI! But sticking your head in the sand isn't going to make this go away. No more surprises; we need to get ahead of this story."

"How are we supposed to do that?"

"Let's see what they're saying on the Internet," she said, removing a laptop from her tote bag and resting it on the kitchen table.

"Do we really have to do this?" I asked, fearing inflammatory on-line posts.

"Yes, we really have to do this. What's the WiFi password again?" she asked.

I told her and watched as her fingers worked magic on the keyboard.

"I get about 8,000 hits when I Google your name plus Atlas and CNBC has already updated their on-line coverage with Colin's report. Does anybody know where you live?"

"Oliver, Liz, Amaryllis, maybe some other people I met at the store . . . Do you think the media would actually show up here?"

"You never know. We need to be prepared for every possibility."

I sat passively while Christine continued her search and when my cell phone beeped, we both jumped. Moving swiftly to answer, I saw it was Liz.

"Liz! How are you? How's Nantucket?" I babbled.

"I can't believe you've been lying to me this whole time!" she screamed.

It was the first time I heard Liz raise her voice. The words rushed out clumsily, but their effect was no less biting.

Chastised, I replied, "I never lied to you."

"Stop it, Mia! You told me you were taking a sabbatical. You acted so professional, *so perfect*, but it was all a game! You're a liar who ran away from shady business dealings!"

"That's not true, Liz! Let me explain—"

Christine, hearing the twinge in my voice, looked up from her laptop.

"So you didn't get fired from Atlas?" Liz asked.

"I did get fired, but not for the reasons they're speculating about in the press."

"Then why didn't you tell me that you'd been fired?"

Taking a deep breath, I answered, "Because you never asked."

"We talked about your past many times! You had tons of chances to be up front with me."

"You always assumed that I had decided to take some time off and, technically, that wasn't far from the truth."

"When Philip saw the report on CNBC this morning, I thought there must be some kind of mistake until I saw my store—and then Amaryllis! You're all over the news and I look like an idiot for hiring you!"

"Liz, I always felt so grateful for the job and I put everything I had into it."

"How can I believe you? I don't even know who the real Mia is anymore!"

Neither do I, I wanted to say. *I've been trying to figure that out since I moved here.*

"I'm so sorry, Liz. I never meant to for you to get caught up in this."

"It's too late for that! I trusted you with my business, my money . . . You can forget about ever stepping foot in my store again!"

She had already rendered her verdict: I was a traitor, a hypocrite.

"Liz, please hear my side of the story," I begged. "I was devastated after I lost my job. I was in dire financial straits and didn't know how I would get back on my feet again, so I came here to sort things out. I haven't been hiding from the FBI or the SEC. I'm not involved in any insider trading. Those are all lies! I've only been hiding from myself. I wanted to put my career behind me and was too humiliated to tell anyone what really happened. But I planned on telling you the truth when you came back. Please believe me."

"Does Oliver know the truth?" Liz asked.

Oliver. I'd wondered—more times than should have mattered—if he was following the news surrounding Atlas.

"Yes, he does," I said quietly. "I told him that weekend we went away."

After a vexing silence, she replied, "I thought we were friends, but you never thought to tell me?"

"I—I didn't know how. I'm so, so sorry."

"So am I. Goodbye, Mia."

Then the line went dead.

I limped back to the table.

"What happened?" Christine asked.

"I just lost my only friend in Overlook," I said, eyes watering.

"I know how fond you've become of Liz," she consoled, "but if she doesn't believe you, then there's really nothing you can do is there?"

"She might have believed me if I'd been honest with her from the beginning."

"Isn't she the one who offered you the job in the first place?"

"Yes."

"Then she believed what she wanted to believe. Given your circumstances, how could she have expected more?"

I sniffled and reached for a napkin to blow my nose. "It never felt right misleading her."

"You were planning on quitting anyway."

"Yes, but it would have been on my own terms. Her finding out like this—it isn't right."

"I know Liz has been a good friend to you, but you don't have time to think about her right now."

"I don't want to think about anything! I just want to jump down a hole and die!" I wailed, sobbing into the napkin.

Christine grabbed me by the shoulders. "Mia, look to me: You have to focus. You're in deep shit—and it doesn't matter that you haven't done anything wrong—we have to think about damage-control." She repositioned her laptop so we could both look at the screen. "Let's get back to work."

Her battle cry exhorted me to get a hold of myself. I took out my own laptop and tried to be clinical, shutting off any sensitivity to personal attacks or untruths. We checked the most obvious websites (CNBC and Bloomberg) regularly, as well as other news and opinion outlets like *The Huffington Post*, *New York* magazine and *The Daily Beast*. These sites rehashed what we already knew, so the Comments section proved the most interesting in gauging public opinion, and I was getting very little sympathy. My favorite entry was in the *New York Post* from a reader in Staten Island: "*That bitch probably made so much money; she never has to work again!*" I laughed until my belly hurt.

"What was the name of that Wall Street blog you used to read all the time?" Christine asked.

"Doubling Down?"

"No, the one with the really cheeky blogger . . ."

"You mean JoJo Katz and Moneymaker.com?"

Christine chuckled. "Yeah, that was the one. We should go on that too."

"She ran that awful video of me and Tripp arguing," I reminded her.

"Well, let's see what she has to say for herself today."

I typed in Money Maker's blog address and saw my name in the headline. Reluctantly, I read it out loud: *"Am I the only one who thinks that Mia Lewis—"*

"Is getting shafted?" Christine finished. She looked up from the screen, eyes alight. "This could be a game-changer!"

I rapped my knuckles on her computer. "You read it. I'm too nervous."

She magnified the screen and spoke:

Much has been made in recent days about the so-called "Mystery Woman of Wall Street," hinting that Mia Lewis's disappearance from the grid is related to the insider trading allegations against Atlas Capital.

Mia Lewis was featured on this blog shortly after her dismissal last year when a video recording of her reprimanding Tripp Armsden surfaced. Many, including myself, found her irate rant humorous, but a slew of new information sheds light on what Lewis was dealing with at Atlas Capital.

At the time the video was made, Lewis was Head of Equities and Armsden reported to her. But when they argued over a trade, he remained while she was told to leave the firm. Let's look at the gender dynamics at work here: **Woman in a position of authority asserts that authority and gets fired.**

Lewis took the honorable approach and stepped back, hoping to live an anonymous life in the countryside rather than wage a very public battle with her former employer. That might have been the last we heard of her, too, had it not been for that inconvenient FBI raid at Atlas Capital, throwing Lewis into the spotlight with every aspect of her life open to scrutiny.

Who cares if she took home a million dollar salary? She earned it with her credentials and years in the business. Who cares if she had a personal shopper? Busy traders don't have time to strut around Madison Avenue.

Amidst this unwarranted scapegoating of Lewis, the two other principals in this saga have been given more breathing room. As of this writing, Atlas Capital Head, Peter Branco, continues to reside at his Litchfield County estate or Upper East Side townhouse or Parrot Cay beach bungalow, while Tripp Armsden was recently sighted having drinks at the Boom

Boom Room.

My own extensive research uncovered an interesting fact about Armsden: He was banned from the securities industry for one year as part of a secret deal to avoid a protracted insider trading inquiry at one of his previous jobs. Yes, my friends, you heard me correctly: **Armsden has been accused of this before.**

Why, then, has the intense focus been on Lewis and not on the men who had much more to gain by trading on insider information? I'll tell you why: **When the shit hits the fan, blame the woman.**

Lewis joins a growing list of top female Wall Street executives who've been bullied and ousted since the financial crisis began, including M&A banker Theresa Breeze, once the highest paid woman on Wall Street. Senior-level Wall Street executives post-crisis are still white and male and, judging by the fervor to discredit Lewis, it won't change any time soon.

"Woo-hoo!" Christine walloped. "I couldn't have said it better myself!"

Shaking my head in disbelief, I said, "I never expected JoJo to rally in my defense. I didn't think she liked me—or anyone else for that matter."

"She knows injustice when she sees it!"

"Her scoop about Tripp is true, you know. The FBI told me all about it."

"Who could have tipped her off?"

"Tripp has pissed off a long list of people."

"Mia, you know what this means, right?" Christine went on. "You finally have an ally in the media, an insider with a popular platform. If other outlets pick up on this, it could reframe the whole story!"

"Let's not get our hopes up," I cautioned.

I don't know what I would have done without Christine in those hours after my identity and whereabouts were blasted in the media. She made her proclamations with such conviction, I almost believed them. Ragged after spending a whole day in front of our computers, we shut everything down and made pasta Bolognese for dinner. Christine searched the Web again later in the evening, but JoJo's story hadn't gained any traction. On top of that, CNBC had already transitioned from business news to its prime-time lineup. We were in an information vacuum, but stumbled upon one of my favorite movies, *Something's Gotta Give,* with Diane Keaton and Jack Nicholson. Lights out and scented candles flickering, I luxuriated in what was probably the most beautiful beach house ever captured on film and imagined the possibility that an independent woman could find love again.

40.

Some sort of epiphany had taken place in the middle of the night. By lunchtime the next day, CNBC ran a live segment with not only JoJo Katz, but Theresa Breeze in their studio. JoJo, my unlikely ally, intimidated, with her brown bangs and black nerdy glasses; while Theresa, my professional girl-crush, carried her demure blonde bob and pearls with panache. Christine and I watched in awe as they weighed in on my predicament and the status of women on Wall Street in general.

"JoJo, what about Mia Lewis's story resonated with you and inspired such a pointed essay on your blog?" asked Trevor Smith, the British anchor.

"I was frustrated by the gender bias inherent in many of the assumptions people—including some in the media—made. There was a rush to judgment that was ridiculous and totally offensive," she replied, looking squarely at Trevor, silently implicating his own reporting.

The camera closed in on co-anchor, Patricia Martinez.

"The Mia Lewis case has sparked renewed debate about women and Wall Street. I don't think there's anyone better-suited to discuss that than Theresa Breeze, former M&A banker, once considered the 'most powerful woman on Wall Street.' She now runs her own hedge fund, Tailwind Capital Management. Now, Ms. Breeze, many people thought your case sent a terrible message about the future of women on Wall Street. Are things better or worse for women since you left your job at one of the world's most prominent investment firms?"

"I've been in business for over thirty years and have seen

a lot of progress, but I would argue that we've gone backwards since the financial crisis," Theresa said.

"In what way?" Patricia asked.

"The facts speak for themselves: There are no female chief executives at the biggest Wall Street banks; few women have been promoted to top positions on management commit-tees—"

"Surely you don't think there's some sort of conspiracy against promoting women to senior-level positions?" interject-ed Trevor, crinkling his brows.

"I'm not implying that at all, Trevor," Theresa said, smil-ing. "But studies show that during times of stress, we close ranks and gravitate towards the familiar. The 'tried and true' becomes important; political savvy and connections become important. Racial and gender diversity are desirable goals, but many executives are putting them on hold until the financial system has stabilized."

JoJo nodded. "There's no denying that women have fared much worse than men in this recession. Over seventy percent of the layoffs in the financial services industry have been wom-en."

"That's pretty ironic, considering middle-aged white men got us in this situation to begin with," Theresa added, chuck-ling.

And on and on they went . . . Trevor Smith didn't stand a chance as Theresa and JoJo presented a barefaced analysis about the glass ceiling on Wall Street. Theresa maintained that once women cracked that glass ceiling, they were often thrown onto a "glass cliff" and assigned senior positions with a higher risk of failure, due to a pre-existing crisis or a lack of support

and resources. Intellectually, I had heard this phenomenon discussed for years, but believed that my promotions—and Peter's
backing—proved that the industry had gone beyond gender
and race. Listening to Theresa, however, I realized I had been
pushed off that glass cliff without a parachute.

After the CNBC segment, Christine and I mined the Internet for more intel and came to understand just how much
the blogosphere was buzzing about JoJo's article. I read editori-
als on the *Huffington Post* and the *Daily Beast* in my defense,
from women whom I admired and considered standard-bear-
ers for female empowerment. Many others—silent heroines
whose jobs didn't make the front page of the *Wall Street Journal*—shared courageous accounts about the gender discrimination they had experienced: promotions that were given to
lesser-qualified men; salaries thirty percent less than their male
counterparts; networking opportunities missed because they
had to rush home to children . . .

"I'm in a very strange position at the moment," I said.
"I've gone from being a pariah to some sort of poster-child for
women on Wall Street."

"Isn't that wonderful? You have the potential to inspire
thousands of other women out there!" Christine said.

"But aren't I doing that from a position of failure, not
success?"

"That's exactly what makes your story so relatable. Nobody wants advice from someone who's never *failed* at anything. Those people aren't credible!"

"I didn't realize how far removed from reality I was until
I got fired."

"But would you trade the wisdom you have today for the

bubble of a year ago? Would you rather live with the fantasy that Peter was fair and just? That you were financially-sound and emotionally-balanced?"

"Well, when you put it that way, I guess I *am* better off today," I said, laughing, just as the doorbell rang. "Who could that be?"

"A reporter? You haven't answered your phone all day, so maybe they've decided to hunt you down."

"Would you mind checking?"

"You want me to answer the door?"

"Uh, maybe not. Go see if there's a car outside first."

Christine tiptoed to the curtained window panel by the entryway. "I see a black SUV and—oh my God!" she screamed, running back into the living room. "They saw me!"

"*They?* Is there more than one person out there?"

"Yes! A really tall guy—tan, dark hair—and a short old man—bald ..."

"That must be Singh and Mannheimer," I said and bolted to the front door. When I opened it, both men sighed in relief.

"Mia, we've been trying to reach you!" Mannheimer said. "But you're ignoring our calls."

"I'm sorry. I just couldn't deal with reporters harassing me over the phone, random people harassing me on the Internet ..."

By now, the cottage had become so familiar that Mannheimer and Singh traipsed right in. I introduced them to Christine.

"How are you holding up?" Mannheimer asked.

"I feel better," I admitted. "It seems like I have some people on my side."

"That JoJo Katz is a piece of work!" Mannheimer said.

As I looked at him, I thought I saw his right eyelid flutter, as though he was winking at me, and a thought popped into my head.

"Mannheimer, did you tip her off about Tripp's previous brush with insider trading?" I asked.

"What? Me?" Mannheimer asked, shocked.

"He did, didn't he?" I said, turning to Singh.

Singh pursed his lips together before replying, "Mr. Mannheimer insists he would *never* leak confidential FBI information about an ongoing investigation. Isn't that correct, Mr. Mannheimer?"

"Of course that's correct!" Mannheimer insisted, but the satisfaction in his eyes didn't match his aggrieved tone. "But that's irrelevant because we have some good news."

"Good news?" Christine piped. "We could certainly use some of that around here."

Singh granted us one of his rare smiles. "We'll be releasing a statement tonight, but I wanted you to hear it from me first: Tripp will be formally arrested today on insider trading charges."

"*What?!*" Christine and I cried at the same time.

"You heard right," Singh said.

"Did he confess?" I asked.

"No," Mannheimer smirked. "He didn't need to."

"We have a recording of him," Singh added. "Much of the evidence against him was provided by a co-conspirator who's now a cooperating witness."

I sucked in my breath. "Peter?"

Singh shook his head. "Tripp's contact was an insider at

an expert network firm."

"We were right!" I said. "Who was it?"

"The tipper was a university professor, someone who sat on the advisory board of Touchnology Systems. He had taught a few engineering courses to one of the company's founders," Singh explained.

I raised a fist in the air. "Yes! I knew it couldn't be Divya Thakur! She was too smart to fall for his tricks."

"An *academic* passed along material, non-public information?" Christine asked. Her parents were teachers and she revered the profession.

"It happens," Singh said.

"Do you know why?" Christine asked.

"For the same reason as everyone else," Singh said.

"Money," Mannheimer answered.

"This professor was popular, respected, and had spent years of his life teaching kids who went on to become rich entrepreneurs and he got a little sick of it," Singh said.

"Jealous would be the more accurate description," Mannheimer retorted.

"But he sat on the advisory board! He must have been getting some kind of compensation for that," I said.

"He got an annual fee and supplemented his salary by consulting for Putnam Dixon, that expert network firm you and Mannheimer came across," Singh said.

"So it was the professor at Cal Tech?" I asked.

Singh nodded. "He saw these start-ups he advised go public or be acquired, making billionaires out of his former students, so he began offering his knowledge and services to investors on the side and, Mia, you know better than any of us in this room—"

"That edge is everything," I finished.

"Tripp wanted that edge and was willing to go to great lengths to get it."

"So in spite of Tripp's past, he wasn't the one who appeared on your radar first?" I asked.

"The SEC was already monitoring Tripp because of his past history, but nothing concrete had turned up. The professor, on the other hand, had been under scrutiny at Putnam Dixon for some time," Singh explained. "He began bragging about a lifestyle that didn't match his professor's salary or the extra income he was earning. He made about $150,000 at the university, maybe another $50,000 consulting. Not chump change, but certainly not enough to buy a second home or take lavish vacations or fly on private jets! Putnam Dixon contacted the bureau after they learned the professor had participated in a meeting with Tripp a week *before* the Touchnology acquisition was announced."

"So you got two for the price of one," I said.

"Something like that."

"What'd Tripp give him in exchange for the information?"

"Cash payments, access to a villa in Parrot Cay and a shipment of Maine lobster!" Mannheimer said.

"You were working on this parallel track all along when you convinced me to trap Peter," I said, more awed than annoyed by the undue pressure the FBI had put on me to cooperate.

Singh looked uncomfortable. "We weren't sure who would break first: the professor, Tripp or Peter. We had to keep all of our options open."

"How'd you manage to turn the professor?"

"We actually approached him about his association with Tripp soon after you left the firm. Naturally he denied everything at first. You rarely get a suspect to admit guilt right away. It took a couple of more conversations about prison time and fines to convince him to work with us in exchange for leniency. He agreed to record his conversations with Tripp and, well, here we are today. I can't be more specific than that. You'll have to wait for the trial."

"And Peter? What happens to him?"

"He hasn't been charged with anything—yet. Depends on what Tripp has to say. Although I'm sure Peter's $750-per-hour attorneys are giving him all the options available and you'd better believe one of them is cooperation."

"Good luck finding the truth," I said. "They'll blame each other, contradict each other . . ."

"A criminal indictment is like the five stages of grief," Mannheimer said. "You eventually reach acceptance."

"Mia, you've spent your entire career in this business, you must have realized by now that these guys aren't as tough as they seem! Slickness eventually leads to stupidity. An indictment and possible jail time can make a grown man shit in his pants," Singh said.

He spoke without irony, as though he had actually witnessed that unfortunate graphic firsthand, and the rest of us doubled over in laughter. Once we got a hold of ourselves again, Christine suggested opening a bottle of champagne to celebrate.

Mannheimer wasted no time proposing a toast. "To Mia—and all the other pushy broads out there!"

I smiled benevolently. Only a crusty old lawyer who had marched with Dr. King could get away with saying something like that.

41.

Arrested at his midtown apartment, Tripp's perp-walk was documented by an audience of reporters and photographers who then trumpeted his sunken features all over the media. He even made the front page of the *New York Post*. Vindicated, I was besieged by calls for interviews to hear "my side of the story," but I only consented to one in-depth profile. In what must have been the ultimate paradox, I was courted by many of the same investment firms that wouldn't give me the time of day a year ago! One managing director hailed me as having those rare qualities of "guts and gumption sorely needed in this stuffy business." *Too little, too late,* I thought and politely passed.

One call I didn't refuse was from Theresa Breeze. Her appearance on CNBC proved it was possible to be married with three children and still raise $400 million to launch your own hedge fund. She also felt secure enough to express her own opinions and had achieved superwoman status in my book. When she asked if I wanted to meet at the Loews Regency Hotel, Manhattan's premier power breakfast spot, I didn't hesitate for a minute.

I indulged in a car service from Overlook to get me to 61st and Park by 8:30AM. Late August, the Loews dining room was quieter than usual, the frenetic energy of networking replaced by an airy calm, but the presence of former New York City mayor Rudy Giuliani and JP Morgan Chase's Jamie Dimon kept things interesting. The maître d' led me across the room to a booth in the back where Theresa was already seated. Reading glasses were perched on her nose as she read the *Wall Street*

Journal. When she rose to shake my hand, I noticed we were both clad in similar navy blue dresses.

Once we had ordered our food, Theresa turned to me and said, "I've been following everything since this whole story broke; I feel like I almost know you! But tell me about the *real* Mia Lewis, the one behind the news items and all that Internet chatter."

Her conversational style immediately put me at ease and I started from the very beginning—growing up with a single mother, her untimely death, my relentless drive to achieve and succeed. I told her about meeting Peter for the first time at Morgan Stanley and how he had mentored me throughout my career. The dining room had thinned out when I reached the sequence of events that led to my firing. Theresa listened intently and didn't cringe when I stated, matter-of-factly, that I had subconsciously allowed Peter to become my father-substitute. With my mother gone, I explained, he had been my only constant; the person I saw every day, the one who measured my moods, shaped my tastes and set my goals. He became the one I did not want to disappoint.

When I finished, she said, "That must have made his betrayal even harder to stomach."

"It did, but I'm glad it happened. Otherwise, I would've just continued to do his bidding," I said, as the waiter topped off my coffee. "But enough soul-searching; I'm ready to start over."

Theresa raised an eyebrow. "Does that mean you're ready to start working again?"

"I've *been* ready."

"Then how'd you like to work with me as a portfolio manager? We're not a huge fund, but we're still raising capital and have had a return of about nine percent so far this year."

"That's almost three times the index."

"And we're damn proud of it! Although I'm both CEO and Chief Investment Officer, I'd love a fresh perspective, above all from someone like you who's had some distance from this business. I'm not interested in running a shop that chews people up and spits them out. I lived the mistakes of my old job and want Tailwind Capital to be a place where we work on exciting things, but also have work-life balance. I don't want to be your mentor. You don't need one; you've been in this business long enough. Your self-worth will come from your individual performance, not from me or anyone else." She paused. "If that vision gels with what you're looking for, then I'd love it if you could give my offer some serious thought."

She was saying all the right things, those intangibles I hadn't been able to articulate at Atlas, but in my exile had come to understand were essential to preserving my sanity. If I wanted to return to this business, there'd have to be a paradigm shift.

"I don't have to think about it," I told her. "That's *exactly* the kind of opportunity I've been looking for."

Our power breakfast flowed into lunch as we analyzed the changing industry and Tailwind's role in it. I hadn't had an intelligent business conversation in almost a year and could almost see the wheels turning in my head again, confirming that I wasn't washed-up or insignificant. By the time lunch was over, we had an informal employment agreement on the table and a start date directly after Labor Day.

I met with a Manhattan realtor and spent two days looking at rental properties before putting a security deposit on a one-bedroom in the West Village with the savings I had accumulated from renting out my Battery Park apartment. It was in my dream neighborhood, with low-rise architecture and charming alleyways. The walk-up lacked the clean lines and smart gadgets I usually preferred, but I was attracted to its irreverent vibe, the contrast between the building's grungy entryway and the welcoming light inside the apartment. My new neighbors would be artists and entrepreneurs and it felt like the place was blessed with a youthful energy.

As my September 1st move-in date approached, I began packing the odds and ends I had acquired in Overlook. I'd been on an erstwhile "austerity plan," but had no trouble filling boxes with new books, porcelain, bric-a-brac from Eclectibles and a yoga mat that had never been used. Another box contained the cozy down jacket, thick sweaters and Ugg boots that had gotten me through the harsh winter. I caressed the scratchy wool on a grey turtleneck and tried to place the last time I'd worn it. It felt like a lifetime ago.

The doorbell's "dingdong" pulled me out of my reverie. I was expecting a FedEx from Theresa with my employment contract and was stunned to find Oliver at my doorstep. My jaw dropped, but I was at a loss for words, so my face must have reflected pure confusion.

"Hi," he said. His features were lopsided, strained into an awkward half-smile.

"Hi," I whispered.

"Sorry for showing up unannounced."

Nerves, swirling inside me, revived the gut-wrenching anxiety of the past few weeks. I thought I had reached a place of peace, but Oliver's presence shook me up again. Flushed, I propped against the doorframe for support. "Can I help you with something?"

"I've been in Barcelona for the past two weeks—"

I must have looked even more confused because he added, "My summer trip with Balthazar. I might have mentioned it to you earlier . . ."

Earlier. Before Sophie.

"Um, yes, it does ring a bell now that you say it."

"Anyway, we landed this afternoon and I'm walking through JFK and see"— he held up the latest copy of *New York* magazine— "this! *You* on the cover!"

I grinned, in spite of myself. "It was the only interview I gave, but I didn't think they'd make it the lead story."

"With a pretty racy title too!"

The piece, "Screwed: The Mia Lewis Story and How Wall Street Treats Women," was far from timid and I was proud of its in-your-face, take-no-prisoners brashness. Unsmiling, with arms akimbo, I had assumed my best "kickin' ass and takin' names" pose in the photo.

"Well, I couldn't have said it any better myself," I replied and walked backwards into the house, tacitly giving Oliver permission to come in. I stopped short, however, of offering him a drink or asking him to sit down.

"It certainly made for some interesting reading," he said.

"Really? You knew most of the facts already," I said, alluding to my confessional in Battery Park and our last weekend together.

"I knew the backstory, but didn't realize how much things had escalated. You've been through so much and I had no idea.

I want to apologize for not being there for you."

"You don't owe me an apology. You don't owe me anything, not after I texted you when I was about to settle with Peter and you ignored me."

"What text?" he asked, puzzled.

"The one I wrote to you three, four weeks ago. But it doesn't matter; you didn't have to come here and apologize. I'm fine—getting on with my life." I gestured to the moving boxes in the living room.

"Mia, I swear I never got your text! I would have never ignored it."

"Then what happened to it?"

"Sophie—"

"Did you honestly come here to talk to me about her?" I snapped. "Because I'm busy and have better things to do with my time!"

Stricken, he shrank back. "No, I didn't. You have every right to be angry with me. I behaved like an ass."

Lowering my voice, I said, "Oliver, you made your choice. No hard feelings."

"Will you at least let me tell you that I made a mistake? I had some misguided sense of duty and what it meant to be a family, so I turned away from the one true thing in my life since Balthazar." He paused. "*You.*"

I lifted my hand, erecting a barrier in the space between us. "Please don't play with my emotions again because—"

"I'm saying that I still love you, Mia."

I wanted to cover my ears. They were words; powerful, unreliable words he had said before.

"When Sophie came back," Oliver continued, "I wasn't

sure if it was a closed chapter. Her guilt, her desire to make up for lost time with Balthazar, resurrected old memories. But I'd been holding on to the idea of something that's been dysfunctional for years. Mentally, I thought I was doing the right thing by trying again, but my heart was someplace else. Sophie knew about you and started checking my phone. She must have deleted that message you sent. I'm sorry."

"What did you tell her?"

"I told her whatever we'd had, whatever we were trying to fix, was over because I was in love with you. She could still be a part of Balthazar's life—I wouldn't deny him that—but that's it."

"Oliver, it's never really going to be 'over' between you and Sophie. You have a child together! And you can't just come back because you realize you made a mistake."

"Mia, I never wanted to hurt you and I don't know if you can understand this—I don't even know if I have a right to ask this of you—but I needed to make this mistake in order to reach this point. I needed to erase any doubts. I don't know if you can forgive me for that, but it's the truth. I'm sorry."

"And Balthazar? What have you told him?"

"My biggest regret is the emotional damage this has had on him, but I've spent the last two weeks explaining that he won't have both parents in the same house. We can't give him a 'normal' life like most of his friends and he seems to have accepted it. I promised him this trip to Barcelona and the last thing I wanted to do was disappoint him again after all he's been through."

"I've thought about Balthazar. I know it's been tough."

"I ended up hurting him again—and you. I've been trying

to figure out a way to tell you how I feel," Oliver waved the magazine in the air. "*This* gave me the courage to do it."

"I'm moving," I blurted out. "I've accepted a job in the city and start next week."

"I see," he said, eyeing the bags and cartons on the floor.

"I had to get on with my life, you know."

"Yes, I know."

"You can't just come back like this. I have a plan; everything is sorted."

"I couldn't *not* come. If you still love me—if a part of you wants to see where this could go—please give us another chance." Searching my face, he asked, "Or have I killed whatever we had?"

"Oliver, I trusted you!" I said, the ache of his rejection searing through my body again. "I was prepared to give up so much for you!"

"Mia, you deserve so much more than what I was capable of. But I'm here now—if you'll have me."

I froze. Slowly, small tremors of recognition, that connection between two damaged souls, crept back. I had been drawn to Oliver since that first accidental encounter at Cupcake de Ville. His quiet strength, the caution beneath his confidence, had made me believe his love—when he finally offered it—was real.

My doorbell chimed one more time.

"I have to get that," I said.

It was the FedEx courier with the documents from Tailwind Capital.

"Is everything okay?" Oliver asked when I returned to the living room, pointing to the box I held. "Were you expecting something important?"

I nodded. "My employment contract."

"So you haven't signed anything yet?"

"No."

The corners of Oliver's mouth lifted in what looked like an appeal or a sign of hope. I felt the complexity of that sign, the grip of unsaid words, a door I could crack open. I thought of my mother and her sacrifices and wondered, not for the first time, if my so-called life would have made her proud. The struggles and success, the piercing disillusionment—they were all part of the journey, weren't they? The material had become immaterial, but my pride—battered and bruised—remained. My eyes found Oliver's and, package still in hand, I smiled back.

Epilogue

For all my years on Wall Street, I never had my own separate, close-the-door-if-you-want-to office before. It felt strange, having the freedom to shut out the rest of the world, but I only did it for client meetings. I also shared an administrative assistant with Theresa and constantly wrestled with what to delegate and what I could do myself. Those first few weeks in my new orchid and book-filled room, I decided that everything about Tailwind Capital exuded elegance and calm, from the landscape paintings in the reception area to the selection of green tea in the pantry. There was no communal television blasting CNBC or a volatile trader spouting expletives. Theresa had a stealth style, but could sting when necessary. I had witnessed that first-hand when she successfully renegotiated lower fees for our Bloomberg terminals.

Tailwind inhabited the ground floor of a twenty-foot wide townhouse on East 81st that had been in foreclosure when Theresa bought it a few years back. It had previously been a doctor's practice with a dedicated entrance, and Theresa's family lived in the three renovated floors above. She had trained her kids well; they rarely appeared during business hours. Theresa usually finished around five or six in the evening, tailoring her schedule around the teachers' conferences, school performances or sporting activities she didn't want to miss. She encouraged me to take a yoga class or go for a run in Central Park when things were quiet, but two months into this new job, I wanted to stay focused.

A total of ten people worked at Tailwind. I was the most

senior portfolio manager and two analysts helped me study the market and craft presentations for potential clients. They were different, this new crop of young financial geniuses, displaying more humility and less of the entitlement that had left a blemish on their generation. They were almost deferential towards me, too; eager to reach consensus and willing to do all manner of grunt work. Maybe it was my age. I had turned thirty-six a little while back and, with my battle scars, I couldn't fairly categorize myself as "young" anymore. I was also a minor celebrity in their eyes, or at least a supporting player in one of the many, many scandals that had rocked Wall Street since the financial crisis.

They had recently asked me about Tripp. Days earlier, he pleaded guilty to conspiracy and securities fraud after admitting he had purchased Touchnology stock based on secret information about its impending acquisition. Under his agreement with prosecutors, he faces up to two and a half years in jail. I was so tempted to speak openly about Tripp's arrogance, his lack of intellect, even his sloppiness. I knew those two twenty-somethings would have eaten it up like kittens to milk, but I stayed impartial, offering only that we had different investment philosophies.

The Mia of last year, the one who had castigated Tripp in public and then thrown water in his face, made me convulse today. I had clearly been unraveling for some time before reaching that tipping point and often wondered what would have happened if I'd stayed at Atlas—chugging along, business as usual, coddled by the system and my paycheck. Would I have become ensnared in their illicit activity and be facing jail time? I believe that I have a firm moral compass, but would desperation or fear of financial loss entice me to go by the wayside? That question often dogged me in the middle of the night and I would stare at the ceiling in my Jane Street bedroom, listening to the clash of sirens and honking cars until I dozed off again.

The professor, Tripp's contact at the expert network firm, had also pleaded guilty for leading a ring that leaked confidential information to traders and hedge fund managers and could spend the next four years in jail. Peter, defiant to the last, insisted he was innocent and claimed no prior knowledge of how Tripp had procured his information. Nevertheless, a grand jury had indicted him for suspicion of insider trading and his case was scheduled to go to trial next spring. It seemed I would never really be free of Peter and expected to be called to testify against him. But I was ready to look him in the eye again; I wanted to thank him for pushing me out, for coercing me to reassess my life.

Some might think it's strange that I'm back in finance, but I couldn't end my career with scandal or failure. Theresa had offered me a second chance and I came to understand that this business is in my DNA. I'm good at what I do; I shouldn't be ashamed to own it. I might not be doing this for the rest of my life, but I need to see if I can succeed without the shadow of absent parents, a manipulative boss or a conflicted lover.

In the end, the choice wasn't about Oliver or my career.

The choice was about me.

Acknowledgements

I worked on this book over many years and am immensely grateful for the knowledge and support I received from so many people. I don't have a financial background, but I am intrigued by the stories behind the numbers. Many thanks to the women in finance who shared their experiences with me, particularly my dear friend, Rhonda Eldridge, whose candor, insightfulness and sense of humor provided inspiration and credibility to the narrative. I express gratitude to my early readers whose encouragement propelled me forward: Kristen Donovan and Malcolm Lindblom. My faith in our friendship gave me the courage to show you the early, cringe-worthy drafts! I will always treasure your interest and confidence in my work. Kimberly Andersson, my sistergirlfriend in Stockholm, provided aesthetic assistance and an intuitive understanding of the main character. Thank you for your trusted counsel.

Supervisory Special Agent David A. Chaves (retired) was a senior FBI Official in the New York Division investigating securities fraud. I'm indebted to the illuminating phone conversation we had as I tried to paint a picture of financial misdeeds, hubris, and their consequences. I'd also like to recognize New York Times and CNBC journalist Andrew Ross Sorkin, whom I've never met but admire, and his incredible reporting about the financial crisis and Wall Street scandals. He made technical facts and figures accessible to a layperson like me. I've also spent so many hours watching "Squawk Box" and "Squawk on the Street," I should probably have an MBA by now!

I've dedicated this book, with love and gratitude, to my

big sister (by thirteen months), Dominique Anglade Neblung. She's a working mom, diligent and devoted to her family. I can't overstate what an important sounding board she is. I admire her strength, loyalty and plain-spokenness. These traits still matter and will win the day in the end. PJ Rizvi is my sister from another mister, my peacock-feathered friend whose quirky mascot—along with some other colorful phrases— managed to find their way into this story. Thank you for never letting me take myself too seriously!

Saul Bottcher's expertise came at a critical juncture in the journey of this book. His positive attitude, advice and helpful feedback empowered me to consider an alternate path. The latter stages of project gave me renewed focus, reaffirming my passion for books and the written word. Most of all, thank you for your faith in Mia.

I am also grateful to Sara Camilli for believing in me since 2004 and for her patience despite my slow output!

And to my family, whom I love without end. My husband, Christian Dahlberg, was invaluable while I researched this book. He educated me on the basic elements of trading; his instincts and input always challenged me to think twice. I hope my children, Yasmine and James, will forgive me for being so distracted at times and remember, instead, how I sat hunched over the manuscript—dreaming, thinking, typing, deleting, editing, doubting, cursing and, finally, letting go. I labored over every word and nothing worthwhile comes without hard work!

About the Author

Jennifer Anglade Dahlberg grew up in suburban New York and graduated from Columbia University. Her first novel, *Uptown & Down* (Penguin/NAL), was published in 2005. She lives in Stockholm, Sweden, with her husband and two teenage children.

To keep up with Jennifer's writing and to be notified of future books, please sign up for her (spam-free) mailing list at jenniferdahlberg.com/mailing-list. You can also follow her blog at jenniferdahlberg.com, or follow her on Instagram at instagram.com/jennifer.anglade.dahlberg.

Uptown and Down

In her dynamic debut novel, Jennifer Anglade Dahlberg explores the headstrong ambitions and fragile dreams of a couple on top—and their drive for success, which tests the limits of privilege, love, and friendship in the most provocative of ways . . .

Nora Deschamps is an editor at a chic women's fashion magazine. Her husband Jeff Montgomery owns an independent record label that's edging into a mega-bucks hip-hop phenomenon. Tracked as one of New York Magazine's "25 Most Exciting Couples Under Forty," Nora and Jeff appear to have it all. But their future is about to be shaken, by Nora's on-the-rise career that's taking an intimate toll on their lives, by a crime that Jeff is powerless to prevent, and ultimately by the secret of a long-ago indiscretion and the revenge that now threatens all they've strived to achieve.

From the uptown high-life to the downside of love, betrayal, and long-standing lies, Nora and Jeff must now fight harder than ever to learn the meaning of trust.

Available from online retailers and local bookstores.

CPSIA information can be obtained
at www.ICGtesting.com
Printed in the USA
BVHW07s0039160718
521689BV00002B/117/P

9 781773 420509